PRA

ELOISA JAMES

"Her style is exquisite, her prose pure magic."
New York Times bestselling author
JULIA QUINN

"A novel by Eloisa is a
delicious treat that shouldn't be missed.
A wonderfully original voice
in romance fiction!"
New York Times bestselling author
LISA KLEYPAS

"Romance writing does not
get much better..."
People Magazine

"A symphony of delights
for romance readers, a lyrically
written love story graced
with richly nuanced characters and
generously seasoned with
the author's incandescent wit."
Booklist on *Once Upon a Tower*

"Are you saying that I'm not a terrible kisser?"

"India."

She drank more champagne and looked at him, wet lips shiny. "I thought perhaps you'd offer me lessons in the art, which I would refuse, of course."

Every man had limits to his self-control. Thorn stood up, walked around the table, and drew her to her feet. "India, my kisses are appalling. Terrible. Would you offer me lessons?"

She looked him straight in the eye and said, "Practice makes perfect." And then she giggled. Lady Xenobia India giggled.

Thorn pulled her into his arms. "You do remember that I plan to marry Laetitia?"

"Do you imagine that a kiss or two might make me want to marry you?" The pure surprise in India's eyes gave Thorn a quick kick in the arse.

The daughter of a marquess would never look to one such as he, no matter how much she liked his kisses. For God's sake, had he learned nothing in his years as the bastard son of a duke?

India put her arms around his neck. "We are friends, you and I. I have no true friends, because I've never had time for them. I never had them when I was little either, because of my parents. You are my first true friend."

Then she kissed him.

By Eloisa James

ELOISA JAMES

Three Weeks With Lady X

AVON
An Imprint of HarperCollinsPublishers

This is a work of fiction. Names, characters, places, and incidents are products of the author's imagination or are used fictitiously and are not to be construed as real. Any resemblance to actual events, locales, organizations, or persons, living or dead, is entirely coincidental.

AVON BOOKS
An Imprint of HarperCollins*Publishers*
10 East 53rd Street
New York, New York 10022-5299

Copyright © 2014 by Eloisa James
Excerpt from *A Duke of Her Own* copyright © 2009 by Eloisa James
ISBN 978-0-06-222389-0
www.avonromance.com

First Avon Books mass market printing: April 2014

Avon Trademark Reg. U.S. Pat. Off. and in Other Countries, Marca Registrada, Hecho en U.S.A.
HarperCollins® is a registered trademark of HarperCollins Publishers.

Printed in the U.S.A.

10 9 8 7 6 5 4 3 2 1

For Linda, in an inadequate attempt
to thank a master of her craft
for hours of analysis, laughter, and mint tea.

Acknowledgments

My books are like small children; they take a whole village to get them to a literate state. I want to offer my deep gratitude to my village: my editor, Carrie Feron; my agent, Kim Witherspoon; my writing partner, Linda Francis Lee; my Website designers, Wax Creative; and my personal team: Kim Castillo, Franzeca Drouin, and Anne Connell. In addition, people in many departments of HarperCollins, from art to marketing to PR, have done a wonderful job of getting this book into readers' hands: my heartfelt thanks go to each of you. And finally, my niece, Nora Bly, was extremely helpful in shaping India's best qualities.

Chapter One

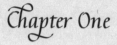

June 14, 1799
Number 22, Charles Street
London residence of the Dibbleshires

"*L*ady Xenobia, I adore you!"

Lord Dibbleshire's brow was beaded with sweat and his hands were trembling. "In vain have I struggled, but I can no longer contain my ardent feelings; I must reveal to you, no, *enlighten* you about the depths of my emotion!"

India managed not to step back, but it took an effort. She tried to summon up a perfect smile, kind but not encouraging. Though she wasn't positive that smile even existed.

Whatever she came up with would be better than an utterly inappropriate shriek of *Bloody hell, not again!* Daughters of marquesses—even deceased and arguably mad marquesses—did not shriek. More's the pity.

The smile didn't seem to work, so she trotted out her standard answer: "You do me too much honor, Lord Dibbleshire, but—"

"I know," he responded, rather unexpectedly. Then he frowned. "I mean, *no*! No honor is too great for you. I have fought against my better judgment and while I realize that there are those who consider your reputation to be sullied by your profession, I know the truth. The truth shall prevail!"

Well, that was something. But before India could comment on the truth (or lack thereof), he toppled onto his knees. "I will marry you, Lady Xenobia India St. Clair," he bellowed, widening his eyes to indicate his own shock at this declaration. "*I*, Baron Dibbleshire, will marry *you*."

"Please do get up," she said, resisting the urge to groan.

"I know that you will refuse me, owing to your inestimable modesty. But I have made up my mind, Lady Xenobia. The protection of my title—and, of course, yours as well—will overcome the ill effects of your unfortunate occupation. A plight to which you were driven, a point I shall make early and often. The *ton* will accept us . . . they will accept *you*, once you have the benefit of becoming Baroness Dibbleshire."

Aggravation marched up her spine like a troop of perfectly dressed soldiers. True, her reputation was tarnished by the fact that she refused to stay home practicing her needlework. But as she was the daughter of a marquess, technically a Dibbleshire would be lucky to dance with her. Not that she cared about such things. Still, her godmother accompanied her everywhere—even now Lady Adelaide Swift was likely within earshot—and if nothing else, Adelaide's chaperonage had ensured that India remain as pure as the driven snow despite her *unfortunate* occupation.

Who would have guessed that taking on the task of ordering people's lives would have tarnished her lily-white wings?

At that moment, the door to the sitting room opened and

her suitor's mother appeared. India's head began to pound. She never should have agreed to Lady Dibbleshire's plea that India refurbish her drawing room, no matter how interesting a challenge it was to strip the room of its Egyptian furnishings.

"Howard, what in heaven's name are you doing?" the lady demanded, making the whole situation even more farcical than it already was.

Dibbleshire sprang to his feet with surprising ease, inasmuch as his center of gravity was quite low slung and hung over his breeches. "I have just informed Lady Xenobia that I love her, and she has agreed to become my wife!"

India's eyes were met—thankfully—by a gleam of sympathy in Lady Dibbleshire's. "His lordship has misunderstood," India told her.

"Alas, I have no doubt of that. Child," Howard's mother said, "every time I think that you have demonstrated the depths of your similarity to your father, you astonish me yet again."

Dibbleshire scowled and looked, spaniel-like, back to India. "I will not allow you to refuse me. I haven't slept for two nights, unable to think of anything but you. I have made up my mind to rescue you from your life of drudgery!"

He reached out his hand, and India nimbly stepped back. "Lord Dibbleshire—"

"You move from house to house, ceaselessly working." His pale blue eyes gazed at her with devotion.

"Dear Lord, Howard," Lady Dibbleshire exclaimed, "if our estate is ever lost, I am happy to think that you will be able to support us by making a living on the stage. However, it is my duty as a mother to point out that you are being rather vulgar."

Apparently, his lordship had confused vulgarity with honor; he gave his mother a ferocious glare.

"Lady Xenobia is our dear and valued guest," her ladyship continued, "who has been kind enough to aid me with restoration of the drawing room, as well as persuading the inestimable Mrs. Flushing to be our cook. For which"— she turned to India—"I shall be eternally grateful."

India had the knack of moving excellent servants into households where they would be appreciated and well paid. Mrs. Flushing had been languishing in the employ of a dyspeptic general, and was far happier cooking for Dibbleshire and his mother.

"And Howard," Lady Dibbleshire continued, "clearly you too are enjoying Mrs. Flushing's menus, given your expanding middle."

He scowled again and pulled at his waistcoat.

India opened her mouth to say something soothing, but at that moment her godmother bustled into the room, accompanied by a stream of words. "Darlings," Lady Adelaide cried, "that lovely Mr. Sheraton has sent a delectable small mahogany table. Jane, you will adore it, simply adore it!" She and Lady Dibbleshire had been school friends; indeed, nearly all of India's clients were her godmother's near and dear acquaintances.

"How splendid," Lady Dibbleshire said. "Where will you place it, Lady Xenobia?"

India had become famous for designing rooms in which furniture was scattered in unstudied, asymmetrical seating arrangements. "I shall have to see it to be sure, but in the grouping under the south window, I think."

"Perfect!" Adelaide exclaimed, clapping her hands. "Your drawing room will be the talk of London, Jane, mark my words."

"We shall come take a look," Lady Dibbleshire replied, "just as soon as I've persuaded my feckless son that your goddaughter has far better things to do than marry one such as he."

"Oh my dear, you mustn't be harsh to sweet Howard." Adelaide moved over to Dibbleshire and took his hand. "I'm certain that India would be ecstatic to marry you, if only the circumstances were different."

"I would never burden your name with the social opprobrium resulting from the path my life has taken," India told him, following up with a smile and a gaze that indicated clear-eyed courage and self-sacrifice. "Besides, I saw Miss Winifred Landel watching you last night, though you were tactful enough to overlook her obvious infatuation. Who am I to stand in the way of such an advantageous match?"

Lord Dibbleshire blinked at India and said, uncertainly, "Because I love you?"

"You merely think you love me," she assured him, "due to your charitable heart. I assure you that you need not worry about my plight. As a matter of fact, I have made up my mind to withdraw from my profession."

"You have?" This from Lady Dibbleshire, whose mouth actually fell open. "You do realize that at this very moment ladies all over England are imploring their husbands to obtain your services?"

But India and her godmother worked like a well-oiled machine when it came to dissuading men from proclaiming their love. "You should ask Miss Landel to marry you," Adelaide said, patting Lord Dibbleshire's hand vigorously. "India is already considering three or four proposals, including those from the Earl of Fitzroy and Mr. Nugent—the one who's from Colleton, not the other one, from Bettleshangler. He will be a viscount someday."

At this news, his shoulders slumped again. But Adelaide glanced at India, a twinkle in her eyes, before turning back. "Besides, I am not convinced that you two suit each other, Howard, dear. My darling goddaughter does have a bit of a temper. And of course you're aware that Fitzroy and Nugent are somewhat older than you. As is India. She is twenty-six, and you are still a young man."

Dibbleshire's head swung up and he peered at India.

"Miss Landel is barely out of the schoolroom," Lady Dibbleshire put in, nimbly taking up the ball. "You can guide her into maturity, Howard."

He blinked rapidly at this idea, clearly reconsidering his infatuation now that he'd learned the object of his adoration was four years older than he.

India suppressed the instinct to pat the corners of her eyes for wrinkles and composed her face to look old. Almost elderly. Presumably her white-blond hair would help; Adelaide was always pestering her to tint it one color or another. "Lord Dibbleshire, I shall hold your proposal sacrosanct, enshrined in my memory." She held her breath.

His lordship's chest swelled and he said, "I commend your intention to retire from this invidious profession, if one can call it that, Lady Xenobia. And I wish you all possible good fortune, of course."

His love for her was dead.

Right.

A few moments later India walked upstairs to a small sitting room that Lady Dibbleshire had designated as her and her godmother's retreat during the renovation process. Catching sight of herself in a mirror, she peered closer to see whether wrinkles indeed radiated out from her eyes. She couldn't see any. In fact, at twenty-six, she looked fairly the same as she had at sixteen: too much hair, too much lower lip, too much bosom.

There was no visible sign of the hard knot in her chest, the one that tightened every time she thought about accepting a proposal of marriage.

She was good at refusing men. It was the idea of *accept-*

ing one that made her feel as if she couldn't breathe. But she had to marry. She couldn't go on like this forever, moving from house to house, dragging her godmother with her.

After she had been orphaned at fifteen and sent to live in Adelaide's disordered, chaotic house, India had quickly realized that if she didn't organize her godmother's household, no one would. And after Lady Adelaide had lavishly praised India to one of her friends, boasting that they would pay a visit that summer and "straighten everything out," India had tackled the friend's household as well. One thing had led to another, and for the last ten years she and Adelaide had made two or three such visits a year.

It was exhilarating to create order from chaos. She would renovate a room or two, turn the staffing upside down, and leave, knowing that the household would run like clockwork, at least until the owners mucked it up again. Every house presented a different—and fascinating—challenge.

But it was time to stop. To marry. The problem was that having sifted through so many households, she had received an intimate view of marriage, without seeing anything that particularly recommended the marital state . . . except children.

That had been the hardest part of her job, finding nannies and refurbishing nurseries for young women her own age. Her longing for a baby had brought her to the decision that it was time to marry.

The only question was who to marry.

Or should that be *whom* to marry?

She was never certain of her grammar, thanks to her father's inability to keep a governess. Servants, it seemed, didn't like going unpaid. Moreover, God-fearing English servants also disliked the fact that their masters danced naked in the moonlight.

India winced at the memory. She had spent years trailing her parents, her vibrant, loving, half-mad parents, longing for affection, attention, even supper. . . . They *had* loved her. Surely.

Everyone's parents had good and bad sides. Her parents had loved her, which was good. They had danced attendance on a moon goddess instead of the Queen of England, which was bad.

They had sometimes forgotten to feed her. That was the worst.

Without question, her fear of marriage really went back to her childhood. Marriage meant trusting a husband to take care of her, instead of taking care of herself. It meant accepting that he would be in charge of their accounts. The very idea of a man like Dibbleshire talking to an estate manager made her shiver.

She swallowed hard. She thought she could get used to living with a man. But could she obey one?

Her father had been very dear, but he had played ducks and drakes with the estate, neglecting to pay the baker's and butler's accounts, as well as regularly forgetting the existence of his only child. He and her mother had died during a trip to London that they took for an unknown reason, although they'd had no money for such an excursion.

It wasn't unreasonable for her stomach to clench at the idea of putting herself in the hands of a man.

Still, she could do it—with one minor tweak.

She simply had to find a man who was sweet and kind, and smart enough to realize that she should be the one to run their household.

If she, Xenobia India St. Clair, expert at turning chaos into order, truly put her mind to the task, how hard could it be?

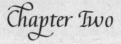

Chapter Two

The same day
40, Hanover Square
London residence of Mr. Tobias Dautry, Esq.

𝐵y right of birth, a duke's eldest son should be sleek and self-satisfied, assured of land and titles by England's laws of primogeniture. He ought to have no worries greater than the threat of split breeches while riding to the hounds, or a mistress who leaves him for a marquess with a better command of his tool.

But that would be an eldest son born within wedlock.

It is an entirely different story if the son in question is illegitimate, born of a ravishing but itinerant opera singer, a woman who had paused at the Duke of Villiers's country estate long enough to give birth to a son and wandered on like a lark seeking warmer climes.

Thorn Dautry was neither sleek nor self-satisfied. Even
when he seemed relaxed, he was alert to possible danger,
and with good reason: he'd spent his formative years ward-
ing off death.

As an adult, he'd become a man who controlled his world
and everything and everyone in it, and he didn't bother to
pretend he didn't know the reason. Not when he was sitting
across from his best friend, Vander, whose childhood had
had just as formative an effect on him.

A deep voice broke the silence in the library. "I don't
approve, Thorn. While Laetitia Rainsford won't make a
terrible wife for some fellow, she's not right for you. Why
in God's name did you choose her?"

Evander Septimus Brody, future Duke of Pindar, was
sprawled opposite, a brandy glass balanced on his stomach. Vander had been Thorn's closest friend since Eton,
when both of them had been bent on proving themselves
with their fists. Their failure to beat each other senseless
had led to a lifelong bond.

Sometimes Thorn felt he and Vander were two sides of
the same coin: he, a duke's illegitimate son who had to fight
off the world's opinion, and Vander, a duke's legitimate son
who didn't fit the mold. Vander was too direct, too male, too
violent to suit the sensibilities of English society.

Thorn raised an eyebrow. Laetitia was widely viewed
as the most exquisite woman on the marriage mart. Her
charms were obvious. "You really can't guess?"

"Oh, I know she's beautiful. And you'd be stealing her
from any number of young bucks who write sonnets to her
nose. But she's not right for you."

"How can you know that?" Thorn was genuinely curious. Vander didn't look like a future duke—his hair
was shaggy, and he had the jaw of a prizefighter, not a
nobleman—and he didn't act like one either. He never went

to balls, so how in the hell would he have met a virtuous young lady like Miss Laetitia Rainsford?

"I was seated beside her at a dinner party given by my uncle. She certainly is pretty enough. But as your wife?"

"I've made up my mind. She's the one." Thorn took a drink, returning his brandy glass to precisely the same spot on the side table. "She is beautiful, well born, and well bred. What more could I want?"

"A brain," Vander stated, his eyes not leaving Thorn's face.

"I don't look for intelligence in bed," Thorn said dryly. In his estimation, Laetitia had all the requisite qualities for bedding and mothering, even if a high degree of intelligence didn't seem to be one of them. "I believe one of the reasons that my factories thrive is that I suit talent to position. In fact, I see no meaningful difference between the two."

Vander snorted. "You think *I'm* harsh? You will have to live with the woman!"

"That's true, but I also live with my butler," Thorn pointed out. "What's the difference, really, besides the fact I don't have to share a bed with Iffley? Laetitia will be the mother of my children, and it is my distinct impression that she is an excellent nurturer. In fact, I met her in the Round Pond in Kensington Gardens, where she was watching boys sail toy boats."

His intended probably wouldn't appreciate the comparison, but Thorn had the notion that she was like a rescued hound, one that would adoringly follow her new master in return for some kindness. That was absurd, given that she was as beautiful as a wild rose, with hair like a Botticelli angel. By all rights, she should be arrogantly aware of her dominion over men. But instead she had a desperate look about her eyes, as if she needed saving.

It was a fair trade, in his estimation. Her beauty in return for his protection.

"You plan to drop your wife at this new estate of yours with a brood of children?"

"I see no reason to live at Starberry Court with her." His own father had taught him little more than how to fence. Thorn intended to be that type of father, and he needn't be in residence to do it.

"A mother does more than nurture her family," Vander objected. "I hear scientists have estimated that half of one's intellect comes from each parent."

Thorn just looked at him. His children would be *his* children, just as his father's were his father's. He and the Duke of Villiers were carved from the same block of marble. It wasn't just the white streak in his hair that had appeared in his and his father's hair after each of them had turned nineteen. It was the set of his jaw, the way Villiers calculated outcomes, even the way he breathed air.

If one wanted more proof, it could be had in the fact that the duke had spawned children with five different mothers, and each of those children was—in his or her own way—a copy of their father. "Of course, I hope that they look like their mother," he added, with a wry look.

"Bloody hell," Vander said, disgusted. "I suppose you'll raise the poor babes as a pack of wolves."

Thorn grinned at that. "You'd better find someone to marry. You don't want your wolves to be puny in comparison to mine."

"I haven't met the right woman yet." Vander took a gulp of brandy, slumping lower in his chair. Thorn never sprawled. Sprawling would put him at a disadvantage; he would lose critical seconds before he could dodge a blow and launch an attack.

"Why don't you ask Eleanor to find you someone suitable?" Thorn asked. His stepmother, the Duchess of Villiers, knew everyone in society worth knowing. Moreover, she was brilliantly strategic and would enjoy determining the future of the duchy of Pindar.

But Vander shook his head. "I want what your father has."

"What's that?"

"You know what."

"You want *Eleanor*?" Thorn was, frankly, astonished. His stepmother was beautiful, intelligent, witty . . . and she was also deeply in love with his father. Eleanor wasn't interested in younger men, nor indeed in any man other than her husband.

He gave Vander the kind of look he reserved for pickpockets just before he knocked them off their feet. "You keep your hands off my stepmother. I had no idea that you had propensities of that nature."

"You should see your face!" Vander was positively howling with laughter. "Your stepmother is a very nice woman," he said finally, more or less recovering himself. "But I don't want *her,* you idiot. I want the type of marriage those two have. I want what Villiers has." He took another slug. "I'll be damned if I'll settle for anything less."

"I don't consider the marriage I'm contemplating to be lesser," Thorn objected. "Just different. My father's life revolves around Eleanor, and hers around him. I can't see either of us altering our habits for a woman. What about all those horses you're training, and the fact you're constantly off to one steeplechase or another? I have no problem imagining you with a wife—but one who is the center of your life? No."

"I would make time," Vander stated.

"Why?"

"You really have no idea, do you?"

"What I know is that Laetitia is remarkably beautiful and she's a lady, which will protect my children from being shunned as a result of my birth. Part of the reason I treasure my stepmother is that she's unlike any other woman I've met. Quite frankly, I've come to believe another such woman doesn't exist."

"She has to, Thorn." Vander came to his feet but didn't walk away, just stood, staring down at Thorn. "I want to love a woman the way your father loves his wife. I don't care if she looks like an apple seller. I want to feel passion for the woman I marry. It doesn't seem too much to ask."

"My father almost married a woman who belonged in Bedlam," Thorn said, leaning back so he could see Vander's face. "It was pure accident that paired him with Eleanor. Are you hoping that the perfect woman will simply wander in your door?"

"If she doesn't, then I'd rather not bother," Vander said flatly. He moved to the decanter and refilled his glass. "If I'm to change my life to suit a woman, she'd damned well better be worth my trouble."

He had a point there. Thorn was fairly sure marriage would be a bother. In order to woo Laetitia, he had been obliged to buy a country estate, although he was perfectly comfortable living in London. What's more, he was taking on a wife when he already had twenty-three servants, along with men working in factories, solicitors' offices, and the rest.

But he wanted children, and for that he needed a wife. He liked children. Children, whether boys or girls, were curious. They liked to ask questions; they wanted to understand how things worked.

"Since you're not planning to change your life, I suppose you'll keep your mistress?" Vander dropped back into his chair, taking care not to spill his brandy.

"I pensioned her off the day after I met Laetitia."

"Then I'll point out the obvious. You are signing up to sleep with no woman other than Laetitia Rainsford for the rest of your bleeding life."

He shrugged. "She will give me children. And I have no doubt she will be faithful, so I'll pay her the same respect."

"Loyalty is one of your few virtues," Vander acknowledged. "The problem with you," he added, staring contemplatively into his brandy, "is your infernal childhood."

Thorn couldn't argue with that. Spending his boyhood as a penniless mudlark—diving into the Thames to search for anything of value in the muck—had shaped him. He had learned the hard way that danger lurked where you couldn't see it.

"You don't trust anyone," Vander continued, waxing philosophical. "Your father should have kept a better eye on you. I'll be damned if I misplace any of my children, even if I produce a bastard, which I won't."

"My childhood made me what I am. I wouldn't trade it to be the pampered son of a duke."

Vander shot him a sardonic look. Thorn was the only one who knew what horrors had lurked inside the Duke of Pindar's country seat.

"I trust my father, Eleanor, my siblings," Thorn stated. "And you. That's good enough."

Frankly, he didn't waste much time thinking about trusting women. And he found it rare that he respected them. His life revolved around his work, and most gentlewomen didn't seem to do anything except their part in bed, though he generally did most of the work there too. That was the nature of it. He wasn't a man to give a woman her way between the sheets.

"I trust you," Vander replied. He added no other names. Not that Thorn expected him to, because he knew there were no other names to add. Vander's face had darkened, and as

Thorn saw it, his friend's darkness was his own business.

"That's why I want a marriage like your father's," Vander continued, staring at the fire through his empty glass. "There have to be more people in the world I can trust than a muscle-bound, sweaty bastard like yourself."

Back when they'd been fourteen, that weak jest would have been an invitation, and the two of them would have pummeled each other until half the furniture in the room had been broken . . . and they'd come out the other side panting and happy.

What's more, that remark, or another like it, would surely have been made on this very day of the year, because it was the anniversary of Vander's mother's death, which he generally spent skating on the edge of violence. Consequently, every year on this day Thorn ensured he was at Vander's side.

Thorn got to his feet. "I'm sick of sitting around with a maudlin romantic, talking about women. Foil or épée?"

Vander rose with no sign that three glasses of brandy had impaired him. Probably they hadn't; he seemed to have been endowed with the ability to burn off alcohol within minutes.

Predictably, Vander chose the heavier blade, the épée. Thorn was the better fencer; Vander had the habit of losing his temper and slashing instead of strategizing.

Once in Thorn's ballroom, they stripped down to shirts and breeches and began circling each other, blades poised.

But even as he calculated every shift in Vander's weight, Thorn kept thinking about marriage. Laetitia wasn't bright, it was true, but frankly, he believed that to be a decided advantage in a wife. His mother had been that rare thing, a strong-minded woman with a vocation, and her art had mattered more to her than her son.

He didn't have any interest in a woman with a profession. He wanted a woman who would never dream of leaving her children—for any reason. Laetitia adored children, and she clearly had no larger aspirations than motherhood. He had decided five minutes after meeting her that she would be his bride, though he hadn't yet informed her of the fact.

Her approval was unnecessary, really, since their marriage was a matter of negotiation between himself and her parents. After meeting with Lord Rainsford, he understood that he would pay dearly for Laetitia's beauty. But more importantly, he would pay the highest price for her birth.

The only remaining obstacle was Lady Rainsford; her parents had made it clear that her approval was necessary.

Vander was fighting like a madman, to the point where he had twice nearly broken through Thorn's guard. His chest was heaving and he was bathed in sweat. But he looked better than he had earlier: less fraught, less furious . . . less grief-stricken.

Good.

Time to go in for the kill. In a coordinated series of strokes, Thorn danced around the edge of Vander's blade, sliced his right arm around and under, feigned an attack, whirled, switched hands, came at him with the left.

Touché.

Vander's response to defeat was a stream of oaths that would have made a sailor blanch. Thorn bent over to catch his breath, watching drops of sweat fall to the floor. He couldn't best Vander in the boxing ring, but he could damn well wipe the floor with him when they held swords. Even better, the air of madness that hung about his friend every year on the anniversary of his mother's death had evaporated.

Thorn pulled off his shirt and used it to mop his chest and face.

"Do you think that Laetitia will like you?" Vander asked.

" 'Like me?' What do you mean?"

"The way you look. Does she seem attracted to you?"

Thorn glanced down at himself. Long bands of muscle covered his body, forming ridges over his taut abdomen. He kept his body in fighting shape, and no woman had yet expressed a complaint. "Are you talking about the scars?" Like every mudlark who survived into adulthood, he was covered with them.

"You never go into society, so you wouldn't know, but Laetitia's just spent the season dancing with a crowd of wand-thin mollies with no need to shave. We're too big, and we'd both have a beard within the day if we allowed it."

"Those men were all at school with us," Thorn said, shrugging. "You're taking marriage too seriously. It's a transaction like any other. I'm giving her a country house; that will make up for my brute proportions."

"Damn," Vander said, pausing in the middle of rubbing sweat from his hair. "You really mean it, don't you? I can't see you as a rural squire."

Neither could Thorn, but as he understood it, children required fresh air and open spaces. His new estate was close to London, and he could easily visit.

"What will you do with yourself there?" Vander gave a bark of laughter. "Go fishing? I can see you fashioning a new rod and selling the design for a hundred pounds, but reeling in a trout? No."

Thorn had just acquired a rubber factory that was losing money fast. For a moment, he imagined a rubber fishing rod—he had to design something profitable that the factory could make—but then dismissed it. "I won't be there often," he said, tossing his shirt to the side. "I'll leave the trout for idiots who fancy shriveling their balls in rushing water."

He was an East Londoner to the core, and he'd only catch a trout if he were starving. Plus, his time as a mudlark had left one indelible mark: he didn't like rivers. Given a choice, he'd never go in one again, and certainly never dive to the bottom.

"I like fishing," Vander objected, pulling on one of the linen shirts that Thorn's valet had left stacked on a filigree chair.

"Good, because I'm inviting Laetitia and her parents to the country in a fortnight or so, and you can come along and fish for your supper. I have to persuade Laetitia's mother to accept my baseborn blood, and you can be proof that I know the right sort. I only hope you've never met each other."

Vander threw his drenched shirt at Thorn's head, but it fell to the floor. Thorn was already heading out the door.

He had a factory to save.

Chapter Three

*I*ndia made an excuse and did not join the Dibbleshires for tea; there was no point in risking yet another passionate declaration from his lordship. Instead, she and her godmother retired to their sitting room, where India began opening the mail Adelaide's butler had sent over by a groom. Letter after letter implored her to cure various ills: a disorganized house, an unfashionable dining room, even (implicitly) a marriage.

But she resolutely wrote back refusals, mindful of her decision to marry. She even refused an offer from the Regent's secretary asking if she would renovate his private chambers in Brighton. The only truly tempting letter came from the Duchess of Villiers. Eleanor was older than India, and mother of an eight-year-old boy, but despite these differences, they had struck up a close friendship. Eleanor was brilliant, well read, and witty without being cruel, and India admired and adored her.

In fact, Eleanor was everything India planned to be, once she had time to read the books she had missed as a child. Someday she would like to invite Eleanor and her other friends to a country house of her own. They would spend lazy days in the shade of a willow, talking about literature. She would understand grammar by then, and never worry about *who* and *whom* again, let alone *lie* and *lay*.

But now Eleanor was writing to ask a special favor. "Adelaide, did we meet Tobias Dautry when we stayed with the Duke of Villiers?"

Her godmother put down her teacup. "No, he was in Scotland at the time. You must have heard of Dautry. He's the oldest of Villiers's bastards, and by all accounts, he owns five factories and is richer than Midas."

"Didn't he invent a blast furnace, or something like that?"

"Yes, and sold it to a coal magnate for ten thousand pounds. I must say, I do feel sympathetic toward Villiers's by-blows. It must be awkward to be brought up as a lord or lady, with expectations of an excellent marriage. Who would choose to marry a by-blow? Still, I hear that His Grace has given the girls outrageously large dowries."

India knew she was cynical, but common sense told her that those girls would indeed make excellent matches.

"Dautry is different from the others," Adelaide continued. "Rougher. I think he was living on the streets when Villiers found him, and he was already twelve years old. Eleanor never managed to civilize him."

"Why haven't I met him?" India asked. What with one thing and another, she had been to hundreds of social events in London in the last few years, although she had never debuted. It was her considered opinion that the queen had no more interest in meeting her than she had in meeting the queen.

"He's a man of business. Knows his place, I expect."

"Well, he can't have avoided society entirely," India said, "because Eleanor writes in this letter that he's courting Laetitia Rainsford."

"Really!" Adelaide's mouth formed a perfect circle. "I wonder how he came to meet Lala? She's so pretty that I would have thought her parents could do better. And Lady Rainsford was one of the royal ladies-in-waiting before her marriage."

"Money," India suggested.

"Money is not everything."

Adelaide could say that because she had never lacked it. India, on the other hand, had grown up on an estate that had been falling to wrack and ruin. In her view, money *was* everything. Or nearly everything.

"Do read to me what she says?"

India looked back at the letter. "She begins by telling me that Theodore beat his father at a game of chess for the first time, which apparently made them both very happy—"

"Goodness me, the child is only eight, isn't he?"

India nodded. "Then she writes, '*I know how much you are in demand, but I write with the faint hope that you are free. His Grace's eldest son, Tobias Dautry, has recently acquired a country estate just outside London called Starberry Court. It likely needs some refurbishing, although Tobias bought it with its contents intact. He is courting Miss Laetitia Rainsford and he wishes to ensure that the house is in suitable condition before he invites her parents to the country. Naturally, I told him that you were the only person I would trust in such an endeavor.*' "

"Eleanor is not happy about the match," Adelaide stated. "How interesting! I suspect that means that the duke is equally displeased."

"What on earth gave you that impression?"

"If Eleanor were happy about Dautry's courtship, she

would say so. And you know how informal Eleanor is; she uses Laetitia's full name. She doesn't like Lala."

"I only met her once, but I thought she was a very sweet girl."

"She's beautiful, but not very bright," Adelaide said with a touch of asperity. "I suppose that explains why the duke and duchess are not in favor. Her parents must have weighed her lack of wits against his unfortunate birth. What did you say that estate he bought was called?"

"Starberry Court."

"The Earl of Jupp's country house!" Adelaide exclaimed. "Supposedly he draped the walls in red damask and invited fourteen Italian women to live with him. The naughty sort of Italians. He held very popular parties, by all accounts. No one ever admitted to going to one, but everyone seemed to know the details."

One quickly lost all naïveté when investigating the antics that could disrupt a badly managed household, so India nodded, unsurprised. "Starberry Court became a bawdy house?"

"Not precisely a brothel, since the services offered were gratis," Adelaide said. "Jupp died last November, I think it was, and everyone said that he was brought low by the French disease. I expect the furnishings are deplorable."

"We could strip the damask in a day or two." A little prickle of excitement went down India's spine at the idea of tackling such a large task. Of course, there was the issue of finding a husband, but surely that could wait for a few more weeks. These days a small army of craftsmen awaited her command. She could have a house painter, a master wood carver, and a stonemason on the doorstep in a matter of days.

"You could likely make it acceptable," Adelaide conceded. "Still, I don't know what Dautry was thinking, buying that particular estate. Given the circumstances of his birth, why buy an estate with such a sordid reputation?"

"It was probably an excellent bargain."

"I wonder if Lord Rainsford is feeling a pinch. His wife is both spiteful and recklessly extravagant. Perhaps Lala is being sacrificed on the altar of parental excess."

"Eleanor goes on to say that she and the duke will be in attendance when Mr. Dautry entertains the Rainsfords in his new house," India said. "She invites us to stay as well. I hardly think that accepting an offer of marriage from a duke's Midas-like son, even if he was born on the wrong side of the blanket, can be termed a sacrifice."

"You're wrong there. Lady Rainsford is one of the most arrogant women on God's earth, obsessed by her connection to the Court. Mark my words: she is mortified to think that one of her daughters is considering marriage to a bastard. What's more, Eleanor wouldn't want any child of her beloved Villiers being less than celebrated. She is ferociously loyal and protective of her husband's motley brood."

India folded up the letter. "But if Villiers champions the marriage—which he must be doing, given that Eleanor will host the house party—it will take place." She was reasonably certain that the duke got everything he wanted, whether that meant marrying his bastard son to a lady or to a royal princess. He was that type of man.

"We should do it!" Adelaide exclaimed. "Lala's so witless that she might spend her whole life dancing attendance on her mother. Eleanor needs our help. That house needs our help. But heaven help her, that girl needs our help too.

"What's more," she added gleefully, "the betrothal will take Lady Rainsford down a peg or two. I can't tell you how many times she's informed me that her family has attended royalty since the time of Henry VIII."

"You make Lala sound addled," India objected. "I think her reputation for witlessness must be overstated."

"She can't read," Adelaide confided. "She told me herself."

"She needn't read once she's married to Midas; three secretaries can read aloud to her. Though I do think her governess should have been more persistent." India had fierce opinions about inadequate education.

"By all accounts, they tried. She still had a tutor as of last year, but she just couldn't grasp it. That must be the real reason the Rainsfords are considering this marriage. If she cannot read, she cannot run a household." Adelaide hesitated. "I wonder if Dautry knows that?"

There was something about this proposed marriage that India didn't like. The mercantile nature of it was jarring.

On the other hand, her parents had married for love—disastrously. Even though her father's estate desperately needed an influx of money in the form of a dowry, he had decided that happiness would solve everything. He had been wrong. Love was a terrible reason for marriage, in India's estimation.

"Eleanor is requesting that we spend the next fortnight at Starberry refurbishing the house, after which they would join us," India said.

Adelaide's expression cleared. "An excellent idea! And it would give you time to do something with your hair before we return to London."

India's hair was thick and hard to handle, as well as being an unusual color, more like silver than gold. One minute Adelaide thought she should rinse it with rosemary extract, and the next with egg yolks. Or better yet, dye it yellow.

India simply instructed her maid to pin it up as best she could. In her experience, women were of the opinion that her hair could be "brightened up," but men seemed to like it as it was. India just thought there was too much of it.

As best she could tell, she had her paternal grandmother's bosom, and there was too much of that too. Fashionable clothing was designed for small breasts, which always caused problems with fitting gowns—but luckily, she hadn't had reason to dress fashionably. In fact, it was the opposite.

She had to wear gowns that promoted respect, but also trust. In order to do her job, the people who hired her must feel she could be trusted with their homes, and dressing in the very latest styles often frightened them.

Consequently, she traveled with three trunks, because she never knew how she might need to present herself. Sometimes the master of a household responded best if she dressed like a duchess, with an emphasis on diamonds. (They invariably assumed that her jewels were family heirlooms, even though India had bought them herself.)

Other times she presented herself as a docile, modest young lady, who valued every word that dropped from the man's lips. And then there were times when the seventeen-year-old scion of the house was clearly going to make a nuisance of himself. She would come to breakfast with braided hair, wearing a dress of brown homespun reminiscent of a German governess.

If she took on Starberry Court, she should probably wear something that minimized her rank. A man who wished to rise in the world and overcome his illegitimate birth would be looking for reassurance. She would have to protect Dautry's sense of *amour propre,* while giving tactful instruction about the manners and style of a great house.

"All right," she said, making up her mind. "We'll say farewell to Lady Dibbleshire and inform Mr. Dautry that we will help him with the renovation. And with catching the woman of his dreams."

"An excellent plan," Adelaide said, nodding. "But India

darling, I must remind you that time is passing. This house cannot be an excuse to put off a decision about marriage."

India's good cheer wavered. She summoned a smile. "The house won't take long."

"You must decide between your various suitors, my dear." Adelaide patted her hand. "They won't wait forever."

"I will," India said, the words hollow even to her own ears. "I mean to find a perfect husband, Adelaide. Just as soon as I have time."

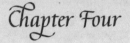

Chapter Four

June 17
40, Hanover Square
London

*I*ndia was happy to see that the Duke of Villiers's eldest son lived in a spacious town house built of white marble, its pillars the perfect size and shape to support its portico. There was nothing she liked more than to be given *carte blanche* in her renovations, and from all appearances, her client had the funds to do so.

But the moment she and Adelaide entered his library and Dautry rose from behind his desk to greet them, she realized she had made a grave miscalculation.

He walked toward them with the effortless confidence of a man who is formidable in every respect, even though he wore no coat or cravat, just a white linen shirt and breeches that stretched over his thigh muscles. Stubble darkened his jaw, and his hair was neither pulled back in a neat queue nor covered by a wig.

He looked like a farm laborer.

Or a king.

India would guess that he dominated any group of men in which he found himself. Birth hierarchy would be displaced by a more primal hierarchy of maleness. He breathed a power brewed from masculinity and intelligence, not from an accident of inheritance.

Still, his bones were knit together with a fineness that spoke of his father, of the Duke of Villiers. In fact, she could see the duke in Mr. Dautry's every lineament: in his high cheekbones, in the brutal turn of his jaw, even in the white streak that punctuated his black hair.

To her horror, India realized that all that maleness had kindled a sultry warmth in her stomach, and her pulse was thumping to a disgracefully erotic beat. She was both shocked and surprised by her body's reaction. She was decidedly not a woman who turned weak-kneed over a man.

The feeling, however, was decidedly not mutual. Indifferent eyes flicked over her, and he turned to her godmother. "Lady Xenobia," he said to Adelaide, bowing, "it is a pleasure to meet you."

Adelaide giggled, a girlish sound that India had heard only once or twice. "Mr. Dautry, I fear you are quite mistaken. I am Lady Adelaide Swift. May I introduce you to my goddaughter, Lady Xenobia?"

No sooner had surprise flashed across his face than it was gone. "I am honored, Lady Adelaide," he said smoothly. He turned to India. "My apologies, Lady Xenobia. I assumed you were Lady Adelaide's companion, judging you far too young to have accomplished the miracles that the Duchess of Villiers credits you with."

His reference to her youth—welcome though it might have been—did not make up for his assumption about her status. The only thing that made her feel better was that she was almost certain that proper grammar would require "*with which* the duchess credits you."

Mr. Dautry bowed to her, though with none of the flourishes that men generally produced when introduced to the daughter of a marquess. Even those who knew something about her father—that is, that he had been as daft as a chicken in the rain—paid obeisance to her title. Yet this man didn't even bother to brush his lips over her glove.

"It is a pleasure, Mr. Dautry," she murmured, wishing that she was wearing a gown that would bring a man to his knees. Irritatingly, that image just sent another streak of heat down her legs.

Of course, her godmother tumbled back into speech. "I could never accomplish any of darling India's miracles, I assure you! Why, when we were at your father's home . . ." Still talking, Adelaide trotted over to a sofa and happily accepted an offer of refreshment. India followed, watching as Mr. Dautry jerked his head at the butler, sending him off to fetch tea.

As Adelaide talked on and on, scarcely pausing for breath, Mr. Dautry's face took on a faint air of boredom. India adored her godmother, although she sometimes found herself dazed by Adelaide's prattle. But that was for *her* to feel, and no one else was allowed to exhibit the slightest hint of ennui in her godmother's company. She gave Mr. Dautry a narrow-eyed glance that said without words that his expression was an impertinence.

He just raised a brow, not a bit abashed.

Once the butler returned with a tray, Adelaide engaged herself pouring tea—a ceremony that she took extremely seriously—and there was finally a moment of silence in the room.

"So, Lady Xenobia," Dautry said, "my stepmother assures me that you are quite proficient at renovating houses."

Proficient? Eleanor would never have damned her with such faint praise. Clearly, this man was not going to be as easily managed as most of her clients.

Temper was ever her failing, and sure enough a spark of it kindled at his insult. "She has informed me that you are *desperate* to refurbish a country house," she replied.

Next to her, Adelaide's brows drew together. There was nothing that Adelaide disliked more than rudeness, and India's tone had been slightly impolite—as had Mr. Dautry's.

He settled back in his chair and gave India the smile with which a tiger greets a gazelle. "Yes, that's accurate. I hate to wait, you see. I am easily bored."

He probably never waited—not for a carriage, nor for a woman, nor for anything.

"I was very pleased to hear that you are planning to marry," Adelaide said, jumping into the charged silence. "Darling Eleanor confided that you have met an irresistible young lady."

India was watching Dautry carefully, and she saw a flash of irony in his eyes. This man found no woman irresistible.

"I have indeed been lucky enough to meet a lady whom I hope to make mine," he agreed. "But, of course, I must first ensure that my house provides a suitable setting for such a treasure."

The man was impossibly arrogant. He deserved to be taken down a peg or two, if only for his condescending reference to Lala as a "treasure."

But that was not her responsibility, India reminded herself. She merely had to be civil long enough to fulfill her promise to Eleanor. She leaned forward and gave him her "approval

smile," the one that promised she liked him, that said she
thought he was marvelous. Men loved that smile.

Dautry's mouth tightened and his gray eyes became distinctly cold. She sat back abruptly.

All right. That didn't work.

"What would you like to have done to Starberry Court,
Mr. Dautry?" she asked, pitching her voice toward crisp
authority.

"I should like it to be habitable in a fortnight."

"I assume the house is in excellent condition? A fortnight is an exceedingly short period of time."

"I have no idea," Mr. Dautry said, draining his teacup
in one swallow.

She frowned. "What do you mean?"

"I sent a man around to ensure that it was structurally
sound before I bought it."

She and Adelaide stared at him.

The irritated look crossed his face again. "It's a house,"
he stated. "In the right location, with a quite large estate attached to it. I was assured that this house is just what a young
lady would desire—or perhaps the better word is *require*.
That is where you come in, Lady Xenobia." He put down
the cup. "By the way, is that truly your name? 'Xenobia'?"

India knew perfectly well that people often thought
her name extremely odd, but they rarely said so. For one
thing, the name was recorded in *Debrett's*. And for another, anyone who had met her father was unsurprised by
her name. She considered herself fortunate that she had not
been christened "Moonflower."

"Yes, it is," she said evenly, and immediately returned
to the topic at hand. "Do you truly mean to tell me that you
have no idea of the house's condition?"

He answered her with a look. Apparently, he was not a
man who chose to repeat himself.

"My dear sir," Adelaide cried, "you can't possibly think to have the house habitable in a fortnight. From what I've heard, it served as a veritable brothel in the last years of its occupancy."

"I fail to see why Jupp's activities, no matter how unsavory, should affect the condition of Starberry Court. There are brothels that are as elegantly appointed as ducal mansions."

India had no doubt that the man had seen the inside of many a brothel. "Lady Rainsford is an extremely fastidious woman," she said. "She judges her behavior above reproach and insists the same of others."

Dautry raised an eyebrow. "I see. Are you well acquainted with her?"

"Her virtues are widely known," India said, leaving it at that. "If you wish to marry her daughter, not a hint of ill repute can be attached to your estate. Even if the walls and furnishings are in decent repair, it will be well-nigh impossible to achieve the correct tenor in a mere fortnight."

"Tenor?" He looked as if he was about to start laughing.

His expression sent pure irritation up India's spine. "Given your circumstances," she said, "your house must be not only charming, but also impeccably refined."

He looked as if he was about to say something derisive, so she added, "Another way to put this, Mr. Dautry, is that every detail must speak to your father's family, and not to your mother's."

At that, his eyes narrowed in a scary way, and Adelaide put down her teacup with a sharp click. "India, dear, there are ways to communicate one's opinion, and I would beg you to be more respectful." She rose, wrapping her lacy shawl around her shoulders. "Mr. Dautry, would you be kind enough to bring me to your butler so that I might powder my nose?"

India knew that by leaving the room, Adelaide hoped to bring an improper subject to a close. But Dautry returned from escorting Adelaide, walked straight back to the sofa, sat down, and said, "I gather you are trying to inform me that Miss Rainsford is above my touch?" His tone still held a hint of mockery, and the last of the simmering heat India had felt on first meeting him dissipated. This man was breathtakingly arrogant and quite dislikable.

"I think we can both agree on that point, Mr. Dautry." Since he was setting her teeth on edge, she gave him a deliberately patronizing smile. "You have made an excellent choice, but your social deficit means that you face obstacles in winning the lady's hand."

He folded his arms across a chest that was far broader than it should have been. He had to be fifteen stone, and all of it muscle. "I'd be grateful to know what considerations *you* think make the lady such an excellent choice," he said. "I suspect that our reasons differ."

Dautry couldn't have made it more obvious that he was prodding to see whether she was too missish to speak the truth aloud.

"It scarcely matters, does it?" India asked, stalling.

For his part, Thorn was reconsidering his conviction that ladies were tedious. This one, in particular, seemed to have a fiery temper that matched Vander's. And she became even more beautiful as her color heightened and her eyes sparked with irritation.

"One might say I fell in love at first sight," he said, quite untruthfully. "I met Miss Rainsford in Kensington Gardens and was so enchanted that I cannot imagine marrying another. But that doesn't explain why *you* consider her such an excellent choice."

She raised an eyebrow, revealing patent disbelief in his declaration of love. But he had managed to goad her into an answer. "Your birth presents an obvious and unavoidable challenge: you cannot marry just anyone. At the same time, your father is a duke, which means that your children—*if* you marry well—will be accepted in society by all but the most rigid sticklers."

"Good to know," Thorn said dryly.

"I fail to see why you are feigning naïveté," she snapped.

"So Miss Rainsford is of birth sufficient to paper over my 'deficit,' as you termed it? I generally think of it as bastardy, but I know there are some ladies who do not care for the word."

Lady Xenobia didn't even flinch. She was dressed in a white, fluttering thing that made her look impossibly young, but it was becoming increasingly clear that, whatever her age, she had a steel backbone. No wonder Eleanor liked her.

"As I'm sure you're aware, Lady Rainsford served as a lady-in-waiting to the queen. Yet her daughter is not pretentious in the least. Hopefully, she will not mind your disheveled appearance . . . much."

"I gather it does bother you," Thorn said, letting his amusement show.

The lady ignored that. "Insofar as Lord Rainsford is not well off, and you have no need for a large dowry, this is an ideal match. I suggest we meet in two days to assess the condition of Starberry Court. I would estimate that the work will take from one to two months, depending on the state of the plumbing."

She was clearly in a temper. Her eyes had turned squinty, which paradoxically just made her more attractive. It was hard not to wonder what all that passion would be like in bed.

When Lady Xenobia had first entered the study, Thorn had noticed her figure and her mouth—no man alive would ignore that mouth. But he had been thinking of this as a cursory interview with a faux-titled charlatan who would demand a great deal of money for beautifying Starberry Court.

Now, though, he had a strong suspicion that if he checked *Debrett's*, "Xenobia" would appear, likely engraved in gold.

His indifference had evaporated. Something about those furious blue eyes was giving him an erection. A very unwelcome erection, since he hadn't bothered to put on a coat when the ladies were announced.

Damn it, there was a reason men wore coats, and his reason was getting bigger every moment. Thank God they were sitting down. He had to get his body under control before Lady Adelaide returned and he was forced to stand.

"That was a very enlightening assessment, Lady Xenobia. And I appreciate your approval of my chosen spouse."

Her eyes flashed again, and Thorn felt an answering throb in his cock. Damn it. "But inasmuch as you are unable to refurbish my house in a fortnight," he continued, "I am forced to reconsider."

"No."

He raised an eyebrow. "I beg your pardon?"

"I said no."

"You seem not to understand me. I'm sure I can find someone to smarten up the house within the next two weeks. I'm grateful for your advice, and I will certainly instruct whomever I engage to remove any trace of debauchery they may find." He couldn't stop himself. "Swinging chairs or a mirrored ceiling, for example."

He had the keen sense that most young ladies would—at the very least—look curious at this glimpse into the further reaches of erotic customs. Not Lady Xenobia. Her eyes flared again, though she took a deep breath, clearly making a valiant effort to overcome her temper.

"No."

"No?" No one contradicted him. Certainly not a woman.

That lush mouth of hers pressed into a flat line and she rose. Hell. That meant he too had to stand. His prick was still trying to burst his breeches, even though he was dueling with a she-devil.

"I am withdrawing my request that you refurbish my house," he said. "Starberry Court merely needs to be made habitable; it needn't be transformed into a residence fit for a duke."

Luckily, she was busy glaring at his face. "You are wrong, Mr. Dautry. If your house is not impeccably furnished and adequately staffed, Lady Rainsford will not agree to this betrothal, no matter how much money you have. What's more, the house is not your only challenge. It will take you at least a month to acquire a wardrobe that will persuade Laetitia's mother you are a gentleman."

Her eyes swept over him, from hair to boots.

Shit.

But she didn't appear to notice anything untoward—other than his lack of a cravat and coat. "You should think of Starberry Court as a background that will disguise who you really are," she continued, seeming to discard the idea that he could conceal his true status with a new coat.

A man would probably spend a lifetime teasing her just to get that heated look in response. Thorn gave her a smile that—he had been reliably told—made women weak at the knees, and therefore was practically guaranteed to make her even more furious. "Do tell me, Lady Xenobia: who exactly am I?"

Her eyes glittered. "Are you attempting to *intimidate* me?"

"Absolutely not. I'm merely attempting to clarify your thoughts on the subject. Because since I haven't managed to sack you—not that I ever officially hired you—I might as well know my new employee's opinion of me."

She looked at him with about as much warmth as you might expect from a wild boar. That was the way it was in the peerage: they were all man-eating carnivores, to his mind. Except his father. And Eleanor. And a few others.

"First, Eleanor hired me, not you. And second, you are the bastard son of a duke," Lady Xenobia said bluntly, showing that she had balls, to put it equally bluntly.

"Do you realize that you are the first lady who has ever said the word 'bastard' aloud to me?"

She looked him straight in the eye. "The word has more than one meaning." It seemed she applied at least two of those meanings to him.

Thorn grinned. "Are all daughters of dukes like you?"

"I'm the daughter of a marquess, not a duke. And precisely what are you implying?"

He saw over her shoulder that Iffley was helping Lady Adelaide with her pelisse. "You are the first person I have employed who refused to be let go."

"I am extremely fond of your stepmother. I promised her that I would help you, and I shall. Your parents are rightfully concerned about your prospects for a respectable marriage."

Thorn shrugged. He was fairly sure neither Eleanor nor Villiers gave a damn who he married. "Eleanor instructed me not to inquire about your fee."

"I never discuss such matters," she said coolly. "My solicitor will contact yours."

"You're a lady, all right," he muttered. She had probably seen the bulge in his breeches without the faintest idea what it was.

"Do come, my dear," Lady Adelaide chirped from the doorway. "I have several more calls to make."

"We shall meet you at Starberry Court the day after tomorrow," Lady Xenobia said, chin in the air, as if she were

Queen Elizabeth addressing Parliament. "First thing in the morning, if you please, Mr. Dautry."

She leaned a bit closer, lowering her voice. " 'First thing in the morning' in this case will signify nine o'clock, Mr. Dautry. Forgive me for the clarification, but I would guess that your evenings are quite . . . tiring."

She *had* seen his erection. And that throaty voice of hers only made him stiffer.

"In the meantime," she continued, "I would suggest that you place yourself in the hands of Monsieur Devoulier."

"Why that tailor in particular?" Thorn drawled, thinking with some satisfaction of the various coats Devoulier had made for him over the years. He might not choose to dress like a peacock on a daily basis, but that didn't mean he hadn't the clothing to do so.

"He excels in making shortfalls less obvious," she said coolly. And damned if she didn't glance at his crotch.

How in the hell did she think his cockstand would become less obvious? And did she think that he walked about like this all day? Actually, he might do so—around her. Her folded arms were making her delectable bosom plump up like a present any man would beg to receive.

Iffley escorted the ladies out of the library, which gave Thorn time to admire Lady Xenobia's bottom before it was concealed by her pelisse. With a sigh, he looked down at his breeches.

As the front door closed, Lady Xenobia's actual words sank in: she had called his cockstand a "shortfall." A *shortfall*? An involuntary bark of laughter erupted from his throat.

No woman—lady or otherwise—had ever complained about his tool. Lady Xenobia hadn't even seen it in the flesh.

That was tantamount to a dare.

And he had never refused a challenge in his life.

Chapter Five

"*I* regret to interrupt you, Mr. Dautry, but a child has arrived." Iffley's voice had a sour ring, as if he were a classical actor forced to introduce a burlesque. "By special delivery," the butler added.

Thorn was wrestling with the design for a band of rubber, to be made at his new factory with all possible speed. He wanted it to be large enough and strong enough to secure a trunk on the top of a carriage, though he had no idea whether that was possible.

He scowled at his butler. "It's a misdirection. Get out." He had to do something about the band's elasticity, as well as rubber's tendency to melt in warm weather.

"She is accompanied by a letter addressed to you," Iffley replied with a sniff. He was endowed with a long, thin nose that gave him the air of a well-bred greyhound, and his sniff ably conveyed both reproach and disdain.

There was only one reason a strange child would show up, unbidden, at his doorstep. Yet it couldn't be a child of his. His father's lamentable example had made him vigilant in that respect. "How old is this child?"

"I would be reluctant to guess at her age; my knowledge of such matters is negligible."

The man suffered from a *folie de grandeur,* in Thorn's estimation. Perhaps he would banish him to Starberry Court. "Where is she now?"

"Frederick is in charge of all deliveries," Iffley said, extending the letter on a silver tray. "Therefore, she is at the service door, awaiting your instructions."

Thorn's eyes fell to the scrawled handwriting and his heart squeezed, then beat faster. "Bloody hell," he said softly. "That bollocking arsehole." Even touching the envelope gave him a terrible feeling in his gut, like the time he ate a pickled herring with a greenish tinge. He'd been too hungry to be put off by its peculiar taste.

"Bring the child," he said.

Iffley left and Thorn forced himself to look at the handwriting again. But he didn't open the letter, as if not reading it would somehow change the information he knew was inside.

Moments later, the door opened and the butler reentered, followed by one of his footmen, Frederick, who carried a little girl of perhaps three or four years. Her hands gripped Fred's lapel so tightly that her knuckles were white. Her face was hidden behind a tangled cloud of yellowish hair, and her legs looked pitifully thin.

Thorn took a deep breath and came from behind his desk. "Well. What is your name?"

Instead of an answer, a stifled whimper broke from the girl's mouth. The sound was infused with terror, and Thorn's chest tightened. He couldn't bear frightened children.

"Here, open this and read it aloud." He handed the letter to his butler, then plucked the child from the footman's arms. "Fred, you may return to the entry. Thank you."

The little girl looked at him for a second; he had an impression of gray eyes and a thin face before she buried her head in his chest. Her bony little back curved against his arm.

"Hell," he said, walking over to a sofa and sitting down, only belatedly remembering that one shouldn't curse in front of children. "What's your name?"

She didn't answer; he felt, more than heard, a sob shake her body.

Iffley cleared his throat. "Shall I summon the house-keeper?"

"Just read the letter to me." Thorn curved his arms around the child so that she sat within a nest, tight against his chest. That had generally soothed his sisters, back in the first days after they'd been rescued by their father and would wake up terrified night after night.

He too had been scared by the huge mansion and the odd, eccentric duke who had appeared out of nowhere, scooped him and five other children off the streets, and declared his paternity. After which His Grace had looked down his big nose and announced that his name was Tobias. It was a name he'd never heard before, and he still didn't like it.

Once Thorn turned out to be the eldest of the Duke of Villiers's rescued bastards, he rarely sat down without having a child, if not two, hanging on him, and the sensation of holding a small body on his lap came back immediately. He stroked the child's back and looked up to find Iffley staring at him, jaw slack. "Read the damned letter, Iffley."

There was a crack as the wax seal broke, and Iffley

cleared his throat. "There has indeed been some mistake, sir," he said, relief ringing in his voice. "Belying the envelope, the salutation is not addressed to you."

But Thorn had the same warning feeling that led him to sell stocks when he met a business owner who was just a trifle too jovial, or one whose teeth shone in the candlelight. "It's addressed to Juby," he said, resigned.

Juby was his pre-rescue name, the name of a mudlark who had lived in the rough and scavenged in the Thames. Juby was, and was not, Mr. Tobias Dautry, the illegitimate son of the Duke of Villiers. And he was, and was not, Thorn Dautry, an extraordinarily wealthy bastard who owned six factories, a couple of houses, and now a country estate.

Now Thorn looked down with a pulse of sadness at the child huddled in his lap. Presumably, another of his band of boys had died. There had been seven mudlarks slaving under Grindel—a rapacious, brutish master—when Villiers had located Thorn. He had been taken to his father's country estate, and the duke had dispatched the other boys to good homes. Grindel had gone to prison.

Even so, Fillibert had died that first year of a blood infection. Barty had gotten in a fight, struck his head on a cobblestone, and had never woken again. Rattles was gone the following year. After that, there had been five left, including himself.

There was an enduring bond between them, forged from surviving Grindel's cruelty, from risking death in the Thames, from coming close to starvation and frostbite more times than he cared to remember. Yet the only boy with whom he'd become true friends was Will Summers. Like Thorn, Will was the illegitimate son of a nobleman, though his father had never acknowledged his baseborn son.

When they were lads, Will had hair like a duckling's

fuzz, an odd yellow that would fluff up in the sunlight after they emerged, shivering, from the Thames, their hands full of scavenged treasures like silver spoons and human teeth—whatever they could find and, more to the point, whatever their master could sell. Will was the stubborn one, persistent to the point of madness, diving into the murkiest water to chase a flash of silver.

Iffley cleared his throat again. "It is indeed addressed to 'Juby,' and signed 'William Summers.' The handwriting is unclear, and it has apparently been exposed to water. It begins, *'If you're reading this, I've lost . . .'* but the latter half of the sentence is indecipherable. Something about the child follows. Her mother is apparently dead, then something about the Americas." He tipped the letter sideways and squinted. "It seems her mother died during her birth."

After Thorn, Will was the best educated: he had won a place at King's, and thereafter had gone into the militia. Which made it only more surprising that his daughter was alarmingly thin and distinctly unclean. She had an odd smell about her, like the inside of a tobacco pouch.

"What is her name?" Thorn asked.

"It notes without reference to a proper name that his wife's sister lives in Virginia, in America. At least—" He caught himself.

Thorn gave him a grim smile. "The child is orphaned but not illegitimate, for which we must all offer hosannas. I was at the wedding, Iffley. It took place at St. Andrew's, with a lashing of ceremonial rigmarole. But I was asking for *her* name, not her aunt's."

The girl's thin back hunched, like a bird putting its head under a wing. She was listening, though she chose not to enter the conversation.

The butler squinted at the letter again. "I don't see a name. From what I see here, you are the guardian and may choose to send the child to America if you wish. There's a bit in here about a silver teapot. Or the top to a silver teapot, which doesn't make any sense, followed by the name of his solicitor. I regret to say that the missive is abusive in nature. Summers addresses Juby as a 'fusty nut.' I believe he also says that he himself is 'ignorant as dirt,' but it could be that Juby is the object of that invective as well. And that's the entirety of the note."

Thorn nodded. "Send a message to my solicitor asking him to find out what happened to Will Summers, member of the militia located in Meryton. And ask Mrs. Stella to attend me." He tightened his arms around Will's daughter and said gently, into her ear, "Will you please tell me your name?"

The child burst into tears. Thorn sighed and stood up, scooping her into his arms. He hitched her a bit higher and followed Iffley into the entry. Frederick stood against the wall. "I gather you accepted this special delivery, Fred?"

"Yes, sir."

"Was a trunk delivered at the same time?"

"No, sir. And the driver took off so quickly that I scarcely had a look at him."

Mrs. Stella burst through the servants' door, ribbons streaming from her cap. His housekeeper had gravity about her, a quality of being bound to the earth by more than the weight of her sturdy form. "Well, who's this?" she asked. "Could it be I see a wee one in need of a bath?"

There was one more sob, and the girl's head shook in violent refusal.

"How about a bowl of porridge?"

Another shake.

"I've always found that cake is very cheering," Thorn remarked.

Mrs. Stella sighed in an exaggerated way. "Well, if you say so, sir. Cake it shall be." And she held out her arms.

No movement.

"*Cake*," Thorn repeated. "Mrs. Stella is a very nice woman, and the cake can only be found in her part of the house."

It took a moment, but the girl raised her head. "I can walk."

"You may have cake only if you tell me your name."

"My papa named me Rose," she said, her voice wavering for a moment.

Thorn put her down and she went to Mrs. Stella, stopping to look up at her. "I don't, in the general course of things, like to be carried," she said, her voice piping but quite clear.

Mrs. Stella smiled and said, "You will have no argument from me. I shouldn't like to be carried myself." They set off through the servants' door, Thorn frowning after them. Will's daughter had a most peculiar manner. As if she were ninety years old and a dowager duchess to boot.

He'd be damned if he'd ship Rose off to America. His father had misplaced all his illegitimate children after consigning them to the care of an unscrupulous solicitor. No, if the aunt wanted Rose, she would have to come to England and fetch her.

But what the devil was he to do with the girl until her aunt arrived, even supposing they could find the woman? Rose couldn't live in his house, no matter how birdlike and—

No.

Thorn went back to his desk and sat down before the design for his rubber band. Even as he worked, though, he couldn't stop thinking about Rose. At length he realized that the easiest solution was to give her to his stepmother, Eleanor. It would hardly matter if the *ton* believed that the Duke of Villiers had spawned yet another bastard.

In fact, he could ask her directly; he had just time enough to stop by his father's town house before meeting Vander for supper. He'd gone straight to his study from a vigorous ride and he smelled like the stables, so he went upstairs to his bedchamber and rang for his valet.

An hour later, he was bathed and had shrugged on a coat as elegant as any the Duke of Villiers had worn. The choice had nothing to do with the way Lady Xenobia's lip had curled when she'd looked him over.

The mere thought of her brought on another irrational flare of desire. Damn it, the woman was the daughter of a marquess. When he'd reached manhood, his father had told him not to look at women in the highest ranks. A cat couldn't look at a king, after all, nor a bastard at a marquess's daughter.

Not that he'd been *looking* at Xenobia.

Though she had looked at him.

Chapter Six

Thorn returned downstairs after bathing, thinking that he'd better see how Mrs. Stella was faring and tell Iffley to send for a Bow Street Runner. He needed someone to investigate what had happened to Will, not to mention what had happened to his daughter's clothing.

It turned out that his new ward had been bathed and fed, and put down to nap in the nursery, a room he had heretofore ignored.

"I was able to find her a little black gown that fit with just a tuck or two," Mrs. Stella reported. "I have her measurements, and I've ordered a proper wardrobe, which should be delivered in a week. You'll have to hire a governess as soon as you can, Mr. Dautry. And a nursemaid, of course."

"Would you see to the nursemaid, Mrs. Stella? And tell the agency that I'd like to interview governesses. Not tomorrow, as I'll take Rose with me to Starberry Court, but the following morning. Where's Iffley?"

Mrs. Stella's mouth tightened. "Mr. Iffley was quite perturbed by the child's arrival. I could not speak to his whereabouts."

Bloody hell. Thorn had the feeling that the agency would have to look for butlers as well. "Ask Fred to send him to me in the library."

Sure enough, Iffley had been packing his bags. "I have compromised my standards enough," he stated, his tone so sour it could have curdled milk. "After giving it some thought, Mr. Dautry, I realized that it matters little whether that child upstairs is yours or another's. The scandal will envelop you both, and the disgrace will extend far beyond the walls of this house."

Thorn resisted the impulse to take the supercilious jack-ass out with a blow to the jaw.

Iffley required no response. "I am one, sir, who prefers to have the distinctions of rank preserved. I compromised my own standards by taking this post; it is with no small amount of shame that I have confessed the same to myself. My eyes are opened to my own ignominy." He clasped his hands, looking to the heavens with an expression of utmost anguish.

Thorn stopped being irritated and started grinning. It wasn't often that one had a private farce performed at no cost in such intimate surroundings.

He sent Iffley away and ran back upstairs to see Rose. When he looked in the door of the nursery, she opened her eyes, which were large and framed by curling eyelashes. Not that they made her pretty, not with the grayish cast to her skin and the way her eyebrows cut across her eyes as straight as the flight of an arrow. She sat up as he walked into the room.

"I must go out this evening," he said.

Rose's lower lip trembled, but she said nothing and laid her head on her knees.

"For goodness' sake," he said, feeling a twinge of guilt. "One cannot take a child to a gentleman's club."

A tear caught the light as it slid over the curve of her cheek.

"Bloody hell," he said, abandoning his intention not to swear in her presence. He sat down on her bed. "Why haven't you got a doll? When I was growing up, my sisters dragged dolls with them wherever they went."

Rose didn't lift her head, and her voice was muffled by her knees. "Mr. Pancras says that there is no useful purpose to a doll. They grow dusty very quickly. He believes that acquiring accomplishments such as Greek is a better use of one's time."

"Mr. Pancras, whoever he is, sounds like an ass," Thorn said. He glanced at the clock on the mantelpiece. "Come on. We've just time to find you a doll before the shops close."

Rose sat up directly. "But the ribbon broke on my right slipper and Mrs. Stella said I can't go outside until I have new shoes."

Sure enough, there was a very tired-looking pair of slippers next to the bed, one of which had only half a ribbon. Thorn helped her from the bed, slipped them on her feet, and tied a knot instead of a bow around Rose's thin ankle, which she viewed with evident disfavor.

He stood, and she looked up at him. She did not hold out her arms, but it seemed he was expected to pick her up.

"Didn't you announce that you don't like to be carried?"

"I make exceptions when I am ill shod."

The child stared back at Thorn as if there was nothing odd about her speech. He gathered her up into his arms and remarked, "At least you smell better now."

He glanced down in time to see cool gray eyes narrow.

"So do you," she said.

Thorn stared down at her. Had she? Yes, she had. "That was not a polite comment," he told her.

She looked off, into the corner of the bedchamber, but her implication was obvious: *he* had been impolite to point out her former odor.

"I apologize for mentioning your condition. How old are you?" he asked, with real curiosity.

Another silence ensued, as if she was debating whether to answer. At last she said, "I shall be six very soon."

"Almost six! I thought you were three. Or four at most."

She regarded him again. Silently.

"My father will like you," he said, grinning.

Her nose tilted slightly in the air, and she did not deign to answer.

"You are a mystery," Thorn said, now striding toward the stairs. "You sound as if you've had a governess. But you're deplorably thin, and you have no clothing. Generally speaking, those things are difficult to reconcile with the having of a governess. Of course, there are always exceptions."

"I never had a governess," Rose announced with a crushing air of condescension. "Mr. Pancras was my tutor."

They had reached the entryway. Thorn took his coat and Rose's shabby pelisse from Fred (Iffley having taken himself off for good), carried Rose outside, and deposited her in his carriage.

"Have you ever met your aunt?" he asked, once they were underway.

"No. As Papa informed you in his letter, she lives in America."

"By all accounts, that's a marvelous place, full of bison."

"What is that?"

"An animal larger than an ox, and much shaggier."

"I am uninterested in bisons," Rose observed. "And I shouldn't like to live in America. Papa said that the ocean was perilous, and that my mother's sister was a whittie-whattie twaddle-head."

At that moment Thorn was struck by the conviction that he was never going to let Rose anywhere near the land of bison. Nor was he going to hand her to Eleanor, as if she were a piece of unwanted china. He was thinking about what that meant for his life when she asked, "Have you traveled to America?"

"I have not. You are very fluent for a nearly six-year-old."

"Papa said I have an old soul."

"Nonsense. You have a very young soul, to go with that lisp of yours."

At this, her eyes narrowed and a little bit of pink stole into her cheeks. "I do not lisp."

"Yes, you do." It was very slight—but rather enchanting.

She turned her sharp little nose into the air. "If I lisped, Mr. Pancras would have taught me otherwise."

"Why the hell didn't you have a governess?" Will had always been peculiar, but it sounded as if marriage, or being widowed, had made him even more so.

"Papa believed that women added unnecessary complications to a household."

"No nursemaid?"

She shook her head. "The kitchen maid helped me dress."

"Where *is* Pancras? Or, to ask the same question another way, why did you arrive by special delivery, and why were you dirty and thin?"

"My father said that in the event of tribulation or strife, I was to be sent to you." She stopped again.

" 'Tribulation'?" Thorn leaned back against the carriage seat. He was used to clever children. Hell, all six of his siblings could talk circles around most Oxford graduates. But it could be that Rose took the cake. "Do you know how to read?"

"Of course. I've been reading ever since I was born."

He raised an eyebrow, and she stiffened.

"Where is Pancras?" he repeated. "Why did he not bring you himself, and why have you no belongings?"

"He couldn't bring me. He had to take the first appointment that was offered to him, in Yorkshire. There was a delivery going from the brewery to London, and it cost much less for my fare than it would have on the mail coach. Plus my trunk went at no cost. I'm afraid that Papa had very little money when he died; Mr. Pancras said that he was a spendthrift."

"Your father didn't make enough money in the militia to permit extravagance," Thorn told her, making a mental note to send another Bow Street Runner after Pancras and, when he'd been turned up, to send him on a boat to China, special delivery. "So you were sent along with the beer."

Rose nodded. "The journey look longer than Mr. Pancras had thought it would."

"What happened to your clothing?"

"When we reached your house, the driver left quickly, and he forgot about my trunk. It was strapped under the barrels. He was quite unkind and wouldn't bring it down at night. I had to sleep in my dress."

A second Runner to find Rose's trunk. "How long was the journey?"

"Three days."

Thorn felt fury smoldering in his gut. "*Three days*? Where did you sleep?"

"The driver allowed me to sleep in the wagon," she explained. "It wasn't entirely proper, but I thought that Papa would tell me not to fuss. Did you know that when he was little, Papa occasionally slept outside, under the stars?"

Occasionally? He and Will had spent a couple of years sleeping in a church graveyard because their bloody-minded master wouldn't let them inside except in the dead of winter. "I did."

"He did not fuss, and neither did I," said Rose, and up went that little nose again. "I don't like to be unclean, and I didn't care for the insects living in the straw. But I did not complain."

Thorn nodded.

"Or cry. At least," she added, "until I reached your house, when I succumbed to exhaustion."

"You succumbed?" Thorn took a deep breath. "When you first arrived this morning, you didn't say a word. Do you know that I considered the idea that you might be unable to speak altogether?"

That won the very first smile he'd seen on her face.

"I talk too much," she informed him. "That's what Papa always says—*said*." Her face crumpled, and smoothed over so quickly that he almost missed it.

"You might feel better if you cry."

"I shall not, because it would make him feel sad, even in heaven."

Thorn frowned, not at all sure how to untangle that.

"Besides, I needn't cry. I am not alone and I don't have to sleep under the stars. I have you in case of tribulation. I'm lucky," she said stoutly. But a tear ran down her cheek.

"You'd better come over here," he said, holding out an arm.

"Why?"

"Because this is a time of tribulation."

They drove the rest of the way to a store called Noah's Ark, Rose nestled under his arm. After a while, Thorn handed over his handkerchief.

The shop turned out to be a wonderful place, crammed with not only dolls but also toy boats, toy carriages with real wheels, and whole regiments of tin soldiers.

The owner, Mr. Hamley, surveyed the two of them and

apparently recognized instantly that while Rose looked like a tattered little crow, Thorn planned to buy her whatever she wished. Consequently, he began treating Rose like one of the royal princesses.

As Hamley introduced Rose to the very best dolls to be found in all England (according to him), Thorn wandered away and discovered the wooden balls meant for playing croquet. He picked one up, tested its weight, tossed it from hand to hand. It would be interesting to try to make a rubber ball. It might even be possible to make it bounce. . . .

He was thinking about that when Rose came to fetch him. She had found the perfect doll, with real hair, bright blue eyes, and movable joints. "I shall call her Antigone," Rose told him.

It seemed like an odd name to Thorn, but what did he know? He distinctly remembered that his sister Phoebe had a girl doll she named Fergus.

Twilight was falling by the time Rose selected an appropriate wardrobe for her new doll. Antigone had a morning dress for making calls, a velvet evening dress, and a riding habit with cunning tiny buttons running up the front in a double row. She had a soft woolen pelisse that was nearly the same green as Rose's, a nightdress, and a little pile of undergarments that included knitted stockings as gossamer as cobwebs. Plus an umbrella.

"Perhaps a presentation gown?" Mr. Hamley asked. He opened a special box lined in white silk. Inside was a white gown that came with several ruffled petticoats and a set of hoops that would make Antigone absurdly wide. It was swagged in white lace and embroidered with tiny dangling pearls.

Rose gasped and reached out a finger to touch the satin. But she firmly shook her head. "It would be wasteful to own a gown that was worn only to meet the queen."

Thorn crouched down and said, "Sweetheart, your father gave you to me because I have more money than I know what to do with. Do you think that Antigone would like to be presented to the queen?"

Rose nodded.

There were no more tears on the way home, and Rose happily danced away to introduce Antigone to Mrs. Stella and the upstairs maid, who would serve as nursemaid until they hired one.

The next morning in the carriage Rose said, with a distinct ring of defiance in her voice, "Antigone and I would have been perfectly happy spending the day with Fred. I dislike the country."

In fact, Antigone did appear to be regarding Thorn with a very impertinent expression, but he merely said, "Until we find a governess, you will go wherever I go, and I need to pay a visit to Starberry Court."

"I find it quite incomprehensible that I should accompany you. Children are to be seen and not heard. Everyone knows that." Rose removed her doll's pelisse, drew a tiny sheet of foolscap from her pocket, and propped it up on Antigone's legs.

"What is she reading?" Thorn inquired.

"Antigone has begun a regime of studying Greek verbs for three hours each day. See?" She turned the paper so that Thorn could see words in a script so small that only a mouse could read it.

"I see no point in learning Greek," he told Rose. "What will she do with it?"

"Nothing. Ancient Greek is no longer spoken."

He shrugged. "Why waste her time?"

She had settled Antigone's paper into place and drawn out a small leather-bound volume for herself. "Neither of us are wasting our time. I would prefer to learn things, even useless things, than do nothing. Would you like me to teach you Greek? Mr. Pancras told me that all gentlemen know the language."

"I am not a gentleman."

She looked him up and down. "I can see that you are not," she observed. "But perhaps if you knew Greek, you would be able to become a gentleman."

"I don't want to," he told her.

Rose nodded and returned to her book.

And Thorn found himself staring down at the design for a rubber-stretching machine with the edges of his mouth curled up.

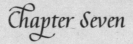

Chapter Seven

Starberry Court
Near West Drayton, Middlesex

The carriage rounded the circular gravel drive and drew to a halt. Adelaide had fallen asleep somewhere along the way, so India touched her knee gently and said, "We're here."

Her godmother opened her eyes and burst directly into speech. "The den of iniquity! Did I tell you that Jupp asked me to dance once, when I debuted? My mother declined on my behalf, of course. He already had a reputation as a libertine."

India gathered her reticule. "Let's hope the house doesn't show too much evidence of his debauchery." She glanced from the window as she waited for their groom to open the door. They had been following Mr. Dautry's carriage for some miles, and now he was stepping down from his carriage. She had forgotten how tall he was. Once again he wasn't wearing a coat, and his waistcoat emphasized the absurd width of his shoulders. Dark hair tumbled over his collar, because he wore no hat. And he hadn't a cravat either.

Hopefully he had summoned Monsieur Devoulier, because unless he began wearing a coat at the very least, it wouldn't matter if she covered Starberry Court in gold leaf: Lady Rainsford would never marry her daughter to a man who dressed like a common laborer.

As she stepped from the carriage, she watched, astonished, as Dautry held out his hands and swung a little girl down to the ground.

"Was Mr. Dautry previously married?" India asked Adelaide, *sotto voce*.

"Not that I know of," Adelaide said, clambering down from the carriage and adding, "Goodness!" once she looked in his direction.

Dautry's bow wasn't as dismissive as it had been when they'd first met. Still, it was the bow not of a courtier but of an assassin: a gesture with edge, with deadly grace.

"Lady Adelaide and Lady Xenobia, may I present my ward, Miss Rose Summers?"

The child dropped a quite respectable curtsy. Who in the world was the girl and, for that matter, where was her governess? It wasn't as if Mr. Dautry couldn't afford one.

"How do you do, Miss Rose?" Adelaide asked, stooping to smile at her.

"I am very well, thank you," she replied, in a manner remarkably composed for one so young. "It is an honor to meet you, Lady Adelaide." She turned slightly and curtsied again. "And Lady Xenobia."

India met gray eyes as cool as pond water, and her heart sank. Those eyes were unmistakable. It seemed that Villiers's bastard son was following his example and raising a child born out of wedlock under his own roof. Lady Rainsford would *not* approve.

Her mind was whirling, so she turned to survey the house. Starberry Court was a charming old mansion built of brick the color of clover honey, with six gabled roofs, numerous stone balconies, and mullioned glass windows. At one time, there had been elaborate gardens, but now high grass brushed the lowest windowsills. The drive still traced a gracious circle, but its gravel was punctuated by small white flowers growing here and there.

"Are there no servants at all?" she asked, her misgivings growing by the moment.

"It doesn't look like it. The estate agent didn't mention any retainers." Dautry began walking toward the door, pulling a large iron key from his pocket, the child trotting beside him to keep up with his long stride.

"Mr. Dautry!" India said firmly.

He and Rose turned in unison, and she looked into two pairs of eyes staring at her with identical impatient expressions.

For a moment, India couldn't even find words. Was he foolish enough to think that Lady Rainsford would accept the presence of a baseborn child in the household? No amount of money would quiet that scandal. None.

Even Villiers, the highest in the land, had been shunned by sticklers who felt his bastards should not have been thrust on society. And Mr. Dautry, needless to say, was no duke. Even if Lady Rainsford allowed the marriage, he and Lala would be rebuffed by all but close family.

"Mr. Dautry, I believe we should have another discussion about your expectations for the house party," India said finally. It was unnerving to find that she was not able to read his eyes.

"Eleanor told me that you would take care of everything. If you can't, I should like to know immediately."

"Did you truly buy this house sight unseen?"

"Do you always need things repeated, Lady Xenobia?" The way he drawled her title made the comment even more irritating. "I am quite sure that I mentioned that two days ago."

"But I had no idea that the estate was in such neglected condition," she said, trying to decide how to address the larger problem.

"I suppose we need to hire a gardener. Or ten."

"You have no staff whatsoever? I must hire everyone?"

Dautry raised his free hand and ran it through his thick hair. It sparked black, like the underside of a raven's wing, and revealed the white streak identical to the duke's. When he dropped his hand, his hair tumbled back into place and the streak disappeared. "If I had the staff, why would I need you?"

He didn't need *her*. He needed an estate manager, a housekeeper, a butler. Servants. A *wife*. And he should have married that wife years ago, so that Rose had a proper family.

"We seem to have misunderstood each other," India said, trying to stop her voice from rising. "I don't build whole households. I assess the weak points in staff, dismiss some people and hire others. My people will refurbish walls and floors, but generally we do a room or two at most. I had no idea your house was completely abandoned, without any servants whatsoever."

The impatience she'd seen in his eyes flared. "Unfortunately, my butler in London proved an arsehole, and I let him go. I can't dispatch him to help you."

India's temper blazed up. "You should not swear in front of your daughter!" she snapped, the single, complicated word tumbling out before she could think better of it.

In the silence that followed, a bird trilled. India's muscles tensed, her body instinctively preparing to run for the carriage in response to the murderous look in Dautry's eyes.

"Daughter? He is not my father," Rose said at the same moment that Dautry snarled, "Rose is my ward."

A stunned heartbeat passed before Adelaide chirped, "Oh Mr. Dautry, you do remember how you mistook Lady Xenobia for a hired companion? And now she has mistaken Miss Rose for something closer than a ward. Such mistakes do happen!"

India's heart was beating so fast that she felt dizzy. No matter how she fought it, her temper always seemed to get the better of her. "I apologize for my error."

"I think Mr. Dautry would make a very good father," the little girl said unexpectedly. She tucked her hand into his again.

India felt her face soften. "I am truly sorry, Miss Rose. I didn't mean . . . well, I misunderstood."

"There is no need to apologize," she said with dignity. "I like Mr. Dautry very much. In fact, I am going to teach him Greek, and how to dance, and he will be better off."

If India had held any advantage over Dautry before, she had just lost it. She had the sudden conviction that if she showed the slightest weakness, Dautry would squash her like an unwelcome fly at the breakfast table. "How fortunate," she said, turning to him. "I shall look forward to seeing the results of this Pygmalion endeavor."

Pure fury burned in the depths of Dautry's eyes. He bent and scooped up Rose. "I would be honored if you were my daughter," he told her, turning away slightly so that the two of them had privacy. "But I know that Will was very happy to have been your papa, and I wish he were standing here with you right now."

India took a deep breath. She had been an idiot. Dautry was an arsehole, to use his own expression. But in the utter absence of any facts, she'd had no right to leap to that or any other conclusion, and even worse, to allow the words to tumble out in front of the child.

What's more, now she couldn't simply walk to her carriage and drive away. She supposed that Rose must have entered Dautry's life in the last few days—which meant that the child had only just lost her father. How could she not have registered her mourning garment? Presumably she had lost her mother too.

Suddenly the missing pieces fell into place. This was why Thorn believed Lala would make the perfect wife. She would. Lala would be an excellent mother to an orphaned little girl. Lala was just the kind of woman who would take a child in need under her wing, give her a home, love her.

Given that, how could India not do her own part?

She *would* renovate the house and stay for the party, just long enough to make certain that the betrothal went smoothly. She would do it for Eleanor, and for Lala. And because Rose needed a mother. And—not least—because she was ashamed of herself.

As Dautry continued to speak quietly to his ward, India moved closer to the house. Happily, the mortar was in decent repair. One window appeared to be cracked, but it was in the servants' quarters and hopefully hadn't resulted in much water damage. The lawns and gardens were overgrown, but a squadron of gardeners could bring them back to a sufficiently civilized state within a week, and something quite beautiful by the date of the house party.

She began the mental list that would dictate her life for the immediate future. She would send her groom back to London immediately to summon her staff. And she'd send a letter to her favorite employment bureau, informing them that she would need twenty, or perhaps even thirty, people.

She had walked to the corner of the house and was peering down the hill at what appeared to be a dilapidated folly when she heard someone approaching. She turned to find Dautry striding toward her. Behind him, Rose was showing a doll to Adelaide.

He had a loose-limbed way of walking that signaled—in her estimation—that Greek would have no effect on his status as a gentleman. He would never be one. But she doubted Lala would care: he was one of the most handsome men India had ever seen.

"Lady Xenobia," he stated, coming to a halt.

Earlier she had thought his eyes inscrutable, but not now. They were still outraged. "Mr. Dautry, I apologize again for presuming that Rose was your daughter," she said.

His mouth tightened. "Your error—"

She cut him off with the same decisiveness with which she might counter an indignant butler. "My error had to do with the fact that your eyes are remarkably similar."

"I fail to see how such a common eye color would lead to such an error, but it is irrelevant. As you say, your talent lies in refurbishing a room or two, and I have an entire house to staff and furnish."

"That has been the limits of my experience to this date," she stated, holding his gaze. "However, I shall renovate this house and find servants for you in the next three weeks so that you can host a party including the Rainsfords, as well as your parents. I shall remain at Starberry Court for one week thereafter, and make absolutely certain that your betrothal comes to pass without Lady Rainsford's mounting a strong objection."

His reply was a string of words she'd overheard on the street but had never heard said in her presence.

She waited him out—precisely as she would an incensed butler.

At last he said, "No."

"Dear me," India said. "I thought I would have to wait for you to learn Greek before you could express yourself in English."

"I can express myself," he said, his eyes narrowed. "Just so we don't misunderstand each other, Lady Xenobia, I have no need of you."

India summoned every bit of self-control she had to keep her voice even. "Lady Rainsford will not permit you to marry Laetitia without my help, particularly after she meets Rose. I will not be the only one to mistake the child for your daughter. Rose will have to remain in London during the house party."

"No."

India frowned at him. "What? Why?"

"She spent three days in a beer cart on the way to London. I refuse to allow her to feel lost or neglected again. She remains with me."

India froze, her heart thumping at the idea of the little girl traveling in such a manner. "Anything could have happened to her!"

"I am well aware of that."

She took a deep breath. "I am very distressed to hear about your ward's arrival, but I feel compelled to tell you that while Lady Rainsford may overlook your unfortunate birth, she will not countenance the marriage if she has the faintest suspicion that Rose is yours. And she *will* have that suspicion."

"My ward has yellow hair," Dautry said, folding his arms. "Mine is black. She hasn't the faintest resemblance to me."

Against her will, India felt a pulse of sympathy for him. "It's her manner," she explained. "I think it would be fair to say that you and she view the world the same way."

"And what way is that?"

"From an invisible throne."

He was still furious, but *he* clearly had little trouble controlling his temper. "If that is the case, and Laetitia's mother disallows a betrothal, I shall look elsewhere for a wife. To resort to a proverb, there are many fish in the sea."

"You haven't time to look for another wife," India said just as bluntly. "You must marry Laetitia before people realize your ward has a distinct likeness to you. Once gossip spreads about Rose, you will be unmarriageable, in my opinion. I would suggest a special license."

Thorn was in the grip of a violent wave of disbelief. Had he previously thought Xenobia a she-devil? The names that came to mind now were far more violent. "Are you to accompany me on my honeymoon as well?" he asked. "Will I be allowed to bed my wife without instruction?"

Damned if that didn't provoke a mocking little smile from her, reminding him that she considered him to have a shortfall in his private parts. "Naturally, you will have all my best wishes for your success," she said sweetly.

As he opened his mouth to say a few choice words that he would likely regret, Rose skipped up and slipped her hand into his. "Shall we see the house now, Mr. Dautry?"

He would be happy to convince the she-devil just how well he could *succeed*. But he clenched his teeth instead and again took out the key he'd been given by his solicitors.

"Has anyone lived here since Lord Jupp died?" Lady Xenobia walked ahead of him, sounding as cool as if the air hadn't sizzled between them a moment earlier.

"No," Thorn said, grimly registering that battling with her had perversely made his cock spring to action—and he'd left his bloody coat in the carriage. Again. "I bought the house with all contents intact. Hopefully, the furniture merely needs dusting."

"It's been a good six months," Lady Adelaide said cheerfully, trotting over to join them.

The oaken door was large and heavy, with stubborn hinges. Thorn was forced to throw his shoulder against it until it swung open with a creaking noise and a rush of dusty old air. They all stepped forward as light flooded the entry hall.

A moment later Thorn snatched up his ward and headed straight back out of the house, his hand clapped over her eyes.

Chapter Eight

The Earl of Jupp had adorned his entry hall with statues.

Of naked people.

Copulating.

India had never seen a copulation before (if that was the correct use of that noun—was it a noun?), but she knew enough to be certain that these statues depicted variations on the act she'd heard described. Just inside the door, for example, was a group of two women and one man, their naked bodies so entwined it was hard to see whose limb belonged to whom. What's more, they were standing, instead of lying down, and there was no bed to be seen.

"Extraordinary," Adelaide said, fanning herself. "I'm almost sorry that my mother didn't allow that dance with Jupp. One has to wonder whether he had these done from life." She moved around the side of a horizontal piece featuring two people carved from a single block of marble.

"The men do not look English," India said, feeling

somewhat proud of the fact that she'd even noticed their facial features.

"Probably Greek," Adelaide said. She peered at a bronze statue. "Do you know, I think there's a chance that this piece is by Cellini?"

India hadn't the faintest idea who Cellini was. Was a "piece" still a statue when there was more than one person involved? Or was that a "composition"?

She moved to stand beside Adelaide, who was staring at a naked man from the back. His legs were extraordinarily hairy. And he had a tail.

India wrinkled her nose. "Is that supposed to be a man?"

"Don't be prudish, darling," Adelaide said. "There's nothing worse than an English lady who doesn't appreciate art, particularly an exquisite bronze dating from the 1500s. The hooves and tail suggest he's a satyr."

"What's a satyr?"

"Half-man, half-goat, from Greek mythology. My governess didn't teach me much about satyrs, because they are invariably naughty." She took a quizzing glass from her reticule, bent over, and peered at the base. "That looks very like Cellini's mark."

The goat man had a beautiful back, muscled in a way that India imagined few English gentlemen's were. And although she probably shouldn't look, his behind was very attractively shaped. Rounded, one might say. And muscled.

"Benvenuto Cellini was one of the most famous sculptors in Renaissance Italy," Adelaide said. "My husband spent a terrible amount of money on a silver salver depicting Neptune. Naked, of course, so it couldn't be used even among friends." She sighed.

The late Lord Swift had been prone to extravagant decisions. Luckily for Adelaide, he died before he could lay waste to the entire estate.

The satyr was not alone. He was embracing a damsel, one arm curved around her waist and the other flung in the air, curving over their heads.

They were kissing.

His lover wore no more clothes than did he.

"Thank goodness your mother didn't raise you to be straitlaced, as you'd likely faint at this," Adelaide commented, taking a closer look at the way the two figures clung to each other.

It was true that India's mother had favored dancing naked in the moonlight over instruction in ladylike behavior. At any rate, the sculpture made her feel more feverish than faint.

"I think the satyr is actually the god Bacchus," her godmother continued. "Do you see that grapevine around his forehead? Or a follower of Bacchus, because it seems to me that the god didn't have hooves."

India was more interested in the fact that she couldn't see below his chest in the front: the satyr and his beloved blended together below the waist.

Adelaide strolled away to inspect a female nude leaning against a surprisingly large bird. "This is presumably Leda and the swan. Do you suppose that Mr. Dautry was aware that these statues came with the house?"

"I had no idea." The sunlight darkened for a moment as Dautry walked through the door. "I damn well wouldn't have brought Rose with me. I've put the coachman in charge of her, but I can't stay long."

Adelaide began chattering to him about Cellini, and India drew out a piece of foolscap and a pencil and began making a list of the statues, the better to ignore the silly, craving ache that the satyr's kiss had aroused.

It was ridiculous.

Absurd.

That whole conversation outside with Dautry hadn't helped. She had never seen a man flaunt an erection the way he was doing—again. Adelaide had made certain that India recognized the signs of male arousal, if only so that no man could surprise her unawares.

But she hadn't known that men were regularly lecherous. In fact they likely wore long coats just to disguise the fact. The thought of Dibbleshire's breeches drifted through her mind; she shuddered and pushed the image away.

There were ten statues in all. She waited for a pause in Adelaide's lecture about Renaissance sculpture, then asked, "Do you wish to keep these pieces, Mr. Dautry?"

He was standing before Leda, who had very large breasts and looked merry, as if swans were just her cup of tea. "Perhaps I'll keep this one," he murmured. But then he glanced sideways at India. He was trying to shock her, the way little boys did when they dropped their breeches.

"She looks like a village barmaid," she said indifferently. "I find the satyr far more interesting."

Dautry pivoted and gave the bronze statue a good long stare. India looked again too. The satyr's hand was curved above his lover in a gesture both exuberant and protective. Unwillingly, she felt another pulse of warmth.

"If they were both female, I would," Dautry said, with a wicked grin.

He was trying to provoke her again, and she refused to give him the satisfaction of appearing scandalized. "Shall we consign the statues to the barn, and you can decide their fate some other time?"

Adelaide turned around, frowning. "Darling, you can't mean to imply that you will actually attempt to put the house to rights. India has never done anything like *this*," she told Dautry, gesturing about. "Her services are more like those of a wife. A temporary wife."

His smile deepened.

"Barring any intimacies, of course!" Adelaide cried.

India rolled her eyes. "Mr. Dautry, I assure you that my clients do not think of me as a wife, temporary or otherwise."

"Actually, that's probably why they're always falling on their knees before you, waving a ring," her godmother said.

"I'm going to pay through the nose for a wife," Dautry said, looking very amused. "It doesn't seem extraordinary that I would have to pay for a provisional one first. According to my solicitor, you charge a sum larger than many dowries."

"That is true," Adelaide said, nodding. "From the moment that darling India decided to help people in a formal way, as it were, she determined that her services had to be seen as an extravagance, or she would not be treated with the respect she deserved."

India decided to ignore this unhelpful exchange. She opened the first door to her left and entered a large drawing room. Its moth-eaten damask curtains had fallen to the floor, and only a few pieces of ramshackle furniture stood against the walls.

"Damned disappointing," Dautry said, following her into the room. "There's nothing very scandalous to be seen here at all."

India turned in a circle. The sofa and all the chairs would have to go straight to the dust heap, along with the generations of mice homesteading within. But the writing desk against the wall needed little more than a good polish to be restored to itself.

"The proportions of this room are divine," Adelaide said, poking at some paneling that had buckled from the wall.

"Unfortunately, I am not going to be able to make a complete tour of the house, since Rose is waiting for me.

Lady Xenobia, can you speculate from the condition of this room whether you could transform the house into a background that will disguise the real me?" Dautry asked.

"I can transform the house, but not you," India replied.

His response made Adelaide's forehead crease. "My dear Mr. Dautry, you'll have to curb your language. Laetitia's mother won't care for it."

"Maybe you should delay those Greek lessons," India said, keeping her voice sincere. "Just until you learn enough English to express yourself properly."

"I suppose *you* never curse," Dautry said, a distinct hint of provocation in his voice.

She was getting to know his measure now: he found her amusing. And not when she thought she was being witty, either.

"Mr. Dautry may not have had all the advantages one would wish," Adelaide said earnestly, "but that doesn't mean that he's less of a gentleman. Why, some of the most gentlemanly men rise from nothing. My butler, for example."

Dautry was terrifyingly attractive when he grinned; a dimple indented one cheek. Who would have thought such a forbidding man would have a dimple?

Without noticing, Adelaide rattled on about her butler and his exquisite manners. He never took the Lord's name in vain. "At least, I've never heard him do so, and I can't imagine that he would." India, having hired him, was quite sure of that.

"I'm afraid it's too late for me to learn that lesson," Dautry said. "And now we'll have to curtail this investigation of the property, because Rose has been in the care of my coachman long enough. Lady Xenobia, I believe that Lady Adelaide would prefer you didn't take on Starberry Court."

"I'm sorry, Adelaide, but I have already agreed to do it," India said, adding, "and I shall not fail." That sentence came out with a bite. The only time she had done so was after she'd had to ward off Lord Mening's son and heir with a penknife, which meant she'd vacated the premises before she'd been able to replace the cook.

"But where would we stay?" Adelaide protested. "Surely not here. Our trunks and our ladies' maids should arrive in an hour or two . . . are we to sleep on the grass?"

"I will take rooms for all of you in the Horn & Stag in Tonbridge," Dautry said. "It's a decent place."

"Splendid," India said.

Adelaide sighed. "I'm afraid that my goddaughter is used to getting her way," she told Dautry.

"Perhaps Rose and her nursemaid could stay at the Horn & Stag during the house party?" India asked, still grappling with the issue of Thorn's ward.

"Absolutely not," he said. "I want her close to me at all times."

"Are there any outbuildings on the estate?"

"A dower house and a gatehouse."

"I could renovate the dower house as well," India said. "She would be very close to you; you could visit her daily. But she would be out of Lady Rainsford's sight, at least until her ladyship had agreed to your betrothal."

"Are *you* ever planning to marry?" Mr. Dautry asked.

"What?" India said, nonplussed.

"Of course she will marry," Adelaide exclaimed, sounding scandalized. "India has more suitors than she knows what to do with."

"Incredible," he murmured. "Miracles never cease. I am always surprised by what my sex will tolerate."

"How odd," India said sweetly. "I myself am never surprised by men. Absurdity is so common that it seems characteristic of your sex."

"My dears, you are squabbling like the children I am

happy never to have had," Adelaide said. "India, I suggest that we retire to the inn and discuss your suitability to take on such a large project."

India should have followed Adelaide out the door, but she didn't move. "You will have to be kinder once you marry Laetitia," she said to Dautry. Something in his eyes told her that he wasn't thinking about his fiancée at the moment. "She will wither if you speak to her like that. She's too amiable to stand up to your sarcasm."

"But that's precisely why I've chosen her," Dautry said, prowling toward her. "Not because of some absurd wish to enter the peerage. If I wanted to marry a woman merely for her title, I wouldn't have chosen Laetitia."

"You'll be lucky if she accepts your offer," India said. "Even she deserves—"

"*Even* she? Are you implying something about my future bride's virtue?"

She scowled at him. "Of course not! Your mind is in the gutter."

"Always. So what did you mean?"

India hesitated. She was shocked to see that he was grinning again, his eyes locked on hers.

"If you're about to inform me that Laetitia is a noodle, I know it already."

"Ah," India said carefully.

"Miss Rainsford has a smile so charming that she's sweeter than honey. She is lovely and, like any red-blooded man, I am, shall we say, enthusiastic to bed her. She will never attempt to change me. She'll greet me every morning with a smile, offer me whatever I desire, and she'll do it cheerfully, because that's her nature."

India was struck by an emotion she had never dreamed she would experience: jealousy of Laetitia Rainsford. No man would ever describe *India* as sweeter than honey.

"Why would I give a damn about the fact that she doesn't know Greek?" Dautry continued. "Or how to multiply sums? I can do that myself."

India pulled herself back together. "I've been in many households in the last decade. I've seen plenty of husbands who consider their wives to be ninnies. Over time, in their arrogance, they leach away the sweetness they once loved."

"They are fools," Dautry said flatly. "A wife is an investment, like any other, and I take care of my possessions. I will coddle Laetitia, and frankly, I would never speak to her the way I have to you, because I've spoken to you the way I speak to a man."

Outrage surged through India's body. "Laetitia will not be your possession," she said between clenched teeth. "She will be your wife. Your partner in life. And for your information, I am *not* a man."

"Indeed? I think you may be a general disguised in women's clothing."

That did it. Lala was sweet as honey, and she was a general. The words that went through India's mind weren't polite ones. "I shall send a note around to your London residence with names of some tradespeople and artisans who should be able to help you," she said tightly.

Dautry shook his head. "I want you."

"You cannot have me. Now, if you'll please move out of the way, I shall join my godmother."

"You promised to make this house habitable so that Laetitia and her family can be comfortable."

"You can't have everything you want."

"You're afraid," he said, taunting.

"There is nothing for me to fear." She placed a hand on his chest and pushed. "I would like you to step away."

"Are you afraid of failure? You can't tolerate being my temporary wife for three weeks?"

India didn't like the way his gray eyes had turned smoky, like the sky at twilight.

He repeated, "Are you afraid that you'll fail?"

"Of course I'm not. Move back, or I will shout for help. My coachman is very large."

"If you did that, we would be compromised," he said, his voice dropping. "Lady Adelaide seems to have forgotten that she left us unchaperoned. Can you imagine the two of us permanently shackled?"

"No, I cannot," India stated. "Now, for the last time, will you please allow me to leave the room?"

"You may not be afraid of the work, but you're afraid of something," he said, not moving an inch. Instead he braced himself against the wall with a hand by her left ear, which brought his face even closer to hers.

India could smell him, a wild, woodsy smell, like soap and wind.

"Thus, I deduce that you're afraid of *me*," he said.

"I am not afraid of you," India said, keeping her voice even. "But I believe that Laetitia could do much better than marry a man who considers her a noodle and wants to treat her well merely because he paid for her!"

At that, he threw back his head and roared with laughter. "You're a romantic! Under all that brass and bluster, you're a romantic!"

India balled up her fist and struck him on the shoulder as hard as she could. He did not flinch at the blow, but he fell backward a step, still laughing. She turned to go, muttering under her breath.

He caught her arm. "What did you say, India?"

She turned her head and glared at him. "Let go of me!"

"Not until you tell me what you said." That dimple again.

"I said that you are a bastard," she told him, straight out.

"You're correct." The man was damnably attractive when he laughed. His gray eyes turned warm. And warm was dangerous because it made India feel warm too.

She wrenched her wrist from his grip.

"If you don't renovate Starberry Court," he called when she was halfway to the door, "I'll inform Eleanor that you called me a bastard and used my birth as the reason you fled."

India froze, then turned around slowly. "That wasn't what I meant, and you know it!" The Duke of Villiers and his wife were fiercely protective of his illegitimate children. Eleanor might forgive her; Villiers would not. And she liked them. She liked both of them.

"But that's what you said. I have you in a corner, India. If you're thinking that my father wouldn't like it . . . you're right. Not only would he not like it; he would destroy your reputation without a second thought."

"You wouldn't!"

"Yes, I would. I want Laetitia as my wife. I don't want to waste time looking for another woman. Her mother is apparently hell-bent on her daughter being kitted out with a country estate, thus I must invite her here before the news about Rose leaks, as you informed me outside. And you have made it more than clear that I need your taste—did you say that it was impeccable? Not just any tradesman can do the job."

"You are blackmailing me. You are a corrupt—"

He cut her off. "What's more, you'll have to renovate the dower house as well. That wasn't a bad idea on your part. Rose can stay in the dower house during the party so that the Rainsfords don't jump to the same conclusion you did about her parentage."

"They won't like it whenever they meet her."

"I do believe I'll take up your idea about a special license. They can meet Rose once I'm their son-in-law."

India didn't know what to think. "Very well," she said, giving in. She would hate it if Eleanor thought she was so insufferable that she wouldn't associate with Thorn due to his birth. "I'll help you."

"You'll stay for the party as well," he said, his voice deep and smooth now he'd got everything he wanted. "I've invited a friend of mine who will likely fall madly in love with you. You need a husband, and he's available."

"I have no need for your help finding a husband!"

"It would only be fair," he said, his voice pious and his eyes dancing.

India curled her nails so tightly into her palms that they dented her skin. "I want an unlimited budget. I'll have to hire half of London to get this done quickly."

"Go ahead. We rich bastards come in three sorts: rich, very rich, and even richer. I'm the last sort."

"Have you any specific requests as regards decoration of the house?"

He shrugged. "I like every color other than red. My father appreciates luxury, and one guest room should look like a king's palace, if possible. Get rid of those naked statues, unless you want to keep the satyr for yourself. It's sad to think of you having grown this old without ever glimpsing a man's arse."

"If you ever say anything like that to me again, I will walk out that door and never return," India stated.

There was a moment of silence, and then he smiled again. It was galling to recognize a drop of admiration in his eyes. "Balls," he said, "you've got them."

"I am not a general!" she said, and then kept going, made reckless by fury. "How do you know I haven't seen a man's arse?"

"If you have, you have untold depths, Lady Xenobia," he said, his amusement clear.

"Lady Adelaide and I will welcome you back in precisely a week," she said, ignoring his provocation. "By then, I will know the full extent of what needs to be done."

"Right. One more thing," he said. "I don't want a bed in Laetitia's room; she'll sleep with me."

"No bed?" India said, incredulous. "Of course I'll put a bed in your wife's chamber. What if she doesn't wish to sleep with you?"

"We'll sleep together." He folded his arms again.

"Your wife—"

"I know. She deserves much better than I."

"*Me*," India snapped.

"What?"

"'I' is ungrammatical; it should be, 'She deserves much better than me.'"

He burst out laughing, so India talked over him. "Privacy is a lady's prerogative, no matter whether her husband considers her—and treats her like—a possession."

"You seem to think that Laetitia won't want to sleep with me," he said silkily. "Dear me, India. You take such a dismal view of marriage; you must at least feign optimism once you accept a man's hand."

She turned on her heel and stamped out of the room, followed by a deep masculine chuckle. "I saw your lips moving," he called. "Didn't you tell Lady Adelaide that you never curse? Or were you talking about her butler?"

Choice words rocketed through India's head.

"Three weeks with Lady Xenobia as my wife," Dautry said, still laughing as he caught up with her. "I can't think of a better prologue to a life with Laetitia."

Chapter Nine

June 20, 1799
The Horn & Stage Inn

Just after sunrise the next morning, India rousted Adelaide from her bed and dragged her back to Starberry Court.

"Why must we be here early?" Adelaide asked, her sentence cut off by a yawn. "I'm in no hurry to see Jupp's statuary again."

"I have so much to do; I can't waste time." India crossed the entry hall, feeling a rising sense of excitement.

Adelaide trailed after her. "The statues look absolutely revolting in the morning light, don't they?"

A bird—or a flock of them—had plainly roosted on the marbles' heads and other bits of their anatomy; all the sculptures were lavishly streaked with white. India didn't care. Her first order of business was to inventory the rooms. After that she would tackle cleaning, with the help of every chambermaid she could find in the village and vicinity.

Adelaide drifted through the entry, morosely holding her skirts above the dust. She loved to accompany India from house to house, primarily because it gave her an opportunity for a long visit with acquaintances. India loved the challenge, but Adelaide loved the company.

"I'm in no danger of finding myself compromised here," India said. "By noon today, I'll be surrounded by laborers, from gardeners to maids."

"That's true enough," Adelaide said, poking at one of the statues with a gloved finger. "I think this one is a copy. It's plaster, not marble."

"Why not return to the inn? You could send my lady's maid back in the carriage and spend the day relaxing in that lovely parlor, reading a book."

"I couldn't leave you alone!"

"Marie would be here in no time, Adelaide. And since Dautry rented the entire inn, your presence will give the innkeeper and his wife something to do."

"Well . . ."

"I insist," India said firmly, taking Adelaide straight back out the door and leading her to the carriage. "I'll see you for dinner tonight, dearest. I'd be most grateful if the innkeeper could send a light luncheon."

Once Adelaide was gone, India returned inside, enjoying the great echoing sense of the house. A surge of excitement bubbled inside her. Furnishing and staffing a great house from the ground up would be the perfect swan song to her career.

She would give Starberry Court a sense of dignity and tradition, with a balance of beauty and comfort. Interestingly, the furnishings that were left in the house did not live up to Jupp's lurid reputation. There was some unfortunate damask wallpaper in one bedchamber, but that was a question of taste rather than depravity. And if Jupp had hung his bedstead in garish red velvet, the cloth had long since been stolen.

She pulled out a piece of foolscap. One sheet would account for every object in the house, and another would list ideas for walls and furnishings. In the next hour, she opened every drawer in the kitchens, wrinkled her nose at the privies, and investigated the butler's pantry, only to find empty shelves lined with felt where silver should have been.

When three women arrived from the village, she promised to pay them half again as much as their regular wage. Her maid, Marie, appeared and professed herself happy to help as well. They all began dragging furniture downstairs, and even throwing some out the windows with the help of Adelaide's grooms.

Dear Mr. Dautry,

I am attaching a list of all the usable furniture discovered in the house. Most important is an extraordinarily beautiful cabinet with pearl-inlaid swans on panels of exotic wood. It bears the mark of the artist Jean-Henri Reisener, who is one of the most notable French cabinetmakers.

As you'll see, the list is short, as unfortunately most furnishings have been damaged or stolen. I will be buying a great many items in the next week and shall have the invoices sent directly to you. I will also be contracting for wall painting and coverings.

Yours sincerely,
Lady Xenobia India St. Clair

Dear Lady Xenobia,

It's nice to know that you haven't crashed through an unstable floorboard and broken your neck. Swans and more swans . . . what have you done with Leda? I can't say that I'm very fond of swans. Did you know that the males bite hard enough to snap a child's arm bone?

Thorn

Dear Mr. Dautry,

I am sending this note back by the groom who delivered yours. In a piece of luck, we discovered that the cellars are intact. You have a quite fine collection of wine, which includes port laid down twenty years ago. When we find a butler, he will have to fill in gaps in the collection, but of course the sediment in any new bottles would not have settled by the time of your house party.

You will also be glad to know that there are no swans in the river that borders your gardens. I put Leda in the attics; a bosom that size might terrify an unwary chambermaid.

Yours sincerely,
Lady Xenobia India St. Clair

Dear Lady Xenobia,

I speak for all the males in the house when I say that Leda's bosom was the best thing about her.

Thorn

"There is no response," India told the groom who had spent the day riding back and forth to London. By all rights, she should throw such a disgraceful missive in the fire.

Instead she folded it and slipped it in her pocket.

Chapter Ten

June 22, 1799
76 Portman Square, London
Home of Lord and Lady Rainsford
and their daughter Laetitia

Miss Laetitia Rainsford, known to her family and friends as Lala, was in the grip of a wave of pure, unadulterated panic. Mr. Dautry would soon arrive for tea. Her mother had already succumbed to three spasms that morning, and Lala felt as if she was on the verge of her very first.

He was coming. Mr. Dautry. The son of the Duke of Villiers. Her suitor. He had made his intentions very clear, although this was the first time he had paid them a call. She had met him a month ago in Kensington Gardens, at which time Dautry had told her plainly that he meant to court her, following that up with an appointment with her father.

She truly appreciated his clarity and decisiveness, because she always found herself confused when people engaged in clever conversation. Society conversation.

She hated society.

"Lala!" She turned to find her mother standing in the drawing room doorway, clutching a handkerchief, looking the very personification of self-sacrifice. "Is that what you mean to wear?"

"Yes, I am wearing this gown," Lala replied, clasping her hands behind her back tightly so that her mother couldn't see that they were shaking. "I'm afraid there isn't time to change it now, Mama. Mr. Dautry will be here any moment."

"I suppose that is the best you can do," Lady Rainsford said, eyeing Lala's hips. "He must not mind overly about your shape, as he has accepted our invitation to tea."

"I am of the impression that he does not dislike my form," Lala said, finding her voice. Her aunt had told her that she had been dubbed the most beautiful debutante of the season, but her mother never said a word about that; she was obsessed with the overly generous shape of Lala's hips. "My figure is not terrible, Mama." Where did *that* come from? She never stood up to her mother.

Surprisingly, Lady Rainsford didn't burst into an angry retort. Instead, she strolled into the room, sat down, and said, "The man's a bastard. Beggars can't be choosers."

Lala swallowed and said, "Mama, Mr. Dautry is no beggar; he is extremely wealthy."

"Daughter! A lady *never* speaks of money in such a direct and vulgar manner." Her mother raised a melodramatic hand to her brow, like a bad actor in a penny drama.

As Lala saw it, given that ladies such as her mother took great pleasure in spending money, the subject could not be outlawed. "Julia heard from a friend that he recently bought a country estate because he is planning to marry."

Her mother straightened. "Which estate?"

"Starberry Court."

Lady Rainsford sank back onto the sofa again, brow creased in a way that would give her palpitations if she caught sight of it in the mirror. "That's the Earl of Jupp's estate—before the line died out, of course. Dautry probably bought it for a song."

"Twenty thousand pounds," Lala said, telling the first huge lie of her life. She had made up the biggest sum she could imagine.

"Well, I suppose his money balances his blood," her mother said, showing no reaction to the sum, though Lala knew she had to be impressed. "Sit down, if you please. You drive me to distraction the way you're looming about. You must remember, dear, that your bottom is better hidden than revealed in the open air."

"I understand you dislike talk of money, Mama, but I also know that Father is feeling very strained by lack of funds and would prefer not to pay for another season."

"Oh, your father," Lady Rainsford said, allowing her head to droop like an unwatered tulip. "When has the man *not* fussed about this or that? My ill health is due to his constant laments."

"Mr. Dautry won't care that I have no dowry," Lala said bluntly. "And he's likely to give Father a very large settlement if we marry."

"Believe me, Lord Rainsford could talk the hind leg off a donkey on that subject," her mother cried. "Neither of you seems to understand what a disgrace it would be to marry my daughter to a by-blow."

"Better married to Mr. Dautry than never married at all." Lala had been beset by suitors all season, but her father had rejected every one. She knew why: he had decided that her beauty was worth a huge settlement. In short, no one had bid high enough to pay off his debts.

"If only you'd eat less, your season might have had an entirely different outcome!" her mother said, her voice becoming a little shrill. "Why, you were seated beside Lord Brody, the Duke of Pindar's heir, throughout six courses. You could be a duchess!"

To Lala's mind, her failure with Lord Brody had nothing to do with her figure. It was because she was stupid. She couldn't follow conversations that pinged like tennis balls, clever expressions flying back and forth. His Grace had looked bored by the end of the first course.

"Father cannot afford another season," she said, going back to the only point that might influence her mother. "Thus, if I don't marry Mr. Dautry, I might never marry at all."

"There's no need to play the martyr," her mother said, clutching her handkerchief in a manner that threatened to shred it. "It's as if you actually want me to have another nervous spasm. I'm sure we all wish you would marry, even if it is to—"

The butler opened the door and announced, "Mr. Dautry."

Lala knew perfectly well that her mother's voice was audible in the entry, even through the door. Whenever she heard that strident tone in the drawing room, she tiptoed up the stairs.

But Mr. Dautry strolled into the room as casually as a lion into its den, Lala thought, with a sudden–-and uncharacteristic—turn to metaphor. Except that lions' eyes were tawny and hungry, and Mr. Dautry's eyes were the color of the sky on a windy, rainy day: cold, without an ounce of sentiment. His rumpled black hair was a bit longer than the fashion, but then, as far as she knew, he had nothing to do with the *ton,* so why should he follow fashion? And yet she noted with relief that his coat and breeches had been crafted by a master. Her mother would never forgive a second-rate tailor.

"It is such a pleasure to see you again, Mr. Dautry," Lala said, risking the revelation of her bottom by rising from her chair. "Mother, may I present Mr. Dautry to you?"

As Dautry bowed, Lala realized that her mother was responding to the masculinity that clung to him like a second skin. Her handkerchief was no longer clenched, but began gently waving about, conveying a sense of fragility.

Mr. Dautry wasn't the man Lala would have chosen for a husband; he was altogether too rough and masculine, with his hard eyes and the way the air seemed to vibrate slightly around him. But that was irrelevant.

As her mother had said, beggars can't be choosers.

Throughout the fuss over the tea tray, Lala told herself that she was not going to sit like a stone, without opening her mouth. She was going to be witty. She had rehearsed some clever things to say, and she had asked her maid to read aloud the *Morning Post*. If the conversation lagged, she planned to say—brightly—"Isn't it marvelous that those terrible mutinies in the Royal Navy were put down quickly?"

Mercifully, she didn't have to blurt it out immediately, because her mother was inquiring about the "dear duchess," Dautry's stepmother, even though Lala knew perfectly well that her mother had, at best, a nodding acquaintance with the Duchess of Villiers.

Dautry was obviously aware that her mother did not move in such exalted circles. At the same time, he didn't seem to care that she was claiming acquaintanceship. Despite Lala's nerves, a smile turned up the corners of her mouth. And Dautry smiled back at her—with his eyes only, but she saw it.

"The duchess is great friends with Mrs. Worsley, is she

not?" her mother was saying. "Mrs. Worsley is so lively at the dinner table. She always leads the conversation."

Dautry did not reply, and neither did Lala. She had learned long ago that replies were not obligatory when conversing with her mother.

"I wouldn't know how to speak as she does, going on and on about affairs of state and matters of high culture. There's something unrefined about it, don't you agree, Mr. Dautry?"

"I find Mrs. Worsley an interesting conversationalist."

"Men *do,* do they not?" Lady Rainsford exclaimed. "That is, she has the trick of talking to every man as if she adored him."

"And every woman as if she loathed her," Mr. Dautry said. "I suppose that I fall on the lucky side of that divide. But I come with an ulterior purpose, Lady Rainsford. Your daughter has told me of your exquisite taste."

Lala had never said anything like that, but she recognized the work of a master and smiled as if she had, indeed, said as much.

"I have recently acquired a country estate, Starberry Court."

"So we have heard," Lala's mother said, adding, with inexcusable vulgarity, "for some twenty thousand pounds." That was typical of her mother: she chastised Lala for mentioning money, but considered her own social position so secure that she could say whatever she wished.

Mr. Dautry clearly did *not* like to discuss his finances. But when Lala looked at him with a plea in her eyes, he did not utter the rebuke her mother deserved. Instead, he said, "That rumor was inaccurate. The sum was close to double that; the lands are quite extensive."

His expression apparently reminded Lady Rainsford just how presumptuous she had been; the handkerchief began fluttering about her face as she peeped over it.

"At any rate," Mr. Dautry continued, "I should be very grateful to have your advice on restorations you might suggest for the estate, Lady Rainsford. I am thinking of assembling a small house party for just that purpose."

"We are frightfully idle in this family," Lala's mother replied, still playing peekaboo with her handkerchief. "Even so, our social engagements keep us running hither and thither all the time. When will you hold your party, Mr. Dautry?"

"In three weeks, if that will suit you."

"I shall look at my engagement calendar." She looked as if she were bestowing a shilling on a vagabond.

Lala could read his eyes without difficulty. He thought her mother horrible. She rose, guessing that her suitor had endured all the intimate time with Lady Rainsford that he could tolerate. "Mr. Dautry, it has been such a pleasure to see you."

Dautry sprang to his feet with the speed of a racehorse.

"You must forgive me for not rising," Lala's mother told him. "My health is a constant concern to those who love me, and I do my best to conserve my energy in order to cause them less worry."

It wasn't until after Dautry had departed that Lala realized she hadn't uttered a word the entire time, other than "hello" and "goodbye." Her heart sank. So much for being clever and funny.

She'd done it again.

"You're such a pea-goose," her mother said, confirming the thought. "How can a man be expected to spend a lifetime with a woman who doesn't make an effort to entertain him? That's the least a wife can do, you know. They feed us, clothe us, take care of us, and in return, we entertain them."

"Yes, Mama," Lala said.

"We charm them with our beauty and our conversation, soothing away the cares of the day."

Lala wished her father were there to hear this lecture. It might be the first thing he'd laughed at in weeks.

"Yes, Mama," she said.

Dear Mr. Dautry,

I have bought silk for the drawing room walls. The cost is approximately £300, but they will send the invoice to you directly.

Lady Xenobia India St. Clair

Dear Lady Xenobia,

The invoice for silk arrived, asking for £350. I also received an invoice from an Italian painter by the name of Marconi, who is charging £150 for painting swallows. Where are these swallows? They must be formed from liquid gold, so I want to make sure I notice them.

Thorn

Dear Mr. Dautry,

The swallows will be on the dining room walls. As you seem to be worried about costs, I had your statues assessed. You will be happy to know that the bronze was indeed sculpted by Benvenuto Cellini, and may be worth a great deal of money. I can arrange to sell the piece, if you wish.

Lady Xenobia India St. Clair

Dear Lady Xenobia,

Offer it to the vicar. If for some strange reason he doesn't want it, I might give it to you as a wedding present.

Thorn

Dear Mr. Dautry,

   The vicar would be gravely offended, and I shall not do such a thing. Nor do I desire a wedding present of that nature.

                                        Lady Xenobia

Dear Lady Xenobia,

   I think I'll call you Lady X. It has such an exotic sound to it; I feel as if I am writing to the madam of a prosperous brothel. (I've never done that before, in case you're wondering.)

                                             Thorn

Dear Mr. Dautry,

   I am named after a queen who conquered all of Egypt, not after a brothel owner. Had you paid attention to your history lessons, you would presumably know that.

                                        Lady Xenobia

Dear Lady X,

   Please do remember that you are my temporary wife, in other words, at my beck and call for the next three weeks. I begin to see a spiritual purpose in all the money I'm spending to tame the Queen of Egypt. My first command is that you address me as Thorn.

                                             Thorn

Dear Mr. Dautry,

We all know you were born on the wrong side of the blanket, but you needn't have called yourself after a bush. It seems unreasonably humble.

Lady Xenobia

Dear Lady X,

You will have to imagine my response. I cannot put it in writing.

My given name is Tobias, a self-effacing name that doesn't suit. I was informed of it when I was twelve, at which point it was already inappropriate.

Thorn

Dear Mr. Dautry,

I like Tobias. It has an intellectual ring. A man with that name should be able to recite ancient Greek poetry.

Lady Xenobia

I rest my case.

Thorn

Chapter Eleven

June 27, 1799
Evening
Starberry Court

India had never been so tired in her life. The house had been gutted and scoured, and the interior walls replastered, the hardest physical labor completed in record time by crews paid treble their usual wages.

What was left now was the more nuanced work of making Starberry Court into a luxurious residence, with a patina of refinement and respectability. That would start tomorrow, when tradesmen would begin arriving with furnishings. But at the moment she could only think about a bath and her bed at the Horn & Stag.

She was heading outside to summon her coachman when the sound of a carriage made her look up. Perhaps one of the tradesmen had decided to beat the crowd.

But then she recognized Dautry's glossy black coach and vaguely remembered that he had mentioned an inspection visit. Watching as he leapt from the carriage, she decided that he looked remarkably like the statue of the satyr. Maybe it was exhaustion making her hazy, but his shoulders seemed just as wide.

The satyr's hair was curlier; Dautry's tumbled around his ears. Presumably, he didn't have cloven feet, but one never knew. He might. There was something about his eyes that was just as naughty. Devilish, really.

She corrected herself: Adelaide had explained that the satyr was not a devil, never mind the hooves and tail. In the back of her mind, she was aware that she wasn't making sense.

"Hell, you look awful," Dautry said, by way of greeting.

She smiled at him. "Why, thank you. How very kind of you to point it out."

"Show me around the place and then we'll go to the inn for supper, because you are about to fall over. Did you sleep last night?"

"Certainly," she said, trying to remember whether she had. She'd been making yet more lists and had been surprised by the dawn. The day had been frantic as the last of the walls was replastered, the kitchen's new slate floor was laid, the privies cleaned . . . All of that had to be completed before the new furniture could be brought in.

Dautry walked through the rooms so quickly that India had difficulty keeping up. "Looks good," he announced when he had seen all the plastering and the new floor in the kitchen. "We need some chairs and tables."

India explained about the tradesmen who would be arriving on the morrow with carts of furniture, rugs, and smaller objects. "I hope to be able to furnish the servants' quarters and the bedrooms from what they bring."

He nodded. "Supper," he said, taking her arm.

She was tall for a woman, but he was taller. And very solid.

"I really must go to bed," she said, feeling instinctively that the less time she spent with her employer, the better.

There was something disturbing about him, and the feeling was all the more intense after their exchange of letters. A taut awareness between them made her skin prickle.

"Supper, followed by bed," he stated.

They left the house, but she came to an abrupt halt next to his carriage. "I can't leave; my coachman won't know where I am."

"Where the hell is he?"

"In the stables, of course."

Dautry jerked his head at his groom, who trotted away. "You're in this house alone? Where's your maid? And your coachman is in the *stables*?"

"I don't make people work all night long," she said indignantly. Then she remembered the first night and added, "At least not without paying them a great deal of money."

"You should not be in the house alone," Dautry said. Without warning he slid his arm behind her knees and lifted her.

India started to protest, but in one clean motion he tossed her onto the carriage seat. He jumped in, swung the door shut, and thumped the ceiling.

Their eyes kept tangling in an embarrassing way, so India tried looking out the window. The cows looked as sleepy as she did.

"You ought to have footmen guarding you at all times," Dautry said. "I'll send a couple of mine out from London tomorrow."

"There's no need," she said, feeling dizzy. "My maid is with me all day, and once the servants' quarters are furnished, I shall be able to hire proper staff. The registry service is sending candidates tomorrow afternoon."

As soon as they reached the inn, she could go to bed. Meanwhile, she kept her backbone straight with pure force of will.

In a smooth blur of movement, Dautry moved to sit beside her. He propped himself in the corner, yanked her against his chest, and ordered, "Sleep."

She immediately tried to sit up again. "This is quite improper! And besides, I don't nap."

"Stuff propriety," he said, sounding impatient. "I don't want to marry you, Lady X, and you don't want to marry me, so who the hell will ever know—or care?"

"I never nap," India repeated.

"Don't nap, in that case." But he didn't loosen the arm holding her against him.

It would be undignified to continue to struggle. And every bone and muscle in her body was grateful to not be sitting upright.

Dautry didn't seem uncomfortable. "Since I saw you last, Rose and I have been getting to know each other. She has added the study of French verbs in the imperfect tense to her Greek. Last night she walked round and round my library, reciting them in that odd voice of hers: '*Nous venions, vous veniez.*' "

India could hear his heart beating quite slowly, like a melody played on a piano far away, in another part of the house. The carriage rocked gently beneath them. "I have no idea what that means," she admitted.

"No Frenchman would understand her either. She has an appalling accent; she sounds like an old dowager butchering the language. I've promised her a tutor, but I can already tell it won't make any difference. I haven't been able to find a governess I like yet, and she's peeved at me."

India was thinking about that as she drifted off to sleep.

When she woke, she was still lying down, no longer in the carriage but in a room with windows open to an evening breeze. The far-off rhythm of Dautry's heartbeat was still there, under her ear. And there was a light pressure on her back from his warm hand simply resting there.

Her heart pulsed momentarily with loneliness, because she couldn't remember anyone ever before putting a hand on her while she slept.

She sat up, peered at him, and said, "Hello." They seemed to be in a room at the Horn & Stag, and something had happened to her hair; it was tumbling past her shoulders.

"I like your hair," he said.

"It's my mother's," India said, in a voice husky with sleep. "There's too much of it."

"You could stuff a pillow with it someday."

She chose not to respond to that absurdity. "What are you reading?"

"A book about Leonardo's inventions."

India had no idea who Leonardo was, but she didn't feel up to asking. The expression in Dautry's eyes as he watched her rearrange her hair made her want to ask him what he was thinking—and run away to her room, both at the same time. Absurd.

She took a deep breath and twisted all her hair around itself. Most of her hairpins seemed to be mysteriously missing.

"I pulled them out in the carriage," Dautry said, watching her fruitlessly pat her head.

"Why on earth did you do that?"

"I was bored." He took a pin from his waistcoat pocket and gave it to her. "Do you know, I think I could make a better hairpin, one that bent in the middle."

India didn't see how that would improve the design, but

it seemed impolite to say so, especially after he'd presumably carried her inside. "I must apologize, Mr. Dautry, for falling asleep in such an unladylike manner."

"Thorn."

"I beg your pardon?"

"You're to address me as Thorn, remember? I already issued a command to that effect. I'm tired of 'Lady X.' I shall call you India, as your godmother does. 'Lady X' sounds like a woman with a repertoire of exotic sexual services to offer. You haven't, have you?"

She gave him a look. "If you'll excuse me, I will retire to my chamber. I will, of course, continue to inform you of my progress."

"You haven't said much about progress," he observed. "Instead, you've sent me bills so large that I could have wallpapered half the East End." He reached over and tugged on the bell.

The innkeeper immediately opened the door. "We're ready for supper," Thorn told him. The man bowed and withdrew again.

"I couldn't," India said, just as her hair uncurled and fell down her back again. Though it was true that her stomach felt as if it were pressing against her backbone.

"If you're going to say some idiotic thing about how you can't eat dinner because a lady shouldn't eat with a man, or some damned thing along those lines, just don't. I'm starving. You're hungry and tired. Furthermore, you're not a lady right now, but in my employ, and I could eat with my butler if I wanted to."

Before she decided whether she was more hungry than tired, or more tired than hungry, the innkeeper bustled in with a large covered salver, followed by two maids with china and cutlery.

After they laid the table, India didn't think about it any

longer. She and Thorn sat at the table and ate oyster stew, followed by roast beef, French beans, peas, and a very good cheese pie. She ate more than she'd eaten in days. She drank two glasses of wine, then sipped a third glass more slowly, as she watched Thorn eat more of everything.

"You have an impressive appetite," she said, somewhat awed.

"As have you," he said, working on another helping of peas. "I like a woman who doesn't nibble like a goat."

"Lala has a very charming figure," she offered.

He looked up and grinned. He had lovely white teeth. "I know."

She was beginning to feel owlish and drowsily content, so she put her elbows on the table. Even not having had a governess, she knew it was deeply improper. Actually, worse than that: maybe it was criminal.

Thorn wouldn't care.

"I think you'll be quite happy together." She poured more wine for him, thought about it, and poured more for herself as well. "Will you tell me about growing up in East London?" she asked, propping up her head with one hand.

"It wasn't fun," he said. His voice dropped in register.

"I didn't suppose it was *fun*. I imagined it was terrible. But I don't know, which is why I asked."

He had curious eyes, a gray that looked almost green in the lamplight. With a thick fringe of black lashes. "Why do you want to know?"

"Why not?" She took a sip of wine, feeling heat pool in her stomach. It was his fault for being so damned handsome. She pushed the thought away. "I am curious about any number of things. Almost every moment, I realize something else I don't know. For example, I don't know who Leonardo was, any more than I understood Rose's French verbs."

"No particular reason why you should know about Leonardo," Thorn said. "He was an artist, though I don't care about that. I'm interested in his inventions."

He was looking down at what remained of the cheese pie as if he were about to take another piece, even though he'd already eaten three. India reached across and took it away. "You've eaten enough. You will grow fat."

"I won't get fat." He growled it.

"You've probably grown a paunch from all the food you've just eaten," she said, enjoying herself.

His eyes narrowed and he stood up wordlessly, pulled his shirt from his breeches, and bared his stomach.

India barely stopped her mouth from falling open. He looked like . . . like something. Like no man she'd ever seen. Not that she'd seen many men. But she knew they were soft around the middle, the same as she was. Thorn wasn't. His torso was rippled with muscle under taut skin. Rather than white, it was sun-browned, and a little line of hair led straight into his waistband.

"I trust I have made my point," he said, sitting down again. "Now I shall have a slice of strawberry tart with cream." He cut the tart and took half for himself. He cut another quarter and put it before her. And then he poured thick cream on top of both plates.

India never ate sweets because she figured that there was about the right amount of her. Besides, Adelaide was convinced that dessert went straight to one's breasts, and India was wary of becoming more bosomy than she already was. Speaking of which—speaking of whom?—her godmother must have gone to sleep wondering why she hadn't returned for supper.

"Eat," he commanded.

She ate. He poured more wine and she drank that too.

"You appeared astonished at the sight of my stomach,"

he remarked, glancing at her from under his eyelashes. There was something sinful in his voice that made her feel muddled.

"If you look at the satyr's waist from the side, very carefully, his torso is almost as rippled as yours," India said.

Thorn burst out laughing.

"Most gentlemen's stomachs are quite different. Lord Dibbleshire's, for example," she confided.

"Who the hell is that?" He had finished his tart, but he leaned forward and stole a forkful from the plate, even though it was the public dish and his fork should never have touched it.

"He's the latest to ask me to marry him," India said, faintly surprised to hear that her words emerged a bit slurred. She pushed away her wineglass.

"How many proposals have you received?"

"Ten. Or perhaps only nine—I think that Sir Henry Damper didn't actually mean to ask me to marry him. He meant something else, but Adelaide appeared and he had to change what he was saying very quickly."

Thorn's eyebrows drew together. "How many have asked you for 'something else'?"

"Oh, a few," India said. "But mostly they ask me for marriage because, you see, it would be much cheaper to marry me than to hire me. I'm very expensive." As he'd done it first, she decided to take a bite from the dish.

"Bloody hell."

"Will you tell me what it was like to live on the streets?" she asked.

"I didn't grow up on the streets," he said, beginning to peel an apple. "I was cared for by a nice woman until I was around six years old, when my father's solicitor took me away and placed me in an apprenticeship."

"All right," India said, thinking this sounded a good

deal better than it could have been. "What did you learn?" She pulled her wineglass back and took another sip.

"It wasn't a real apprenticeship. My master was an old bastard who had a group of boys and forced us to do whatever he wanted."

Her glass froze in the air.

"Not that. We were mudlarks. Do you know what that is?"

"As I told you, I hardly know anything."

He shook his head. "You're an odd duck."

"No, just an ignorant one."

Dautry leaned forward. "Who gave me a primer on the differences between plaster, paint, and silk for walls?"

"Those things are not important."

"What is?"

"How to speak correctly. In French and Greek. Knowing who famous people are, like Leonardo." She said his name carefully. "And Cellini. You say that with a *chee* sound in front, but you don't spell it that way."

"That's important?"

"I suppose you wouldn't know, because mudlarks don't have tutors. Do they?"

"Definitely not." He began to cut the apple into precise slices.

"What does a mudlark do?"

"Scavenge things from the Thames."

"Do you mean that you went swimming?"

"Sometimes. But mostly we waited for low tide and waded into the mud to pick up whatever we could. Sometimes we found silver spoons and coins. But most of the time it was teeth, scraps of iron, buttons. Even handkerchiefs."

India stared at Thorn in horror. "That's awful! And it could have been dangerous. Were you in danger of drowning when the tide came in?"

"Broken glass was a bigger problem. It lurks in the mud,

and if you're unlucky with your foot or your hand, it will slice you, as easily as I'm slicing this apple."

"'Slice you'?" India whispered. "*Slice* you?" she said, louder, because she didn't believe in whispering, even when the word was frightening.

"Infection took a lot of the boys." He was watching her over his glass. "There are corpses in the water, and if you went into the water with an open wound, you were likely to get infected."

"What?" She shouted that. She didn't mean to; it just came out of her mouth. "He made you go in the river when there were dead people in there? Did you *step* on them?"

"No."

"That's despicable!" she cried. "Despicable! How did he force you to wade into the mud?"

"He was a violent man," Thorn said, without a trace of emotion in his voice. "Though he never hit me. I would have killed him, and he knew that."

"You should have."

"I would have, sooner or later. Just to make him stop shouting at us." The memories didn't appear to bother him much, but they had to, somewhere deep inside.

But the story explained for her why Thorn wanted to marry Lala, besides the obvious fact of her beauty. She was such a sweet girl: she would make him feel better. She would smooth over all those bad memories.

India told him that, leaning on her elbow again. "Lala is just right for you. She's like sugar icing. She'll make it all sweet again."

He looked up at her, a bit squinty-eyed. "What are you talking about? Make what sweet again?"

"Life. She's the perfect antidote to such a terrible experience." But there was one more thing she wanted to know. "Did he feed you enough?"

The look in his eyes was sardonic, as if she were an idiot. Which she was. *Whom* she was?

"I hate being hungry," she said. But really, there wasn't much to be said about it, and she knew it as well as anyone, so she stood up, just catching the edge of the table before she lost her balance.

"And I never drink to excess," she added.

"You're more interesting when you do. What do you know about being hungry?"

India ignored that. "I must go to bed. The carts will begin arriving at six in the morning. I promised a twenty percent bonus for every piece I take."

He drained his glass. "Bloody hell."

"You're supposed to stand up as soon as I do," she said, letting go of the table and heading toward the door. "It's never too late to learn, Dautry. Lala will expect you to stand in her presence."

Then she jumped, because somehow he had got himself to the door before her. "I'm not Dautry," he said, a big hand curling around her upper arm.

"No, you're a bastard," she said obligingly, and giggled. "To be honest, I never said that word aloud before I said it to you."

He turned her around so they faced each other. Her hands naturally came up to rest on his chest.

"I'm *Thorn,* not 'Mr. Dautry.' Can you remember that?" He gave her a little shake, as if she were a poplar tree and the wind had swooped by.

"Some married couples don't even address each other by their Christian names!"

"Thorn isn't my given name, remember? Tobias is."

He looked rough and dangerous, like a man who would threaten to kill an evil master and mean it. "Tobias is not the right name for you," she said, leaning in a little bit to make her point.

The corners of his mouth quirked up. "I agree."

"A Tobias would drink hot cocoa for breakfast and go bald. And I think he would wear flannel drawers, which I find truly abhorrent. You don't wear flannel drawers, do you?"

His body went still again. "What do you know about men's drawers?"

"Oh, for goodness' sake," she said, stepping away from him because she was within a second of leaning forward and putting her cheek against his chest. "I know precisely the amount of fabric required to make a pair of drawers. Unless the man has a large stomach, in which case, I don't know how much fabric is needed, and the tailor must measure. But I have to say that I don't like the idea of flannel."

"You'll be glad to know that I don't wear it."

"That is irrelevant to me." She added, just to make the point, "Mr. Dautry."

"India."

"Yes?"

"You're mine for another two weeks. I'm Thorn at meals and in letters. Not in public."

They would likely never eat together again after Starberry Court was finished, since she scarcely knew Lala.

"I suppose," she agreed.

His eyes caught hers.

"All right—*Thorn*," she said irritably. "Using nicknames makes me feel as if we're siblings. Next you'll expect a kiss goodnight."

Something changed in his eyes, and India suddenly felt a bit more sober.

"I wouldn't say no." His hands slipped down her back.

"Are you offering to make me your mistress?"

He was silent for a second, then said, "No. But I am wondering if you have ever been kissed."

"Of course I have!"

He bent his head, and his lips touched hers.

India was curious, very curious, so she stood still as the kiss happened. Then it was over.

"Well, that was nice," she said, feeling a little trickle of disappointment. What had she expected? Kisses were kisses and nothing more. Three men had kissed her. Four, including Dautry. None of the kisses had been terribly interesting.

He pulled her closer, which set off a feeling of alarm. "I must go to my bedchamber now," she told him.

"Did that kiss make you desire to marry me?" he inquired.

"No. Though it was very nice, of course. I think Lala will be very happy with your kisses."

"I'm not married *yet,*" he pointed out. "Nor betrothed, because I wouldn't be kissing you if I was."

"Good," she said promptly, and forgot she was standing in the circle of his arms, his hands warm on her back. "Do you know that I once saw Mr. Bridewell-Cooper kissing the vicar's wife?"

"A bold choice. My guess would be that the gentleman has kissed many women who aren't his wife."

"Will you do the same?" For some reason, the answer mattered. Probably because Lala was such a dear, and not all that bright. Other women had to look out for her.

His expression turned dark. "Absolutely not."

"That was just the right answer," she said, giving him a lavish smile, her best smile. She stood on her toes and brushed her mouth over his, just as he had. "I quite like being friends with a man. It's very interesting." Then, because she felt tipsy and chatty, she added, "And I am glad you kissed me. It was very nice of you."

Apparently, she'd done something wrong, because he

scowled and pulled her against him. "If I'm your friend, India, I can't leave you thinking that was a kiss."

"Why not?" she asked, confused.

He bent his head.

This kiss was different. India felt as if she were in a dream, one in which Thorn's eyes closed, and she glimpsed his thick, black lashes. And then his tongue slid between her lips.

She'd never dreamed that a kiss could be so intimate. His tongue was *there,* in her mouth, as if he were talking to her. As if they were talking to each other. Silently. It made her shiver, and he pulled her even tighter.

India decided that she really liked kissing. It was *fun,* she thought dimly. Very . . . very . . . something.

"Damn it," he growled, pulling back.

"What?" she said, giving him another big smile. "I like this. It's quite nice."

" 'Nice'?"

Her smile dimmed. "Didn't you like it?"

"India." He stopped. "No."

"Why not?"

His eyes were on hers, and she actually caught the precise moment he decided to be honest. "You're not good at kissing, India. In fact, you're downright terrible."

Her heart thumped and her arms fell away from his neck. "Oh." She'd have to remember not to kiss her future spouse until after he proposed.

"India—"

That's all she let him say. He was probably going to offer her lessons, or some other absurd thing that only a man would think up. She ducked around him to leave, before realizing that her inadequacies weren't his fault. She turned and said, "Thank you for telling me, Thorn. I'm sorry about—"

That was all she managed to say, because he reached out and pulled her toward him once again. A large hand clamped on her bottom—where no man had *ever* touched her!—and he growled in her ear, "I'm not done yet."

His tongue swept into her mouth. She could actually feel his hunger deep inside her body, making her skin tingle. The hand that wasn't holding her against him came up and gripped her hair in his fist, tugging her head back.

A little whimper broke in her throat, and without thinking she bent her head sideways and brought her own tongue out to taste *him*.

The moment she did that, he groaned and his arm tightened around her. That kiss . . .

That kiss did things. To her, to her body. He was surrounding her, all hardness to her softness. The feeling made her hot and restless, and she made that little sound in the back of her throat again and pressed closer to him. She didn't know why she hadn't liked kissing before. It was tremendously interesting. It was more than interesting. It was . . .

Thorn cursed and pulled away from her.

India stood there, feeling feverish. "I must be very drunk," she said, pulling herself together.

He was staring at her, eyes gray-green and wild. "*Damn*."

"Good night," she said, and added, "this did not happen, Mr. Dautry."

" 'Mr. Dautry'?" He growled it.

India realized that her heart was beating fast and her knees felt weak. She cleared her throat. "Right. Thorn. Not that this will happen again." She walked out the door with admirable steadiness and got herself upstairs and into her bed.

When she woke up in the morning, she lay for a while trying to decide whether she was still a bad kisser, or whether he'd taught her something. But when she ventured down to breakfast and learned that Thorn had set off at the break of dawn without even leaving a letter, she concluded that that spoke for itself.

The truth stung. Perhaps even more sharply because she had no idea what she should have done differently. But over the years she'd learned that not everyone could be good at everything. She finally decided to put the whole subject out of her mind, into the same box as her childhood—things better left unexamined.

Just as she made that decision, Adelaide walked into the breakfast room.

"I understand that you and Mr. Dautry supped together last night," she said, helping herself to a serving of coddled egg from the sideboard. "I suppose I ought to have chaperoned you, but this wicked cold kept me in bed all day. And in truth I don't worry about him, since the dear man has such an infatuation with Lala. Do you know that he told me that Lala was his ideal woman, perfect for him? *Lala*? I am as generous as the next person . . ."

In the back of India's mind, the sting got a little sharper. One had to suppose that Thorn had kissed Lala—how else could he have deemed her perfect?

After a struggle, India managed to control a bitter pulse of jealousy by telling herself that jealousy was unbecoming. Unladylike.

She ignored the part of her that didn't give a damn about being a lady and just wanted Thorn to consider *her* kisses perfect.

Dear India,

> *Today I received an invoice for Aubusson carpets. Are you nailing them to the roof in lieu of slate?*

There isn't enough floor space in the entire house for this number of rugs.

> Thorn

P.S. I am sending this letter by one of my footmen, Fred. He's a country boy. I told him that you are not to be alone in that house at any time. The groom will return with your reply.

Dear Thorn,

The carpets are an investment for future generations. Lala's mother will appreciate the furnishings, even if you don't.

> India

P.S. Fred is a lovely fellow.

Dear India,

You do realize that I won't be marrying Laetitia's mother, don't you?

> Thorn

Dear Thorn,

Count your blessings.

> India

Dear India,

I received another collection of invoices, and now I am rethinking marriage altogether. I'm not sure it's worth it. Did we really need that much champagne? Not to mention the barrel of Colchester oysters, the knitted stockings, and the pound of Fry's drinking chocolate?

                                        Thorn

Dear Thorn,

Of course you must marry. Many men your age have already been inconsolable widowers, wooed, and won their second wives. You are a laggard in that respect.

                                        India

P.S. The stockings are for your footmen (three begin next week), the oysters for Lady Rainsford (who adores oyster soup, according to Adelaide), and the chocolate for me.

Dear India,

You must be living for pleasure, considering that pound of chocolate. I think I'd prefer to remain unmarried and develop a gluttonous lust for chocolate. In bed. The oysters throw a strange light on Lala's mother; you do know what they are good for, don't you?

                                        Thorn

Dear Thorn,

I have heard something of the virtues of oysters, but I believe that they need to be fresh to be efficacious in that respect. I'm surprised that you have need of such a remedy, but I shall hasten to lay in an order for regular shipments whenever you are in residence.

India

Dear India,

You injure me; truly, you do. I would display my virtues, but I'm sure that, as the virtuous woman you are, you might faint.
Or not.

Thorn

Dear Thorn,

I see enough wilted vegetables in the regular course of things.

India

Dear India,

You have thrown down the gauntlet in terms of my vegetables, and my supposed shortfall. I could have proved it to you the other night.

Thorn

Dear Mr. Dautry,

There was no other night. You were dreaming.

                    Lady Xenobia India St. Clair

Dear India,

I'll be there tomorrow for another inspection of your progress.

                    Thorn

Chapter Twelve

India could glimpse sanity on the far horizon. Soon the drawing room walls would be covered with Lyonnaise silk, hand-painted with apple blossoms. One of her favorite Italian painters would finish work in the dining room by afternoon; he had first painted it gray-green, and now he was almost done gilding the painted swallows that swooped across its walls.

India had sent Adelaide—whose taste was impeachable—back to London to choose furniture from Thomas Sheraton's and Jean-Henri Reisener's showrooms. They would have to accept whatever was available, but she had a very good relationship with Mr. Sheraton, in particular, and was reasonably optimistic that he would give her whatever he had and tell his customers that the pieces they'd ordered had been delayed.

A man specializing in Italian glass had arrived the day before, carting with him a true treasure: an enormous Ve-

netian blue-glass mirror, along with the alabaster mantelpiece that would be installed after the silk was on the
drawing room walls.

And she had borrowed a master gardener from Lord
Pendleton's estate in the next county. (Pendleton was still
very grateful to her for the successful birth of his child,
in which frankly—since she hadn't been the woman in
labor—she had played no real part.) The sound of men
working in the gardens drifted through the open windows.
Already the lawns had been weeded, neatly mown, and
rolled smooth enough for a tennis game. The flowerbeds
had desperately needed pruning; now they looked present-
able, though rather bare.

When Thorn jumped from his carriage that evening, she
was waiting respectably in the drawing room, rather than
leaning in the doorframe like a night-walker. She had also
taken the time to bathe and put on a gown without a speck
of plaster or dust or paint on it.

The moment Thorn walked into the drawing room she
could tell that something was wrong. His body was vi-
brating with pent-up emotion as he strode toward her. She
started to drop into a curtsy, but he leaned forward and
brushed his lips over hers. As if they were siblings. Not
that she had a sibling, but she imagined they kissed like
that.

"We must be quick, India," he said without further
greeting. "Show me the floors you've paved in gold, and
I'll be back on the road."

"You are not merely walking through the house and
leaving!"

"Yes, I am."

She shrugged. "Fred plans to serve the dinner sent by
the innkeeper here, if that changes your mind. We might
begin in the ballroom. It turned out well." That was an

understatement. The walls had been stuccoed in the faintest pink, and the decorative molding was gleaming white. She'd had wall sconces installed with pale green blown-glass shades, a tint that matched the delicate chairs. She thought it was perfect.

He walked through the door, looked around, and said, "It looks good. What's next?"

India's mouth fell open. She put her hands on her hips. "This room is not *good*!"

"It isn't?"

"It is utterly gorgeous. It is better than Versailles. It is better than any ballroom you've seen before!"

A germ of amusement lit up his eyes, which just irritated her more. "It's hardly my forte," he said, not sounding in the least apologetic.

"I had workmen in here day and night! The night before last, none of us slept because—"

At that, his scowl matched hers. "What do you mean, you didn't sleep?"

"Francisco and I had to paint the stucco before it dried," she explained. "If you don't finish painting—"

He took a step toward her. "*Francisco* and you?" His voice dropped a level, and all that anger he was carrying in his body channeled right into his words. Maybe he wasn't as controlled as she'd thought.

"Francisco Bernasconi," she said, holding her ground. "He's a master of stucco, the best in all England. Three or four years ago, he showed me how to do it, and now I always help."

"I didn't hire you to do manual labor!"

"It's one of the reasons I'm successful," she explained. "If I have to, I can bake bread. I can show a cook how to make mayonnaise and not break it. I can paint stucco, I can move furniture, I can—"

"The hell with that," he growled. "How old is this bloke?"

India frowned. "That is irrelevant."

"It's not irrelevant. How old is he?"

"Barely thirty, I suppose. But his age doesn't matter: what matters is that he trained in Florence under a *maestro*. He's an artist."

"I suppose he's in high demand?"

"Always. It was a miracle that we were able to get him here on such short notice."

His eyes flared. "He came because he's in love with you. I suppose they all are."

"Francisco has never said a single inappropriate word to me, ever. You do him a huge injustice to suggest it!"

He looked at her lips and then straight down her body. "Were you wearing that?"

"Of course I wasn't wearing this gown!" India was beginning to feel truly incensed. Thorn had been in a mood when he'd arrived, and now he was being absurd—as if he were jealous or protective, which he had no right to be.

"Well, at least that's something," he muttered.

"What are you talking about?" she shouted at him, now losing her temper altogether. "I didn't wear this gown, because I wore another gown, and what does that matter anyway?"

"He watched you bend over. All night long."

"I wasn't bending over!" she retorted. "Not that it makes any difference."

He closed his eyes for a moment. "India, tell me that you weren't on your knees."

She didn't speak to that, because of course she had been on her knees. Francisco and his men worked on the upper walls, on the delicate leaf work around the moldings, and she worked below. "You are an extraordinarily rude man," she said, turning to leave. "I'll show you the dining room walls, after which you can return to London."

"Those walls were painted by another Italian—Manocchi, wasn't it? Did he too give up everything when you begged him?"

"Mr. Marconi and I have worked together many times, and he is very loyal," India said, tossing her head because she didn't like his tone. She looked over her shoulder and said, with distinct satisfaction, "Moreover, you paid him half as much again his usual rate."

"He is in love with you as well," Thorn stated. "Bloody hell."

"I can see that you'll just make rude remarks about the dining room, so you might as well get into your carriage now."

"I changed my mind. I'm having supper with you," he said. "We'll stare at the birds on the walls while we eat. I want to make sure to get my money's worth."

Chapter Thirteen

Thorn's day had started badly and had become progressively worse. Rose informed him at breakfast that she hated the governess he'd hired, after which she disappeared. Two hours of rising panic ensued as the household searched for her; it wasn't until Mrs. Stella unearthed her from her hiding place under his desk in the library that he knew she was safe.

At that point he had lost his temper, after which he felt even worse because Rose burst into tears and said that her father never shouted. He didn't doubt this was true. Will might have been stubborn, but he was always sweet-tempered.

He wasn't. He was a prick, who'd just behaved like a prick to a little girl who didn't deserve it.

They had ended up in a big chair as he rocked her back and forth and tried to explain himself. "The idea that you were lost in London made my gut turn cold. In fact, it's something of a personal triumph that I didn't curse like a sailor."

Rose raised her tearful face from his chest and said, "It's very ill mannered to congratulate oneself. Particularly when one is at fault." A little pause, and she added, "Do you think that Papa was sent to heaven because he was a saint?"

"From what my solicitor discovered, the British militia doesn't train their men well enough. One of them made a mistake, and your father died as a result." He probably should have lied and said that Will was too good for this world. Which would have made Will roar with laughter and call him all number of names.

Once Rose was promised a governess she liked and handed back over to Mrs. Stella, Thorn went to his rubber factory, only to be told that it was impossible to produce bands of rubber large enough to hold trunks on top of a carriage. Even after three hours of trying to think their way around it, he and his manager couldn't make it work.

Yet now, here with India at Starberry Court, he was smiling. It was a miracle.

"Show me the dining room, India," he repeated. "I'm bloody well starving to death."

It seemed that India was a flouncer when she was cross, given that she flounced her way into the dining room ahead of him, which allowed him to appreciate her truly fine curves from behind. That put him in an even better mood.

Enough so that he poured praise on the swallows, painted by some poor dauber who was obviously in love with India, though she never noticed him. He had figured out that the proposals she'd mentioned—of marriage and otherwise—were likely just the tip of the iceberg when it came to men in love with Lady Xenobia India St. Clair.

She should wear a warning sign on her back. Before you

knew it, you'd be in too deep to recover, find yourself on your knees mumbling nonsense, too taken by the way she burned with life and passion to save yourself.

He himself might have ended up in the same bind if he hadn't decided early on in life what type of woman he wanted to marry. Laetitia was exactly right. She would love him and their children in an uncomplicated way.

India, though, was complicated. Everything about her was complicated. There was even something about her childhood that he didn't understand. "Where is Lady Adelaide?" he asked, remembering her supposed chaperone.

"She's gone to London to pick out furniture. Mr. Sheraton is far too grand to send pieces here for my consideration; Adelaide has gone to coax him into giving us pieces that he has made for others."

"Is that legal?" he asked, not really caring.

"Of course it is." India grinned, apparently having forgotten that she was cross at him. "You'll pay him much more than he would have received, so everyone will be happy. Well, except the original purchasers. But he'll make them other pieces. Everything that comes from his workshop is superb. I told Adelaide that we'll take whatever he will give us."

She sat down and began removing the tops from serving dishes arranged down the middle of the table. "Your kitchens should be operating very soon now. The chimneys have been repointed, and there are two new stoves. I am still negotiating with the cook, but I am hopeful."

Thorn sat down opposite her. "Did Lady Adelaide know that I was coming to see the house?"

"Yes, of course. She asked me to give you her best."

"She felt no need to chaperone?"

"Your frank adoration of Lala has put you in the category of an elderly uncle. I think of it more as brotherly love. Given the way you greeted me with a kiss."

He shot her an ironic look. "I have enough sisters as it is, India."

Fred carried in yet another platter. "Berry tart, Lady Xenobia," he said cheerfully. Clearly he and India were now the best of friends.

"Thank you, Fred," India said. She turned to Thorn. "Did I mention that I found a marvelous butler called Fleming, who will arrive tomorrow? Three new footmen should be in residence very soon, and Fred can continue as head footman—unless you'd like to take him back to London."

"I think I'd rather port him back and forth with me," Thorn said. "He's a useful fellow. Just bring the food, Fred, and we'll serve ourselves. No, wait a moment! I want a bottle of that champagne."

"That's for the house party," India protested.

"I'll be damned if I waste all that wine on Laetitia's mother. I've been to tea again since I saw you last, and the woman is a shrew."

She said nothing, which meant she agreed. Hell. No wonder he had sensed Laetitia needed rescuing.

"Champagne," he repeated.

"You'll find bottles in the cellars, Fred," India said, putting a slice of chicken on one plate, half the bird on another, and handing him the latter. "How was your day?"

Thorn didn't feel like confessing that he'd shouted at Rose. "I spent most of it at one of my factories not far from here that manufactures galvanized rubber. We've been trying to create a band strong enough to hold a trunk on top of a carriage, but it won't work."

"Is that why you were cross when you arrived?"

"I was not cross," he told her.

"Irritable? Moody? Gnashing your teeth?"

She was an imp, and the disturbing thing was that he'd like to kiss her into silence.

"What does 'galvanized' mean?" India asked.

"Galvanization is a process that stops rubber from melting." He took a bite of chicken and forced his attention away from the swell of her lower lip.

"Why can't you make the band work?"

"It's too large for our machines." Frustration leaked into his voice.

"Would you be able to make a smaller band?"

"What for?"

"Rubber is elastic, isn't it? I would love a band I could put around bundles of paper and playing cards. Would it be possible to make a band large enough to put around a box, if not a trunk?"

"Possibly."

"Unless a box is extremely well made, the top allows dust to seep inside. It would be wonderful if a band would hold a box together so that the contents didn't become dusty. For example, I like to have shelving built in the attics of any house I work on, with boxes . . ."

A half hour later, Thorn emerged from a haze, during which he had drilled India with questions about every possible household use for a band of rubber. He looked up from the paper on which he had been jotting down possible dimensions to find that she was smiling at him, cheek propped on her hand.

He was struck by another impulse to kiss her, this time so strong that his body froze for a moment. "I'm being an idiot," he muttered, shoving the paper into his waistcoat. He poured them both glasses of champagne from the bottle Fred had unearthed. "Let's drink to India's band of rubber."

" 'Rubber band' sounds better," she said.

He raised his glass, quite certain that his factory would survive after this. "Twenty-six men were in danger of losing employment, but your rubber bands will prevent that."

The champagne India had bought tasted like apples and had a powerful kick. He still preferred brandy, but this wasn't terrible.

"Enough about rubber," he said. He realized his eyes kept drifting over her lush breasts, and his sense of self-preservation abruptly kicked in. "What are you looking for in a husband, Lady Xenobia India St. Clair?"

"He must be kind and very calm," she said readily to this complete non sequitur. "And I'd prefer that he do something with his life and leave me to run the household."

"My dear," Thorn said with a grin, "he'll *do* something. I can promise you that."

His comment didn't seem to scandalize her in the least, perhaps because she was tipsy again. Lady Xenobia had many virtues, but an ability to handle her liquor wasn't one of them. He poured the last of the champagne into her glass and reached over to ring the bell.

"Did you know that many men are incapable in private?" She eyed him. "Are you?"

"No." That word came out more forcefully than necessary. Even though her talk of wilted vegetables and shortfalls—and now incapabilities—*sounded* like a challenge, India was almost certainly a maiden. True, Lady Adelaide was not proving to be the most assiduous of chaperones, but an innocence about India suggested she had never succumbed to the many men who sprawled at her feet.

"Marriage is not about that," India said. "Marriage is an understanding, a contract governing behavior and, hopefully, advantageous to both sides, but the advantages to each partner must be weighed. That's why I—" She stopped.

"Why you what?" Thorn asked.

"I was fifteen when Adelaide asked me to organize the household of a friend of hers," she explained. "I accepted payment because my father had left me nothing but a title.

Without a dowry, I was unlikely to make a good match, let alone an excellent one."

"Therefore you earned your own dowry."

"Yes."

She beamed at him, and Thorn felt a chill down his back. When India forgot to smile like a lady . . . He shook it off. "I would say that you now have enough negotiating power to marry whomever you wish."

She was toying with her glass, her slender fingers playing with the stem as if it were an instrument. The sight made his groin tighten, and he wrenched his attention back to the subject of her ideal spouse. "The most important consideration has nothing to do with title," he said. "Personal traits make it possible for a marriage to succeed."

She cocked her head. "That is very wise of you."

"I have my moments." He grinned at her. "I'm well aware that Laetitia wouldn't suit everyone, but she's right for me. Have you met your perfect man yet?"

"To be honest, I'm generally too busy to give men much thought."

To Thorn's mind, that was one reason she had been successful. Wives instinctively realized that India posed no threat to their marriages, even as their husbands acquiesced to her every request.

She had a Cleopatra face, the kind that made men fall on their knees. He'd bet that after she gave a man the glimmering little smile she had on her lips at this very moment, he would simply give her *carte blanche* to do as she would with his house—precisely as he himself had.

"My husband will have to be good at kissing," she said, her eyes pure, slumberous devilment. "I've been told that I'm not very good at kissing, and I will need to marry an expert."

"India," Thorn warned. This game they were playing was dangerous.

She wrinkled her nose at him and looked so adorable that he tossed back the rest of his champagne, letting the cold wine burn a little sanity into him.

Fred arrived with a second bottle, while India handed Thorn a slice of apple pie and took a piece of berry tart for herself. After Fred left, empty plates in hand, Thorn said, "India, you are not bad at kissing."

"You said I was." But there was a little smile in her eyes.

"Our second kiss wasn't just good," he said, "as you obviously know. It was . . ."

He couldn't find the words.

"Are you saying that I'm not a terrible kisser?"

"India."

She drank more champagne and looked at him, wet lips shiny. "I thought perhaps you'd offer me lessons in the art, which I would refuse, of course."

Every man has limits to his self-control. Thorn stood up, walked around the table, and drew her to her feet. "India, my kisses are appalling. Terrible. Would you offer me lessons?"

She looked him straight in the eye and said, "Practice makes perfect." And then she giggled. Lady Xenobia India giggled.

Thorn pulled her into his arms. "You do remember that I plan to marry Laetitia?"

"Do you imagine that a kiss or two might make me want to marry you?" The pure surprise in India's eyes gave Thorn a quick kick in the arse.

The daughter of a marquess would never look to one such as he, no matter how much she liked his kisses. For God's sake, had he learned nothing in his years as the bastard son of a duke?

India put her arms around his neck. "We are friends, you and I. I have no true friends, because I've never had time for them. I never had them when I was little either, because of my parents. You are my first true friend."

Then she kissed him. She was tipsy, and a lady, and unchaperoned. . . .

But she wasn't a bad kisser.

She tasted like berry tart, like sparkling wine, like a woman . . . like India. She leaned into him, buried her fingers in his hair, closed her eyes, and let herself go. There was no tension in India's body when she kissed; she fell into the act with the same passion with which she seemed to approach everything.

It was the most erotic thing he'd ever experienced. Even so, he kept a strict rein on himself. His hands slid along her arms and felt skin as smooth as satin.

He lifted up one slender arm and placed a kiss at the inner curve of her elbow. She caught her breath, so he licked her there. A small, remote voice in the back of his mind reminded him that they could only kiss.

Nothing more.

He had never paid attention to arms before. Now he put a kiss on the delicate blue veins of her inner wrist and felt himself hardening even more, as if he could come merely from the taste of her.

When he straightened, she wound her arms around his neck and began kissing him again, her tongue retreating, setting his blood on fire, dancing forward and making his mind explode with images of what she might do with that tongue. . . .

That's when he knew he had to stop. It was one thing to kiss India. She was unlike any other woman he'd met: curious, brave, and independent. She was a friend. But he couldn't take it too far.

He didn't want to ruin everything.

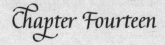

Chapter Fourteen

Dear Thorn,

    I am enclosing an invoice from Thomas Sheraton for several thousand pounds. He was kind enough to give you furniture that had been crafted for another customer; I knew that you would wish to repay his generosity by giving him a generous supplement, thus I added it to the invoice. Mr. Sheraton asked me to give you his sincere thanks.

India

Dear India,

    The bill from Sheraton was crippling, but in comparison, the cost of a "blue mirror" was truly aston-

ishing. Do you wish to appear blue? Do I? Is this a reference to blue blood? Do I give a damn that the mirror is Venetian? No, I do not. Return it.

                                        Thorn

Dear Thorn,

One does not "return" a work of art. You are striving to enter the upper ranks, and you will simply have to trust me to create a worthy atmosphere.

                                        India

Dear India,

Return the damn mirror.

                                        Thorn

Dear Thorn,

You'll be happy to know the mirror and mantelpiece have been installed and look splendid.

In other news, I have managed to secure you an excellent cook. I had to lure him away from Lord Pistlethorpe's household, and you will be paying him somewhat more than his normal wage. But given your boast that you are—I hope I have this right—more than a "rich bastard," I knew you would not hesitate, because excellent food can make an otherwise uncomfortable house party bearable.

He arrived with his kitchen crew in tow, and I hired them as well. I trust that Lord P does not send you a challenge, but if he does, I've no doubt you will be the victor at fisticuffs or something of that nature.

India

Dear India,

You may keep the mirror if you could restrain yourself from filching staff from other households. I have indeed heard from Pistlethorpe, who is not pleased.

By the way, we used to call him Mortar-and-Pestle at school, owing to his nocturnal activities.

Thorn

Dear Thorn,

I have no idea what you are talking about with reference to Lord Pistlethorpe, and I don't wish to know.

Your new butler, Mr. Fleming, unfortunately cannot be in residence until the day before you and your parents arrive. I have also engaged four upstairs maids, two downstairs maids, a scullery maid, and a stablemaster. We are on the lookout for a bootblack and two hall boys.

The gatehouse has been cleaned, with some very basic furnishings installed, as I did not know whether you would care to hire a gatekeeper.

India

Dear India,

I was referring to a man's wish to pleasure himself under the covers in the dark. Pistlethorpe treated his tool to a vigorous dubbing nightly in such a manner that every boy in the house knew it. Do women do the same? Were you sent to school?

I suspect that marquess's daughters are too delicate and precious to leave the parental eye, but I have no idea. My sisters were kept at home, but then we were all special cases.

Thorn

Dear Mr. Dautry,

You may not write me in this manner or I shall cease to send you notice of what I am doing with your estate. I will simply forward the bills.

Lady Xenobia India St. Clair

Dear India,

I surmise from the irritation in your letter that ladies do not lie about at night touching their softer parts, which is a huge loss on their part. You should try it. It's greatly relaxing, and you seem prone to vexation.

Thorn

Mr. Dautry,

I enclose the following invoices: £100 for wax candles, £50 for lye soap, and £200 for gold braid.

Lady Xenobia India St. Clair

Dear India,

If you intend to fleece me out of house and home, at least send along a word or two to blunt the pain. Surely what I wrote was not so horrendous? I was under the impression that you and I were becoming friends, in a strange sort of way. But I am sorry if you are genuinely offended; I suppose ladies don't want to hear of such things, even in jest. What the hell is all that gold braid for?

Thorn

Dear Thorn,

I have no objection to being friends if you at least attempt to be witty rather than vulgar. The gold braid trims the dining room curtains. They were hung today and they are magnificent against the silk walls.

India

Dear India,

I'm not very good at wit. It's probably to do with growing up on the streets. Can you forgive me? I didn't say that I lie about pleasuring myself while thinking of you, after all. It was merely a polite inquiry.

                                                        Thorn

Dear Thorn,

   Why on earth would I share such private informa-tion with you? This is a genuinely curious question.

                                                        India

Dear India,

   I know from the tenor of your letters that you do it. Put the satyr in whatever room you've chosen. I'm sure he'll be inspirational, and I don't want him any-where near me. I've no mind to look at a man's arse.
   I wish I was coming to Starberry tonight to see the gold-braided curtains myself. I would try to get you tipsy again; I have fond memories of our meals together.

                                                        Thorn

India had hired a housekeeper whom she'd had her eye on for some time—an excellent maid working in a London house where her abilities were underappreciated. She was younger than most housekeepers, but she had a stern back-bone and would stand up to her new master. And perhaps as importantly, she would be a warrior on Lala's side.

Over the years, India had realized that servants played an important part in a marriage, and not simply because a good cook made everyone in the house happier.

Lala's bedchamber was, in India's considered opinion, precisely what any lady would want. She had ignored Dautry's instructions and given her a bed with barley-twist posts, hung in pale yellow silk embroidered with pansies. There was a graceful desk under the window, where the mistress of the house could glance out across the back lawn, with a view all the way to the willow trees that graced the riverbank. The bedchamber was a refuge, a place that would echo and replenish Lala's sweetness.

She had also purchased a large Sheraton wardrobe, with shelves of different depths on which to place evening gowns, day dresses, and even a special shelf for a presentation gown.

Some parts of the estate would necessarily remain untouched, at least until the house had its own mistress. The dairies and the brewhouse were still in wretched condition; the nursery was clean, but bare; she had barely looked at the library, other than acquiring a few comfortable chairs and a few boxes of books. She meant to organize the shelves, but that would be all.

The privies were now clean, but even so she had set in motion the establishment of Bramah-designed water closets, with a float system for the water tank. She'd never seen one, but she'd read about them, and although they were very new, and very expensive, she determined they should be placed throughout the house, even though it would happen after the house party.

After spending a decade living in the margins between householders and servants, she had a keen understanding of the fact that life would be immeasurably better for chambermaids if chamber pots could be retired forever.

Because Dautry had given her no direction as to livery, she toyed with the idea of putting his men in a deep red, simply to vex him, but in the end she chose overcoats made of Italian wool in a blue just a touch darker than a robin's egg.

Since the gardens had been ruthlessly pruned, they could not furnish blooms to adorn the house. Her solution was to trade an exorbitant donation on the part of Mr. Dautry to the parish church, which desperately needed a new steeple, for the head gardener's freedom to take whatever he needed from the flowerbeds that stretched behind the vicarage.

Already the house was beautiful: glowing, elegant yet homelike, comfortable as well as luxurious.

Dear Thorn,

    I offered the satyr to the village church, as you suggested. The vicar was so offended that you have had to make a major donation to repair the church steeple. Perhaps the Cellini should be relinquished to the Bank of England, where it could wait in a vault for your further instructions?

India

Dear India,

    Is the dower house progressing? I think Rose would like a rocking horse. She told me today that Antigone does not like the new governess (the second I hired), and when I found the time to investigate, I learned that the lady had already given her notice. We shall arrive with a nursemaid and the much-beloved Antigone.

Thorn

Dear Thorn,

    I have completed the mistress's bedchamber, which

means the house is very nearly ready. I was unable to find a rocking horse here; perhaps you can locate one in London? The dower house awaits Rose.

India

Dear India,

I shall arrive in three days, Rose in tow. I sent my new butler out for a rocking horse and he found only a rocking cow. Rose thinks the cow is stupid, and I have similar concerns about the new butler. She named the cow Buttercup.

Thorn

Dear Thorn,

A good milking cow is never a bad investment; your future offspring might like her.

You will be happy to know that the privies are now functioning, and the bedchambers furnished. Yesterday Lady Adelaide and I left the Horn & Stag and moved to Starberry Court.

India

Dear India,

Did I tell you that I've invited my friend Vander, the future Duke of Pindar, to the house party? I know the two of you are a perfect match in that you have the bluest of blue blood. Lately, I've been thinking that I should give him advance warning.

It's the least a man can do for the brotherhood.
Like wearing garlic to ward off a vampire.

                                              Thorn

Dear Thorn,

   I'm worried that after Laetitia gets to know you
a bit better, she'll choose the local doctor—a very
handsome young man—over you. I summoned Dr.
Hatfield to warn him of Lady Rainsford's imminent
arrival. As you may be aware, her ladyship requires
daily medical attention for any number of ailments.
I promised Hatfield two pounds for each day that he
dances attendance on her.

                                              India

Dear India,

   That's probably the first expense of which I
heartily approve. Here's hoping that Hatfield can
keep the lady in check. I met her only twice, but I
live in fear.

                                              Thorn

Dear Thorn,

   You really mustn't speak of your future mother-in-
law in such a jocular manner. Perhaps you should
begin an earnest study of polite manners. It would
be a shame to do all this to the house, only to have

*Lady Rainsford take a virulent dislike to you. As she
is bound to do if you don't play your cards better.*

           India

Dear India,

   *You are my trump card. I expect your next career
will be in matchmaking. At any rate, I am just back
from meeting Laetitia in Kensington Gardens, and I
am too much at ease with the world to squabble with
you. I am feeling like a lucky man.*

           All the best,
           Thorn

For some irrational reason, India had kept all of Thorn's
notes. She liked the way his sentences tore across the page in
a strong, slanting hand. By this point, she had a quite a pile,
as they'd kept messengers going back and forth to London
for days. But she tossed this letter in the library fireplace.

Of course, she was glad that he was happy. Thrilled.
Lala would be able to coax him into displaying his dimple
on a daily basis. Lala was adorable, that's what she was.
Adorable the way little bunnies and babies and all the
sweet little things in the world were.

These days, India felt herself to be the very opposite
of adorable. She looked haggard. She was so exhausted
that she felt as if a horse had ridden over her. Everywhere
she looked, she saw more things that needed attending to.
Indeed, as she watched Thorn's letter burn, she realized
that the space over this fireplace needed a painting.

A family portrait would be perfect: perhaps Lala and

her children in the garden, and Thorn leaning against a tree just behind them, with that fierce look he had, and the contained power of his body.

She shook her head, taking herself out of the room nearly at a run. She wouldn't answer his letter.

In fact, she shouldn't answer any more letters at all.

Dear India,

You will be happy to learn that I have solved the problem of the governess. I found a tutor instead, a young sprig by the name of Twink. He graduated from Cambridge about three and a half minutes ago, but he's a good fellow. He laughs, which Rose needs.

Her nursemaid's name is Clara. She's a good girl from the Highlands and will probably fall in love with Twink, but there's nothing I can do about that. They will both accompany us to Starberry C. and stay in the dower house.

Thorn

India had spent the whole of the afternoon in the library, sorting through books in order to shelve them, and she still wasn't finished. In her opinion, a library was the heart of a house. A library's book-filled shelves conveyed the impression that a family has lived in one place for generations: curious minds bequeathing their collections for their descendants to read.

Obviously, Thorn didn't have that.

Nor, it seemed, had Jupp. Either he hadn't owned many books, or an especially literate thief had ransacked the library, since most of the bookshelves had been bare.

Never mind: India had bought three large crates of "miscellaneous books" from the Temple of the Muses bookshop in Finsbury Square, and they'd arrived that morning. The shelves had been scrubbed and oiled; now they gleamed in the June sunlight, waiting to be filled. India began by emptying the crates and piling the books on the floor according to subject matter: literature and poetry (of which there were very few) here, military history and the like (at least fifty) over there, householdry and farming (three tall stacks) across the room. There were books of essays, books of sermons, and fourteen Bibles. (Apparently the bookseller hadn't thought she'd actually *look* at her purchases.)

When she had them sorted, she turned her attention to the books that remained of Jupp's collection in order to distribute them among the piles.

It was at that point—and perhaps she should not have been surprised—that she discovered his naughty books.

The first one she picked up was called *Memoirs of a Woman of Pleasure*. That was followed by *Venus in the Cloister: or, The Nun in Her Smock*; *The Rape of the Sabines*; and *The Amatory Adventures of Tilly Tucket*.

"Tilly Tucket"? What sort of name was that? India sank to the floor and opened the book at random, finding herself staring at an engraving of a frolicsome couple. Like a silly chambermaid, she gasped and slammed the volume shut, opened it again, and examined precisely what was happening.

She could feel her cheeks were pink by the time she put the book to the side; perhaps she would buy a bookshelf that locked. After one quick look at *The Rape of the Sabines,* she dropped that one onto a pile destined to be thrown away, followed by a few others that were equally horrid.

But then she picked up *The Genuine and Remarkable Amours of a Light Gentleman* and turned to the first page.

The book followed the adventures of a young man called Francis Feather. "Feather" turned out to be not . . . feathery. In fact, she had no idea that men's parts were so large. Feather's was easily the size of his lower leg. It didn't seem anatomically possible.

The volume was lavishly illustrated, and there was definitely something riveting about the engravings. In one, for example, Feather and his inamorata were making love on a table.

She could tell it was a dining table, because a teacup and two plates had smashed on the floor, presumably owing to the frenzy of their activity. It made her think differently about household cleaning, though surely the depiction was merely there to shock.

Adelaide had explained that these things happened under the covers, in the dark. Once in a while.

Well, maybe Adelaide hadn't specified that, but India had inferred it.

Feather observed no such restrictions: in another engraving, he was depicted on a riverbank, and when he did appear in a bed, he had a woman nestled on each side, just like the Greek statuary now residing in the attic.

At that point, India turned back and began reading the actual story. She only came to herself thirty minutes later, when the light was slanting low through the library windows. Pushing her hair behind her ears, she realized that her fingers were trembling.

It was an interesting book, she told herself. Merely interesting. She closed it, willing herself to forget the images inside. It was just that the engravings looked so, well, erotic . . . and the women didn't appear to be shy or ashamed. They appeared to be very jolly.

Eager, even.

Though how could they possibly be? It wasn't physically

possible. But there was that picture of the table, with the woman's head hanging off the edge, her hair sweeping the floor. That had to be ecstasy on her face.

It was hard to tell. India opened to the page again and turned it upside down, the better to examine the woman's face.

Her mouth was open. Was she in extreme pain, or was she experiencing pleasure?

She was mulling this over when a noise broke her concentration and she looked up. Thorn stood in the doorway, regarding her. She slammed the book shut and scrambled to her feet, feeling like a child caught sneaking bonbons. "What on earth are you doing here? You aren't due for two days!"

Thorn raised an eyebrow. "You didn't answer my last two letters. I thought I'd better make sure you hadn't collapsed with exhaustion."

"Of course I haven't," India said, dropping her arm so the book was hidden by the folds of her skirt.

"I've been at the factory all day, so I stopped by on my way back to London." He looked around at the stacks. "Tell me you're not trying to organize these books."

India cleared her throat. "Just in a general way, by subject. I'll put the literature in one section, histories in another."

"I suppose the library is one good thing that comes from owning a country estate." He walked over to the table and picked up a book on animal husbandry. "I can send out the books I have sitting around in London. They've outgrown the bookshelves in my library and are stacked against the walls, much to my housekeeper's dissatisfaction."

India casually slid *Remarkable Amours* on top of a stack of books describing travel. Thorn picked a book from another stack, and looked at its spine. "Are these all books of sermons?"

"I'm afraid so," India said. "That stack and the one over there, and all those on the far table."

"Jupp never fails to surprise. Get rid of those, will you? That will leave space for my London books."

India nodded. "What books do you enjoy?"

"Anything I can get my hands on, though not sermons. What else is in here?"

The naughty books came to India's mind, but she had no idea how to refer to them. "Let's see . . . There is a short stack of grammar books, two of Greek grammar and three of German."

Thorn turned up the lamps fixed to the walls, and another on the mantelpiece. "I suppose I can give those to Rose. She's such a solemn little thing that she'll probably work through them in a matter of a week."

"I found a couple of children's books that she might like. I put them in the dower house."

"We've already made two trips to Hatchard's bookshop," he remarked casually, returning to the table and picking up a travel narrative.

India felt her insides clench. If he glanced at the next stack . . .

"I didn't think that you would conduct such errands yourself," she said, edging closer to the questionable volume and leaning her hip against the table. In a moment, she would nonchalantly pick up the entire stack and carry it over to a shelf.

"Rose's governesses have barely stayed in the house long enough to unpack. But from now on, Twink can take her to the bookshop. You know, you could have simply piled these books onto the shelves." He laughed at the expression on her face. "I gather you're a perfectionist."

"I wouldn't be very good at this profession if I weren't."

"It's odd to hear a lady speak about a *profession*," he said, turning over yet another book.

"You must not talk to many," she said tartly. "You are surrounded by women who work very hard at various enterprises."

"But they aren't ladies," he said, with perfect truth. He turned his head and looked at her from under his lashes. "And even more than not being ladies, they aren't daughters of marquesses."

"There's nothing about my father's title that renders me incapable of work."

"Clearly that's the case. But don't pretend that you're not unusual, India." He'd reached the bottom of the stack of books. "This is the third book about Italy. I'm starting to think that Jupp bought that Cellini in his travels."

"In fact, I think those books came from a bookshop," she said. "I found only twenty or thirty books here, so I had to add to your library."

Thorn looked up with a bark of laughter. "You bought some poor bugger's books to make it look as if I had ancestors who knew how to read?"

"No one is trying to disguise the provenance of the house and your ownership of it," she objected.

He snorted.

"We are simply demonstrating that you are a man of discernment," India told him.

Before she could stop him Thorn leaned over and picked up Feather's book. He turned the pages, an entirely wicked grin on his lips. "I see that I am very discerning indeed. You *are* showing unexpected depths, India."

"Thanks to Lord Jupp, you have many such volumes in your new collection," she muttered, gesturing toward the stack on the floor. She could feel color rising in her cheeks again.

"Damn," Thorn said, turning the pages. "This is an adventuresome little volume."

"I threw a couple of them in the bin," India said defiantly.

"Good."

She hesitated, then: "Aren't you curious about what they were?"

"There's sickness in the world, India. I saw some of it as a boy, more as a man . . . I don't want it in my house, or anywhere near Rose."

India loved the way he was protecting Rose, so she smiled at him, a wide smile. Unguarded. Unusual for her.

He frowned. "India."

"Yes?"

"No wonder all those men are scrabbling at your feet to marry you. You could seduce a saint with that smile." He looked back at the book and turned another page. "Did you enjoy Mr. Feather's undertakings?"

"I merely glanced at the volume."

His mouth quirked. "I stood in that doorway for a good five minutes before you saw me. I was squinting, but it looked to me as if this was the picture you found most fascinating."

At that, heat flooded her body. Propriety demanded that she run from the room, but she remained where she was.

Thorn turned the page upside down, just as she had. "What on earth is so fascinating? Except the size of Feather's tool, which definitely falls in the category of an optimistic daydream."

India filed that comment away to think about later. Who would wish for something that large to come anywhere near her most delicate parts?

"Do tell, India," Thorn said, laughing aloud now. He turned the picture the other way.

"I was trying to see whether she was enjoying herself," India confessed.

"See how her hands are flying out into the air like that?

In my experience—which is not slight—she's having a fine time. Screaming, I would guess."

Another wave of heat concentrated between her legs. "'Screaming'?" She didn't know whether to be horrified or envious.

"With pleasure," he added, turning the pages. "Feather is giving her everything she wants. Hell, look at this one." He glanced up, his eyes alight with mischief. "She's screaming here as well."

India looked at the engraving for a good minute before she realized what Feather was doing with his head between the lady's legs. And yes, the lady did seem to be experiencing an acute level of happiness. And her mouth was open, as Thorn noted.

She snapped to herself again. "We shouldn't be having this conversation. It's wretchedly inappropriate."

Thorn shook his head at her. "Nothing wrong about it, India. You and I are friends."

That stopped her on the very edge of flight. "Friends? You look at books of this nature with your *friends*?" Frankly, it was a scandalous notion.

"No, only with you. Come take a look at what he's doing here. I've never tried it."

"No!"

"I'll come to you, in that case." India rapidly backed away, until she found herself stopped by the bookcase.

"I don't want to see it!"

Thorn stopped just in front of her, trapping her with his large body, so close his shoulder rubbed against hers, and she could smell his spicy, fragrant male smell, even hear the sound of his breathing.

"I suspect you've had to live like a nun in order to avoid being tossed from society, haven't you? How old are you?" He looked her up and down. "Twenty-two?"

India sighed. "Twenty-six."

"You've had to wrap yourself in virtuous white for twenty-six years. No wonder you're retiring. That's hellish."

His smile, she registered, was dangerous to her peace of mind. And her virtue. She cleared her throat. "I must return to work, Thorn. And this conversation did *not* happen."

"You mean that nuns aren't allowed to ogle Feather's better parts?" Thorn grinned at her. "I like this picture; don't you?"

India glanced down and discovered that a young lady was bouncing on top of Feather, their bodies connected only by his extraordinary . . . whatever. And they appeared to be lying on a tree limb. "No!" she exclaimed.

He closed the book and dropped it on a shelf, leaning even closer and bracing his right arm over her head. "Those pictures are exaggerations. You do know that, don't you, India?"

She scowled at him. "The matter is irrelevant."

"It's not irrelevant, because you're about to marry. During my years at Eton, I saw hordes of men starkers. I can tell you this, India: whoever you marry will not compare to Feather."

India felt, irrationally, that she should defend her future husband. "You don't know that," she objected. "I'm sure that he will be . . . everything that a man should be."

Thorn's grin was making that hot and muddled feeling spread all over her body. "It's really irrelevant," she repeated crossly.

"Maybe before you decide on the man, I should take him for a dip in the horse pond and take a discreet glance. It would be awful if you went to your wedding night with images of Feather in mind, only to discover your beloved is the size of a thimble."

"He won't be!"

"How would you know? I would feel terrible if a book I owned corrupted you and consequently you never enjoyed your marital life."

India gave him a little push. "Back away, if you please. I'm going to my chamber."

"I know; you're about to tell me again that this conversation never took place. Do you know that you're the first female friend I've ever had?"

"I don't think we're friends," India observed.

"In that case, what are we?"

She ducked under his arm and walked away without answering, because there was no good reply to that.

He shouted when she had almost reached the door. "India!"

She turned.

"You forgot your nighttime reading!" The book hurtled through the air, and she instinctively put up her hand and caught it.

That smile again.

Chapter Fifteen

Early the next evening
The drawing room, Starberry Court

"India, darling, I insist that you go to bed early this evening," Adelaide said. "You look half-dead."

India felt a pulse of pure shame. The truth was that she had stayed up far too late, absorbed in the exploits of Francis Feather. "I cannot. I have only one day left before the duke and duchess join us."

"I am exhausted myself," her godmother said. "I shall take supper in my room, and I recommend you do the same. When do Mr. Dautry and Rose arrive?"

"Tomorrow morning," India said.

"That young man will have to mind his language in the next week. I'm astonished that dear Eleanor wasn't able to do more with him. After all, he lived in their house from an early age."

In India's estimation, it wouldn't matter at what age Thorn had entered the duke's house: it would have been too late.

"Of course, he *is* his father's son," Adelaide continued. "Those eyes are his father's, and that hair, all the rest of it."

"But for the personality," India pointed out. "I have always found the Duke of Villiers to be as courteous as he is witty."

"That's because you know Villiers only after he married. Years ago he reveled in upsetting people: imagine the scandal when he first appeared in society after bringing six illegitimate children, from five different mothers, to live under his roof."

"I don't believe that Mr. Dautry is emulating his father's footsteps by strewing children across the countryside," India said.

"I agree." Adelaide walked out of the drawing room, heading for the stairs. "In my experience, people whose parents led irregular lives tend to be quite conservative. Just look at you, my dear."

India followed her up, automatically checking to make sure that every speck of dust had been removed from the shining banister. "What have I to do with this? I am not the product of an irregular union."

"Of course you are not! Your parents were married in St. Paul's Cathedral on an absolutely beautiful day, though it did rain later in the afternoon, as I recall. But they were not, shall we say, entirely traditional in their nurturing, were they?"

As most parents didn't send their children out into the woods to forage for mushrooms for supper, India offered no defense of them. Still, "I don't think my parents' eccentricities made me conventional," she observed.

"You guard your heart," Adelaide said, reaching the top and pausing. "Don't you, child? You talk about choosing between your various suitors as if you were choosing dining room chairs."

"How else should I do it?" India replied, stung. "That's what my father would have done, if he were alive and if he had been an entirely different man." She was all too aware that had her father still been alive, she might well have been running around his estate without proper shoes to this day, unless she'd been married off to a cowherd.

"With your dowry and title, you have your choice of men. I'm merely saying that you could choose on the basis of love, if you wish." Adelaide turned into her bedchamber, rang the bell, and sat down before the fireplace.

"That did not work well for my father and mother." India, who had followed Adelaide into her room, bent over and kissed her on the cheek. "You do know that it was the best day of my life when you took me in, don't you?"

Adelaide smiled, but shook her head. "It wasn't the best day of your life, it was the worst, because your dear parents had left you. They didn't mean to, but they left you."

Personally, India felt that parents who'd spent their time being artists and worshipping the moon—as opposed to ensuring that their daughter had been properly fed and clothed—had left that child years before they'd run away to London and died in a carriage accident.

But she also knew that Adelaide preferred to believe that the marquess and his wife had been merely flighty. Eccentric. Different.

She kissed her godmother again and went to her own room, falling onto her bed. Unfortunately, as soon as she lay down she proved to have more than enough energy to think about the way Thorn made her feel: silly, and feminine, and weak in the knees. Which was absurd.

She rolled over on her back, biting her lip. She had to stop thinking about him. He was a man who knew what he wanted, and he wanted Lala: a girl who was lovable and uncomplicated, like sunshine. And beautiful. India wasn't falsely humble about her own looks, but she didn't have Lala's perfect features and sunny blue eyes.

What's more, India had a hard shell, built up over those lonely days while her parents had cavorted and she'd been hungry and hadn't known what to do with herself. When there had been no cook, and no footmen, and nothing but a huge, decaying house.

She sighed and rang the bell to ask Marie to fetch her some supper. It was stupid to feel slighted by the fact that Thorn wanted to marry someone else.

It wasn't as if *she* wanted *him,* after all.

The next morning Thorn decided to ride to Starberry Court, leaving Rose, Twink, and Clara to follow in the carriage. He was well aware that he was irritable. To begin with, the rubber band machine had broken down yesterday, a disaster that followed a morning drive with Laetitia that left him a little concerned.

She hadn't said a word. Not a single word. She'd just sat next to him, her hands folded, as beautiful and as mute as an English rose.

India was no English rose. She was a wildflower, something brighter and uncultivated that stirred your heart with its beauty.

Tomorrow, when Laetitia arrived for the house party, she would surely have more to say for herself. Perhaps she had simply been lulled into a companionable silence by the trotting horses, or the fresh air.

As he dismounted before Starberry Court, the great front door opened and a man—clearly a butler, given his lack of gloves—emerged, two footmen at his heels.

The butler bowed. "Mr. Dautry, my name is Fleming. Lady Xenobia engaged me to serve as your butler, should I prove satisfactory."

Thorn handed Fleming his coat and listened while the man told him that the Ladies Adelaide and Xenobia had not yet risen. After that he asked Fleming enough questions to get the lay of the house; incredibly, in all his visits he'd never managed to go above the ground floor. It seemed the family chambers were situated in one wing, and the guest rooms were in the other. "Isn't the nursery generally on the third floor?" he asked.

"Lady Xenobia believes that modern mothers prefer a less old-fashioned arrangement," Fleming stated. "Her ladyship converted a large sitting room in the family wing to a nursery, with a small attached chamber for the nanny."

Thorn headed up the stairs, thinking about India's restoration of Starberry Court. She hadn't simply painted the walls; she had actually made decisions about how he and his new family would live their lives.

He strolled into the nursery, amused to find a large rocking chair on the hearth, flanked by a smaller rocking chair and a tiny chair obviously meant for Antigone. Rose would be delighted.

What's more, India had lined an alcove with bookshelves and stocked them. Rose would love *The Adventures of the Six Princesses of Babylon*. He picked up a book of fairy tales and looked at the painting of Cinderella on the cover. Lala was prettier. Hell, India was prettier than that.

Though India wasn't conventionally *pretty*. Not with her odd combination of white-gold hair and darker eyebrows. And the beauty mark just next to her lip. She looked like a sensual painting, like one of those Titians for which the painter used his mistress as the model.

Of course, Titian's mistresses had sleepy, placid expressions, nothing like India's. She was a pain in the arse, but something about their exchange of letters was as much fun as sparring with Vander. But subtly different—probably because she was a woman.

Back in the hallway, he opened the door to the master bedchamber. He had told India that he disliked red; naturally she had papered his walls a dark crimson. Once inside, he saw she'd had an alcove built there as well. But whereas Rose got books, he got the Cellini.

Strolling over to inspect, he realized that India had turned the sculpture in such a way that anyone lying in the bed had an unobstructed view of both figures, their mouths barely touching in a kiss, their bodies entwined.

There was a note stuck to the satyr's shoulder.

Dear Thorn,

> *I tried to make this room a refuge for those of passionate sensibilities. Perhaps it will inspire you to new heights.*

> *India*

He snorted. But he pulled the note off and tucked it in his pocket. He was keeping her letters, if only for the novelty. He had never corresponded with a woman before.

The guest rooms were on the opposite side of the house. No self-respecting person would be in bed at this hour in the morning, so Thorn decided to rouse India. It wasn't hard to guess which bedchamber was hers; there was a faint trace of her perfume lingering outside the door.

Light filtered through the curtains, and Thorn could see

that the bed was hung in translucent amber silk; he only barely made out a sleeping figure through it. Pulling back the bed curtain gave him a peculiar feeling, as if he were discovering an enchanted princess. Like one of the stories India had bought for Rose.

She was curled on her side, all that pale hair of hers spread across the pillow. Surprisingly, she looked sweet in her sleep. But still erotic: her lips were naturally ruby colored, and he could just see her beauty mark. It was a mark that made a man look harder at her lower lip, made him dream about what that mouth could do.

Hell.

The funny thing was that looking down at her now made him think back to when he was a mudlark, before the Duke of Villiers had come out of nowhere and declared himself to be his father. He had never seen a woman with skin like India's, like the inside of a flower petal.

He hadn't even known such women existed. As the daughter of a marquess, India was everything he wasn't, and everything he would never be. All that privilege and birth was bred in the bone, and it showed in her face.

With a sudden surge of irritation, Thorn sat on the bed, expecting the motion would wake her. She opened her lips and made a funny little huffing noise, flung an arm above her head, and slept on.

Once, when he was a boy and it was cold, just beginning to snow, he'd seen a girl in a warm woolen coat whose mother had held out her hand and said, "Come on, sweetheart." The girl hadn't even seen him, but she'd walked away with all the love he'd never known.

No wonder sitting beside India made him feel every inch the mudlark. She'd had all that: all that money and gloss and love and protection.

He reached out and shook her shoulder, and not terribly gently either.

She opened her eyes, and the look in them went straight to his cock. She had a hazy look about her, as if she'd just made love for hours. As if she was waking after a night of it, and she wanted still more.

As if . . .

Her eyes popped open all the way and she sat up. His hand went over her mouth. "Please don't scream. God knows the last thing either one of us wants is for you to be compromised. I will never marry a woman just because society thinks I ought to." His voice came out harder than it should have.

He dropped his hand.

Her eyes had lost that hazy sweet look, and for a second he felt a pulse of regret. Instead, she was glaring at him. "What are you doing in here?" she hissed. "Don't you dare think that because you employ me, you have the right to personal services!" She began to grope around behind her.

Outrage surged up his back. "You think I would come to your bedchamber for that?"

"You wouldn't be the first!" she snapped. She brought up her arm, and damned if she wasn't wielding a club, covered in flowered flannel. "Touch me again and I'll hit you!"

"What the hell is that?"

"An iron bar that I will use on your skull if you don't get off my bed and out of my room!"

"Are you telling me that some man dared to enter your bedroom and accost you? Is that what you're saying, India?" Their eyes met, and he reached out and took the weapon away, weighing it in his hand. "This wouldn't do very much. It wouldn't stop a man who was truly determined."

"It did what it had to," India replied proudly.

"Who?" He knew his voice came from his throat like a gunshot. "Who did that?"

"I took care of it."

"*Who was it*?"

"That's none of your business!" She picked up all that gorgeous hair of hers and swept it behind her shoulders. "Now, you—"

He bent over and growled it, right in her face. "India, who dared to come into your bedroom and frighten you?"

"Besides you?" But she added, "Sir Michael Phillips. I struck him in the ear with my iron bar." Her smile made her eyes light up. "He complained the next day that he had lost his hearing and wouldn't be able to sing in tune!"

Thorn fought back another growl. The bastard was going to be taking the castrato part once he got his hands on him. But there was no need to disclose that fact to India.

"Phillips, who has a house in Porter Square? Went to Oxford? Silly little beard that only covers half his chin?"

"Yes," she said, pushing more hair behind her shoulders. "Adelaide and I visited his mother, because she had influenza. After she was out of danger, he seemed to believe that I would take care of him as well."

"Anyone else do that?"

She frowned at him, so he put it a different way. "Where did you get the idea of the iron bar, India?"

"My godmother keeps one just like it in her bed when she's traveling. In an inn, for example. A woman should always be prepared."

If a woman didn't have a man sleeping at her side, she probably should have an iron bar. In fact, it wasn't a bad idea. In fact . . . he might be able to make bars for just this purpose.

"What are you thinking about?" she asked suspiciously.

"Manufacturing iron bars, for the self-defense of ladies,"

he said readily. "I have a factory that could make them. We could use scrap metal. Perhaps with a slender end for women with smaller hands."

She stared at him a moment, then broke into laughter. "Is that how you made your untold millions?"

God, she was gorgeous. Dangerously so. He wrenched his mind back to the reason he'd invaded her privacy. "India, would you care to explain what that statue is doing in my bedchamber?"

"Don't you like your room?" she asked, a naughty smile glimmering in her eyes.

In fact, he did like it. And she knew it. "The walls are red," he pointed out.

"The devil should have a lair that suits his disposition," she replied, obviously unperturbed. "A background, you might call it."

"You'll have to change it."

India shook her head. "I'm finished appointing the house. Your guests begin to arrive tomorrow, and I must ensure that Lala's mother adores you, which frankly will be a bigger challenge than the whole house put together."

"Bedchamber aside, India, you did a hell of a job. The place is dazzling."

She sat up straighter, and a hank of her hair fell over her breast. The lock was long and curly, and the breast was as lush and delectable as it appeared when she was dressed, though she tended to wear gowns with all the appeal of a governess's.

He had to get out of her bedchamber. "Right," he said, jumping to his feet. "I'd better go prepare for Rose's arrival. She'll be along in the carriage presently."

For one second, India looked disappointed, but then she said regally, "You ought never to enter a lady's chamber."

"Vander arrives tomorrow," he told her, ignoring her

rebuke. "That's Lord Brody, future duke. Don't wear that dress I last saw you in. Haven't you any gowns that might seduce a man?"

"I'm not going to seduce Lord Brody!" India said, brows drawing together like a thundercloud.

"I'm friends with Vander, but I can't guarantee that he's anything much in bed," Thorn said, grinning. "If you like his looks you should try the merchandise first. I've never been partial to tow-heads, myself."

"I am ignoring you." India swung her feet out of bed and poked around with her toes for her bedroom slippers. She had the prettiest feet he'd ever seen: slender and white and silky looking. And her ankles were as delicate as the rest of her.

An image of the scars that slashed across his thighs popped into his mind. Her head bent as she poked her feet into her little slippers; all he could see was her incredible hair.

She straightened up. "You must leave now. Marie, my maid, will arrive soon."

"Does she simply walk into your room in the morning?"

"Of course."

"She'll have to change that once you're married."

India didn't even glance at him as she went to the dressing table. He didn't like to be ignored, so he said, "Vander might be a morning man."

She turned around as she pulled on a dressing gown, and he saw faint puzzlement in her eyes. "A man rolls over in the morning and finds himself ready," he explained. "He wakes up hungry, and if there's a soft body next to him, he'll make her a happy woman. Which he would want to do without a maid interrupting."

Her face flushed pink. Thorn grinned and decided to leave with that thought. He got himself out of the bedroom and downstairs to alert Fleming to the existence of Rose—

only to discover that India had informed him about everything, including the need to keep Rose's presence in the dower house a secret for the time being.

He spent a half hour poking around the kitchens, butler's pantry, silver closet. "Where the hell did she get all this stuff?" he asked Fleming, staring into a closet full of silver platters. Some had great domed lids; some, little feet.

"Lady Xenobia is acquainted with Messieurs Hannam & Crouch. She trusted me to visit their store on Monkwell Street and acquire the basics for a household of this size."

Thorn picked up one of the platters, one without fussy little feet. Of course, he'd seen silver like this on his father's table. The duke did not believe in hiding his silver under a barrel, as it were.

But he had never thought about owning any himself. The piece he had in hand was an oval with some decoration.

"This seems good enough," Thorn said.

"The platter has a gadrooned border, and the field is engraved with a diaperwork pattern," Fleming said. "A crest could be added at a later date, should you wish for it."

"You might as well get to know me, Fleming. The answer to that is, when hell freezes over."

"Quite right, sir," the butler replied, without flicking an eyelash. He took the platter and handed it to the footman, who had been trotting after them like a puppy. "Put this in my pantry, Stevens."

"Why?"

"We have handled it, and the platter must be polished before use."

Thorn was losing interest in silver. "I don't give a damn whether it's polished or not, as long as it has food on it."

"I gained that impression, sir, when you paid Hannam & Crouch, although they neglected to send you an inventory of the objects you had bought." Fleming's tone was wry; Thorn suspected they would get on very well.

He shrugged. "You realize I'm a bastard? It gave my butler in London indigestion, until at last he left for the good of his immortal soul."

"I too am a chance-child, as we call it in the Highlands," Fleming said.

Thorn broke into a crack of laughter. "How in hell did she find you?"

"I have served under the Marquess of Pestle, and most recently as head footman to the Duke of Villiers."

"Ah, she stole you from my father."

"Everyone in service knows of Lady Xenobia. If a man would like to move households, he hopes, if not prays, that she will pay the house a visit. I met her two years ago, when she spoke to every person in His Grace's household. She did not forget my ambition to be a butler."

"Does she always speak to every person in service?"

Fleming nodded. "From the butler to the scullery maid. You can imagine that she learns quite a bit about the household."

She was brilliant, that woman.

As Thorn entered the library, the image of India in her bed came back into his head. He would have guessed that ladies wore white flannel to bed, perhaps with a bit of lace around the neck and the wrists. To cover up.

India had been wearing pale blue silk. And there had been a lot of lace, and it hadn't been doing much to cover anything up.

A crunch of carriage wheels interrupted that interesting train of thought, so he went out to greet Rose. She climbed down, clutching Antigone and looking uncertain. He probably should have traveled with her, even though Twink and Clara were descending from the carriage as well.

Thorn stopped and held out his arms. "Rose!"

Her face was tight, and he waited while she thought about it. Finally, she trotted toward him, and he scooped her up. "How's my girl?" he asked her.

"I am not your girl," she said, with that awkward earnestness that characterized her.

"You most certainly are," he said. "On loan from your papa."

"Oh." She looked unconvinced. Thorn had never had trouble persuading members of the female sex to like him. Until, that is, he met Rose. She held herself apart, no matter how much he tried to charm her.

"We're off to the dower house," he told her, hating that fact. He understood the necessity, but it didn't suit him to hide Rose away, as if she were someone to be ashamed of. It made her seem like a by-blow, whereas she was the perfectly legitimate product of holy matrimony.

But when he had informed Laetitia about Rose and the dower house, she had nodded instantly. "My mother is . . . difficult," she said, her voice barely above a whisper. He knew what she was really saying: she needed him to rescue her, and he would.

"Where is Lady Xenobia?" Rose asked now.

"She's in the house, I expect," Thorn said. "Would you like to see her?"

Rose nodded vigorously. "I know that she will want to see the progress that Antigone has made."

Thorn glanced at Fleming.

"Lady Xenobia will undoubtedly join you in the dower house, Miss Rose," the butler said. "For a visit."

Chapter Sixteen

Miss Laetitia Rainsford was supervising as her mother's maid packed Lady Rainsford's trunk for transport to Starberry Court. This was not because Abigail needed supervision but because her mother insisted, and Lala had learned long ago that it was easier to do as her mother willed than try to resist it.

"Take care with that gown," Lady Rainsford said, from where she reclined on a day bed across the room. "That is Valenciennes lace on the sleeves."

Abigail already knew that, and always took care. But Mama liked to catalogue the valuable things in her possession. Almost as much as Mama liked to catalogue her ailments. But not quite as much as Lala liked to make unkind comments in the back of her head, where no one could hear them.

It was a sin, and she knew it. She nodded, and said, "Yes, Mama," and watched as Abigail painstakingly folded the

gown between lengths of white silk to keep the lace from
snagging or wrinkling.

"I'm still unsure about this visit," her mother said fretfully. "A bastard, to call a spade a spade! My daughter
marrying a child of shame. Who would have thought it?
Not I, not when I was the most beautiful woman in the *ton*,
and I chose your father to wed."

"Mr. Dautry *is* the son of the Duke of Villiers," Lala
ventured to say, not for the first time, nor even for the tenth.

"Who is as scandalous as his offspring," her mother
said, raising a hand limply in the air and letting it fall. She
had applied a paste of cucumber and fuller's earth, guaranteed to eradicate all wrinkles, to her face that morning.
It had dried solid, and now it had begun crackling like the
bed of a dried-out pond.

"Your father should be appalled at the very idea of link-
ing his blood with such an immoral man as Villiers, let
alone a bastard slip from the tree."

Abigail had finished the gown and was placing a last
layer of silk on top before closing the trunk's lid. "Papa
is quite impressed with Mr. Dautry's holdings," Lala reminded her mother. She had been repeating two concepts
over and over: "duke" and "wealth."

But she dared not utter any of the things she'd like to say,
which included pointing out that no one considered her more
than a pretty face, if not a dunce. And that her father was weary
and gaunt with anxiety about money. And that he needed Lala
to marry quickly, and not cost him another season.

Frankly, her mother should have been kissing Mr. Dautry's feet. It was a miracle she'd met Mr. Dautry, given that
he hadn't attended the usual events of the season. He'd
never seen her stumbling along in a conversation, trying
to find the right words, trying to come up with something
witty or even merely fitting, and failing. She would try to

say something, and her face would begin to feel tight and she could feel color creeping up her neck.

But Mr. Dautry didn't seem to expect her to be clever, which made it all easier. He was so interesting that she found herself actually paying attention to what he said.

He wasn't a man she would have selected if she'd been given a choice. She liked men who were far less aggressive and masculine. For almost two years before she'd debuted, she had been infatuated with their vicar, who had a slender, intelligent face and no hair on his head at all. She attended church so regularly that her mother started calling her Goody Two-shoes.

"Dautry is rich," her mother said fretfully. "But who would have thought that I, *I*, would have to sell my daughter in the open marketplace to a bastard with a purse of gold? My exquisite daughters should have been snatched up by the highest in the land the moment they debuted."

"Mariah had four excellent offers," Lala reminded her, ringing the bell to summon footmen to collect the trunk.

Her mother's clayey face cracked into a smile at the memory. "Yes, Mariah is a true beauty. What a wonderful season she had! Everyone was whispering about her, casting wagers about who she would accept . . ."

Lala didn't know why there had been any speculation: her father had simply accepted the largest offer for Mariah's hand. Unfortunately, he didn't think that any of the men who had proposed to Lala had offered adequate recompense for her beauty. Instead, he held out for a better offer—and then the season was over.

The very thought of having to endure another season made her heart pound. If Mr. Dautry didn't marry her, she'd have to go through all of it again, knowing everyone was whispering about her, not because she was beautiful but because they thought she was a simpleton.

She had even overheard some girls giggling and calling her "a spoony Sally." She hadn't entirely understood what they'd meant—who was Sally?—but it was obviously no compliment.

Abigail opened the bedchamber door and stood back, letting the footmen fetch Lady Rainsford's trunk. It would be sent on immediately, allowing the gowns to be aired and re-ironed before they followed tomorrow afternoon.

"I just wish you would be a little more vivacious, Lala," her mother went on, taking no notice of the men's presence. Lady Rainsford was not one to notice servants unless she wanted them to do something for her. "Though to be fair, it's hardly your fault that you're daft, but you *could* do something about your hips."

Lala clenched her teeth and willed herself not to cry. It would be ridiculous to get teary simply because two footmen were watching.

"It gives you such a lubberly air," her mother went on relentlessly. "I swear it would be easy. If you would just stop eating for a couple of weeks, you could have the same slim figure as your sister. We wouldn't be scraping the bottom of the barrel like this, lowering ourselves to visit the house of a by-blow."

"The Duke of Villiers will attend the party, Mother," Lala said, adding with some desperation, "and I'm certain that he will be greatly offended if you allow your feelings about his son to be evident."

"No one can say that I'm not the soul of tact," her mother said, with a blithe disregard for the truth. "Abigail, I'll thank you to shut the door after the footmen. There's a draft coming in that will likely go to my lungs and finish me off before I manage to get my last daughter off my hands."

She swung her legs from her bed and pointed to her silk

wrapper. Lala draped it around her mother's bony shoulders.

"I should like a tisane, brewed with a touch of honey. Meanwhile, it is time for you to take a brisk walk around the park. Three times a day, remember, and you haven't even been out of doors today. It's already ten in the morning. Laziness is the downfall of your figure."

Lala had been dancing attendance on her mother since daybreak, but she bit back a comment. There was no point. No point.

She kept repeating that to herself until she was out the door and heading to Kensington Gardens.

Chapter Seventeen

"*I* need a bonnet," India told her maid, Marie, after Fleming conveyed Rose's wish that she pay a visit to the dower house. She never went out of doors with a bare head; it was one of the rules she had read in a book about being a lady. In the absence of maternal advice, she had practically memorized the book at an early age.

A short time later, she was walking down a gravel path, cursing herself for having chosen such an elegant—and thus tiny—hat. The warm breeze was already teasing her hair out of its place; she could feel tendrils around her neck. And with her hair, that meant the whole thing would fall apart by the time she reached the dower house.

She was about halfway to her destination when she encountered Thorn and Rose, strolling hand in hand on the path. Thorn held a child's hoop in his other hand.

"Lady Xenobia," he said, quite as if he hadn't been sitting on her bed a mere hour ago. "It's a pleasure to see you."

Rose curtsied and said, "It's a pleasure to meet you again, Lady Xenobia."

India wrenched her eyes away from Thorn's face—he was the sort of man who commanded all one's attention—and looked down at the child. Of course, she was still wearing mourning black.

But this time India saw no resemblance to Thorn. Instead, she saw grief lingering in Rose's eyes. She knelt down and said, "Good morning. How is your friend Antigone this morning?"

"She is not a friend," the child replied with dignity. "She is my doll, but I pretend that she is my ward."

"I gather that Antigone has lost her mama and her papa," India said. "I'm sorry. She looks very elegant in her beautiful pelisse, although perhaps a little sad."

"She hasn't had a mama for a long time," Rose said. "But she is lucky to have me. That makes her lucky, lucky as a lark."

"My mother and father died as well," India said, responding less to Rose's reply than to the emotion in her eyes. "I still miss them. It does get better, though it never really goes away."

Rose's lips pressed together in a way that India recognized: she, too, had realized quite young that crying didn't help.

"I see that Mr. Dautry is carrying a hoop," India said. "Are you very good at rolling it?"

"No," Rose replied. "I do not have the control to make it stay up. I told Mr. Dautry this, but he bought it anyway."

"I am quite adept with a hoop," India said, straightening up. "Shall we try together? We can leave Antigone with Mr. Dautry. Do you have the dowel? Excellent! Now we must find a nice flat bit of path, because even the faintest bump will send it spinning off into the grass."

"Antigone and I shall find our way back to the dower house and await you," Thorn said gravely.

By the time she and Rose bowled their way back to the dower house, India's hair had tumbled down her back, and her cunning Italian shoes were pinching her toes. But never mind: Rose's cheeks were pink, and she was talking so much that India hadn't said more than a word for the last five minutes.

India limped up to the front door and pushed it open, ushering Rose in before her. The entry led directly into a small, cozy sitting room, where they found Thorn reading a newspaper.

Rose ran to him, leaned against his knee, and told him of her last, triumphant bowl, in which the hoop had rolled all the way down the path until a tiny rock had sent it askew. He put the paper aside immediately, wrapped an arm around her, and bent his head to listen. It was such a tender scene that India's heart caught.

Characteristically, Thorn hadn't stood up as she entered, the way a gentleman ought. Instead, he looked her over, then drawled, "It looks as if you ran around the house three times backwards, India."

Rose said in an urgent whisper, "Mr. Dautry, you must rise in the presence of a lady."

"That is just what I was thinking," India said, unpinning her little hat.

"Are you sure she's a lady?" Thorn asked, rising. "She's all pink in the face, and her hair is a mess. In fact, she looks a fright." His eyes were alight with teasing laughter. "Dear me, Lady Xenobia. Please don't tell me you'll try to seduce Vander with that gown. You look like an old maid put by in lavender."

"That is a most objectionable comment," Rose exclaimed, before India could say anything. "What's more, it's not enough to stand up; you must also bow."

"I generally don't bother," he said carelessly. "And Lady X knows it. I promise I'll be gentlemanly around Laetitia, however."

"Mr. Dautry hopes to marry Miss Laetitia Rainsford," Rose told India, putting her hoop to the side. "I have been trying to give him the benefit of my advice, because my tutor was quite knowledgeable about matters of deportment and rank."

"To my dismay, I've discovered that my ward could hire herself out as a governess tomorrow," Thorn said. "Lady Xenobia, your face is as red as a tomato, if you don't mind my saying so."

"It's hot outside," India said, frowning at him as she took a seat. "And before Rose feels the need to correct you again, I'll point out that it's quite impolite to compare a lady to a vegetable or, indeed, make her feel inadequate in any way."

Thorn dropped into a chair. "Why should you feel inadequate merely because you are an attractive shade of red?"

Rose looked from Thorn to India. "I am going to put my hoop away in my room. I shall ask Clara to bring some lemonade, Lady Xenobia."

"You have charge of a very interesting little person," India said, after Rose left.

"She's a dowager duchess in the making." Thorn stretched out his legs and put his clasped hands behind his head. "Seriously, India, is that what you intend to wear tomorrow?"

"And if I am?"

"I thought we had agreed that you should entice Vander, otherwise known as the future duke?"

India stared at him. Somehow they'd fallen into a relationship that she'd never imagined having with a man, not ever. Perhaps it was like a brother and sister. Except . . .

occasionally she glanced at him and he was so handsome that it made her shiver all over. "Do you speak to your siblings this way?"

"Absolutely."

"Do they find you as maddening as I do?"

He grinned at her, and her annoyance went up two more notches. She, who had learned to keep calm in the face of domestic chaos, was always losing her temper around him. It was infuriating.

"My siblings adore me."

"Odd," she said flatly.

"Let's discuss your gown. It's more interesting."

"Why don't we discuss what you will wear instead?" She looked him over, nice and slow, to make her point. "Lady Rainsford will not appreciate that woodsman look you've adopted."

"I shall throw on some decent clothes tomorrow. At the last minute." When Thorn was amused, his voice dropped and took on a rough edge that made him sound even less gentlemanly.

"Rose looks much better," India said, changing the topic to something less provocative. "Less drawn and less frightened."

"I force her to eat apple tart for breakfast," Thorn said. "Though what she really likes are Gunter's ices. Every afternoon."

India smiled at him.

"What did I do to deserve that?" Thorn asked, looking both quizzical and completely unmoved.

"Anyone would be happy to see how well you care for your ward," India said. "Your mother would be—" She broke off, realizing she had no idea who Thorn's mother was or what she would like.

"Never met her," Thorn said promptly. "She was an

opera singer, and presumably not maternal by nature, given that she left me behind with Villiers—clearly not a model father."

"Oh."

"What was your mother like?" he asked.

An image of the marchioness flashed through India's mind, her hair long and free, dancing naked under the moon. What was there to say? "She was quite original."

"From what I've heard, she was mad as a March hare."

"An unkind assessment," India said. She raised her chin defiantly.

"I investigated your background after I knew you would be around Rose," he explained. "Before that, I had decided that anyone calling herself Lady Xenobia was obviously a crook, so I didn't bother to inquire about your antecedents."

"You're not the first to have deduced that from my name," India conceded.

"What father names his child Xenobia, instead of Margery or Blanche?"

She hesitated.

"I'm guessing that madmen are not as parental as one might wish," he said, leaping into the silence.

"My mother had a tendency to forget I existed," India heard herself saying. She'd never told anyone that uncomfortable truth. It wasn't just that people would feel sorry for her; keeping silent made it feel less real. "But she did love me," she added. She always told herself that.

"My mother did not feel the same toward me," Thorn said easily. "According to my father, she thought I was a pretty baby, though. I looked better in those days, or she had a temporary flash of maternal feeling."

"She left you in a warm, safe place where you would be cared for."

"There is that."

He had his arms stretched across the back of the sofa, and he was so good-looking that India's heart skipped a beat. It was stupid, but there was something wonderful about the way he had made himself into Rose's father. He would never leave behind a child of his.

"My parents died in London," she went on. "But I didn't know they were there or why they had left home. They had neglected to tell me they were leaving."

His eyes darkened. "Did you think that they had abandoned you altogether?"

"I wasn't sure." It was a relief to put it into words. "Sometimes they would leave home, but they generally told me where they were going, and they'd never been gone for three whole days."

"You never found out what they were doing in London?"

She shook her head. "No one knows. My father was driving the curricle because we didn't have a coachman, and he went off Blackfriars Bridge. From what they told me, he tried to rescue my mother."

"Neither of them survived?"

She swallowed, feeling the same old lump of grief going down her throat again. "He wouldn't have wanted to live without her." It was stupid, stupid, stupid, to feel that her father should have wanted to live for her. Half the time he didn't even remember she was alive.

Thorn reached out and grabbed her wrist. Then he pulled her forward, and she toppled onto his lap.

"What are you doing?"

He wound his arms around her, and India stopped thinking about her parents.

"Your father and mother should have told you they were leaving," he said into her ear. "They should have wanted to make sure you were safe. I can see that they weren't wonderful parents. But I am absolutely sure that they loved you."

"How can you know?" India said, her voice cracking.

"I've been in the Thames a thousand times," he said. "The water is murky at the best of times, and it would have been stirred up by the carriage and horses. A person gets turned around trying to swim in the muck, and there's a wicked current slashing around the curve just past that bridge. Boys would dive down and never come up, and we never knew what had happened to them."

India's eyes were prickling, and she turned her cheek against his shoulder. "I—I think they might have been leaving home for good."

"Why do you think that?"

"We had no money, but my mother did have some jewelry."

"You implied once that you had been hungry as a child. They allowed you to go without food, although they had jewelry they could have sold?" His voice was incredulous.

"The set was given to my mother by her grandmother," India explained. "She couldn't sell it."

"She could," Thorn said bluntly. "She should have."

India's mouth wobbled. She had thought that sometimes, but it was terribly disloyal. "She planned to give them to me. Except she must have changed her mind, because they took them to London, and obviously they were going to sell them. I realized later that they must have decided to go to the Barbados. They always talked of it."

His arms tightened around her, and he asked, "Where was Lady Adelaide during your childhood?"

"She was married and living in London. She had no idea what it was like in the country." India used to dream that a fairy godmother would arrive, bringing beautiful gowns, or perhaps just a clutch of eggs . . . but it never happened. One day rolled into another, and when one was worrying about food and the coming winter, anxiety made the days blur together. There were whole years of her childhood that she couldn't quite remember.

Anguish tightened in her chest. Thorn must have realized, because he dropped a kiss on her hair just as the first sob struggled out of her mouth.

"I n-never cry," she gasped five minutes later.

"It's all right," he whispered, his deep voice as soothing as the caress of his hand on her back. "There are parents who make terrible decisions, India, but that doesn't mean they don't love their children. I do not believe for a moment that your parents scooped up those jewels, planning to leave you behind."

"Father loved the idea of sailing for Barbados," India whispered.

"They would not have left without you."

"Why did they take the jewels? They were kept behind a loose stone in the fireplace. When Adelaide came to take me away, I went to retrieve them. And—and they were gone."

"Perhaps they were stolen," Thorn suggested.

"No, Father had taken their leather bag as well. It wouldn't fit behind the brick, so it was always left in a drawer in the side table. No thief would have known that." She drew in a ragged breath. "For some reason, they took the jewels and left before daybreak without saying goodbye. But I'm—I'm used to it now."

Thorn didn't believe she was. He had never known his mother, and even so, the fact that she'd abandoned him had left a sting. India's parents sounded even more irresponsible. "They loved you, and they wouldn't have left the country without you," he repeated.

"How can you possibly say that with such certainty?" She was starting to sound a little cross, which he took to mean that she was coming back to herself.

He'd bet his fortune that her parents fell in love with her the moment they saw her. But love alone didn't make people good parents. He had a shrewd sense that Vander's mother had loved him, but you couldn't convince Vander of it.

"Because you are who you are," he said, smiling even though she had her cheek pressed to his shoulder and couldn't see his face. India hadn't the faintest idea how many people loved her, from her parents to Adelaide, to her workmen, to all those men who had asked her to marry them. . . .

"They shouldn't have!" she snapped, sounding more like herself. "They should have woken me and told me where they were going."

"Very true."

"I cannot believe I told you all that," she said, sighing and straightening up. "I've never mentioned it before. It seems disloyal to their memory."

"Given what is already known about your father, I doubt that anyone would offer praise of his parenting skills," Thorn said dryly. "I take it the jewels were not found on their bodies or in the carriage?"

She shook her head.

"You never told your godmother? No one instituted a search for the jewelry?"

"No."

Thorn's disbelief must have shown in his face.

"Adelaide was wracked with guilt after my parents' death," India said defensively. "Because she hadn't visited in more than a decade, she had no idea about the state of our house."

"It wouldn't have taken much to hire a Bow Street Runner to look into the matter," Thorn pointed out, making a mental note to do just that himself. If the Runner found nothing to report, India need never know.

"My godmother lives in a cheerful world. She works hard to keep it that way. And she deserves it, because her marriage wasn't very happy."

Thorn was on the verge of saying something extremely impolitic about godmothers who didn't protect their god-children, when India gently pushed away his arm and rose to her feet.

"I must wash my face before Rose returns." But she turned around at the door and gave him one of her smiles, the kind that shone from her eyes. "You're such a good friend, Thorn," she said. "Thank you."

She left him thinking about the ways he wasn't a good friend.

Not at all.

Upstairs, India stared at herself in the glass. Her hair was disheveled, her eyes were swollen, and her throat felt scratchy from all that crying, but all the same . . . she felt a weight had lifted. It was stupid, but it was a relief to have told Thorn. The cold, squeezed part of her heart had eased.

He made her feel warm and safe for the first time in years. Years and years.

Rose was back in the sitting room by the time India returned. "I must leave you both," India said. "Fleming will wish to consult with me before the duke and duchess arrive tomorrow."

Rose looked a little disappointed, but she hopped to her feet and dropped a curtsy. India knelt down in front of her. "You do understand why you must stay in this little house, don't you?"

"It would be disadvantageous for Mr. Dautry's plans to marry Miss Rainsford if her mother believed I was a child born out of wedlock. So I shall stay out of sight."

"You're very gracious," India said, putting a hand lightly on Rose's head.

"I met Miss Rainsford," Rose said.

"She is a charming young woman," India replied.

"She told me that she doesn't care to read."

India paused, then rallied. "Then you can read *to* her, just as you read to Antigone. I think you'll be comfortable here. I shall stop by every day and see if there's something I can bring you and Antigone."

"Mr. Twink and I are working on English grammar, because he says it's important to learn that before turning to Greek," Rose reported.

India felt a little pulse of jealousy, which was entirely absurd.

She glanced over Rose's head. "Thorn, will you return to the house before supper?"

He shook his head. "I'll stay with Rose as long as I can, if only to make sure that Twink doesn't drown her in past participles."

India had no idea what those were, so she merely nodded.

"Don't forget to hunt out a better gown for tomorrow, India," he ordered.

She rolled her eyes.

"I think Lady Xenobia looks quite nice," Rose said.

"She looks like a nice nun," Thorn said. "She needs to go a different direction in order to catch Vander."

"Why do you sometimes call each other India and Thorn, and other times, Lady Xenobia and Mr. Dautry?" Rose demanded. "It isn't proper."

"We're quite good friends," Thorn said easily. "The best of friends, in truth."

India felt a wobbly smile on her mouth. He was right, of course. She had no other friend like him in the world.

" 'Informality is the vice of the masses,' " Rose announced.

"Hell's bells, who told you that?" Thorn asked.

"My former tutor, Mr. Pancras," Rose said.

Thorn snorted. "That man is quickly becoming my worst enemy."

"If people call me Rose, and you Thorn, then we are Rose and Thorn." The child curled her lip in disdain. "I prefer Mr. Dautry. It's far more dignified."

India smiled at her. "I like Rose and Thorn."

"I do not agree," Rose replied, quite politely. "But I realize that I am too young to be heard on the subject."

At that, Thorn burst out laughing, and India slipped out of the house while he was tickling his ward.

Chapter Eighteen

*L*ate that afternoon, India finished the final preparations for the arrival of the guests. The Duke and Duchess of Villiers were due to arrive in the morning, with Lord Brody, Lady Rainsford, and Laetitia following in the afternoon or early evening. It seemed that Lord Rainsford would not come at all; Adelaide had discreetly confirmed that the lord and lady were only rarely to be found under the same roof.

All chambers were aired and ready; flowers would be placed in each room first thing in the morning. Between India, Fleming, and the housekeeper, they had planned the week like a military operation.

"The duchess will serve as Mr. Dautry's hostess," India reminded Fleming, checking through a list of wines that would be offered.

"Yes, my lady," the butler said.

"I suppose there will be any number of crises, and you

may come to me if you must. But please make sure that the other guests don't know, Fleming."

"Absolutely not, my lady. Lady Adelaide will take supper in her room again tonight," Fleming informed her.

India's exhaustion fell away. That meant she and Thorn would dine alone, without a chaperone. Adelaide's conclusion that the two of them needed no chaperoning was erroneous, but India had not objected.

Beginning tomorrow, there would be no more kissing— or, for that matter, weeping—in Thorn's arms. Once Lala entered the house, India would revert to being merely a family friend.

But for tonight . . . a prickling excitement rushed over her. Thinking about the moment when Thorn had caught her up and taken her mouth without even asking sent a wash of heat down her legs.

Neither of them was betrothed. Yet. Tonight, no matter how improper, they could still kiss. She started up the stairs with unbecoming haste and forced herself to slow down. When Marie arrived, she requested a bath. She stayed in the bath a good ten minutes longer than she wished, because the only thing she really wanted was to rush downstairs and find Thorn.

To talk to him.

Or, perhaps, not to talk.

By all rights, she should wear a simple gown to supper and save her more seductive clothing for the arrival of Lord Brody. But instead, she put on her most becoming gown. It was the color of the pearly inside of a seashell, with a low drawstring bodice and a light overskirt of loosely woven linen that pulled away in front.

She felt naughty in it. Not prudish or old-maidish.

Marie helped her put on a pair of slippers whose heels would put her head just at Thorn's shoulder. At last India descended, telling herself that she would allow a single kiss. Or maybe two kisses. But no more.

Fleming stood at the bottom of the stairs. "Lady Xenobia," he said, bowing. "Mr. Dautry is waiting for you just outside." He pushed the front door open for her.

Of course. They would eat in the dower house with Rose. There would be no kisses. It was silly that India felt such a crushing sense of disappointment.

Thorn was leaning against the stone lion at the edge of the drive, waiting for her. "Rose is surrounded by paper dolls," he said once she joined him. "I have been informed that my presence is neither required nor particularly desired."

"I thought we would dine with her," India said.

He took her arm, and they began walking not toward the dower house but in the other direction altogether, away from the house and down the hill. "Clara has a dab hand with a pair of scissors, and Rose is happy," he said. "I thought that perhaps in all your frenzied attention to Starberry Court you missed the fishing hole."

"I do not care for fishing," India said, "particularly not when I'm wearing one of my favorite gowns."

"We shan't actually fish," Thorn said, looking surprised. "I don't even own a pole."

"And this is most improper," India added.

"I thought we put that nonsense away, at least between ourselves."

"You don't understand. The house is full of servants now. We could truly be compromised if anyone saw us by ourselves at dusk."

He kept walking, drawing her forward. "Who would see us?"

"Any of the servants—and gossip of that nature would

spread like fire through London. My reputation would be ruined. In fact, we must return to the house immediately."

Thorn just grinned. "Don't worry. I would tell Vander that nothing happened between us."

"It's not just that," she said, trying to explain in a way he would understand. "My life—any lady's life—is made up of morning calls, and musicales, and balls. I would be thrown out of society. No one would receive me or send invitations. That's what it means to be ruined."

They reached the bottom of the hill. "The life you describe sounds damned tedious. I can't picture you just going to balls and making calls, India."

She smiled wryly. "I have trouble imagining it myself."

"Hell, I should ruin you just so you don't get caught in such a boring life. It would be my good deed for the year." He pulled her around and his mouth was on hers—not coaxing, as when they'd first kissed, but hot and demanding. This time his mouth was a burning command, a direct order that she relinquish all control.

India opened her mouth to him without hesitation, aware that her body had been longing for his taste and his touch, aware that she instantly started shaking, just a little. Aware that her arms wrapped around his neck as if she were drowning and only he could save her.

When he pulled her even tighter, she cried out, the sound muffled by his mouth. His leg pushed forward, between hers, and she ground against him, electrified.

There was a rough groan and a curse, and Thorn snatched her up, took one long stride, and released her. India shrieked and fell, landing not on the hard ground but on a stretch of canvas suspended in midair.

"It's a hammock," he said, laughing down at her. "Haven't you ever been in a hammock?"

She looked up at the ropes that held the canvas above the ground. "No! We can't do this. I need to—"

Thorn lay down beside her in a practiced gesture that revealed he'd spent night after night in hammocks.

"Is this what mudlarks sleep in?" she whispered, hardly able to shape the words because of the searing heat of his body settling against hers.

He shook his head, dusted her mouth with his. "We slept on the ground between graves, in the churchyard. Nice and quiet there."

"When were you in a hammock?"

"Aboard ship," he said. "I made one voyage with the East India Company."

She meant to ask something else, but his hand had cupped her head, just enough to turn it to his mouth. And after she fell into the potency and storm of his kiss, that hand moved. . . .

It trailed along her throat, a caress that seemed almost innocent. India squirmed closer to him, her arms pulling him on top of her, parts of her hungry in a way she'd never imagined.

But she couldn't think about it, because their kiss was wet and hot, and so fierce that her head tilted back and the hammock enveloped them and pushed their bodies together, as close as the satyr and his lover.

Thorn's hand drifted below her neck, and a sound broke from India's throat as his touch rounded the curve of her breast. She tore her mouth from his, an involuntary cry floating into the air.

He muttered a curse and his mouth covered hers, just as his thumb rubbed across her nipple, sending a streak of golden fire through her. India's cry was swallowed by his kiss. Not that she consciously realized it, because she could only think about his hard, warm body pushing against hers as she arched shamelessly toward him.

When Thorn gave her breast another rough caress, India's heart stopped beating for a moment. When it started again, it was racing. She bent one of her knees and pushed it between his thighs, and this time the groan was *his*.

"I want . . ." she whispered, breaking off. But the raw words came from her throat, willy-nilly. "You and I."

He was tugging gently at her bodice, which gave way instantly. He lowered his head again and kissed her collar-bone. India felt a shiver rock her entire being as she waited for his lips to drift lower.

"You and me," she corrected herself, letting her fingers slide through his hair, thick and soft and far too long for a gentleman. She loved that he wasn't a gentleman. No gentleman would topple her into an open-air ship-bed, kissing her so intimately where anyone might see them.

Her fingers trailed down his neck, drifting out to caress his shoulders. Thorn let out a husky groan at her touch. The only other sounds were the sleepy grumble of the river and the songs of nesting birds.

No one would know. No one would hear. She tried to pull his head down to kiss him again, but he pushed up on one arm, steady in the hammock even as it rocked.

"There is no *you and me*," he stated.

"There's you and me in this hammock," she returned. And she moved her leg to touch that hot, vital part of him. At her touch, she saw darkness in his eyes, like the madness in her blood. "Please, Thorn. *Please.*"

He leaned closer and said against her lips, "What are you asking for, India?"

The hammock was swaying, and with it, his body against hers. The muscles in his shoulder rolled under her fingertips, the fine linen of his shirt sliding over his skin.

His lips opened against hers, and again his hand rounded

her breast and put delicious pressure on her nipple. India clung to him, her belly strangely hot, her legs trembling.

She liked the feeling.

Very much.

When Thorn raised his head again, she saw a flare of wildness in his eyes.

"I want all of it," she said, and gasped, because his fingers were skimming her side, the intimacy of that touch undeniable. "You and me." She blinked. "I mean, you and I."

Thorn had pulled aside her bodice again, his mouth descending to her breast. She arched her back and moaned. "I need. . . . Oh Thorn, I need . . ."

He moved to the other breast, and she lost control of whatever it was she had meant to say. One of his hands was sweeping up one of her legs, leaving raw hunger in its wake. The fever swept over her again: she wanted his taste, his smell, his consuming, ravishing kiss.

A foggy thought occurred to her: if she was going to play the trollop, she might as well *do* that. She let her leg fall open, inviting his caress.

Thorn's teeth grazed her nipple and at the same moment his fingers curved inward. She was writhing against him, words flowing out of her mouth, an endless stream of pleas that would have embarrassed her except . . .

They didn't.

It felt right. Like a natural thing, like the right thing. "I know you're a gentleman under the skin, for all you say to the contrary." The words caught in her throat. "But I'm asking you, Thorn. I'm—"

"What are you asking me for?"

He was looking down at her seriously, as if one hand wasn't resting on the soft skin of her inner thigh. Her body was frozen, waiting for those fingers to inch higher.

"A gentleman would stop now," she said, daring him.

His fingers drifted another inch, stopped again. The feeling raged through her, and she trembled from head to foot.

"A man who didn't care about society would continue, because the woman in his arms was—was agreeable," she whispered.

A dusky chuckle drifted into the air. " 'Agreeable'?"

His fingers drifted again, and the air whooshed from her lungs. "Please," she said, her voice a thread of sound. She hated whispering. She just couldn't seem to find the breath to make a forceful demand.

"Be sure of what you ask for," Thorn said, his voice dark. "If you continue to beg me, India, I *will* seduce you, and I won't be sorry. But I won't marry you simply because my cock has been inside you."

India's heart quickened at his words, although she should have been outraged that anyone would say such a vulgar thing to her. But she wasn't outraged. She was exhilarated.

"I do not want to marry you," she said, being as clear as she could. She had managed to tug his shirt free, and the warm, sleek skin of his back was under her fingers. "I don't even like you very much."

"I like you," he muttered against her lips. "But I have as good as committed myself to marry another."

India was tired of talking about marriage, or indeed of talking at all. She wiggled down, which made the hammock sway, just enough so that her face was under his. "I want to do all the things in that book."

His mouth quirked, even though his eyes were hungry. "*All* of them?"

She thought about it for a second, and nodded. "Except the one with two women. I'm not interested in that."

"Damn," he muttered, but she saw laughter in his eyes.

"You taught me how to kiss, and that didn't make me

want to marry you. Now you can teach me this," she said, feeling as if she were about to jump out of her skin. "If you won't, just tell me, because—"

The fierce look he gave her made the words catch in her throat. "Because what?"

"Because I'll find another man who's not a gentleman," India said, not letting him intimidate her.

"You'd find another man," he said, slowly and ominously.

Though he looked as if he were about to pounce on her, India didn't flinch. Thorn liked to boast that he wasn't a gentleman, but he was about to behave like one. He was going to refuse her. He wouldn't take a lady's dearest possession, her virtue.

She slid her palms up his back, under his shirt, and announced, "I am not a virgin." She was whispering again, but really, how could a woman say such an outrageous thing, other than in a whisper?

She wasn't accustomed to lying, and it was surprisingly difficult to lie to Thorn.

He stared down at her silently for a few long minutes, and at last said, "Do I have to find some scoundrel and kill him for taking you without your permission?"

She shook her head. Something imperceptible changed in the air around them. He shifted his weight, just slightly, but it was so delicious that a shudder coursed through her.

"I will not do this in a hammock," he stated. His mouth drifted across her cheekbone and she felt the heated touch of his tongue.

She said, with a little gasp, "All right."

"However, we can *begin* in the hammock," he said, his voice like a purr. And with that, his hand swept up her leg and didn't stop. Didn't dandle and caress, or trace patterns on her inner thigh. Instead, it went straight to her sweetest spot, which had in truth never been touched by anyone but herself.

Now his fingers slid into her softness, plundering her without asking permission, taking what they wanted. Fire rushed up her body as he unerringly pressed down in just the right spot. India opened her mouth to scream, but he put his lips over hers. With the kiss, and what he was doing with his hands . . . she squirmed under him, breathless, unable to keep her legs from moving. Her fingers tightened on his back, thinking dimly that she wanted his weight, that feeling, the way it was when he—

One of his broad fingers sank into her and she tore her mouth from his because she was on fire and the sounds in her throat had to come out. . . .

And she came. Like that. In a hammock. The orgasms she gave herself were nothing to this one, not with Thorn beside her, one muscled leg pinning her down, the hammock swaying, his fingers . . . his tongue in her mouth.

"Thorn," she gasped, not knowing what she wanted to say. "Thorn!"

His fingers slipped away and the hammock lurched. Then all his delicious weight was on top of her, elbows on the sides of her face, and he was kissing her with a fierce, consuming hunger that turned her nerves to fire. She had just come, and already she was shaking, her heart pounding, her hands flying over him. Instinctively she pushed up against his heat and strength.

He tore his mouth away, but India was beside herself, her breath coming in little sobs. Thorn wound a hand in her hair and pulled her head toward him. His lips brushed hers, the hammock swayed, and his body ground against hers. A desperate sound broke from her throat and drifted into the air.

"You will not be able to be quiet, will you?" Thorn asked, his eyes smoldering. "You will never be silent."

India didn't know how to reply. Her mind was clouded, absorbed by the chiseled contour of his mouth. She arched toward him again and licked his lower lip.

His eyelids dipped, and he answered his own question. "Never. You're in it with your entire being, aren't you, India? All of you."

India was certain of only one thing: she was completely uninterested in a comparison of herself to other women. She felt at once satisfied and unfinished, replete and hungry. "I can be silent," she said with a gasp.

A half smile curled his lips. He tilted his hips. The hammock rolled and his weight pressed between her legs. A moan slipped from her throat.

"You're lying," he said, whispering it against her throat as he nipped and kissed her. "There aren't many women like you, India."

"Oh for goodness' sake," she cried, exasperated. "Are we to make love in this hammock?"

"No."

Her heart plummeted into her slippers, and her hand slid from his back. "Oh."

"We shall make love in my bed," he murmured. "In that red bedroom you made for me."

"I can't make love to you in that bed!"

He chuckled, and she felt the quake of it against her skin. "Yes, you can."

"Making love in your bedchamber would be wrong."

"Wrong how?" It was miraculous, the way he could maneuver in the hammock without making it turn over and dump the two of them on the lawn. He pulled away her bodice again and the pale cream of her breast fell into his hand, overflowing his palm. She couldn't see what he was doing because his hair fell forward.

But she could feel.

What she felt made her start to pant even as she tried to explain. "Your bedchamber is for your wife. For a man and his wife. We're not that, and this is just one night, so . . ." Her voice trailed off when she forgot what she was saying.

Thorn raised his head and swiped a thumb across her nipple. She squeaked. "I can't make love to you outdoors, India. That means my room." He rolled fluidly from the hammock and pulled her straight into his arms. Just like that, they were both standing.

"Not in the house," she managed.

"Why not?"

"As I just said, the house . . . the bedchamber is for *you* and your wife," she tried again, stumbling into words as she tried to read his eyes. "You'll make memories there, and I don't want any of those memories to be—" She broke off awkwardly.

He gave her that ironic half smile of his. "Lady Xenobia India St. Clair, are you telling me that I'm not allowed to bring a mistress to Starberry Court?"

"I am telling you precisely that." She folded her arms over her chest. "I made a home for you. You mustn't sully it."

" 'Sully it'?"

India was starting to feel distinctly querulous, as well as faintly ridiculous. Had she really allowed a man to put his hands between her legs . . . in the open air? It seemed that she had. The excuse of "an error in judgment" didn't quite cover that foolishness.

She shook out her skirts, wondering if her hairpins were all lost. "I think we should—"

Her words stopped in a little squeak, because suddenly she was over Thorn's shoulder and he was striding back up the hill. "Put me down!" she insisted. "Thorn!"

He just laughed. "We'll be at the gatehouse in a moment.

And by the way, I'm not a man to ever keep a mistress after I'm married. And I should also tell you that I have never made love without a French letter: you will face no danger of an unwanted child from me."

"The gatehouse?" One of his hands was holding her bottom, cupping it tightly, and it felt . . . She began wiggling. "You must let me down. This is absurd!"

"You're surprisingly light, considering your curves," he said cheerfully, and that hand curled a bit tighter.

India pushed herself away from his back. "Are you saying that I'm fat? Let me down!"

His long strides had taken them from the grass onto the gravel path leading to the gatehouse. "Thorn!"

"I'd have to investigate more closely to know whether you're carrying extra weight," he said, his tone silky smooth.

"You certainly will not!" India wrenched herself up at precisely the moment that he swung her to her feet, so she lurched backward and fell against the door of the gatehouse. She looked up at Thorn, prepared to blister his ears as he had never been scolded before.

But he was looking down at her, and her words evaporated.

"I want you," he stated. "I shall have you, Lady Xenobia India. We're not contemplating marriage, because you will marry better than I, and I am all but promised to another. But we shall give each other pleasure tonight. Have you any clarifications to add?"

She shook her head, unable to move her eyes from his face. Everything she did, all her adult life, had been regulated and disciplined, and directed toward the best possible marriage.

This had nothing to do with marriage.

This was for *her*.

"Do you know, I've never made love to a woman I trusted," he said conversationally.

"What?"

"You understand a contract," he said, reaching behind her to push open the door. "You are not trying to entrap me, because I know damn well that you're wet between the legs thinking about me, not my money."

He made her sound like a loose woman. Which, it seemed, she was.

Or rather, she would be as soon as she did this, because ladies did not make love to men to whom they weren't married.

Ever.

She watched as he pushed open the shutters to let in the fading sunlight. He turned to look at her, and she was surprised by the ferocity in his eyes. "I will ask once more if someone took your virtue by force, India." His voice had gone low and ominous again. He was ready to fight—no, to *squash*—every man who had offered her insult.

"No," she said, giving him that new smile that existed only for him.

He said something she didn't hear, and then she was in his arms and they were kissing again, so frantically that she couldn't breathe. His shirt was already out of his breeches, and she slid her hands around his waist. He pulled back and threw the shirt over his head.

He was magnificent, bunched muscle narrowing to a waist without an inch of extra flesh on it. Not at all like her body. She frowned and reached out, tracing a white slash across his abdomen with her finger.

"My body's covered with scars," he said, glancing down.

"I'm sorry," India said softly, bending to put a kiss where her finger had been. Then she straightened, turned, and climbed the narrow stairs to the bedchamber that she'd furnished for a gatekeeper, should Thorn ever hire one. The room held little more than a bed big enough for a man and his wife.

She had pushed open one shutter when a pair of hands slid around her waist and Thorn's body came hard and warm against her back. "May I unbutton your gown?" His lips were on her neck, and she leaned back against him and reveled in a feeling of being outside herself.

She didn't feel like Lady Xenobia, daughter of a marquess. At this moment, she was just India, just herself, making love to someone who had no expectations of her other than her own pleasure.

"Yes," she said, her voice so husky that she cleared her throat and tried again. "Yes, you may."

The shell-pink gown fell to her feet, followed by her corset. India turned about slowly, aware that her chemise was transparent. Compared to many fashionable women, she was generously shaped. When one grows up hungry . . . well, she liked to eat, and she made no apologies for that. And even though she sometimes thought she had too many curves, she didn't care enough to go hungry again.

"Damnation," Thorn growled.

India felt a smile form on her face without her volition. Her shape might not suit current fashion, but Thorn obviously appreciated it. She reached down, just as he had done with his shirt, pulled her chemise over her head, and tossed it aside.

Chapter Nineteen

Thorn took one look at India, who stood before him wearing no more than a pair of silk stockings tied just below her plump thighs, and knew that the control on which he had prided himself since he bedded his first woman was about to break. He wouldn't be able to make love to India by hovering over her on rigid arms, analyzing the way her head turned, or the sounds that came from her mouth.

He was going to lose control and feast on her body. She had gorgeous breasts, a slightly rounded belly, lush hips, and legs that didn't stop.

The curse that came from his mouth was heartfelt. It wasn't just her body. It was the way she was looking at him, slightly amused, confident, with desire in her eyes. Her long hair was tousled and fell around her shoulders and over one breast. She looked like a dream, like Venus herself come to earth.

"Why do you smell so good?" he asked.

"My perfume is scented with moonflower. Aren't you going to remove your breeches?" Her voice rolled over his skin like heated honey.

Her lips were dark cherries, swollen from his kisses. He wanted to push her onto her knees and beg her to take him in her mouth. Thank God she wasn't a virgin. No virgin ever looked at a man as she looked at him now, as if she could lap him up.

He had to pull himself together. "I suspect you don't need me to tell you how beautiful you are?"

Her lips curved, and the only thoughts in his mind were outrageous. He reached down and pulled off his boots.

"A woman can never hear that too often."

"You are damned incredible," he said bluntly, wrenching down his breeches and drawers in one movement, keeping his eyes on her.

She seemed entirely at ease. The thought that she must have stood like this before more than one man flitted through his mind, but he brushed it away.

Her eyes drifted down his naked body and caught at his groin. Her tongue touched her bottom lip, and he nearly groaned aloud at the sight of that pink tip, his cock sending a wild pulse of lust through him.

"Do you really want to try everything Feather did with his various inamoratas?" he asked, forcing his mouth to form words.

Her eyes came back to his face slowly, heavy-lidded but not sleepy. She let a smile answer him.

"Let's start here." He took a step forward and they were skin to skin, a second later tumbling on the bed. He bent one knee so he didn't crush her with his weight, and then he was touching her everywhere, his mouth following his hands.

Her breasts: making her cry out.

Her belly: making her pant.

Lower still: making her moan.

A second later he was kissing her in her sweetest private place. He nudged her legs aside, took one more look at her eyes, hazy with desire, bent his head, and tasted her, making her scream.

Ordinarily, he would have been analyzing what every touch did to her. But this time it was as if he was doing it for himself. Her taste was like a drug setting his body on fire. His fingers curled into her hips so hard that he'd leave bruises, he gave her one last caress, and she exploded. Again.

Generally, Thorn entered a woman with due attention to her state of readiness and her state of mind. He was respectful.

But now he was driven by a need and hunger that knew nothing of respect. He pulled on a sheath, his hands rough and urgent. Rearing up, he pushed India's legs farther apart, bent her knees, and thrust into her in one long stroke. She was hot and tight, and wet. His mind went blank for a moment, his entire being focused between his legs.

He came to himself for a fleeting moment of sanity and looked down. India seemed . . . stupefied. But not with pain, thank God. Some women found him uncomfortable.

"You *must* be as large as Feather," she said, her voice husky with unmistakable pleasure.

He drew back, watching her face, thrust again . . . she arched her head back and actually shrieked. And before he had done more than thrust home one more time, he felt her tightening around him, her body shaking, little pants coming from her mouth.

He looked down and caught sight of the two of them. Connected. All her dainty, duchesslike pinkness and the tool of a rough bastard like himself. It was hardly possible, but he thickened even more.

"Damn it, India," he whispered, leaning down to kiss her carefully, with reverence. Her mouth opened under his, hot and wet and urgent, and he completely lost his mind. He didn't brace himself on his elbows, the better to assess his bed partner. He didn't listen for the catch in her breath or watch for a tremble that might reveal she was close to finding pleasure yet again.

He did none of that. The horse had broken its lead line and was away. His mind spun to white, his senses narrowed to the soft perfection of her, the lush beauty of her breast in his hand, the way her body clasped his.

He began going faster and harder than he remembered ever going. She was clutching him, her legs curved around him, her arms around his neck. His hands were on her hips, holding her still as he thrust into her, grunting because the pleasure of it was so acute that it was like pain burning up the back of his thighs, deep in his balls.

But he held on, managed to hold on by some thread of control until . . . she threw back her hair and a cloud of white-blond silk flew about her shoulders. He heard her cry as if it were a command. His hips jerked with a force he'd never felt before, emptying him into her, thrust after thrust.

Until he had no more to give.

Chapter Twenty

The following morning

India rarely hesitated when it came to dressing. Her wardrobe was organized, mentally if not physically, into categories that corresponded to their purpose, whether that was to cow a bumptious butler or soothe a nervous lady.

But she hadn't any gowns that would simultaneously usher in a betrothal (the dark violet muslin with buttons?) and flirt with a potential husband (the rose-colored muslin with a low bodice?). Frankly, all her bodices felt precariously low. In the last two years, waistlines had crept ever upward and necklines downward—and India was well endowed. Very well endowed. Lately fashion had become annoying, and something she'd prefer to put out of her mind.

At length she made up her mind. "I'll wear the sprigged

muslin with the embroidered roses this morning," she told her maid. "And tonight, the French silk."

Marie's eyes widened. "Finally, you will wear the French silk!"

"With amethysts in my hair," India said, remembering that she had to appear a proper candidate to become a duchess.

Marie handed her a jar of lotion, and India began swiftly rubbing it into her legs. She felt different, as if she'd paid a visit to a foreign country and come home speaking a new language.

She and Thorn had lingered in the gatehouse until she'd had to go home or risk exposure. They'd been lucky, because she'd darted in a side door and made her way to her bedchamber without being seen. Marie had been surprised to find her already tucked into her bed, but she made the excuse that she'd been exhausted.

And frankly, she had been. After hours in Thorn's arms, she had felt as limp as a piece of velvet; she'd slept with a dreamless intensity that she hadn't experienced since she was young.

But now it was all different. Whatever she and Thorn had had between them was over. Lala and her mother were due later that afternoon, as was Lord Brody. The Duke and Duchess of Villiers would arrive, and the last thing she wanted was for Eleanor to think that she was a hussy who would roll about with Thorn in the open air.

That was a private memory. She knew that she would never again have such a wonderful night. That was it.

It was over.

Thorn had used sheaths every time, and he never suspected that she was, in fact, inexperienced. So there would be no consequences, other than the gift of an utterly delightful, sensual memory that she could tuck away and examine later in life.

She'd had a *lover*. Most women gained a husband, at some point or another. But few, in her opinion, had a lover. The thought made her smile.

"It's nice to see you happy," Marie said, as India handed her back the jar of lotion. "I've never seen you work so hard," her maid continued. "But Starberry Court is just perfect. Everyone says so, from the bootblack to Mr. Fleming himself. It's exquisite."

"Thank you, Marie," India said, feeling a bit guilty because she was happy for all the wrong reasons.

She had to stop thinking about the gatehouse. Last night was like a fairy tale, like something that happened to a stranger, not to herself. Though every time she sat down she had to suppress a wince. Clearly it *had* happened to her.

Thinking about Thorn made her nipples harden, and her belly take on a liquid, hot feeling. That was what loose women, who made love not for coin but for pleasure, presumably felt all the time. The women in Feather's book.

She had a lot of newfound sympathy for them. This was like being hungry: it felt urgent. She wanted to find Thorn and pull him into a spare bedchamber and demand that he ravish her. No. That was *over*.

From now on, she would be virtuous. As soon as the house party had concluded, she would return to London and make a decision between her various suitors.

Unless, of course, Lord Brody was as charming as Thorn seemed to think he was. In that case, she might choose to be a duchess.

An entirely virtuous duchess, of course.

After India was dressed, she tried to look at herself as critically as possible. She was going to conduct a courtship under Thorn's eyes. She knew he would watch her and Lord Brody.

He didn't think her clothing was feminine enough. Not sensual enough, with all his talk of generals and the like. A deeply feminine part of her wanted to prove him wrong. The bodice of her muslin gown was pleated and caught up just under her breasts, and constructed in such a way that every pleat made a statement about her best assets. She wore slippers made in Italy with pointed toes and slender heels. And she carried a blue reticule sewn with metallic threads.

"Do you think I should wear some lip salve?" she asked Marie.

He maid looked up, startled. "You?"

"Yes, me."

"Why? You are beautiful."

Marie genuinely believed that every man in the vicinity would fall in love with her mistress. India opened up one pot of salve after another, until she found her favorite shade of peony pink.

"I see no need for lip salve in the morning," Marie stated.

What she didn't understand was that most men wanted a woman like Lala: a woman who didn't say much—and what she said was uttered in a whisper.

India never whispered. She considered whispering girlish. The truth was that she was more likely to yell, at least around Thorn.

Plus, she had a straight nose, instead of an adorable little tip-tilted one. Her hair was too thick and wouldn't stay up properly. And her lips were too big, though she had the idea that applying pale pink color helped with that problem.

She knew they were too big because she'd been called "fish-lips," back when she was a child trading mushrooms at Mr. Sweatham's shop. She would bring him a box of mushrooms from the forest, and he would give her flour and bacon in trade. He always gave her more than the mushrooms were worth, but her pride was never as big as her stomach was empty.

She could still hear that derisive hiss in Sweatham's son's voice when he would say, "There's Lady Fish-lips!" or even worse, "Charity Fish-lips!"

The memory was a steadying influence. Her immediate goal was to see Lala betrothed to Thorn.

After that, she would find just the right husband.

Chapter Twenty-one

By the time the carriage drove up to Starberry Court, Lala was ready to throw herself in front of the horses. Her mother had been suffering from heart palpitations for three days, until she had declared the previous day that she simply could not make the trip to Starberry Court.

It wasn't until Lala's father said that he could no longer afford to feed his family that Lady Rainsford gave in. His lordship was probably exaggerating, but he made his point.

Today her mother spent the entire trip from London pointing out that if Lala ate less, her father wouldn't be so concerned about feeding the family. Never mind the fact that Lady Rainsford couldn't seem to stop buying bonnets and shoes and even new gowns. And it was the mistress of the house who insisted they have three courses at every meal, as in other fashionable households. And it was Lady

Rainsford who retained a doctor to visit the house every single day, the better to listen to her heart.

"I cannot believe that Dr. Belview refused, utterly refused, to accompany us," she said fretfully as the carriage turned down a long drive that Lala thought must lead to Starberry Court. "He is appalling disloyal! I am strongly considering reminding him of his Hippocritical Oath or whatever that is called."

Lala sat next to the window, biting her tongue. The line of trees opened up, and Starberry Court came into view. She gasped.

Her mother didn't notice, since she was busy patting her forehead with an infusion of lavender, which someone had told her was efficacious for headaches.

The house was huge, with imposing wings stretching to the left and right. Two carriages were drawn up on the gravel circle, and a number of footmen milled about in front of the door.

Panic gripped Lala. She could not do this. She simply could not do this. This was not the simple country house she had expected from Mr. Dautry, who didn't always wear a waistcoat when he walked in the park.

This really was the estate of an earl or a duke. The mistress of this house . . . The mistress of this house would need to be not merely smart, but brilliant. Accomplished. She would have to be able to read.

Her mother finally glanced out the window. "It's like a bandage," she said, making even less sense than usual.

Their carriage was slowing.

"A bandage covering a suppurating wound, the wound of bastardy," Lady Rainsford clarified.

Lala's heart sank. "Mama, Mr. Dautry is a perfectly respectable businessman. It is not his fault that the duke was not married to his mother. You *mustn't* speak in this way before him."

Lady Rainsford straightened. "Your father threatened me last night."

"What*?*"

"He threatened me. He said that if you don't marry the bastard, he will not pay for another season." Her voice trembled. "Even though it goes against every part of my nature, I will abandon my daughter to . . . to the filthy lucre of ill-gotten gains." Her hands were pulling at her lace handkerchief again.

Lala's hands itched to slap her parent. The impulse was so wrong that she hardly knew what to do with it. "Mama," she said, taking a deep breath, "I beg you to calm yourself."

The carriage had stopped now, and any second their groom would open the door. He would find her mother with a wild tinge to her eyes, pulling, pulling at her handkerchief. Lala dropped onto her knees on the carriage floor, her hands over her mother's restless ones. "Mama, you want me to be happy, don't you?"

That got her attention. "Of course I do!"

"I want to marry someone and not have to go through another season," Lala said, whispering it. "I truly do, Mama."

In the nick of time, sanity poured back into Lady Rainsford's eyes, and Lala awkwardly retook her seat just as the door opened.

"Why, you shall have him, dearest," her mother said, sounding almost like a normal woman.

Lala swallowed hard and climbed down from the carriage. Whoever had traveled in the other two carriages had already been escorted into the house. The butler ap-

proached and introduced himself, bowing as they shook
out their skirts. Lala liked him immediately, just from the
way he took their measure with a practiced glance and at
once paid her mother lavish attention.

By the time they entered the house, her mother was con-
fiding all the details of her palpitations, and Fleming was
reassuring her that the village doctor would be more than
happy to pay a call every day.

"He is not an untried practitioner," he was saying now, as
a footman took their pelisses. "Dr. Hatfield is well known
and respected in these parts, but also in London. One of
the youngest members of the Royal College of Physicians,
as I understand it. I'll take the precaution of sending a message asking him to pay you a visit this afternoon, Lady
Rainsford, so that we can make absolutely certain that the
arduous nature of the carriage ride caused no problems."

Lala felt as if a ten-stone weight had lifted from the back
of her neck. Fleming opened the drawing room door and
ushered in her mother as tenderly as if she were a day-
old chick. It was a measure of what a bad daughter Lala
was that the only thing going through her mind, other than
gratitude, was a bleak guess that if she married Dautry, her
mother would probably move to this house in order to bask
daily in Fleming's gentle ministrations.

At which point Lala would move to Dautry's London
house, and everyone would be happy, she thought, pushing
away a wave of panic.

She saw Mr. Dautry the moment they entered the room.
He was taller than everyone else, and remarkably male,
which gave her a sensation that verged on dislike. Why
couldn't he have been a mild fellow, only a little taller than
herself?

Her feeling of dread grew when she glimpsed Mr. Dautry's father, the man who might be her father-in-law some-day. The duke was wearing a coat of patterned dark green, which was not extraordinary in itself except for the fact that it was lined in a misty purple silk that showed in the coattails and where his cuffs turned back.

She wanted to run from the room, but he was strolling toward her, followed by the duchess, and there was no-where to hide. Lady Xenobia started to her feet as well, stooping to help Lady Adelaide.

Confronted by the entire party, Lala dropped into a curtsy before the duke, so deep that she almost turned her ankle, then straightened just enough to turn slightly and curtsy again before the duchess, who wore the most beau-tiful morning dress that Lala had ever seen. It was made of white chambray, with an overdress of pale yellow silk closely fitted across the shoulders and bosom. Her Grace certainly didn't look like a woman who had an eight-year-old child. Her figure was exquisite.

She couldn't make herself meet Mr. Dautry's eyes, after she curtsied to him. Lady Xenobia was there too, so Lala just kept curtsying until she nearly curtsied to her own mother by mistake.

As they all exchanged greetings, panic started boiling up inside her, bubbling like molten chocolate in a pot. She didn't *want* a father-in-law like this, one whose cold, gray eyes looked her over and obviously found her wanting.

He would be able to deduce that she couldn't read. She knew it.

But he was standing just before her, while her mother informed the rest of the company about the horrors of their journey. So Lala took a deep breath and said, "I trust you had a pleasant journey, Your Grace?"

"Very," he said. "I suspect this will seem odd to you,

Miss Rainsford, but when one is the parent of an extremely active eight-year-old boy, nearly every carriage ride that does *not* include him is a joy."

"Ah," Lala said. She could think of nothing else to say. "Where is the boy at the moment?" she blurted out.

"Eton."

In the dreadful silence that followed, Lala remembered her plan. "Isn't it awful about Napoleon taking Venice?"

"Awful is one word for it, Miss Rainsford. I was more interested to read in the *Morning Post* that in a mere three years the Doge had allowed the Venetian fleet to dwindle to three hundred and nine vessels. No wonder Napoleon's fleet took the city. Did you read that particular article?"

Lala gulped. "No, I'm afraid we don't take the *Morning Post* on a regular basis," she said. "My mother is quite fond of *Bell's Weekly Messenger*."

The duke bowed his head, and another silence ensued. Then he said, "My wife is an inveterate reader of novels; there are evenings when I can scarcely persuade her to retire to bed, as she is deep in a romantic tale."

Lala opened her mouth to say . . . to say what? "*I can't read*?" "*I never read*?"

Luckily Lady Xenobia turned from the cluster of people surrounding Lala's mother and cried, "Your Grace, please tell me that you are not castigating your wife for an innocent enjoyment of novels! I told you last month that if you would merely embark on the first chapter of *Sicilian Romance,* you would soon find yourself trembling in the middle of the night, unable to stop turning the pages."

"If I am trembling in the night, it has nothing to do with literature," the duke said, giving Lady Xenobia a teasing smile.

Lala blinked, but Lady Xenobia quirked up one side of

her mouth and said, in a mock severe tone, "There is nothing worse than a duke who is determined to be clever."

"I always think that parents should be seen and not heard," Mr. Dautry said, looming up at his father's shoulder as Lady Adelaide took Lala's mother off to a comfortable seat. "Don't tell me that you are telling Miss Rainsford ribald jokes. I shall disown you."

His Grace's cold eyes warmed when he smiled at his son. Father and son were nearly identical, except that the duke's hair was more generously streaked with white. They had the same large bodies, and the same air of supreme control. As if each knew every muscle in his body and how to use it.

"A chip off the old duke," Lady Xenobia said, laughing.

Mr. Dautry slung an arm around his father's shoulders and grinned at her. "Surely you are not implying that I have achieved a level of elegance akin to dear papa's? You astonish me, Lady Xenobia."

Lala felt ill. How could these people be so informal with each other? She'd never seen such behavior, and certainly never imagined it happened in dukes' families. She wouldn't dream of putting a hand on her father's sleeve, let alone embracing him, or addressing him in such a jocular fashion. She had never wanted to be elsewhere more desperately in her life.

"Surely you are not asking for my opinion of your coat?" Lady Xenobia asked Mr. Dautry. Her eyes were dancing, and Lala had the strong feeling that there was a private jest between them. The duke was looking from one to the other, evidently as unenlightened as she.

"I always desire the truth from women, especially beautiful ones," Mr. Dautry said. "Though I should tell you," he added silkily, "that I have received little disparagement."

"I am always startled by how naïve gentlemen can be," Lady Xenobia replied. "In fact, I quite admire your coat, Mr. Dautry. Would it be a creation of Monsieur Devoulier?"

"I forced Tobias into his workroom for a fitting at age fourteen," the duke put in, "and now Devoulier simply sends him coats at regular intervals."

Shoulder to shoulder, the duke and his son looked like an illustration in *Gentleman's Magazine* of handsome gentlemen wearing the very latest fashions. Lala stood beside them silently, her stomach twisting, listening as best she could for a moment when she might contribute something to the conversation.

But it was impossible. The subject had changed from men's haberdashery to a school friend of Mr. Dautry's, a man named Wilberforce.

"Oh, Wilberforce," Mr. Dautry said dismissively. "His bark is bigger than his willy."

Lala wasn't even entirely sure what a "willy" was.

Happily, Lady Xenobia said, "On that less than polite note, I shall now take Miss Rainsford to Lady Adelaide, who is very much looking forward to chatting with her. Try to behave yourself, gentlemen."

There was nothing disappointed in the Duke of Villiers's eyes when he looked at Lady Xenobia. Well, there wouldn't be, would there? She was brilliant, and there was something luscious about her beauty spot, for all that Lala's mother insisted it was vulgar.

Lala dutifully followed Lady Xenobia across the room, consumed by the feeling that this party would be even worse than the season. At balls, one didn't have to engage in true conversation, because the next dance was always about to begin. She simply smiled prettily at her suitors, while they rattled on about whatever they wanted: willies and Doges, for example. Not dogs, *doges*. Whatever they were.

She had just greeted Lady Adelaide, who was sitting beside Lala's mother, when the door opened again and that nice butler announced, "Lord Brody."

The gentleman had tousled hair and piercing blue eyes underlined by dark shadows, which suggested to Lala that he'd stayed up all night. Doing something naughty, no doubt.

Like Mr. Dautry, he was not the type of man with whom Lala wanted to associate. No matter how striking he was.

Sure enough, Mr. Dautry went over and pounded him on the back by way of greeting, as men did with their friends. Lord Brody started laughing; he was probably the clever type as well. Mr. Dautry said something in that smoky voice of his, and Lord Brody replied, "horny as a peach-orchard boar," a comment that she didn't understand at all.

So Lala turned back to Lady Adelaide, her mother, and Lady Xenobia. It was easy to follow their conversation, because her mother never allowed an audience to go to waste. At present she was detailing her palpitations and what the doctor said about them.

Mr. Dautry's drawing room was as elegant as that in a royal palace. Lord knows how many servants were employed on the estate: she'd seen several footmen, and one had to assume that any number of maids were about as well.

As a child, she had dreamed of living in a smallish house with a picket fence and a little kitchen garden. Like every one of her dreams, that had smashed against the rocks. Her mother—notwithstanding her objections to Mr. Dautry's base birth—was obviously impressed by Starberry Court, and thrilled to be rubbing shoulders with the Duchess of Villiers.

Lala would have to marry Dautry and live in this perfectly frightful museum of a house, crammed with fancy furniture and servants.

Dautry was bringing his friend across the room toward them. "Lady Rainsford, Lady Xenobia, and Miss Rainsford, may I present an old friend of mine, Lord Brody? Lady Adelaide, I believe you have met this reprobate before."

Lord Brody dropped back and made his leg, bowing to Lady Adelaide, whom he greeted like a favorite aunt. As he bowed to Lala's mother, she became girlishly vivacious, recounting the time when they met before. "In fact, you shared a meal with my darling daughter!" she said.

Lady Xenobia showed no overt signs of being awestruck to meet a future duke, but Lord Brody was obviously intrigued by her. He bent his head to the side, as if he saw something he'd never seen before.

Lala knew why, too. Lady Xenobia was astonishingly lovely, with more hair than Lala had imagined one woman could have, all of it piled on top of her head. Plus, she'd painted her lips, and with her beauty mark, and the way her upper lip formed a perfect bow . . . She was probably the most sensual woman Lala had ever seen.

Her mother's sharp elbow dug into her side. "Why are you staring at Lady Xenobia?" Lady Rainsford hissed. "You're making a fool of yourself!"

Lala turned hastily back to the conversation about palpitations, only to find that they had moved on to talk of female ailments. Her mother dated all her problems to the birth of her two daughters.

Mr. Dautry, Lord Brody, and Lady Xenobia were having

such a lively conversation that they kept breaking into laughter—even Mr. Dautry, who usually looked as if he never smiled, let alone laughed. After a bit, the duke and duchess joined them and all five stood about being clever, while Lala sat, hiding her bottom in a chair and thinking about how she'd like to plummet through the floor into the wine cellars.

"The blood!" her mother said, fanning herself. "You would not believe the blood!"

Lady Adelaide looked queasy; she had no children, and she probably didn't welcome these details. Lala had heard it all before. She had already decided that if she ever gave birth, she was going to drink a gallon of laudanum and wake up the next morning.

The door opened again, and the butler entered. Lala began wondering if anyone would notice if she choked due to lack of air and died right there. Probably not. Though her mother might notice, insomuch as it would diminish her audience.

When Lala looked up again, she discovered, standing directly in front of her, the very embodiment of the man she had always wanted to marry. He wasn't young, but he wasn't old either. His eyes were navy blue, with wrinkles at the corners that showed he knew how to smile. He was almost bald, and she could tell with one look that he wouldn't have a hairy chest. And he wasn't as imposing as Mr. Dautry. He was probably only a few inches taller than she was.

The butler was introducing Dr. Hatfield and the doctor was bowing and saying that he would be most happy to treat her mother while she was in residence at Starberry. In fact, if she agreed, he would like to conduct a preliminary consultation now.

Her mother's eyes shifted, and Lala could see that she

was rethinking the seriousness of her palpitations; after all, she was sitting with Lady Adelaide, while a duke and duchess stood close by.

"My mother will not agree to see you, Dr. Hatfield," Lala said, standing, "because she would never put her health in front of the enjoyment of others. But I must insist that you do examine her; she had palpitations all morning in the carriage."

Lady Adelaide bounced to her feet as well, likely happy to be released from a discussion of childbirth gore. "Our health is tremendously important after we reach the change of life, don't you think?"

Lala's mother gave Lady Adelaide a look so disdainful that it could have frozen lemonade. Her ladyship didn't appear to notice, and somehow all three of them, followed by the doctor, left the room and went up the stairs. Lala wasn't quite sure why Lady Adelaide was escorting them, but she was grateful for it; her mother was always more restrained in the presence of other ladies.

Once they were in Lady Rainsford's bedchamber, Lady Adelaide seated herself to the side while Lala stood by the bed and watched. Dr. Hatfield went through the various motions that she'd seen forty or fifty doctors do in her lifetime. He asked questions, listened to her mother's chest, and took her pulse.

Her mother talked on and on. Dr. Hatfield had looked at Lala only once, swiftly, when her mother explained that even though it might lead to a palpitation that could prove the end of her, her maternal desire to see Lala settled in life had led to the enormous step of leaving Dr. Belview's care for a week.

Dr. Hatfield had beautiful eyes and a long, lean face that matched his lanky body. He was perfect: masculine without being overly so. Watching, Lala tried desperately to keep her breathing slow and even, because it wasn't panic she was feeling now. It was something else, something far more pleasurable.

When the doctor straightened, Lala held her breath. This was the point at which medical practitioners either ruined everything by announcing that Lady Rainsford wasn't ill at all, or patted her mother's hand and told her that she needed rest and good care, then charged two pounds and promised to return the next day to collect another payment.

She wanted him to be the first sort. But she also wanted him to be the second sort.

He did neither. Instead, he turned to Lala. "Miss Rainsford, what do you think?" he asked.

She gulped. "What do I think of my mother's health?" No one had ever asked her that.

"I find that the most perceptive observers of the ill are family members. A daughter can understand, better than a stranger, her mother's condition."

Somehow, Lala found her tongue. "My mother is quite ill," she said firmly. And that was true. When her mother got that spiraling look in her eyes and her voice rose, no one could doubt that something was genuinely wrong.

Dr. Hatfield nodded, his eyes grave, and turned back to his patient. "I shall visit you again tomorrow morning, the better to monitor your health, Lady Rainsford. I think you would do best to stay in your chamber and rest for at least two to three days. I'm afraid this visit will be far too taxing for your heart."

Lady Adelaide jumped to her feet. "There is no reason to be concerned, Dr. Hatfield. I will be sure to keep your patient comfortable and happy. My dear Lady Rainsford, you will join the party in a few days, when you are feeling stronger."

"Oh, I couldn't!" Lady Rainsford rarely spent time in

bed. There was, Lala thought cynically, no audience in a bedchamber.

"You must think of your health above all else," Lady Adelaide said firmly. "I shall check on you regularly throughout the day, and Dr. Hatfield will visit every morning. That nice butler Fleming can appoint a footman to wait in the corridor, so your maid will be able to ask for anything you might like."

"Oh, there's no need for that," Lady Rainsford said. "Lala can simply run down the stairs."

"Oh, but dear Lala will be with the party," Lady Adelaide said, smiling brightly. "I know that the last thing you would want is to prevent your darling daughter from enjoying the country."

"I recommend absolute quiet," the doctor said. "Peacefulness. You may ask your daughter to read to you for an hour in the afternoon if you wish, but other than that, I should like you to remain quite calm and entertain only an occasional visitor."

Lady Rainsford laughed, and before Lala drew a breath, she said, "My daughter can't read, so *that* won't happen."

"*I* shall read to you," Lady Adelaide said swiftly, as Lala tried to blink back tears of pure humiliation.

Her mother wouldn't reveal such a thing in front of Mr. Dautry. Would she?

Dr. Hatfield met Lala's eyes and asked kindly, "I trust you do not have a problem with your vision, Miss Rainsford?"

She shook her head miserably. If only stupidity could be cured with spectacles, she would wear them happily.

Dr. Hatfield bent over the bed once more, hand on her mother's wrist. "I am quite worried by the agitation of your pulse, Lady Rainsford. Those with a weak heart often overtax themselves, not realizing that their loved ones would actually prefer that they live a long and happy life."

Lady Rainsford opened her mouth again, but this time Lala jumped in. "Mama, I must beg you to take advantage of this opportunity to rest and recover from the journey. This chamber is charming."

Indeed, it was. A tall window stood open to the warm afternoon breeze, which carried in the fragrance of flowers. The walls were covered in a delicate patterned silk, and the rug on the floor glowed in the sunlight.

Lala had never been in such a tasteful bedchamber in her life, and she didn't think her mother had either. Well, at least not since those lauded days when her mother had served as a lady-in-waiting to the queen. Lala happened to know that her term of service had been a mere two months, but to hear her mother tell it, she had been the queen's most beloved companion.

"You needn't worry about your daughter," Lady Adelaide was saying. "I shall chaperone her fiercely, my dear, *fiercely*. I have done the same for Lady Xenobia, and I am proud to say that, even given Lady Xenobia's adventuresome constitution, not a hint of scandal has ever been breathed about her."

"Well, as to that," Lala's mother said, her voice sharpening, as it did when she was about to impart unpleasant news.

But Dr. Hatfield moved forward and said, "Lady Rainsford, I do not want you to stir from this bed for two days or I cannot be responsible for the consequences. Do you understand me?"

Lala saw her mother's eyes grow large.

"Yes, Doctor."

He bowed once again and headed for the door. Lala hurried after him, glad that she had her reticule, because she needed to pay him. And thank him, if she could think how to phrase it correctly.

In the end, it wasn't hard to thank him, because he refused to hear it. And he refused payment as well, but merely looked at her and asked, "What happens when you try to read?"

His eyes were so sympathetic that Lala told him the truth. "Nothing happens," she confessed. "I can see letters and numbers, just like anyone else. I simply can't remember which ones go where. I'm too—I'm too stupid for that." The last part came out in a whisper, even lower than she normally spoke, because she wished she didn't have to say it. Not to a man like this.

He had taken his hat from the butler and put it on. But he looked down at her, with his serious face and those beautiful navy eyes, and said, "Miss Rainsford, I am quite certain that you are not stupid."

That was very kind of him. If untrue. "Please don't suggest that you can teach me to read," she said, noticing out of the corner of her eye that Fleming had taken himself away, and they were alone in the entry. "My parents paid dearly for tutor after tutor, but I simply can't do it."

"No, I suspect you'll never be able to read," he said briskly.

Lala swallowed hard. She knew it; everyone knew it. Still, it was painful to hear, especially from him.

"You're likely not seeing the letters in the same order as everyone else. Or you see them in a different order each time."

"I do see them in the same order as others. I can read aloud the individual letters." She could feel her cheeks glowing. "At any rate, Dr. Hatfield, I want to thank you again for your kind attentiveness to my mother. I know she'll look forward to seeing you tomorrow."

Lady Xenobia popped her head out of the drawing room and said, "Good afternoon, Dr. Hatfield! I trust Lady Rainsford is simply weary from the journey? Lala, once you have seen the doctor off, I thought you might join us. We're starting a game of whist, and you can partner Mr. Dautry." She disappeared again.

"Can you play?" the doctor asked.

Lala shook her head. The numbers on playing cards rattled around and slid off the cards, the same way that letters did from pages. "I'll make an excuse." She began to drop a curtsy, but he caught her arm.

"You needn't curtsy to a country doctor."

Another stupid mistake. By now, she was probably as red as a brightly painted children's ball. "I apologize."

"You needn't apologize either." His hand tightened. "You're to *partner* Mr. Dautry?"

She met his eyes, knowing that her utter misery was undisguised. "Yes," she whispered, managing a wobbly smile. She'd never had such an odd conversation in her life, but the important thing was that Dr. Hatfield wasn't disgusted by her inability to read or play cards. By her stupidity, in other words.

She could tell from the way he looked at her. Just as she could tell that he felt sorry for her, because he had guessed she was supposed to marry Mr. Dautry, and he didn't think they'd suit.

"I'm going on rounds this afternoon," he said. "Would you like to accompany me?"

"Rounds?"

"I go about to see my patients." He jerked his head toward the open door and his vehicle, a dilapidated black carriage.

Lala looked down at her morning dress and her slippers. His gaze followed hers.

"Of course you don't," he said, his eyes going flat. "Miss Rainsford, I apologize for such an untoward request. I must bid you good day."

"I couldn't go without a chaperone," she said, a little breathlessly.

His mouth tightened.

"Just a maid," she added. "And my bonnet! Wait, please wait. Just a moment."

Fleming miraculously reappeared and produced her bonnet as well as a maid, because Lala didn't have a lady's maid. And asking if her mother's maid could accompany her would ensure that Lady Rainsford learned of her daughter's improper excursion.

She was almost in the carriage before it occurred to her that she ought to leave notice with someone other than the butler. She ran back to the house, ignoring the fact that Dr. Hatfield would be able to see her from behind, and said breathlessly to Fleming, "Please tell Lady Adelaide that I've gone on rounds." She turned without waiting for an answer.

Which meant that she didn't see Fleming smile as he closed the door behind her.

Chapter Twenty-two

As India dressed for dinner that night, her mind kept veering toward Thorn. She gave herself a silent scolding and made herself think about Lord Brody instead, but two minutes later she found herself slipping back to a memory of the way Thorn had kissed her good-night after they'd walked home from the gatehouse.

Probably many women had memories like these. The fact that she'd been happier in the hammock, in his arms, than she'd ever been in her life . . . that was irrelevant. He belonged to someone else. He *wanted* someone else.

Not her.

Maybe if she told herself that daily for the next year, she would stop thinking about him.

Even so, she dressed with more care than she had dressed for anything in her life, not allowing herself to think too hard about why she was determined to be—what was the word Thorn had used? Delectable.

The gown she put on was very nearly indecent, only because fashion and her bosom were not in agreement. It was made of transparent rose-tinted silk that swooped in drapes around the bodice before falling to the floor. But there wasn't much bodice. In fact, the top only barely kept her covered and the sleeves were no more than a frail length of gauze. Marie bound up her hair in the front, with one of the newest bandeau, and left all the rest of it to tumble down her back.

"It would be better if I could get your hair to take a curl," Marie fretted. She was fixing rosebuds to India's hair.

"I think it looks quite well," India said. Marie had shadowed her eyes with kohl and painted her lips a darker rose than her gown. Her only jewelry was a bracelet, a thin band of silver decorated with an amethyst, very high on her right arm. "Should you add a few of those amethyst pins?" she asked, standing up and turning slightly in order to see her back in the glass.

"Just a few," Marie agreed, nimbly setting to work. When she was done, each rosebud had a tiny sparkle, a flicker of purple light that highlighted the unusual color of India's hair.

India slid her feet into narrow slippers embroidered with spangles, with ribbons that crossed her ankles, just in case a gentleman caught sight of her legs.

She made herself think about Lord Brody as she went down the stairs. Thorn was right. Brody was a far better catch than the men who had courted her to this point: he was powerful and graceful at the same time. You could take one look at him and know that he would fight off a marauding elephant.

What's more—and even more importantly—she felt instinctively that he wasn't a bully. He would respect his wife and allow her to make most decisions on her own.

He would be a peaceful and calm husband, unlike Thorn, whose wife would probably find herself quarrelling with him once a day.

When she reached the entry, Fleming escorted her to the drawing room and announced her, quite as if they hadn't been working side by side for the last week.

Everyone turned around when she entered. Eleanor and Adelaide smiled; the duke looked surprised. Thorn was standing at the mantelpiece with Lord Brody. He froze when he caught sight of her, and his whole face changed.

India let a little smile play on her lips, because she liked the look in his eyes.

The duke and duchess walked across the room while she was giving Thorn a silent lesson in all the ways he had been mistaken in his assessment of her wardrobe. His Grace bowed, and drawled, "I will take the advantage of my age to say what every man in this room is thinking, Lady Xenobia. You look extraordinarily beautiful."

India smiled at him and dropped a curtsy. Eleanor leaned forward and whispered, "I'm seeing a whole new India."

"I am retiring," India explained. "I felt some new gowns were called for."

"At this rate, you will cut a swath through the *ton,*" the duke remarked. "Perhaps I should warn the unsuspecting men in my club."

"Oh, I don't know," the duchess said, her eyes dancing. "My guess is that India will be affianced before the next season begins."

"I see no need to rush," India told them.

Lord Brody joined them. "Lady Xenobia," he said, dropping into a bow as he took her hand and kissed it. "You take my breath away. That," he said, straightening, "is a tired remark, but nonetheless true."

Thorn strolled over, but his face was not nearly as admiring as Lord Brody's. He bowed, but he didn't add a flourish, nor did he kiss her hand.

"Lady Xenobia," Lord Brody said, turning his back on Thorn. "Would you walk with me?"

India took his arm and let herself enjoy the sensation of walking away from Thorn, so that he could see her hair down.

Lord Brody shared Thorn's overtly masculine air, but at the same time, he was civilized. They moved slowly around the room, talking of his stables. Before she knew it, India was offering suggestions. They had just rounded the corner when she said, "For example, why do stalls always have swinging doors? It would be much easier to negotiate a horse out of a stall if the door slid, instead of swinging open."

She looked up at that moment to discover Thorn blocking their path.

"No one told me this was the time to promenade," he said, his tone growly and irritated.

India wrinkled her nose at him. "Thorn, don't you agree that stalls should have sliding doors rather than swinging ones?"

Brody made a sharp movement and—too late—she realized that she had betrayed an entirely scandalous intimacy. "Do forgive me for addressing Mr. Dautry with such familiarity, Lord Brody. He and I are quite like siblings, as I have long been friends with Her Grace."

That was true . . . and not true. It was true that she had been friends with Eleanor for years. It was most decidedly *untrue* that she had sisterly feelings for Thorn.

"In that case," Lord Brody said, "I insist that you use my Christian name as well. Would you do me the honor of addressing me as Vander?"

"His real name is Evander," Thorn told India. "We both arrived at Eton as boys, whereupon Vander had to pummel any number of boys who thought it amusing to address him as Eve."

"Did you always win?" India asked Vander, delighted to think of the two of them as boys.

He looked at her with a warm light in his eyes that was remarkably attractive. "The only one I couldn't beat was Thorn. And that's because he's an underhanded fighter—as you can imagine."

India raised an eyebrow. "Indeed?"

Thorn rocked back on his heels, and the look in *his* eyes wasn't warm but scorching, and made her think about the night before. And Feather's exploits. "Those fellows were bound by the rules of civility," he said, drawling the words so that he sounded exactly like his father, the duke. "I never have been."

Vander intervened. "Lady Xenobia," he said, "I would love to discuss sliding doors, but I see that Lady Adelaide is summoning you."

"You look exquisite!" her godmother cried a moment later, squeezing India's hands. She bent close and whispered, "And both those young men are completely smitten, my dear."

"You are mistaken," India replied, as softly. "We both know where Thorn's affections lie, and I have barely met Lord Brody."

Adelaide chortled. "Oh, really? What do you think they're discussing right now?"

India glanced over her shoulder to see that Vander and Thorn were indeed talking to each other with unhappy looks on their faces. One might even say angry looks.

"You've set them against one another," Adelaide said happily.

"They are probably discussing the weather," India said firmly. "I haven't said hello to Lala yet, and I must inquire about Lady Rainsford's health."

Lala and Eleanor were seated in chairs that India had arranged before the great windows looking toward the back gardens. She and Adelaide joined them, and discovered that Lala—who, in India's experience, was almost always silent—was babbling about having accompanied Dr. Hatfield on his rounds.

"The baby," Lala was saying, "is no bigger than a scrap." She cradled her arm to show Eleanor the size. "But she has a tuft of red hair, and she was quite good at nursing!"

"Did Dr. Hatfield allow you to see a child being born?" Adelaide asked, scandalized.

In the normal course of events, no young lady was allowed to witness something so indecorous. Last year, however, Mrs. Carlyle had demanded that India hold her hand, and Adelaide had given in. India had found it fascinating. A bit terrifying, but fascinating.

"Certainly not! Little Martha is two weeks old," Lala said.

Her eyes shone, and she went on to discuss the medical aspects of the mother's confinement in a way that made India seriously rethink the commonly held presumption that Miss Laetitia Rainsford was missing a carriage wheel, if not two.

This must be what Thorn sees in Lala, she thought, losing the thread of the conversation when Lala went on to tell Adelaide and Eleanor the proper treatment for scabies. No one in society had glimpsed this side of Lala, but Thorn must understand her better than anyone.

When the dinner gong sounded, the duchess took her husband's arm and said to Thorn, "Darling, please accompany Miss Rainsford to the table. Lord Brody, would you be kind enough to offer an arm to both Lady Xenobia and Lady Adelaide?"

Adelaide chattered all the way to the dining room; India silently held Vander's other arm. He glanced down at her and his smile widened. Thorn, on the other hand, was obviously still cross; as he pulled out Lala's chair, he snapped India a look that held more than a hint of fury.

Though what he had to be angry about, she didn't know.

True, Starberry was no longer her concern, but she couldn't help but notice how well the staff had followed her directions regarding the table setting. Lush white peonies in low baskets graced the middle of the table, and the linens—she had bought three different settings—were slate-blue Japanese silk brocade that accented the gray-green walls.

She slid her fingers from Vander's arm as he pulled out a chair for Adelaide, and in the second before he turned back to her, Thorn appeared at her side and said, "You're sitting beside me."

He whisked her around the table so that she was opposite Vander. "That was extremely impolite, even for you," India observed when he sat down between Lala and herself.

"In truth I am showing my first signs of civilized behavior," Thorn said. "If that bodice falls off your milky way, I shall throw my napkin over you before Vander ogles you even more than he already is."

"He is not ogling me!" India hissed.

"Bosh," Thorn retorted. "He's eating you alive and you're oblivious."

"There's no call for *you* to—" India began, but then she realized that the duke, seated at her right hand, was listening with apparent interest. "Please forgive me, Your Grace," she said, turning her shoulder to Thorn.

"I too find my son to be extremely irritating," the duke

said. "I have nothing but sympathy. Do tell me, Lady Xenobia, who painted the swallows on the walls?"

During the meal India talked primarily with the duke and also with Vander, who completely ignored the protocol that dictated one should not speak across a table. They began by talking of Italian painters, but quickly turned to the duke's new silk top hat.

"I was hoping to cause a riot by wearing it in public," he said in a disappointed tone. "But not even one woman fainted."

"Am I to infer, Your Grace," India asked, enjoying herself enormously, "that your attire regularly causes loss of consciousness?"

Eleanor clapped her hands, and it turned out that Vander had a most appealing laugh, low and husky.

"You injure me, my dear," the duke protested. "Not long ago, John Hetherington wore a top hat and caused a riot. He was fined five hundred pounds for creating a public disturbance. *I* wore a similar top hat to the opera a mere six months after his, and not even a dog barked at me."

"London is used to you being in the very forefront of fashion," his wife said soothingly, but there was a twinkle in her eye.

"I grow old, I grow old," the duke said, not mournfully. "Soon I shall wear flannel waistcoats and my trousers rolled, and all this elegance will be naught more than a distant memory."

India laughed at that, as did Eleanor, both of them perfectly well aware that when the duke was laid to rest—hopefully many years from now—he would be the best-dressed corpse in all England.

"Do you own a top hat, Lord Brody?"

"I'm decidedly *not* in the forefront of fashion," he said, grinning at her.

"I suppose we're lucky that you're even wearing a

cravat," the duke said. "The younger generation takes no pride in their appearance."

"I'm properly dressed," Vander protested. But anyone could tell by looking at him that he wouldn't be caught dead wearing lace cuffs like those peeping from the duke's velvet sleeves.

After that, the conversation wandered, from the new smallpox vaccine, to the new book of poetry called the *Lyrical Ballads* that the duke declared to be audacious, shocking, and ultimately tedious. The duke's dry witticisms and Vander's sardonic parries kept making the three of them break into laughter.

Thorn, Adelaide, and Lala, on the other hand, were engaged in a serious discussion of childhood mortality in the countryside. India found it a particularly unhappy topic, because two years ago she had spent a month with Lady Brestle, who was experiencing a difficult confinement. Alas, she'd lost the child.

India had been the one to order the coffin—a box so tiny that it was painful to think about. She removed the rough cambric the village carpenter used to line it, and replaced it with the finest azure silk she could find, because that was the color of the family's crest.

She did not want to think about that baby. Instead, she wanted to flirt with Lord Brody under her lashes and look speculatively at his shoulders, and wonder whether he kissed the way Thorn did.

She suspected that no one kissed the way Thorn did, not with his roughness and heat . . . but if any gentleman did, she thought Vander might be that gentleman. Perhaps she would kiss him tonight, and then she would have grounds for comparison. With that thought, she gave him a smile that made him raise an eyebrow and then give her a surprisingly attractive, rather crooked, smile in return.

When dinner concluded, the ladies retired to the sitting room for tea and the men took themselves off to the library for brandy. India listened to Adelaide's chatter for a short time, before excusing herself. She wanted to drop by the dower house, just to make certain that Rose was comfortable and happy.

In the entry she told Fleming that she'd like the pony cart in order to drive herself to the dower house for a visit. As she pulled on her gloves, Lord Brody walked out of the library.

"That was a quick brandy," she observed.

"Thorn deserted us—characteristically rudely, without explanation—and the duke began a game of chess with himself, a pursuit that is profoundly tedious to watch. Where on earth are you going at this hour, Lady Xenobia?"

"I mean to take the pony cart for a turn around the estate."

"Excellent! I shall join you. Fleming, my coat, if you would."

A minute later, despite India's protests, they were sitting side by side in the cart. She tried one final desperate appeal. "Lord Brody, I fail to see why you are accompanying me. This is not entirely proper."

"We are in the country, not town. And no lady will venture alone into the darkness while I am here," he said, as the groom standing at the pony's head stood back. "Fleming didn't like it. One must always listen to the butler; it's the fundamental rule of polite society."

Fleming had gently made his disapproval clear.

"Thorn wouldn't like it either," he added as they began to head toward the dower house.

"*That* is irrelevant," she said, turning her nose up slightly. "Mr. Dautry takes advantage of our long acquaintance. I begin to think he is a bully."

At that, Vander gave a shout of laughter. "You *begin* to think? Thorn gets his way. Always. He's been that way since our first term at Eton, when he was the only one I couldn't thrash."

"Men are quite odd," India said, thinking about that.

"We've had each other's backs ever since," he said, glancing down at her. "Where would you like to go, Lady Xenobia? And may I say that if you are planning to visit Miss Rose, I would like to meet Thorn's ward. I know his secret."

"It was my idea to house the child apart from the party," India confessed, "but I feel terrible about the necessity."

"If I were Thorn, I would tell the woman to go to—" He checked himself. "To keep her opinions to herself."

"If he were to do that, he wouldn't be able to marry Lala," she told him. "He told me that she's perfect for him. And he meant it." She glanced at Vander. "Lala is not as unintelligent as most people think, and Thorn recognizes that."

"Indeed?"

"She's very sweet," India went on, although it was oddly painful to admit it. "I believe they'll have an excellent marriage."

"You do?"

"Thorn pretends to be cynical, but I believe he's infatuated," she said. "It's very romantic."

"I must be losing my touch," Vander said rather obscurely, giving her a grin that made his teeth flash in the growing dusk. "You become suspicious in the horse racing world, you know. You stop thinking that people might actually mean what they say."

She touched his hand. "Can you take the path to the right, please? We're almost at the dower house. If you're referring to Thorn, it's my impression that he wouldn't bother lying to anyone."

The smile in his eyes made her squirm a little, and she had the odd feeling that he knew it.

The pony cart drew up to the dower house and Vander jumped down, reins in hand. As he fastened them to the hitching post, Thorn pushed open the front door.

"We came to say good-night to Rose," India called.

"You're just in time," Thorn said. "Her nursemaid is waiting upstairs to give Rose a bath."

Vander came around the cart, and before India quite knew what was happening, his hands spanned her waist and he was swinging her to the ground.

"Come along, then," Thorn said impatiently.

Vander looked down at her for a second longer, then his hands dropped and he and India followed Thorn inside.

Once Vander and Rose had been introduced, Vander launched into a story about a faraway land where paper dolls walked and talked like anyone else. "Their mama is called Lady Cuttenclip," he told Rose. "She doesn't just create dolls. She makes them cunning little hats, pelisses, shoes."

"Ladies do not, as a matter of course, make clothing," Rose observed. "Is everyone in this land of the same status?"

Vander looked distinctly startled. "Surely we need not be so doctrinaire? My sisters are assuredly ladies, and yet they spent hours designing gowns for their dolls."

"Did you design clothing for paper dolls?" Rose asked, turning to India.

"No, but that was merely because I had no paints as a child. I would have enjoyed it."

Rose looked at her thoughtfully and then turned back to

Vander. "How does Lady Cuttenclip acquire paints for her dolls if the world is made of paper? Do they trade paper coins?"

"Yes, of course," Vander said.

"I have very little interest in being a modiste," Rose announced. "I should rather create a paper house with a nursery and a fireplace with burning logs."

"The shelves will be full of tiny Greek texts, of course," Thorn said, laughing.

Rose looked up at India. "Perhaps you could help, since you had no paints when you were small. If you wished, you could make a gown, but I shall make a schoolroom."

India found herself promising to come back at teatime the following day. Vander invited himself, pointing out that since Lady Cuttenclip was his creation, they couldn't do without him.

Rose smiled at that, and India realized that she had dimples. Two of them. She wasn't a pretty child, per se, but those dimples . . .

"My papa used to tell me a story at night," Rose said, turning to India again. "Mr. Dautry isn't good at storytelling."

"I would be happy to tell you a bedtime story," India said, holding out her hand. "I expect that Rose's nursemaid is waiting, gentlemen, so why don't you return to the house, and I will join you later? I worry that the other guests will find it odd that the three of us have disappeared."

"You are not going about the grounds by yourself at night," Thorn stated.

"I've been doing precisely that for weeks," India pointed out.

Vander intervened. "I am happy to wait for you, Lady Xenobia. Thorn, your parents will be wondering where you are."

"It would be quite improper for you to escort India," Thorn said, folding his arms across his chest. "In fact, you shouldn't have accompanied her here without a chaperone."

"Yet it wouldn't be improper for *you*?" Vander said, clearly irritated.

"No."

Since Thorn didn't elaborate, India said, "Mr. Dautry and I are such old friends that we don't concern ourselves with propriety."

"You are feeling protective?" Vander asked Thorn.

"No one is going to compromise India under my roof," Thorn said.

This was barked more than stated, but Vander's eyes cleared and he gave Thorn one of those slaps on the back that men give each other. "I was wrong, earlier," he said. "I apologize."

"We'll bid you good-night, gentlemen," India said. She took Rose away, but not before she heard Vander saying that Thorn had done him the greatest favor of his life.

She smiled all the way up the stairs and through story time, a new experience for her inasmuch as that her mother had never contemplated such a thing. Taking inspiration from Vander's paper dolls, she came up with a world of civilized rabbits. Runnebunny was a rascal bunny, hopping all over the place and stealing everyone's cabbage. But he also had the longest ears and the blackest eyes of any rabbit in the county.

"Your story is rather babyish, but I do like Mr. Runnebunny," Rose said sleepily. "He's just like Mr. Dautry."

"Hmmm," India said, pulling up Rose's covers. "Well, tomorrow, I'll tell you more about Lord Parsley, and I'm sure you'll like him just as much. He's far more civilized, and you know that's important in a bunny."

"I don't care," Rose said, snuggling down into her covers, her doll in the crook of her arm. "Antigone and I think that it's better that a bunny be able to steal lots of cabbage to ensure that his baby bunnies don't go hungry."

India lingered for a moment, thinking that she had inadvertently managed to make her story appallingly revealing. Then she kissed the sleeping child on the cheek and headed down the stairs.

Chapter Twenty-three

Thorn drank two glasses of brandy while he waited for India. He had never felt so damned undecided. In point of fact, he was never undecided. Ever. Generally, he decided which path was best, and took it.

He knew instinctively that Lala was the woman for him. She was warm and sweet and uncomplicated. It was unfortunate that she was also a little boring, especially now that she had learned about infant mortality; Thorn was completely uninterested, but he could live with it.

Her affection would bind his family together. Moreover, her concern with infant mortality suggested that she would make every effort to nourish and raise their children in the best possible fashion.

India, on the other hand, was like a dissected map, one of those new puzzles she had bought for Rose. No piece seemed to fit with another, and half of them hinted at some unknown country, rich, deep, and undiscovered.

Even though he had deliberately invited Vander to his house party, when his friend had thanked him for introducing him to India, his eyes betraying an intensity of feeling that Thorn had only seen when Vander was at the races . . . well, then Thorn had contemplated killing him.

Ridiculous.

He was losing his mind. He took another gulp of brandy. It was probably all a matter of competition with Vander. India was one of the most beautiful women he'd ever seen—and she was the daughter of a marquess, intelligent, witty, and rich to boot.

Not to mention the fact that he'd never enjoyed shagging a woman more. Simply looking at her made him fall into a black well where there was nothing but her smell, her taste, the stroke of her fingers.

One should never succumb to one's lowest instincts. Thorn had learned to curb his desires, to relegate strong emotions to a category labeled "interesting." Lala would be his wife, whereas India was, and India would be, his friend.

It was odd, having a woman as a friend, but if she married Vander, he would see—

Before he knew it, he was out of the chair, his body taut as a bowstring. His imagination had fed him a picture of India in that blue nightdress, smiling at Vander on their wedding night. With a curse, he hurled his glass directly into the fireplace, shattering it.

"What on earth are you doing?"

He turned to find India in the doorway, looking confused. The rich smell of brandy spread through the room. In one stride he was face to face with her, and then she was in his arms. He didn't bother with civility, not this time. He didn't coax her lips open, but took her mouth with all the pent-up force of a man who's just imagined the unimaginable.

His tongue conquered her mouth, claimed, possessed, made it his own. His. *His.*

Not Vander's. Never Vander's.

One arm clamped tight around her and then he was tasting her, tasting India, and her mouth was sweeter than he remembered, their kiss hotter, wetter, deeper. By the time he dragged his mouth away, he had backed her against the wall, his hips grinding into her softness, one hand bound in that gorgeous hair. His body was roaring with heat and fire, muscles taut, ready for the command to take her to bed. Hell, take her to the floor, to the sofa, even just against the wall.

Just take her.

He looked down to dazed eyes and cherry lips. Reality came crashing into his mind, and he jolted back with a curse. India swayed precariously when he let her go, so he reached out and caught her, carrying her to the sofa.

He meant to sit opposite, but somehow he ended up with her in his lap.

She hadn't yet said a word.

"India," he said, and hesitated.

She turned her head, her lips only a breath away from his. "What *was* that?" Her voice was as unsteady as her legs had been, and he thought she was trembling. Just a little, but trembling nonetheless. "We agreed there could be no repeat of last night."

She deserved an honest answer. "Competition," he confirmed.

There was a flash in her eyes—surely not pain? But when she spoke, her voice was steady. "Competition? Over me?"

"Competition between myself and Vander," he said, forcing the words out.

"You are competing for me?"

She pulled back, the better to see his eyes, and Thorn was appalled to discover that he didn't even like that small distance between them. Some part of his mind thought talking was a waste of time, and he should kiss that little indent at the base of her throat. Lick it. And lick his way down the curve of her breast.

He wanted to know if she tasted as sweet all over, every inch of her. There were parts of her that he hadn't had time to kiss the night before.

"It's instinctual," he explained, pulling his mind back from the bed. "Vander is my closest friend, and one of the few people I trust in the world. I've measured myself against him since we were at Eton."

"When he was unable to pummel you into the ground," she said, faint distaste in her voice revealing just what she thought of this sort of male conduct.

It *was* idiocy. It was also, unfortunately, the way he was made. "Vander and I are slightly cracked in that respect," he acknowledged, ignoring the fact that he was playing with her hair.

"You just kissed me because you are competitive with Vander?"

"Yes," he said bluntly.

"That's ridiculous!" she said, sitting up straighter, which pressed the curve of her bottom against his legs. And his cock.

"It makes sense to men," he managed, which was pretty miraculous given that he was in the grip of a lust stronger than he'd ever experienced.

"Men are absurd," she said flatly. "You shouldn't be giving in to the impulse to kiss a woman merely because your friend showed interest in her."

"It's not just that," he said, as his gaze caught on her rosy lips. Without thinking, he rolled over, tucking her beneath him, his body rejoicing as he sank onto her soft curves.

"Bloody hell," he whispered, sending the words straight

into the warmth of her mouth. "You make me lose my mind, India."

She didn't reply, just slid a hand in his hair and pulled his mouth down to hers.

Thorn was no gentleman. He never had been, and he never would be. Still, even as he shifted his weight, just enough to run a hand over India's lush breasts, his conscience started nagging.

He couldn't go . . . where this was going. But he couldn't stop either, because the moment his hand touched her breast, she gasped and her head arched back, exposing a neck as lovely as the rest of her. Leaning forward to kiss it made his hips press into her, bringing a wave of lust more ferocious than anything he'd experienced since adolescence.

He smoothed a hand down her throat, a whisper-soft caress, and kissed the curve of her jaw.

"India," he whispered.

"What was that?" she replied, and he could tell she steadied her voice with difficulty. "More competition?"

"You're damned beautiful, India. There's no red-blooded man in the world who wouldn't want to be in my place. Hell, I feel sorry for all those men who fell in love with you, house by house. You probably ruined them for married life."

Her mouth was bruised a deep red by his kiss, and he found he hadn't the heart to care. Her lips curved in a slow smile, and he felt that smile in his own body. Between his legs. "Your hair is like the white of the sun if you stare straight into the sky."

"My hair is not white," she protested. "I'm not that old yet. I think I would enjoy your competition if it wasn't for the fact that I'm the bone you and Vander are squabbling over." She corrected herself before he could respond. "No: *over which* you and Vander are squabbling."

Thorn didn't want to think about Vander. "What was wrong with the way you said it the first time?"

She frowned. Then her brow cleared and she said, "Of course you wouldn't know, because you were a mudlark. If I end a sentence with 'over,' that's ungrammatical. At least, I think it is."

Thorn started winding locks of her hair around his fingers. He'd never felt anything so silky in his life. "If you were a trollop, I'd pay a bloody fortune to have all this hair of yours sliding over my bare skin."

"Thorn!"

He'd shocked her. A bit. "Why are you worrying about grammar? Who cares if a sentence isn't exactly right?"

"I do. And you ought to as well. It's hard to catch up because I hadn't a governess, and it must be the same for you. You're behind. You must catch up."

"Why?"

It was a simple question, but her brow knit. "Because it's important."

"To be perfect?" He was quite aware that perfection was outside his grasp. What's more, he saw perfection in his father and thought it was over-rated.

"The best you can be," she clarified.

"So why didn't you have a governess?"

Her face changed, and he didn't like her expression. He leaned down and took her mouth again, a reckless, raw kiss that made their tongues mimic what their bodies might do. When at last he jerked his head back, they were both breathing fast, hearts pounding against each other's body, probably in unison, he thought hazily.

"Now tell me," he whispered, running his fingertips along the curve of her jaw. "Why didn't you have a governess?"

Her eyes were half closed. "We couldn't afford one. My parents never wanted one, because my mother thought society's strictures were tiresome." Her voice lilted when she said the last sentence, as if she were quoting a woman long dead.

"I knew there had to be a good reason I grew up on the streets," he said, bending his neck so that his mouth could trace the same path as his fingers. "Not knowing any of those strictures means I've never had to worry about them."

She turned her head, and his lips brushed her cheek. "I find it hard to imagine you worrying about any rules, social or otherwise."

"We can't keep going like this, India, or we'll find ourselves in bed again," he said honestly. "And we cannot do that."

"Of course we can't," she said, not moving. "The last thing I want to do is to be forced to marry someone who is only kissing me because of a childhood rivalry."

"And I am to marry Lala," he said gently.

"I would never do anything to stand in the way of your and Lala's union. Do you know, Thorn, I think that if the *ton* saw her the way she was tonight at dinner, she never would have been labeled a simpleton?"

"A simpleton?" That took him aback.

"Obviously, *quite* untrue," India said, "and I shall squash those rumors just as soon as the new season begins. Lala bloomed tonight. I think her mother might be responsible for some of her problems."

Thorn didn't want to talk anymore about his future wife. Or think about her, though he had to admit that he didn't like the word "simpleton."

India's thoughts were going in a quite different direction, because she got a crooked little smile on her lips and said, "Unfortunately for your competitive side, Thorn, I like Vander."

The smug feeling in his gut evaporated.

"You were absolutely right about him," she went on, apparently not noticing that he'd gone rigid. "He's manly, the way you are. He's interesting and amusing and smart. And you saw how wonderful he was with Rose earlier; he'll make a wonderful father."

Thorn briskly rolled both of them to a sitting position. "If you accept Vander's offer, India—"

"He has made no offer!" she protested.

"If he does, you must *never* tell him that we were intimate. Never."

"Because of your competition?"

"Because of the kind of friends we are." He and Vander were welded together like brothers, and a fracture would be deadly. In fact, he had an uneasy feeling that whether or not Vander learned the truth, the very fact he had slept with his future wife might shatter their bond.

"Very well," she said, pushing her hair behind her shoulders. "I really must get back now, Thorn. Adelaide will be wondering where I am."

Looking at her, Thorn suddenly understood what could lead a man to break all the rules of civility in order to bind a woman to him. Put India's intelligence and passion together with her shapeliness, her mouth, her laugh, even that beauty mark . . . she was enough to drive a man to madness.

"You must tell me the moment that Vander proposes," he said.

She frowned. "Are you saying I need your blessing?"

"We must not kiss after you are promised to another."

"You're implying . . ."

He grinned at her, Lala wasn't his yet, and India wasn't Vander's yet. So he kissed her.

But something still bothered him. "You were not walking easily earlier today," he said, tracing her lower lip with his finger.

India's eyes had a desirous look that made him long to

push her backward and simply thrust into her. Not that he would, but he wanted to.

Oh God, did he want to.

"I didn't what?"

"When you walked around the drawing room with Vander . . . your movement was rather stiff."

The dazed expression in her eyes disappeared; she straightened and scowled at him. But her lip was swollen from his kisses, and her frown just made him harder, hungrier. Still . . . he had to know.

"You walked as if you had been a virgin last night," he said flatly.

It was one thing if Lady Xenobia India was a loose woman, practiced in the arts of shaking the sheets, taking her pleasure where she would. He would never fault a woman for that, any more than he would fault himself.

But if he had seduced a virgin . . . Actually, there was something oddly relieving about the thought. He'd have to marry her. They would fight all the time. They'd probably make each other miserable. But he would have no other choice.

"India?" It came out like a command, though he had meant it only as a question.

She picked up a heavy fall of silky hair and pushed it behind one shoulder. "I fail to see why I should share the history of my intimacies with you. As I told you, I was not a virgin."

He watched her carefully. "I don't know if I believe you."

She jumped to her feet. She looked outraged, like Juno fighting with Jupiter. This could be his life. He couldn't help himself, and grinned at her, which just made her angrier.

"You are insisting that I say this aloud again? Then I will. You were *not* the first."

Well, that was definite. Thorn was well aware that his pang of disappointment was absurd. He had forced her to admit something that no lady would wish to announce. He was an oaf, a thoughtless, mannerless oaf.

"I'm an idiot," he admitted. "I thought you were walking stiffly."

She gave him one last furious glance and turned on her heel. "I shall return to the house in the pony cart, and you can find your own way back, Mr. Dautry." With that, she was gone.

Thorn climbed the stairs and entered the nursery. Rose was curled on her side, arms around Antigone, all that duckling hair of hers spread over the covers. He leaned down and kissed her good-night.

Instead of returning to the main house, he walked to the gatehouse, to the bedchamber where he'd bedded India the night before.

He stripped to the skin, because that's the way he always slept, and slipped naked between sheets that still had the faintest scent of India. She had called her perfume "moon-flower." He'd never heard of it.

They probably didn't have moonflowers in London; certainly there were no flowers down by the Thames. He lay awake, hands behind his head, staring at the ceiling for a long time.

Perhaps it was time to put the Thames behind him. He was tired of measuring his life by whether a mudlark would have known what a moonflower was. Who cared? At the heart of it, the really important point was that India smelled like a woman beneath that delicate trace of flower.

Not just any woman, either: India. Spicy, sweet, bold, desirous.

He'd never had a woman like her before. Even thinking of the way she moaned, low in her throat, made him harden to the point of pain.

Yet his life was planned. There was no space for a

woman who made him feel unmoored. He had to shovel all this feeling back into a hole in the ground and bury it.

It wasn't healthy. Some madness was making him imagine, over and over, the journey from the gatehouse to the main house. A quiet trip up the stairs, a left turn, and straight to India's bedchamber.

She slept deeply, and she wouldn't wake when he entered the room. Not until he drew back the covers and slid into the bed, naked, ready, his hands slipping beneath her nightdress. Even the thought of *touching* her limbs made his cock throb.

And that slapped him back to reality. Had he lost his mind? One woman and one night, and he forgot reason and logic? He wasn't a gentleman, but that didn't mean that he didn't have an obligation to Lala.

He did.

Plus India was exactly what Vander wanted. They would have a marriage like that between his father and Eleanor. Exactly what Vander had talked of. Their children would have India's hair.

He and Lala . . . well, they wouldn't. She wasn't a simpleton, the way everyone in the *ton* thought, but she wasn't India, either. They would have children as well.

It was unfortunate that the thought of babies with Lala's timid expression, even if they had her dazzling beauty, made him feel slightly queasy, but that was the truth of it. He would be kind to his wife, and she would follow him about the way a duckling follows its mother, quiet, docile, obedient . . . sweet and fluffy.

Thorn reared up, punched his pillow violently, and lay back down. No more kissing India, touching India, making love to India . . .

That was for Vander now.

Chapter Twenty-Four

The next day India didn't see Thorn until evening. She spent a less-than-wonderful morning talking to Lala and her mother, who had come downstairs for a few hours before retreating back to her bed. And in the afternoon she helped Rose create an elaborate schoolroom from paper, complete with a bookshelf and fireplace.

"Where on earth have you been?" she asked, as Thorn came into the drawing room before supper.

"The factory. Look at this, India." He pulled something from his pocket and showed her a queer-looking string that seemed to form a closed circle, without a knot or seam.

"What is it?"

"It's your band."

"What?"

"The band you wanted. Made of rubber. We were able to solve the problem once we made it small, which I never considered." He gave her a smile so glowing that India's heart actually thumped.

She took the band and stretched it. "This is brilliant," she said, muttering because she was thinking of all the ways she could use it. "Can you make me more? I'd like one about half this size, and one twice as large too."

He started laughing, which caught the attention of the whole party. They all came over and stood around, admiring the band.

Lala was particularly enthralled. Her eyes became very bright, and she came up with a plan to put the ear trumpet Dr. Hatfield used to listen to people's chests on a band around his neck. "He kept putting it down," she told everyone, "and some houses are not as clean as they might be."

"Does the ear trumpet have articulated joints?" Thorn asked her, after which he and Lala got into a long discussion about whether it would be possible to create a flexible tube, using Thorn's galvanized rubber, that would preserve sound better than the current model.

Eleanor had invited Dr. Hatfield to dinner as a thank you for his faithful attendance on the convalescent Lady Rainsford; once he arrived and they were all seated at the table, Thorn brought up the ear trumpet again.

Secretly—and shamefully—India became rather cross as she watched Lala become a shining, smiling woman who easily held the attention of her end of the table. Vander had made no bones about finding the subject boring—that is, until Lala pointed out that if the trumpet was modified to have a longer tube of rubber, one might be able to listen to horse's hearts. Or even stomachs, to see whether they might have colic.

Thorn wasn't seated beside India tonight; he was across the table. Their eyes met once, and he gave her a little frown. She turned away and managed to get into an interesting conversation with his father about the recent income tax Pitt had established.

When supper concluded, and the women retired to the drawing room, India tried to decide whether she could sneak away to pay another visit to Rose. If she went to the dower house once again, Thorn might assume that she was sending him a message. Flirting with him.

Instead she sat down and wrote Rose a little goodnight story about Lord Parsley, which she gave to Fleming with a request that it be delivered to the dower house.

She felt a bit wistful, remembering how she had told Rose that she would tell her more of the story in person.

But it was better this way.

The last thing a motherless little girl needed was to form an attachment to a woman she'd never see again.

Chapter Twenty-five

After breakfast the following morning, Lala went upstairs and seated herself on a hassock in her mother's bedchamber, appearing to be a dutiful daughter while in reality she dreamed of being a country doctor's wife. It wasn't as if Dr. Hatfield lived in a hovel. He had pointed out his house to her, and it was a perfectly respectable house in the middle of the village, with a picket fence and likely a garden in back.

If they were married, he would help her with the accounts. True, he'd said she would never learn to read, but he didn't make it seem like a criticism; his words didn't lash her the way the various tutors her father had hired had done.

No one ever understood that she had spent hours and hours trying to memorize letters that twisted into little dragons and leapt off the page, or slid sideways as if water had suddenly drenched the ink. No amount of staring or repetition would stop them from moving.

"If you don't do something, you will lose Mr. Dautry," her mother remarked, from the bed.

Lala started.

"Did you hear what I said?" Her mother's voice was rising, which was never a good sign. "My maid has told me everything that's going on in this house!"

"I did hear you, Mama," Lala said. "You are concerned that Mr. Dautry is no longer interested in me." She couldn't bring herself to point out that a few days ago her mother had been appalled at the very idea.

The problem was that Mr. Dautry was a terrifying man. The idea of marrying him made her shudder, though she was not afraid that he would say cruel things to her. He was frighteningly large, overly masculine—but not cruel. He might feel silent scorn for her, but he would never speak the words aloud.

"I think that Mr. Dautry and I are forming an acquaintanceship," she said lamely.

"Apparently the servants think that Dautry is tupping that hopeless excuse for a lady, Xenobia St. Clair," her mother replied acidly.

"Mother!" Sometimes her mother was the perfect embodiment of a royal lady-in-waiting, and one could not imagine a vulgarity crossing her lips. And sometimes . . . she wasn't.

"Don't be a fool, Lala. You're not a child in the schoolroom any longer. Even in the short period I was downstairs I saw the way his eyes followed her across the room. And Brody's as well. She's had Dautry, mark my words. No man looks at a woman that way unless he's known her between the sheets."

"Mama, you mustn't," Lala cried. "Don't say these

things. Lady Xenobia is all that is good and kind. I know that she supports Mr. Dautry's courtship of me. She as much as told me so!"

"She's playing a sly game. She doesn't want the bastard, of course. She can do better, and she's going for the duke. I wouldn't be surprised if she were sleeping with both of them."

Lala gasped.

"At the same time," her mother added.

There are times in a woman's life when she has to make a stand. But years of feeling stupid and fearful crowded in on Lala, and she couldn't think of anything to say that would have an effect. Her mother wasn't even looking at her; she was propped up in her bed, looking at her face in a small hand mirror.

Without a word, Lala got up and left the room, closing the door precisely behind her. She went downstairs and asked Fleming for her pelisse. "I shall accompany Dr. Hatfield on his rounds," she told him. "I would like a carriage brought around immediately."

Lala never said imperious things like that. Never.

She did not permit herself to cry in the carriage on the way to the village, and when she reached the doctor's house, she stepped out and waved the carriage away, even though the groom wanted to approach the house for her.

Her heart was pounding. He had to be home.

He was not home.

A harassed-looking maid opened the door, and almost screamed, "I'm sorry, but the doctor can't help right now, miss. He's gone out on a birthing, and the waiting room's full." Lala heard a cacophony coming from the room just off the entryway, a baby wailing and people barking at each other.

He wasn't there. Still, he would have to return at some

point, and she had nowhere else to go but Starberry Court—and she did not want to do that. Besides, without a carriage, she had no way to return until the doctor appeared.

She walked past the maid into the entry, and took off her pelisse. "What's your name?" she asked.

"Sarah," the maid said, taking Lala's pelisse. "But, miss, really, unless it's an emergency, you mustn't wait. The doctor's been out all night, and I don't know when he'll be back. It wouldn't be proper for you to be in there with the rest of them."

"I shall see if I can help," Lala said briskly. "Why don't you bring some tea?"

"*Tea*?" Sarah was clearly at the end of her rope.

Lala opened the door to the waiting room and took a quick glance. Then she said, "Please bring some hot water, Sarah, and some cotton bandaging. Let's see if we can get that boy's knee cleaned up before the doctor returns."

Dr. John Hatfield was weary to his very marrow. He'd been up all night and had nearly lost the child. Even now, he wasn't sure the infant would survive.

His house would be erupting with patients, as it always was on a Sunday. The poor of West Drayton waited as long as they possibly could to see a doctor; when they had their half day, they skipped church and the public house, and came to him instead.

He really should hire an assistant. He'd tried twice, with men just completing their medical training at St. Bartholomew's, but they never stayed long. They learned what they could from him, and then left for London or Bath, where people could actually afford to pay for a doctor's care.

The worst of it was that since his visit to Starberry Court the night before he couldn't stop thinking—for the first time in his life—that perhaps *he* should go to London. But each time, the thought was met by scornful reality: proximity wouldn't bring him any closer to Miss Laetitia Rainsford.

The distance between them was insurmountable. And the fact that he saw a look in her eyes that echoed the longing in his heart . . . that was irrelevant. A woman like her—astonishingly beautiful, intelligent, with luscious curves, the daughter of a lady (no matter how much of a harridan that lady might be)—wasn't for him.

He was disheveled and exhausted, and he still faced a waiting room full of patients who would run the gamut from merely irritable to dangerously ill.

Sarah was nowhere to be seen when he stepped into the entry although, to his great surprise, he heard none of the usual crying or cursing coming from his waiting room. First he would see which patients were desperately in need of help. After that, he'd try to find something to eat, because he'd had nothing since four o'clock the previous afternoon.

He braced himself for whatever he might find on the other side of the waiting room door, pushed it open, and stopped short.

She was there.

His patients were arrayed around the room, sipping tea as if they were at a party—well, all except that small boy with flushed cheeks, who definitely had a high fever. And *she* looked across at him with a smile that sent a bolt of lust all the way to his knees.

John wasn't a man who lost control of his loins . . . and yet he was abruptly glad that his coat was cut unfashionably low. Miss Laetitia Rainsford was so damned beautiful.

Walking gracefully toward him, she counted off the patients on her fingers, described their conditions, and explained that there were no urgent cases. There was nothing he had to do this very moment, and therefore he should restore himself before attending to them. He glanced around and saw all the patients nodding at him. Miss Rainsford had bound up an arm and put a patch on an elderly man's forehead.

He still hadn't said a word, and an uncertain look crossed her face. "Cook has a hot meal waiting for you," she said, sounding a bit hesitant.

Still, he didn't speak.

He did the only thing he could, given the burst of feeling that spilled through his entire body. He caught her in his arms, and kissed her so hard that she bent over his arm.

But her arms wrapped around his neck, and she kissed him back.

He was dimly aware of cheering, but Dr. John Daniel Hatfield didn't give a damn.

Chapter Twenty-six

*L*ady Rainsford descended from her bedchamber just in time for luncheon, which was enough to make India want to flee home to London. She hadn't realized how profoundly disagreeable the woman was until she discovered that Lady Rainsford's voice dominated whatever room she was in. Before the meal she talked on and on about the way society was degenerating into (if you listened to her) little better than a pack of wolves.

Fleming announced that Lala was confined to her chamber with a severe headache; all India could think was that if Lady Rainsford had been her mother, she would probably develop chronic migraines.

Luncheon was given over to a lecture on the medieval practices of royal ladies-in-waiting. All of which was meant to ensure that the entire party was made aware that Lady Rainsford had married beneath her.

At least, that would be India's summation.

"I cannot approve of the way Lady Rainsford talks about her own daughter," Adelaide said to India after everyone else had escaped the table, leaving the two of them. They had all fled back to the drawing room except Thorn, who had taken himself off somewhere, and Lala, who had missed the meal.

Lady Rainsford had made a point of instructing Fleming not to bring her daughter a plate in her room, saying with a laugh that Lala's hips were large enough.

"I can't stand her," India said fiercely. "My mother wasn't perfect when it came to nurturing, Adelaide, but at least she never tried to eat her young."

"You're exaggerating," Adelaide said. "Somewhat."

"Poor Lala wasn't even in the room to defend herself, and her mother as good as told us that she was eating them out of house and home!"

"Extremely unkind."

"And she said that Mrs. Peters, who everyone knows is grieving the death of her little girl, was being maudlin merely because she wears black and wept on the street."

"That was not compassionate," Adelaide agreed. "I also do not like the way that she looks at you, dear."

"She's decided that I'm a hussy," India said, not caring at all. Lady Rainsford was right. She'd done naughty things—in a hammock, and in a gatehouse. But rather than being shamed, she felt proud of herself.

"I shall have to have a word with her," Adelaide said. "She has single-handedly ruined several reputations, and I'm quite sure she's noticed that Thorn is in love with you."

"*What?*"

"Well, he is, darling. As is Lord Brody. Poor Lala doesn't stand a chance, which may be behind her mother's irritation."

"You are entirely mistaken," India told her. "Thorn has every intention of marrying Lala."

"Reluctantly, I have to agree. I had no idea that Lala was in such desperate straits at home," Adelaide said. "I know Mr. Dautry prides himself on his lack of gentlemanly characteristics. But in fact, I would judge him one of the most gentlemanly men I've had the pleasure to meet."

"I agree."

"Therefore, he will marry Lala, because it is the most honorable thing to do. And you, my dear, will be very happy with Lord Brody."

India swallowed hard. "Of course."

"I suspect that Lala and Thorn will not be as happy together. Yet I worry not about them, but about you. This situation is why society puts strictures on people's behavior."

Her godmother drew India to a halt. Everyone had entered the drawing room before them, and the corridor was empty. "A woman gives away her heart along with her virtue," Adelaide said softly. "A man does not. Society's strictures protect women's hearts as well as their reputations."

Apparently, India's fluffy, affectionate godmother grasped a good deal more than she let on. With a kiss Adelaide disappeared into the drawing room, leaving India staring at the wall.

Surely Adelaide was wrong about Thorn's marriage to Lala. His childhood had been awful, and he needed sweetness in his life. It wasn't as if India could give that to him herself. She didn't have a kind, forgiving nature like Lala's—obviously, since she was still furious at her parents for their neglect and abandonment.

And yet she wanted Thorn to choose *her*, rather than Lala. It wasn't just his body, or the way they made love. It was the brilliant way he invented things such as the India rubber band, merely because he had bought an ailing factory and needed to save the jobs of twenty-six men.

It was even the way he had seen who Lala was, when the rest of them—the whole *ton*—had ignored her. He'd realized that Lala was bright, and that she needed rescuing.

India couldn't even put into words the way he was with Rose. It was as if he'd walked straight into being Rose's father, and the little girl would never know how lucky she was to have had two fathers who loved her, protected her, and treasured her.

India almost groaned aloud. Adelaide was right. She had forgotten to guard her heart.

It seemed she'd given it away, without noticing.

Chapter Twenty-seven

*T*hat evening at dinner, Vander lavished attention on India, but she couldn't bring herself to care. She felt listless, as if the world was hurtling on without her. Probably she'd end up married to Vander. And Thorn would marry Lala.

Obviously, he hadn't spent the afternoon at his factory, not given the way Lala looked. He must have spent the afternoon with her, and never mind the fact that she was supposedly confined to her room with a headache.

Right now Lala was sitting at the dining table, rosy and glowing . . . Did she really think that they wouldn't notice the love bite on her neck? Lala had tucked a fichu into the bodice of her gown, but India wasn't stupid. She could recognize a woman who had spent the afternoon kissing.

Or more.

The worst was that India felt like such a light-skirt, as Adelaide would call it. A slut, to use a baser term. Thorn had spent the afternoon seducing another woman, and she still wanted him.

Luckily, this evening he wasn't seated beside her; he was at the head of the table, and she was quite a bit farther down. So far away that she dared to look at him under her lashes.

She kept meeting his eyes, which was embarrassing. But every time, a stab of lust would go through her and she would shift in her chair, her legs restless. Mortifyingly, he caught her doing it. He knew what she was feeling.

Once he actually laughed aloud after their eyes met, which made her mind reel.

Men were incredible. How could he look at her in that way, after spending the afternoon with Lala? You only had to look at her to know that she was in a happy daze, that she felt loved and appreciated.

India narrowed her eyes at him and then looked to her right, at Vander.

"Are you sparring with Thorn?" Vander asked.

"Absolutely not," India said, taking a swallow of wine. "Though if I could, I would spar with him for having disappeared for hours. It's hardly the conduct of a good host."

Vander's eyes rested thoughtfully on Lala, and India's stomach pitched. Of course everyone guessed where their host had been, or at least, what he had been doing.

"I believe we may be thinking the same thing," she said, summoning a smile.

"And that would be?"

"I expect Thorn has asked Lala to be his wife," she breathed. "Just look at her." Lala was absentmindedly lining up her silverware, a little smile playing around her mouth.

"I'm not convinced," Vander said, his eyes going to Thorn.

"She has a mark on her neck."

Vander looked back at India, one side of his mouth quirked up, and she felt herself blushing. She probably shouldn't even know about love bites. "She does look happy," he agreed.

Lord Brody was handsome. And he wasn't baseborn either, though she didn't give a damn about that. Still, other people did. If her parents were still alive, and if they had cared about such things, they would have preferred she marry Vander.

He even smelled good, like wind with a touch of rain, probably because he spent most of his time on a horse.

She made up her mind. She would not humiliate herself by making calf's eyes at a man who was marrying another woman. Vander was handsome and strong and *perfect*. She smiled at him. The big smile, the one that Thorn hated.

Vander didn't hate it. He smiled back, and his eyes crinkled at the corners in an entirely attractive way. India reached out blindly, picked up her wineglass again, and began to ask Vander about his stables.

She did not look again at the end of the table. She kept her shoulder turned, as a matter of fact. She held on to her dignity with all the strength she had, and she lavished smiles on Vander.

He was her future, and Lala was Thorn's future, and that was that.

When Eleanor rose, all the ladies rose with her, and the room hummed with quiet chatter and the swish of gowns brushing the marble floor. "The ladies will join me for tea in the small drawing room," Eleanor said.

India had designed it for precisely this purpose. It was a beautiful, feminine space, with clusters of settees and even a game table in the event that someone wanted to play piquet.

"Good evening, gentlemen," Eleanor said cheerfully, taking Adelaide's arm and ignoring the way Lady Rainsford was hovering, indicating that she would like to stroll beside the duchess.

India stopped to have a chat with Fleming, who revealed that there hadn't been quite enough soup spoons, and that the second downstairs maid had tripped on the back stairs and sprained her ankle.

"She's a bit clumsy."

"She'll improve," India said.

Thorn appeared at Fleming's shoulder and said, "What in the hell are the two of you discussing?"

Just like that, India's heart sped up and began beating loudly in her ears. He was cross again, but that wasn't what made her pulse race; it was the pure maleness that blazed out of him, even standing as he was in the shadowy corridor, half hidden by his butler.

"Merely an insufficiency of soup spoons," she said. "Thank you, Fleming."

The butler bowed, giving Thorn a sharp-eyed glance. India wouldn't be surprised if he knew everything. Butlers always did.

"You needn't worry about my soup spoons," Thorn said, taking a step closer. His jaw was set, and his eyes were saying something . . . she wasn't quite sure what.

India was transfixed by his closeness, and it took a moment for his comment to sink in. Of course, she didn't. He had a wife now. Or as good as one.

"I understand," she said, head high. "I will give Lala the direction of the silversmith who created your design."

He made a growling sound. "Leave it."

"Oh. Well, I'll be joining the ladies." And she nodded toward the door to the small drawing room.

But instead of allowing her to pass, Thorn took another

step toward her. India reflexively stepped backward, only to discover that he had herded her into a tiny room off the corridor designed to hold footmen's livery.

Proper cabinetry had yet to be fitted, and as a temporary measure, India had concealed the alcove with a misty gray hanging. Now the curtain fell closed behind Thorn as he gently pushed her all the way into the tiny room.

There was scarcely room for both of them, and light filtered dimly through the loose linen weave. She looked up at his scowling eyes and something broke open inside her heart, just a little bit.

She'd fallen in love with a man with cool gray eyes, the very same color as the fabric at his shoulder. She had created the perfect setting for him without even knowing she was doing it.

"Thorn," she said, "I must join the other ladies; they will be wondering what became of me."

"You stopped looking at me," he said, frowning at her.

"I had no reason to look at your end of the table."

He braced one arm on the wall above her head, leaning closer. "You looked at me earlier." He sounded as if he were speaking through clenched teeth.

It was embarrassing to find that the merest glance at his lips made her knees feel weak. But she managed to summon up her self-respect. "You should be spending time with Lala. Go!"

He paid no attention. "Do you know that most people find me intimidating?"

Meeting his eyes made India drag in a deep breath and begin to turn sideways, to dart toward freedom. But his body closed in, and his mouth came down on hers. Their kiss was deep and wet—not sweet, but scorching, as if there was no air in the world other than what she took from Thorn's lips.

It was silent, this desperate kiss, so insistent that she

could actually feel her lips becoming bee-stung. His hand shoved into her hair, and the pins that had held in place a pyramid of elaborate ringlets tinkled to the floor.

"No," she gasped. But his mouth found hers again. She hardly registered that she had launched herself away from the wall, and she was now plastered against him, as close as if she were trying to melt into him.

In fact, she didn't notice at first when his hands slipped under her skirts. Not until she realized that they were cupping her bottom, hitching her higher and backing her against the wall again. Her legs instinctively curled around his hips as he pushed his pelvis against her, sending flames arcing down her legs.

She said something in a shamefully weak voice. It might have been "No." But even worse, it might have been "Yes."

Whatever it was, he ignored her. His fingers slipped into the silky tuft of hair between her legs. The moment he touched her, her lips opened in a cry that he caught with his mouth.

His kiss and caress tumbled her into a haze: her head spun and she couldn't see or even breathe. She clung to him, his clever, clever fingers igniting a fever in her blood. Need rose in her like a dark storm.

"No!" she whispered hoarsely, pulling away from his kiss. "You cannot spend the afternoon with Lala and then come to me. You cannot seduce me while you're betrothed to another."

He met her eyes, his face strained with desire but confused. "I am not betrothed to anyone. I have said nothing about marriage to Lala or any other woman."

India stared at him. It was hard to think when her body was shaking. His fingers had stilled, but they were still there, touching her. "You're sure you're not betrothed? Even informally?"

He shook his head. His eyes had darkened to the color of a storm over the sea, and his fingers started that caress again, touching her in a teasingly regular pattern that made her body oddly lax and tense all at once.

As if she was waiting . . . waiting for something.

"I have spoken to Lala's father, but given the circumstances of my birth, he declined to consider the matter unless I received Lady Rainsford's approval. I never asked Lala for her hand." The words grated from his throat, and India believed him. Whose fault was it that Lala was dreaming about marriage to Thorn? Probably every other woman in London was dreaming about Thorn.

The thought drifted away, because Thorn lifted her with one arm—her weight seemingly nothing—and unbuttoned his breeches with the other, pulling himself free. She gasped when their bodies came together again, her thighs instinctively tightening around his hips.

"I did not spend the afternoon with Lala," he growled at her, his voice jolting, as if he were in a runaway carriage. "I was at the rubber factory, trying to make that damn machine work."

"Oh," India breathed as he nudged her softest, most private spot.

"May I?" he growled, his eyes holding hers. Her arms tightened around his neck. She could no more say no to him than she could tell the sun not to rise. She wiggled against him at the very same moment he drove into her.

She would have screamed but his mouth covered hers again, a frantic kiss in time with the rhythm of his rough thrusting. Wild pleasure flared in her limbs as he kept going and going, an arm around her back to protect her from the wall.

They were both mad, India thought dimly, not really thinking, just feeling: the strength of his arm holding her up, the way they were connected, and the powerful way he was pumping into her, as if she were life.

And then . . .

And then she was coming, her head falling backward, her body jerking as if she were falling into a well full of stars, a deep one. The stars flew out to the very end of her fingers. It was so pleasurable that it was almost painful. And it kept going and going.

Thorn groaned, braced himself against the wall and—

It was different. It *felt* different. He was deep inside her, his breath rasping, his hips pumping. His breath was harsh and his control lost.

He was like a man starving, a man possessed. And with that thought, she was coming again, succumbing to the rhythm of his hips . . . the rhythm of his heart.

A moment later, India's breath was still sobbing from her chest; he still had an arm around her bottom. But he was leaning his head against the wall, gulping air. They stood together in silence, her body blissful and her mind blank.

At length, reason returned, bringing abject terror with it.

"Thorn, you didn't use a sheath," India whispered. "You forgot!"

She heard a sharp inhalation, and then his response, a word she'd never heard before. But she knew what it meant. It meant he dropped her to the floor as fast as a child might drop a cat. Unlike a cat, she landed wrong, lurching on one of her elegant little Italian heels, and managing to stay upright only by grabbing his sleeve.

He didn't notice.

She knew what he was thinking. Now she would force him to marry her. Trap him, and keep him away from sweet, dizzy Lala. She wouldn't.

"I have *never* lost control before," he growled.

"I'm certain everything is fine!" she said, chirping like Adelaide. "My mother tried for years to have another child and never succeeded." She let go of his sleeve and shook down her skirts, ignoring the fact that her legs were throbbing.

"My father has six bastard children," he stated. "If my father had married your mother, you'd probably have seventeen brothers."

"Nonsense," she said, frowning. "May I remind you that Eleanor has borne only one child? I am aware that you have strong feelings on this subject, but I can reassure you that all will be well. Adelaide told me . . . well, conception has to do with the time of the month, and rest assured, you are not going to be a father."

He stared down at her, his mouth tight.

Humiliation was welling up inside, and if it made its way out, India would likely burst into tears.

It was one thing to have a romantic *affaire,* a sweet memory of a single night's bliss. But Thorn hadn't even brought her to a bedchamber, but had simply shoved her behind a curtain and pulled up her skirts, as if she were no more than a night-walker.

The worst of it was that she'd liked it. She had practically begged him to do it, even knowing that he was marrying another woman. And that Lala was dreaming of their marriage.

She'd done that to herself, betrayed her own standards. Self-hatred crept up the back of India's throat like acid.

She had always scorned her parents, but they had never done anything like this. They had danced naked but their intentions were pure, even if the villagers had never understood. Her mother and father had truly believed in Diana, the moon goddess.

They hadn't engaged in a sordid affair, thrown up

against a wall when any servant might walk by. They respected each other; no, they adored each other. They might have been eccentric, but they were married.

For the first time in her life, she had behaved in a way that shamed her parents, rather than the other way around.

"I must go," she said. At least she had the tears under control.

"We have to talk," Thorn said, his voice a low rumble.

"We cannot! Anyone might walk down this corridor at any moment!"

Their eyes met, and she saw as he grasped her unspoken point: her lips were swollen, her hair down her back . . . she even smelled like the two of them. "I am going to my room," she stated, "and this did not happen. It will *never* happen again."

She jerked her arm from his grip, threw open the curtain, and ran toward the back staircase as quickly as she could. When she made it to her bedchamber without being caught, she had the impulse to send up a thankful prayer to the goddess Diana.

Just in case.

Chapter Twenty-eight

Thorn felt as if a bolt of lightning had struck a crowded street and he was the only one in its path. Sensation rushed through him: strong, sharp, biting.

What in the hell was happening to him? Had he truly lost his mind? After India began ignoring him during dinner, there was no further point to the meal. He kept glancing at her, but she turned her shoulder to him, laughing and talking with Vander.

He had been closer than he wanted to admit to dragging her out from the room, carrying her straight to his bedchamber, and losing himself in her. Only his tight control had kept him in his chair.

But after dinner, when he'd seen India talking to Fleming, he hadn't been able to stop himself. He'd treated her as if she were no more than a trull, a woman taken wordlessly by a ruffian who tossed her a sovereign afterwards. Took, moreover, without using a sheath or giving a thought to the consequences.

Naturally she had looked at him with betrayal starkly written on her face. The first time they'd made love, he had promised that she would never face the possibility of carrying a child out of wedlock.

Now he slumped against the wall, a string of curses running through his mind. He would marry her; that went without saying.

But he couldn't get over the fact that he had neglected to use protection. It hadn't even occurred to him. Even though it was an unshakable tenet of his adult life that Thorn Dautry never bedded a woman without using a French letter.

Finally he tucked in his shirt, buttoned his breeches, and went to find Fleming. He needed to obtain a special license.

Fleming's bushy eyebrows flew up when Thorn told him to send Fred to Doctors' Commons in order to request a special license from the Archbishop of Canterbury.

"I believe the fee for a special license is five pounds," the butler said, taking the twenty-pound note Thorn handed him.

"The archbishop will have to leave the license blank, since I am not there in person," Thorn said. "The clergy do not like to do that, by all accounts. Twenty pounds should be sufficient persuasion, proffered as a donation to the poor, of course. Make sure Fred understands that."

"Yes, sir," Fleming said, bowing. "Fredrick is most reliable. I shall send him straight away."

Thorn nodded and glanced over his butler's shoulder, only to meet his father's fascinated eyes. "A special license?" His Grace drawled. "And I thought my eldest son was lamentably conservative. I pictured you in Westminster Abbey. I suppose I should be grateful that you are not contemplating Gretna Green."

"The cathedral would never allow me through its doors," Thorn said.

"They damned well would take you," the duke stated, his eyes darkening.

Thorn hadn't the energy to discuss the consequences of illegitimacy with his father. He had to find India and inform her that they would marry as soon as the next day. Wasn't there some rule that nuptials had to be conducted before noon? They could marry the day after tomorrow.

"May I inquire as to the name of the bride?" his father asked.

Thorn met his eyes. "I'd be very surprised if you didn't know."

A satisfied smile played around his father's lips. "I suspect that I do." He fell back a step and swept one of his magnificent bows. "Son. You do me proud."

Thorn made one of his own perfunctory bows in reply.

Then he retired to his room, brooding over the fact that a blindingly foolish slip would result in marriage to India.

Which meant, in turn, living with India every day, coming home to the amazing hunger that matched his own. The thought sent fire searing through him. India's sweet arse beside him in bed, India's blue eyes glazed with desire, begging him for relief, India's intoxicating moans.

He scarcely touched her, and she was already wet. You couldn't fake that. A woman could fake many things, but not that.

And he trusted her, as much as he'd trust anyone. He even liked her.

She was almost like a man, though her mind worked in fascinatingly different ways from his. India rubber bands were going to be an enormous success. He knew it in his bones, and he was never wrong about business.

After a bath, he dressed and walked down the long corridor to India's room. He entered without knocking and closed the door behind him.

She was curled in a chair reading a book, her face bent to the page. A wall lamp cast a glow over her shoulders, turning her hair to a river of white gold.

With just a glance, he began to harden again, even though he'd just had her, barely an hour ago. Likely their whole life would be like that. He would spend years dragging his wife into corners, into the hammock, into their bedchamber.

He would never grow tired of making love to India. He knew it instinctively, with every fiber of his being. Once they married, her lush body would be his, his for the taking, for the asking, at any time. What's more, she would laugh and scold and argue with him.

Perhaps that was even more important.

Thorn stood in the doorway, struggling to control the emotions raging through him, when India said, without looking up from her book, "I'd much prefer that you didn't walk into my bedchamber without invitation. And I have no intention of extending that invitation."

She was angry. Of course she was. He had explicitly promised that he would never put her at risk of bearing a child. He still didn't believe it had happened. At the same time, all he wanted to do was pull her nightdress from her body, sweep her onto the bed, and thrust inside her.

Without a sheath.

He had spent his youth learning the intricacies of pleasuring a woman from an assortment of females. He had been with many women, more than he cared to remember, knowing that someday he would bind his wife to him with his lovemaking, satisfying her in ways that would ensure she never left him.

Or, more to the point, never left their children.

With India, everything he had learned about slowly bringing a woman to pleasure flew out the window and all he could think of was—one thing.

"A husband needs no invitation to enter his wife's bedchamber," he said, his voice coming out husky and rough. Surely she too understood that they now must marry.

"What a husband does or doesn't need is debatable, but it hardly matters in this instance, as you are not my husband," she said, turning the page. She finally looked up at him. "In case you are wondering, Thorn, you will never be my husband."

"Considering the fact that I had you against the wall a mere hour ago, you are quite likely carrying my child," he replied, knowing that his voice had dropped an octave.

Another woman would have winced or been embarrassed. He could have sworn he saw yearning flash through her eyes. But then it was gone; he must have imagined it.

India's mouth tightened. "I am not carrying your child."

"You cannot know that."

"No. But I can be reasonably certain."

"There is no certainty in these things. I have sent for a special license, and we will be married on the morrow or, at the latest, the day after."

She blinked, apparently shocked. Did she think that he would simply saunter away after that?

Finally she put that damned book to the side and came to her feet. "Thorn, I will not marry a man due to a momentary foolishness. You are essentially promised to Lala. You have spoken to her father, whether he declined to answer or no. She is dreaming of your future life together.

The fact that I acted like a whore does not compel you to marry me."

He was frozen for a moment, then he found himself standing before her, hands on her shoulders, giving her a gentle shake. "Do not *ever* say something like that about yourself. You are nothing like a whore."

India stared back at him, her eyes flat. "Well, it's true that I didn't charge you for my services. But I don't think that Lady Rainsford will care about that distinction."

"Lady Rainsford is a monstrous woman," he bit out.

"She is your future mother-in-law," India observed. "Our unfortunate behavior does not and should not compel you to marry me—and neither does it mean that I am compelled to marry you. You appear to have forgotten to propose, but you needn't bother. My answer is no."

Thorn felt astonishment roaring down his spine. "Your answer is yes."

"Do not think for a second that you can force me into marriage!"

India turned blindly away from Thorn's black expression and walked to the mantel. The truth could not be avoided. He deserved better than she, someone sweet and soft. She swallowed hard.

And *she* deserved someone who loved her, not someone forced by his sense of honor to marry her. Tears threatened again, but she managed to choke them down.

"India," Thorn said from behind her, the bite in his voice easing.

She had to cut him off before he persuaded her, because it would only be his conscience talking. She refused to be sacrificed on the altar of any man's conscience.

Not when it would change the course of her whole life. Not . . . not loving him the way she loved him, especially if he grew to hate her because he lost his "ideal" wife.

He would hate her, if not now, then later, after the plea-sure of illicit encounters in hallways had worn off. She would rather die than live that way.

"At any rate," she said, steeling her voice. "I've changed my mind. I am not giving up my profession. I have decided to accept an offer from the Prince of Wales; I shall reno-vate his private quarters at the Royal Pavilion in Brighton."

His eyes narrowed. "You will not go anywhere near that fat lecher's chambers."

She gripped the mantelpiece, using it to keep herself up-right as she turned to face him again. "I shall go where I wish. And I would be daft not to accept the job. Perhaps after that, I shall marry—but never because of a moment's indiscretion. My parents were neglectful, as you know. But they loved each other. I didn't realize until recently how important that was, and I shall certainly not marry a man who doesn't even think he has to propose."

"I would have proposed." It looked as if his lips were scarcely moving.

"When? After we were married? You walked into this room and informed me that you had sent for a special li-cense. Acceptance on my part had nothing to do with it. You felt that there was no reason to ask me, because our marriage wouldn't have been about *us*. It would be about the possibility of a child."

He didn't deny it. She hated that his tacit agreement hurt.

"Please leave," she said.

Thorn was staring at the carpet, but after a moment, he looked up, his eyes burning with frustration. "You will not defy me in this, India. Our irresponsible actions have left us with no alternative. Regardless of what you say, you cannot deny the possibility that we conceived a child."

That, more than anything, demonstrated that he didn't love her. To him, she was no more than a woman who engaged in irresponsible behavior. A sob nearly forced itself from her throat before she choked it back.

There was only one thing that would stop Thorn from marrying her, she knew. She would have to say it. That horrible thing.

"You are doing this because of the possibility of a child. As I have told you, I am quite certain that there is no child. But if there is"—She hesitated, her heart beating so hard that she felt faint.—"I will do as your mother did."

She saw the blood drain from his face. "Are you saying that you will leave the child to me, just as my mother left me with my father?" he asked incredulously.

She nodded jerkily, uncertain whether her expression betrayed the truth of how utterly an action like that would destroy her. Surely he wouldn't believe her capable of that.

But no, she could read condemnation in his face. He knew her no better than did Lord Dibbleshire. Like his lordship, Thorn accepted whatever she said.

He would hate her now, she understood that. But it had to be.

"I am sure that you will be an excellent father," she said, forcing the words out of her mouth. "Rose adores you."

Thorn's gaze burned into her. "You love Rose, although you've met her only a few times. You would never leave a child, your own child. You are lying."

"I assure you that I am not." She almost turned away again, but she straightened her backbone instead. "You do not know me, Thorn, nor do you love me," she said, letting go of the mantel and standing tall, hating that she had to swim in such selfish, shallow waters to accomplish what had to be done. "I have earned the right to marry someone who loves me. I deserve a man who treasures me."

"I treasure you!" His voice was sharp.

Like a flash fire in a poorly run kitchen, fury and anger

and utter despair raced through her. "You made love to me without protection! You made love to me virtually in front of the woman you plan to marry, and where any servant might have happened by. You do not treasure me!" There was a moment's silence while she pulled her crumbling self together again. "It is not entirely your fault. I have repeatedly made stupid choices."

His eyes narrowed. "What are you talking about?"

"Did I really seem experienced to you?" She whispered those words because they were burning in the back of her throat. "Did I truly?"

He swallowed, and she saw his throat ripple. "You *were* a virgin?"

She didn't answer.

"There was no blood."

"I bled for two days after the first time I rode a horse without a saddle. I was twelve."

"You lied to me?"

She felt her mouth curl into an ironic smile. "I wanted you. And you would not have . . . have taken me if you thought me experienced, would you?"

His silence was the answer.

"You see," she continued steadily, "I wanted you enough to lie to you. But I would like to marry someone who *knows* me. Who loves me. A man who does not barge into my room and make demands of me or, for that matter, tup me against the wall."

"So you'll take Vander?" His voice was a growl, but his eyes were direct.

She raised her chin. "Perhaps."

"He doesn't love you."

"Doesn't he?"

"He *wants* you! That's not the same as loving you."

She had to swallow and clench her teeth in order to keep

from crying. She nodded. "I know that. After all, you and I *wanted* each other. And look where that got me. Please leave, Thorn."

Her throat closed, and she really couldn't say anything else. It was just as well that he dragged his hand through his hair, raked her with another furious glance, and left without a word.

Chapter Twenty-nine

Thorn avoided India the following day by spending most of it working in his library; he even took luncheon there. "Working" was not precisely accurate: he kept losing himself in thought, staring blindly at the desk as ink blotted whatever letter he was trying to write.

He could scarcely believe India's claim that she would give up her child. And yet, every time he decided it had to be a lie, her greatest lie . . . his common sense, his reason, his understanding of the world, sent him reeling back the other direction, toward believing that she told the truth.

India was evidently a version of his mother: a woman who sampled erotic pleasures and moved on, leaving a child behind in the dust caused by her departure. Like India, she'd had a profession that defined her. That she loved. They were both brilliant, creative women who put their professions before their personal lives.

And yet . . .

He thought of the conversation during which India had told him of her parents' leaving for London. The way she had wept on his shoulder, her shuddering sobs telling him that she'd never revealed that pain before.

Thorn knew how it felt to be abandoned, whether unthinkingly, as his father had done to him, or selfishly, as his mother had. A woman marked by that pain would never—could never—give away her baby.

He simply did not believe it. By the time the afternoon was drawing to a close, he was convinced India had lied to him. He had gone over every minute, every second of the time they'd spent together, reviewed every word they'd exchanged, her every glance.

And he'd thought through their conversation of the night before. She believed he wanted to marry her only because of the child they might have conceived. Perhaps she truly believed that he would be happier married to Lala. Certainly, she felt guilty because Lala was wandering around looking like a dazed lamb in love.

He supposed that if he were a gentleman, he would feel guilty too. But he wasn't and he didn't. He had never promised a damned thing to Laetitia Rainsford. In fact, they had never even spoken in private, other than two encounters in Kensington Gardens, and a carriage ride. Every time he came close to her, she shied away.

Even if he hadn't met India, he would have been reconsidering that union, because Lala's mother wasn't merely unpleasant; she was loathsome. He didn't want his children to have a grandmother like that. Besides, he was only one bawdy joke away from Lady Rainsford's rejection of his proposal.

No, he didn't feel guilty. And if India felt guilty, she could find a different husband for Lala. Hell, he'd be happy to supply a dowry. There was no question that India would be as talented at matchmaking as she was at organizing.

He went upstairs to bathe, still thinking hard. Being married to India would be like trying to harness a storm at sea. She was one of the few people in the world who had no fear of him, a woman who whipped around to face him, hands on hips, eyes narrowed, and told him exactly what she thought.

He grinned at the thought of it.

"Cravat, sir?" his valet offered. Thorn nodded. He might as well dress properly when asking a lady to marry him. She wanted a proper proposal; he could do that.

He planned to kiss her before uttering a word, though. If he merely touched her arm, a little shudder would go through her body. Her eyes would darken, and her tongue would touch her lips, preparing for him. And after he raised his mouth, she would cling to him, her eyes hazy.

If he kissed her before proposing, she wouldn't have the willpower to resist him.

With that thought, he glanced down and wrenched off the coat he had just put on. "I'll wear the dark blue one instead," he told his valet. It was longer and would cover what needed to be covered. She wasn't the only one caught in a sea storm, after all. He only had to glance at her, or realize she was in a room, and his prick would rise. And stay up too.

She did something to him, something that eroded his control and turned him into a frenzied brute with one idea in mind. He quickly buttoned the longer coat before his valet could reach out to help.

There was a scratch on the door and his valet opened it. A footman held out a small silver tray. "A letter for Mr. Dautry."

Thorn held out his hand, recognizing India's handwriting. It was bold and delicate at the same time, ornate and yet easily legible. Very like India herself.

Dear Mr. Dautry,

I did not want to lose any time in informing you that the event about which we both felt concern has not come to pass. I trust you can find another use for the special license.

With all best wishes,
Lady Xenobia

He stared at the sheet for a moment before realizing that it didn't make a damned bit of difference. India wasn't pregnant this time, but she would be the next, or the time after that.

If he had to pull her into that alcove and take her again *sans* sheath, he would. In fact, he would do it without hesitation. Obviously, she was upset by his mutton-fisted proposal, and she'd come up with a deception in order to put him off. He had to make it clear immediately that he saw through her ploy and wanted her for herself, not for the baby who didn't exist.

He ran his fingers through his hair and walked from the room to look for her. She wasn't in her chamber, so he went downstairs.

She was in neither of the drawing rooms, nor in the ballroom, dining room, or breakfast room. Where the hell was she?

He was heading toward the servants' door to see if she was counting the soup spoons when he heard a raised voice outside the house, unmistakably the arrogant tenor of Lady Rainsford.

He followed the clamor to the front door, from which position he could see the lady in question standing in the drive, holding forth to an audience made up of Fleming, at the top of the steps, and his father, stepmother, and Vander at the bottom.

Just then his father shifted to one side, revealing two more characters in this little drama: India was there too, her face defiant, holding Rose tightly to her side.

"I know evidence of depravity when I see it," Lady Rainsford was saying, her voice shriller than usual.

Damnation. He ran down the steps. Eleanor reached out and put a hand on his arm. "Stay calm," she said in a low voice.

Lady Rainsford's raisin-sized eyes narrowed at his approach. "There he is! I suppose you hoped to conceal this child, Mr. Dautry? The evidence of your *debased* and *corrupt* nature!"

India watched Thorn approach with an overwhelming sense of dread. She had dealt with every sort of household crisis; she had soothed women driven to hysterics by their husbands, servants, and children.

But it was all different when the tempest resulted from a decision she had made; after all, *she* had suggested Thorn keep Rose hidden away. The dower house had been her idea. She felt paralyzed, as if she had somehow found herself on a public stage without being told her lines.

"You invited me and my daughter here under a pretense!" Lady Rainsford screeched. "Had I not uncovered your shame, my daughter might have married you and been ruined—utterly *ruined*. How long did you think to disguise the presence of your by-blow?"

"I am not Rose's father," Thorn stated. The look in his eyes made India shiver.

Lady Rainsford seemed unaffected. "Poppycock! She was tucked away in a separate house, just as my maid informed me this morning. I could scarcely believe it myself, but here she is. If this child of shame were truly your ward, there would be no need to conceal her existence. I think we can all agree to that!"

India felt another pulse of guilt; she should have guessed that Lady Rainsford would employ her maid as a spy. Then she felt Rose's thin shoulders trembling under her hands, and her guilt was replaced by outrage.

How dare the woman say such things in front of a child? She was despicable. She had to be silenced.

Lady Rainsford moved to a new target, the Duke of Villiers. "And *you*! I suppose you were applauding your son's attempt to dupe those of us who take marriage vows seriously. Is Christian morality a mere jest to you, Your Grace?" The last two words were not meant as a title of respect.

The duke didn't speak, but his expression was terrifying. He stepped forward, and India could tell that his intervention would only make the situation worse.

"This has nothing to do with Mr. Dautry," she cried, cutting off Villiers before he could reply or, worse, throw Lady Rainsford into the nearest hedge. The duke ignored her, moving forward like a predator.

Lady Rainsford merely snorted, her eyes returning to the little girl trembling under India's fingers. "She's the image of her father, and I don't mean that as a compliment."

Utter fury ripped up India's spine. "You are a vile woman," she snapped, "as are your disgraceful allegations. Rose is *my* daughter, and no concern of yours!"

She scarcely believed that she had blurted out those words, even as they came from her mouth. But silence fell.

Blessedly, silence fell.

Lady Rainsford's expression was incredulous. "She is *your* child?"

India drew a deep, stunned breath. There was no turning back now. "Yes," she said defiantly. "Mine. You should cease your unpleasant insinuations, Lady Rainsford. Mr. Dautry is innocent of your charges." She pulled Rose even closer.

"I always knew you were no better than you should be!" the lady said, her mouth twisting with distaste. "People driveled on about how wonderful you were, but there were those of us who knew that only a light-skirt would accept money from a man. The way you moved from household to household, I wonder if you even know the father's name!"

Her words struck with the bitterness of a poisoned dagger. In that instant, India grasped what her hasty remark would mean for herself, for her own reputation. Her heart dropped to her feet. Would she never learn to think before she spoke?

Thorn took a step toward Lady Rainsford, the rage in his eyes controlled but savage. "I want you out of my house within the hour."

"I surmise that you are indeed the father," the lady snapped, "since you protect this fallen woman!"

With one impulsive comment, India had destroyed years of guarding her reputation. Lady Rainsford would spread her malice across all London. Thank goodness, Adelaide had retired to her room for a rest. Not that it mattered.

She was ruined. Utterly ruined.

She swallowed hard; it felt as if a giant hand had just squeezed her heart. Any chance she had of making a life with Thorn was over. He, more than anyone, couldn't marry a ruined woman; their children would be pariahs after Lady Rainsford spread her malicious story.

But suddenly, unexpectedly, Vander, who had been standing silently beside her, wrapped his right arm around her shoulder. "Lady Rainsford," he said in the frosty voice of an insulted nobleman, "I should be very careful about what you say next. You are speaking about my wife."

India started, but Vander tightened his arm in a silent warning.

"Rose is *my* daughter," he continued, his voice dropping into the register of a civilized but homicidal maniac. "We have chosen not to reveal our marriage because of my father's unfortunate circumstance."

His large body warmed India's back, for all the world as if they were truly a family. Her mind whirling, India numbly registered that the Duke of Pindar's confinement owing to insanity was scarcely a plausible reason for a clandestine marriage.

But Vander hadn't finished. "If you again insult my wife—the woman who will someday be the Duchess of Pindar—I will have you thrown out of society, Lady Rainsford. Do not doubt it."

Another stunned silence shuddered through the air.

"I am finding this so enjoyable," the Duke of Villiers said, his smoky voice completely unamused. "All this drama, and we weren't even charged admission. Surely, this is my cue? Lady Rainsford, I see no reason to wait for a further insult. I intend to make certain that you are never invited to another event in the rest of your natural life. I believe that it will be one of the few good deeds I've done in a misspent life."

Lady Rainsford took in a harsh breath. Her eyes popped out a little so she looked like an angry frog as she looked from Vander, to the duke, to Rose. Finally back to India, standing in the shelter of Vander's arm. "I don't believe it!"

she shrilled. She was clearly too beside herself to consider her family's place in society.

"I will hardly produce my marriage lines for one such as you," Vander said with contempt.

Faced by the united front of two ducal families—and the prospect that she had grievously insulted the future Duchess of Pindar—Lady Rainsford exhibited a fledgling instinct for self-preservation and commenced a babbling apology.

A moment later she faltered to a halt, confronted with five pairs of icy-cold, unsympathetic eyes.

Eleanor stepped forward, taking advantage of her silence. "Lady Rainsford," she said, her tone grimmer than India had ever heard it. "You will no longer be welcome at any event at which you might reasonably expect a member of the family of the Duke of Villiers or of the Duke of Pindar to appear."

Lady Rainsford opened her mouth, but Eleanor held up her hand. "If the slightest rumor ever emerges regarding Lady Xenobia or Miss Rose—as well as your vile and sordid accusations—we will not only put it about that you are stark raving mad, Lady Rainsford, but I will also allow my husband to wreck havoc on your finances. You and your husband will retire to the country in abject poverty. Your maid will do no more spying, because you will not be able to afford her. Have I made myself absolutely clear?"

"Yes," Lady Rainsford said, with an audible gulp.

"You forgot 'Your Grace,'" Villiers stated, his voice a cutting blade that made it clear that the woman should address his wife as would a servant, not an equal.

"I think . . . I think I shall look for my daughter." Lady Rainsford scurried up the stairs and back into the house without another word.

Chapter Thirty

$\mathcal{F}$ ive adults and one child kept silent until Lady Rainsford rushed through the front door past Fleming, who had ensured that no other servants had witnessed the scene.

Rose spoke before anyone else. "I am *not* your child!" she cried, looking up at India. "I don't like that woman." Her little face crumpled, but she managed to halt the tears. "I don't like the way people keep speaking as if my father didn't exist. My father was Will Summers, and just because he is dead doesn't mean that he didn't exist!"

Then she twisted out of India's hold, taking a step toward Thorn. "You shouldn't give me away like that," she cried, her voice rising. "I don't want to be their daughter. I don't even know them!"

For his part Thorn was in the grip of a rage that was only barely in check. What was India doing, declaring that Rose was her daughter? And Vander? Why in the hell had Vander made the claim that he was married to India?

India was *his*. Not Vander's.

She would never be Vander's.

But he looked down at Rose and realized all that would have to wait, because Rose was his as well. She was the bravest little girl he'd ever known, but her lips were quivering and her eyes were terrified. Almost certainly Lady Rainsford had called her names before he arrived, ones that she didn't understand. She had been surrounded by shouting adults—and she thought her guardian had given her away.

He scooped her up into his arms and turned away from the adults silently watching them. "I did not give you away, Rose, and I never will. It was all a misunderstanding." He began walking toward the dower house. "Let's go home and we'll ask Clara for some hot cocoa. Where is Clara, by the way?"

"That lady came and told Clara to stay," Rose said, a sob breaking from her chest. "She brought me back to the house. But Lady Xenobia came outside just as she arrived, and they had an argument."

"Did my parents and Vander come at the same time as Lady Xenobia?"

"No, they came just before you. Lady Rainsford is most unpleasant." Her legs clung to his side, but her rigid backbone told its own story.

"She is not a likable woman," Thorn observed, in one of the world's great understatements. He pushed open the door of the dower house. "What you need to know, poppet, is that you are and always will be your papa's daughter. Did you know that I saved Will's life once?"

She stirred in his arms, but he didn't release her. He just strode over to the sofa and sat down, keeping her on his lap. "We were around eight years old. It was winter, and there were ice floes in the Thames."

"Did you have to go into the icy water?" She sounded slightly less distressed. "Papa told me that he used to fish spoons out of the river."

He nodded, tightening his arms around her. "If we didn't jump in ourselves, our master would throw us off the dock."

"That is a despicable thing to do," Rose said. Her hand curled around his forearm.

"He was the same sort of person as Lady Rainsford," Thorn said. "Not someone you would wish to know. The amount of food Grindel gave us depended on what we brought him. Some of the boys were too small and too frail to go into the water when it was icy, so the big boys had to earn food for all of us."

"Eight years old is not very big," Rose observed.

"Your papa was the type of boy who never gave up. He dove and dove that afternoon," he told her. "He was certain that he had felt something at the bottom of the Thames, something big down in the muck. Something that might make Grindel happy enough that he would let us sleep indoors."

There were no words adequate to describe Grindel. Not for the first time, Thorn wished the man were still alive so he could kill him in memory of the boys who hadn't survived.

"I wish Papa hadn't been stubborn," Rose said. "Did he find that big thing?"

"The last time he went down, he didn't come back up. I stood on the dock and watched the spot where he dove, and I didn't see any bubbles. I didn't know what to do. The Thames is dark and murky at the best of times, and in the winter, it's like Hades down there."

"What's Hades?"

"A terrible place. A place where a boy might find himself cut to the bone by a piece of metal sunk at the bottom, or he might come face to face with—" He caught himself. "—with a fish."

"A fish wouldn't scare me!"

"We were city boys, and we knew very little about fish. For all we knew, they would nibble our toes."

"Did you jump in after Papa?"

Thorn nodded. "I did. It was so cold that I felt as if the ice were eating my bones. I kept going because Will was down there somewhere. Finally I saw just a flash of his yellow hair, the same hair that you have."

"What was he doing?"

"He was stuck," Thorn said. "His foot was caught in a net dropped by a fisherman. I almost didn't get him out in time, but we managed. And we made it back to the dock."

The truth was that the Thames had damn well nearly taken both of them that day. He still had no idea how he got Will back to the dock.

"Did you have to sleep in the graveyard that night?" Rose asked. She had forgotten to keep her back stiff, and her cheek nestled against his chest as if she had always been his child.

"We did not. After your father warmed up, he unclenched his fist. And he was holding the top of a silver teapot."

"You mean that little round piece?"

"Exactly."

"Was that enough so that all of you could have supper?"

"It was. Grindel let us all sleep inside for the next week, because it kept snowing."

"It must have been a very costly teapot," Rose said.

"It had a crest on it, which meant its owners would be

grateful to have it back. But the more important point is that Will and I shook hands the next morning, and Will said that he owed me. And that someday he would pay me back by giving me the most valuable thing he owned."

"What did he give you?" Rose tilted her head back and looked up at him.

"You." Thorn smiled down at her. "He gave me you. *You* were the most valuable thing that Will Summers ever owned in his entire life. He couldn't stay with you, Rose. But he remembered his promise, and he mentioned it in the letter he sent to me."

"Oh." Her voice sounded terribly sad.

He put his cheek down on her soft hair, remembering Will and his stubborn, brave nature, seeing how beautifully it had come out in his daughter. "Now you are mine," he told her, "by gift from your father. You mustn't ever think that I would give you away, Rose. I am proud that you are mine."

"But you put me in the dower house." Her voice quavered. "And that lady said that I was hidden away, and she made it sound awful."

Thorn had to unclench his back teeth before he shocked Rose with his opinion of Lady Rainsford. "I should never have agreed to it," he said. "I will never do anything like that again."

"But if you keep me as your ward, you can't marry Miss Rainsford," Rose said anxiously. "Her mother thinks that I am Lady Xenobia's daughter."

"I shall not marry Laetitia. I had already made up my mind about that."

Rose nodded and began pleating his cravat with her small, nimble fingers. "Miss Rainsford wouldn't have been able to read me bedtime stories."

"Laetitia is quite intelligent," Thorn said, stroking

Rose's hair. "I think she can't see letters well enough. She probably needs spectacles."

"Does that mean that Lady Xenobia isn't really married to Lord Brody either?"

"Absolutely not."

"Lady Xenobia can read." The words hung in the air for a moment.

"That is true." Thorn thought about India's flamelike intelligence, the brilliant way she assessed problems before moving decisively to solve them.

Although he wished she hadn't stepped forward and claimed to be Rose's mother. She had made matters infinitely more difficult, though her claim was nothing compared to Vander's. After all, once India and Thorn married, Rose truly would be her daughter. But she would *never* be Vander's wife.

Rose dropped his cravat, hopped from his lap, and ran over to where her doll lay. "Will you tell Antigone and me stories about my papa over supper? Please?"

Thorn wanted to go to India immediately. He had to inform her that they were getting married, and to hell with what Lady Rainsford would think—though he was fairly certain the woman would never breathe a word about the afternoon. His father would ruin the Rainsford family without a second's thought, and obviously she had understood that.

But Rose was at his side, Antigone clutched in her arms, her tears hardly dry. India would still be there after Rose went to sleep.

"Please?"

"Yes," he said, standing up and taking her hand. "Shall we find Clara now?"

"You won't leave while she is getting me ready for bed?"

That was just what Thorn had thought to do. He was

desperate to find India and make love to her, this time as his affianced wife.

But Rose, who had been brave in so many circumstances, still looked haunted, and (for once) younger than her age. Her huge gray eyes were anxious. "I will be in the nursery waiting for you," he promised. She smiled, and her dimple appeared.

Once Rose had been bathed and tucked in bed, Thorn set about plucking stories from thin air, stories about brave, intrepid mudlarks. Will starred as the bravest and best diver, the champion retriever of silver spoons and gold coins. Thorn said nothing of teeth, tin buttons, or rat skeletons.

Rose loved every detail. The pinched look in her face went away, and he could see that she was shaping a mythology around her father. That struck him as a good idea. When he had learned, at age twelve, that his mother was dead, he had been angry at her; it had felt like a second abandonment. Perhaps Rose would also feel anger at some point, but less so if she thought of Will as a hero.

Of course, Will's death was entirely unlike that of Thorn's mother. It was more like the death of India's parents: tragically bad luck. He didn't know why India's parents were in London the day they died, but he'd bet anything that their trip had nothing to do with flight to the Bermudas. They might not have been attentive parents, but he couldn't imagine them deserting her.

Hell, he couldn't imagine anyone leaving her.

Including himself.

Now he had to make her understand that fact—and Vander as well. Thinking of Vander made his blood race. His jaw clenched, and a fresh wave of raw, uncontrolled possessiveness surged through him.

Losing control was unacceptable. But for the first time in years, he wasn't sure he could keep his emotions in check.

It was twilight by the time Thorn strode into the house. He was tired and angry, worried about Rose and frustrated by the mess Vander had made of things. He nodded at Fleming and headed upstairs to find India, so focused that at first he didn't even register a bedchamber door opening.

But the moment Vander stepped into the corridor, the tension that had coiled in Thorn's gut for the last hours detonated. He literally saw red, lunging forward and slamming Vander against the wall. "What in the bloody hell did you think you were doing out there?"

"Do you mean when I saved the damsel in distress?" Vander retorted in a low, furious voice, jerking from his grasp. "I mean to marry India. It was simply a preemptive gesture."

"I'll be damned if you will!" Thorn exploded into motion and they came to blows with the force of a cannon firing, reeling back into Vander's bedchamber.

They crashed to the floor, knocking over a small table, then rolled across the floor with undisciplined fury, the only sounds harsh breathing, occasional thuds as a blow landed, the slamming of the door when Vander's foot caught it, a crash as another delicate table was upended. This one held a crystal decanter. It didn't shatter, but its stopper came off, and pungent brandy poured out and soaked into the carpet.

"Why did you say you were married to India?" Thorn snarled, pinning Vander momentarily. Vander twisted from his grip, his shirt ripping away from its sleeve. Thorn slammed back into him, crushing him to the floorboards with his arm across his throat. "Damn you, answer me."

"Because I *am* marrying her," Vander shouted. With a violent lunge to the side, he freed himself again. "The whole household is buzzing with the fact that you have obtained a blank license in order to marry Lala; I'll take that off your hands. I'm marrying India in the morning."

Thorn's answer was more a howl than a reply. Two minutes later, he had Vander pinned again. He hadn't bested Vander at fisticuffs in years, but by God, he was winning this time. "India is *mine*," he roared, knowing he was on the verge of losing his final shred of control, every lethal instinct honed in childhood loosed by fury.

"I safeguarded her reputation after you allowed it to be savaged by that harpy," Vander bellowed back. "You can save Lala from a fate worse than death—living with her despicable mother—but I shall marry India. Because *I* was the one who stepped forward to protect her, you unmitigated bastard!"

Vander's words struck with twice the force of his fists. Thorn's hands loosened and Vander wrenched himself away, rolling to sit up, back to the wall.

Thorn's right eye was swelling shut, and remnants of his shirt hung from his neck. He pulled his collar free and cast it aside. "You shall not marry her," he said, his voice hoarse. "I don't care what you announced: I am the only man who will ever marry India."

"You slept with her," Vander said flatly. "You cock-proud arse, you slept with the most desirable woman in England—don't tell me you didn't, because a blind man could see the way you look at her—and you didn't ask for her hand? And when her reputation was trodden into the mud by the devil herself, you said nothing. Are you out of your bloody mind?" His voice had risen to a shout again.

"That's none of your business," Thorn replied. Every inch of his body trembled with ferocity.

"Bullshit!" Vander leaned his head back against the

wall, chest still heaving. "I'd marry her with or without Lady Rainsford's provocation, you jackass. I made up my mind to propose after no more than one look at her and a single conversation, let alone a kiss. And you slept with her as if she were a mere doxy, and then let her reputation be smeared into the ground."

"I asked her to marry me last night," Thorn snarled. "She refused me, so I could hardly claim to be married to her. I planned to ask her again."

"You asked her to be your wife *after* you slept with her? You thought that Lady Xenobia India St. Clair would marry you because you were gracious enough to offer your hand after bedding her? Why would she want to marry you?"

"She might have been carrying my child," Thorn said tightly. But a bitter chill was sweeping through him. Vander was right. Why the hell would India want to marry him?

Vander made a guttural sound of disgust and spat his words. "You didn't use a sheath? What in the hell were you thinking?" His eyes glittered at Thorn in the darkening room.

"I don't think around her," Thorn said, telling him the truth. "When I asked her to marry me, she refused. She said that she'd give me the child if we had one." Vander— more than anyone else in the world—would know what that meant to him. The agony that her comment roused.

But Vander just snorted. "You believed her? Damn it, Thorn, you don't really want her. You don't even know her!"

"I didn't realize she was lying to me until later," Thorn said tightly.

"She baited a trap and you fell into it. You might have had a chance with her—after all, she took you into her bed—but that's gone."

Images tumbled through Thorn's mind: Rose looking up at India as she read her a book, and India telling him about her parents' desertion. Vander was right. She had tested him, and he had failed.

He stood up, slowly, knowing that he would be covered with bruises in a few hours. They had gone at each other like rabid animals.

Vander still sat against the wall, his arms on his knees. Without raising his head, he said, "She's mine, Thorn, and the sooner you get used to it, the better. You treated her like a doxy, and you didn't protect her when she needed it."

Every word struck Thorn's gut like another blow from a balled-up fist.

Then Vander looked up, pushing back hair soaked with sweat and brandy. "You had your shot, and you lost. I'm going to marry her. I'll leave it to you whether we remain friends." He got up, lurching slightly, one hand pressed against his side, and left without a backward glance.

Thorn walked into his own room reeking of spirits, with vision only in his left eye.

The hell with it. That dream was over. He'd had it for, what, half a day? The dream that India was his, that he could marry a woman like her: brilliant, glowing, beautiful . . . funny. As wild in bed as she was elsewhere, the kind of woman who lunged at life, fear be damned, and embraced it.

But Lady Xenobia India was a lady. And he was a bastard, who had behaved like a bastard. Of course she didn't want him. She'd let him down kindly, in fact.

He sank into a steaming bath and forced himself to face the truth. He would offer his hand in marriage one more time, if only to prove to India that his proposal was motivated by far more than the possibility of a baby.

But it was a useless gesture. Daughters of marquesses didn't marry bastards, not in any part of England that he'd heard of. India would marry Vander. She was meant to be a duchess. They would be happy together, shining, beautiful examples of England's peerage.

He got out of the bath and dressed swiftly. If he was going to ask a future duchess to marry him, he would do it like the gentleman he wasn't. Not by dragging her into an alcove and treating her like a whore. No, he would go on one knee, he decided, tying his cravat in a Gordian knot.

And once she rejected him, that would be that. He would lose his oldest and truest friend and the woman he loved in one blow. Suffocating darkness welled inside him at the thought.

By now it was nearly time for the evening meal; presumably India would be downstairs, sipping a sherry with the others. He briefly wondered if Lady Rainsford had departed for London or was still cowering in her room, then he discarded the thought. He didn't give a damn what happened to the lady or, frankly, to her daughter.

He descended the stairs, planning to draw India to his study—respectfully—in order to request her hand in marriage. His father was waiting in the entry.

"I'm sorry, but I can't speak now," Thorn said, heading for the drawing room.

"*Son*."

Something in Villiers's voice made Thorn pause and turn back.

"You are looking somewhat the worse for wear."

Thorn gestured impatiently. "Surely you heard the uproar."

"Fleming did a fine job of keeping everyone on the ground floor." The duke's face was expressionless, but his eyes weren't. "They took the special license, Tobias. If you leave now, you can catch them; they won't be able to marry until morning. They went to Piggleston, where the parish church has a resident vicar."

Thorn felt as if a hammer smashed into the back of his neck. The feelings that coursed through him had nothing to do with civilization and everything to do with carnage.

He was going to *kill* Vander. Murder him. Tear him limb from limb.

Blood began pounding through his limbs, and suddenly he knew, with absolute certainty, that he could murder his closest friend without turning a hair. The hell with being respectful to India. She was *his,* and no damn duke was going to have her, not if he had to rip her away from Vander at the altar and throw her into his carriage.

"Right," he said, turning to the door, his mind churning. He had to get on the road, find them, kill Vander, and marry India.

Of course she left with Vander. What else could she do? Thorn had never claimed her, not really.

"My carriage is waiting," his father said.

Indeed, the duke's traveling coach stood in the drive, horses stamping their hooves and grooms standing at the ready.

Thorn nodded to his father, caught a flash of wicked amusement in his eyes—yet another sign of the duke's warped paternal instincts—and climbed into the carriage, directing the coachman to the largest inn in Piggleston. He spent the next few hours alternating between berating himself and suppressing stifling waves of anger at Vander. Finally, the horses trotted off the post road and moved onto cobbled streets.

When they pulled into the courtyard of the Coach and Horn, Thorn leapt down and roused the innkeeper. But though he handed out five-pound notes as if they were ha'pennies, every man he talked to, at all three inns in Piggleston, swore up and down that no couples resembling Vander and India had been seen. By that point a muscle was jumping in Thorn's jaw, and his face was apparently so distorted by rage—not to mention his black eye—that men fell back as he approached.

There was nothing more he could do. He'd marked the location of the church, and he would be there in the morning to stop the wedding.

India would not marry Vander, if Thorn had to assault the vicar at the altar.

He took a room, but he couldn't lie down. Every time he pictured Vander and India on a bed together, scorching pain shot through him. The memory of her face when she lied to him and he believed her . . . the scorn on her face when she told him that she'd been a virgin, though he hadn't noticed.

That was why she would marry Vander. He had broken what they had . . . in fact, he was afraid that he had broken *her*.

She hadn't fought back against Lady Rainsford's ugly insults. She hadn't said another word after coming forward to claim Rose as her own. That wasn't like her.

He stared into the dark, waiting.

Planning.

Chapter Thirty-one

India lay on her back, staring up at the bed canopy. She felt like the ice princess in the fairy story, the one with a frozen heart. Someone had carved out the inside of her body and replaced her heart with ice.

Evidence of that? Next to her was a valiant and handsome lord, a fairy-tale prince. She should have been indescribably happy at this moment.

Vander was on his side, head propped on one hand, watching her. She knew he had a sweet expression, because she'd glanced at him. She also knew that he was able to keep his mouth shut, because he wasn't saying anything. And she knew his body was as muscled as any medieval knight, because there it was, albeit clothed, next to her on the bed.

There was no unmarried woman in all England who wouldn't secretly want to lie next to a future duke while he gazed at her with that expression. It was scandalous to invite him to do so, of course, but she was determined to erase the memory of Thorn lying beside her. Not that Thorn had ever given her a worshipful glance, because he hadn't.

Vander must have gotten tired of waiting for her to speak, because he reached out and gently put a hand on her wrist. It was a large hand, but she didn't think it was quite as large as Thorn's.

Thorn's body was traced all over with scars. Like a warrior's.

Again she reminded herself that Thorn had never looked at her the way Vander was now. Vander seemed to think she was wonderful.

Thorn looked at her as if she were mad, and sometimes, as if she made him laugh. The rest of the time he looked at her with such raw desire that he seemed ready to throw her to the ground.

Well, he'd done that, hadn't he? He had taken her like a sluttish housemaid, downstairs, where anyone could have caught them. She couldn't have been the first woman to fall into Mr. Dautry's snare. She was sure of it. There were probably broken hearts strewn all over England.

"India," Vander said quietly. He began tracing a soothing pattern on her arm.

She glanced at him again, just to confirm that he was as handsome as she thought. He was. Many English gentlemen had jaws and chins that receded in a steady slope right down to their necks. Vander looked like one of those Greek statues she'd put in Thorn's attic. They would have beautiful children together.

What's more, he gave her a feeling of safety. He was big and bold, and he would frighten off Lady Rainsford or anyone else who thought to attack her. He would be a good husband.

She could do this.

She could sleep with him. And marry him. Surely.

"In the scene with Lady Rainsford, you were like St. George killing the dragon," she said, managing a weak smile.

"Alas, the dragon is not dead."

"It was very honorable, though, the way you announced that we were already married."

"It is the desire of my heart," Vander stated, his eyes intent on hers.

In the last hour, he had said all the respectful, adoring things that Thorn had never said or thought. What's more, Vander was on the same bed with her, and hadn't tried to kiss her. He cherished and respected her.

They would have a fine marriage.

Above her, the bed curtains were gathered and pleated into a pretty rosette. She was done with lying. "There was a slender chance that I may have been carrying Thorn's child," she said, not looking to the side. "It did not come to pass."

Unable to resist, she turned her head. Vander's jaw was clenched.

"Are you disgusted with me?" she whispered.

"I am grappling with a wish to murder my closest friend."

"I led him to believe that I had experience," she said drearily. "It's my fault."

"How could anyone believe that you are a loose woman? You are like a treasure that a man could spend his life un-wrapping."

"Thorn believed me. And then when he announced that we would marry, I refused and told him that I would give him our child when it was born." Tears pressed on her eyes and made them ache. "He believed me. Both times, he believed me."

Vander leaned closer. "He's damaged, India. I don't want to make excuses for him, but that's the truth. Once we marry, any child you carry will be mine." His eyes lightened and his mouth curved into a smile. "In fact, let's make love right now."

He was trying to make her feel better, so India smiled at him. But tears were beginning to spill from her eyes. "Thorn desires me, but he doesn't love me."

Vander sighed. "He's my best friend, but he's also an ass, who took advantage of you. He never should have slept with you, let alone without using a French letter."

Hot tears ran down India's cheeks. "He said . . . he said he couldn't control himself around me." The sympathy in Vander's eyes was like a kick in the stomach. "I suppose that's what men always say."

This day had definitely been the worst of her life, other than the day she had been told of her parents' death. "You rescued me from Lady Rainsford," she said, a little sob breaking in her chest. "He just stood there, watching."

"That's not quite true. To be fair, I thought he would strangle the woman."

India had forgotten the moment when Thorn's face went black and he moved toward Lady Rainsford, fists clenched. "But you told her we were married and forced her to stop calling me names."

Vander pulled a handkerchief from his pocket. "Thorn may be unable to see you clearly," he said, gently wiping away her tears, "but I can."

India was bent on telling him everything. "After . . . after she had said those things to me, and I—" She faltered to a halt.

"Why *did* you say that Rose was your child?" Vander asked.

"I wasn't thinking. I got angry, and I wanted Lady

Rainsford to stop ranting. But it's probably just as well. Thorn wants to marry someone sweet and kind. He told me that Lala was perfect for him."

"Are you in love with him?" Vander's warm brown eyes were nothing at all like Thorn's wintery gray ones.

"He made me feel beautiful, and he listened to me." She managed to shrug. "I sound like the seduced virgin in a melodrama, don't I?"

Vander ran his fingers down her cheek. "I cannot tell you what Thorn is or was thinking, India. All I know is that you are unlike any other woman I've ever met. You're exquisite, and brilliant, and brave. *You* are perfect for me."

"I'm not like this," she whispered, wiping away another tear. "I don't cry. Even when my parents left me, I didn't cry." The sympathy in his eyes was humiliating. "And I don't whisper either!"

Thorn didn't love her. He didn't care. He believed her lies, even when she told him—stupidly told him—an absurd falsehood that a stranger could have seen through.

It was over, absolutely over. She simply had to make herself believe that.

"All I can say is that I'm deeply grateful to the loathsome Lady Rainsford," Vander said. "I had the chance to proclaim that you were my wife. And it felt good, India. It felt right. You are my future duchess. Let's see how it sounds: Hello, Your Grace."

His thumb rubbed her bottom lip, and his eyes flared.

"Hello, wife."

Chapter Thirty-two

*T*horn arrived at the church door at six o'clock the next morning. The door was locked, and the village square was hushed and silent. The only sign of life came from the bakery across the square. Since there were no benches he took a seat on a gravestone, and waited.

He had never been one to ride to the hounds. But that was because he saw no point in chasing after animals, when the world of humans was so predatory. Now his entire body was poised for the hunt, waiting for the moment when either the vicar or India would appear. Either one.

But no one came. After some time, the baker's door opened, signaling that fresh bread was available. As if on cue, villagers began to appear, greeting each other as they headed across the square for a fresh loaf. A few of them glanced at him, sitting with his arms folded, but they said nothing.

Thorn was quite certain that neither his dour expression nor his battered face was welcoming. Moreover, by now his instincts were starting to tell him that something was wrong. If he were Vander, he would take India to the church first thing in the morning.

Unless they were still in bed. Unless . . . His jaw clenched again. If India and Vander were truly together, and India was happy, he would leave. He would probably leave England altogether.

It could be that his father had made a mistake. They had traveled to some other town, which is why he'd been unable to find mention of them at the inns.

As he considered what to do next, two women trotted toward the church across the square. Just as they came by him, one said, "If the groom is handing out shillings, I want to be there. Walk a little faster, woman!" They disappeared down the street to the right of the church.

His mind went blank. It seemed he was too late. He walked after the women and discovered that there was a small chapel attached to the parish house. Three or four chattering villagers were walking away from the door, looking with satisfaction at the coins they held in their hands.

He stopped the same woman who had rushed past him a moment ago. "Have I missed the wedding?"

"Yes, sir, you have," she said cheerfully. "Friends of yours? What a shame. And I'm sure they would have liked to have you with them, as my husband had to act as one of the witnesses." She jerked her head toward the chapel. "Go right in, sir. They're signing the book in the back, but they'll be out in a moment."

Thorn followed her gaze. Opposite the chapel was his own damned carriage.

He was too late.

He was too late, and it was his own damned fault. Why

hadn't he realized that he'd never felt lust like that before—which meant it wasn't just lust? He wanted *her,* all of her, from the tips of India's toes to all that gorgeous hair.

Now he would never wake up next to her, roll over, take her sleepy mouth. He would never hold their first child, born in wedlock or not.

The thought nearly drove him to his knees, there in an unfamiliar village where it was starting to drizzle. He had never felt despair like this before—not when he was a mudlark, not when he learned his mother had died without ever returning for him . . . never.

One foot followed another to the door of the chapel. He would see her once more, and after that he would leave the country. Vander would understand. Vander would know precisely what Thorn had lost.

As he reached the door, a flock of people emerged: the vicar, the sexton, a parishioner, another parishioner . . .

The bride.

Chapter Thirty-three

$\mathcal{L}$ala had never been so happy in her life. In fact, she was fairly sure that she'd never had any idea what joy *was*, because anything she'd experienced to this point had been a pale, sickly imitation.

She tucked her hand into John Hatfield's and looked up to see him smiling at her. She couldn't help but sigh: who would have thought that such an intelligent man would ever want her, Lala? And yet he had told her that he didn't believe she was stupid at all, but that something was wrong with her vision that prevented her from seeing print correctly.

"It's like being blind," he had told her the evening before. "How could that be considered your fault?"

Around him, Lala *felt* intelligent. She was hungry to learn everything she could about babies, and illnesses, and the work of a doctor. She couldn't wait to meet his cook, and learn how to run her own household.

"Are you quite certain that you won't mind the fact that Starberry Court will never be your home?" John asked now, his eyes on hers.

She laughed. Her mother and father would likely disown her, but she didn't care. She had her husband and his lovely house. She would go on rounds with him, and feel useful for the first time in her life. No: she would *be* useful.

She would feel loved. And she would *be* loved.

He bent his head and kissed her. "I never imagined that a woman would give up a duke's son for me."

Lala's smile only grew wider. She would have paid a fortune to avoid marriage to Mr. Dautry. Yet intuition told her that it would be better if she didn't clarify that for her new husband. Let him think that earls and dukes had regularly thrown themselves at her feet, and she had rejected them all. For him.

They walked from the chapel together, husband and wife.

She froze in the open doorway.

He was there, looking like an angel of death. There was a moment of silence as she and John stood at the top of the steps, Mr. Dautry at the bottom, arms crossed.

Mr. Dautry's face was drawn and she couldn't read his expression. Lala found herself instinctively trembling. His face was battered, as if he'd already been in a fight.

John said, "If you think to sue me for alienation of affection, you'll find that I own very little in the world. I have nothing of value other than Laetitia, and I will not give her up." The words rang out in the morning air.

Dautry was staring up at them, his jaw clenched. He looked like a devil, standing there with his hair tumbling around his ears and no cravat to be seen. At the same time, he looked as if he'd taken a tremendous blow.

She had never imagined that he loved her so much. Lala

moved a bit closer to her new husband, clinging to his arm.

"We are fast married," John continued. "Laetitia is now Mrs. Hatfield." He sounded completely calm, even though he was confronting one of the richest men in all England, one whose fiancée he had stolen. Well, she hadn't quite been his fiancée, but very nearly.

Mr. Dautry shook himself, like a dog coming out of the rain. "In that case, allow me to be the first to congratulate you." His voice was oddly hoarse, but the words were clear enough.

They walked down the steps. Her husband gently released her arm and the men shook hands, somewhat to her surprise.

"I suppose you used the special license?" Dautry asked.

"I shall, of course, reimburse you," John said, nodding.

"Consider it my wedding present."

"That is remarkably gracious of you." John bowed again.

"Did you inform Lady Rainsford of your intentions?" Mr. Dautry asked.

"Lady Rainsford and I do not always see eye to eye," John replied.

"You astonish me," Mr. Dautry replied.

John smiled at that. "We had a candid exchange on the subject of my wife's intelligence, after which Laetitia and I bade her mother goodbye."

Lala slipped her hand back into the crook of her husband's arm and beamed at Dautry. "I fully expect to be disowned, and she will not pay us a visit for a long time, or indeed, possibly ever."

"A consummation devoutly to be wished," Mr. Dautry stated.

Lala had no idea what he meant, but John gave him a lopsided grin and said, "I hope that if Lady Rainsford decides to visit, I will choose to *be,* instead of Hamlet's *not to be.*"

Lala leaned her head against John's arm as they watched Dautry stride back down the street.

"I think he means to be a patron to you," Lala said. "Perhaps I shall ask him to sponsor a small hospital in the village. He has the money for it, by all accounts."

John looked down at her, a thrilling frown on his face. "I won't have you spending time with that man, Laetitia. He obviously adores you, since he drove all the way here in an attempt to stop your wedding. God knows what would have happened if he'd arrived an hour earlier."

Lala shivered. When they first walked out the door, Mr. Dautry had looked ready to murder John. But once he understood it was too late, he'd shown himself to be a gentleman.

"He will marry," she said, beginning to walk, because she couldn't wait to travel back to their own house. "Once Starberry Court has a mistress, I'll speak to him about a village hospital in West Drayton."

"I don't like the fact that the lord of the manor once loved my wife, even if he does marry someone else. I don't want you ever to be alone with him," John ordered.

The look in his eyes made Lala feel warm all over. "Kiss me," she breathed, stopping in her tracks.

John glanced down the deserted street, then he pulled her into his arms. He dropped a sweet buss on her lips, but when they opened beneath his, it all changed.

Mrs. John Hatfield stood in that empty street for twenty minutes, while her husband gave her a kiss so deep and passionate that they both forgot where they were—at least until the heavens opened and they had to dash through a downpour to the carriage, laughing all the way.

Chapter Thirty-four

India woke early in the morning, still exhausted. She wished she were excited about marrying Vander and becoming a duchess someday. She truly did. She had allowed him into her bedchamber the previous evening, thinking that perhaps she would find herself seduced.

It had made sense at the time: if she found herself enticed by the handsome lord with adoration in his eyes, it stood to reason that she would stop thinking about Thorn.

But in the end they hadn't even kissed.

She would never be Vander's wife. She just didn't feel that way about him.

Thorn, though . . .

He would likely be at breakfast. Her heart started beating quickly at the thought. Presumably, he no longer wished to marry Lala after Lady Rainsford's behavior.

Not that it meant he would turn to her; likely he wouldn't.

She would wish him well in the future, in a dignified,

yet friendly, manner. The only thing she had left was her self-respect, and even that was in shreds and tatters.

Still, she felt better after a bath, not to mention dressing in a close-fitting gown with a violet overlay and a low bosom. It felt as if she were going to war—in which case she might as well dress with her own version of armor.

But in the breakfast room, no one was to be seen besides the butler. "His Grace and Lord Brody have not yet risen," Fleming announced, escorting her to a seat.

"And Mr. Dautry?" India asked, trying to give her voice a carefree lilt.

"Mr. Dautry is not at home."

She hadn't expected that. She paused while unfolding her napkin and looked up. "Not home? Where is he?"

"I'm afraid I'm not at liberty to say, my lady." Then he added, "He departed in the Duke of Villiers's carriage last night."

"Why didn't he take his own carriage?"

The lines next to the butler's mouth deepened. "It was in use."

India frowned. Fleming was Thorn's butler, of course, but in a certain way, he would always be hers too. After all, she had hired him. "For heaven's sake, Fleming, surely I might know who was using Mr. Dautry's carriage?"

The butler closed the door to the breakfast room and lowered his voice. "It was Dr. Hatfield and Miss Rainsford, my lady. At Mr. Dautry's request, I sent a man two days ago to acquire a blank special license from the Archbishop of Canterbury."

Not even by a flicker in his eye did he reveal that the license had been meant for India and his master, even though he had to know the truth. Years of experience had taught India that butlers always knew a household's secrets.

"Shortly after the confrontation with Lady Rainsford

outside the house," Fleming continued, "Dr. Hatfield requested a meeting with the lady, and I'm afraid that there was a further exchange of words in the library."

"Lady Rainsford had a very distressing afternoon," India observed, not bothering to feign dismay.

"Yes, my lady. Unfortunately, she made a number of vehement—one might even say vituperative—remarks before retiring to her chamber. The door to the library was open, and it was impossible not to hear the exchange," he added.

India waved her hand impatiently. It would have required superhuman restraint *not* to listen. "Was Miss Rainsford in the library as well?"

"No, she was not. But the Duke of Villiers was. After Lady Rainsford departed, His Grace offered Mr. Dautry's special license to Dr. Hatfield, and the doctor accepted it."

India gasped. "He *did*? Did he inform Mr. Dautry that he was doing so?"

"At that time, Mr. Dautry was in the dower house with Miss Rose." Fleming hesitated, and added, "I fear that His Grace may have underestimated Mr. Dautry's feelings with regard to Miss Rainsford."

"I see," India said, her voice faint.

"When Mr. Dautry returned to the house, I was below stairs. But I understand that on learning of the elopement, he made off with all speed in an attempt to catch the pair before the wedding took place."

India's heart stopped for a moment. Thorn had gone after Lala. He had desperately tried to stop her marriage to another. He must truly love Lala.

She herself had been nothing more than an available body.

If she was going to become a fallen woman, at the very least she could have kept her heart whole.

But no . . . she never stopped loving her parents, even when they forgot to feed her, and she probably wouldn't stop loving Thorn either. Right now, she felt like a wounded animal. It *hurt* to love someone like this.

Despite herself, her eyes filled with tears and her lip trembled. Fleming discarded his butler's code of conduct and put a hand on her shoulder, his eyes deeply sympathetic.

"I'm all right," she said, swallowing hard and not even trying to hide the pain. "I'll be fine. I think . . . I think I shall return to London immediately, if you would be so good as to summon my carriage, Fleming. My maid can follow with my godmother whenever Lady Adelaide wishes to make the journey."

It was only by a miracle that she managed to avoid bursting into tears before she climbed into her carriage. And the fact that Fleming pressed four fresh handkerchiefs into her hand showed that he knew precisely when those tears would escape.

As it turned out, India cried from the moment the carriage entered the post road, all the way to London. "It's all right, Peters," she told Adelaide's alarmed butler, upon her arrival back home. "It's been a-a-a very trying day."

What woman wouldn't have fallen in love with Thorn? He was seductive and yet tender and sweet. He had genuinely listened to her, and created the India rubber band on her design. He was bawdy and rough and *real,* in a way that true gentlemen never were.

Even though he wasn't a gentleman by birth, he had always been scrupulously honest. He hadn't meant to sweep her off her feet. He had looked her in the eyes, more than once, and told her that their relationship was temporary, and that he planned to marry Lala.

A sob wrenched her chest. The stupid thing was that

men had tried to tumble her for years. They'd assumed that since they were hiring a woman and paying a woman, bedding that woman came as part of the package.

She had failed herself. She had forgotten the safeguards she put in place years ago, the lessons she learned from her father and mother about life. About love.

Now she felt as if a vital organ had been gouged out of her. Who would have imagined that love could hurt like this?

She had to build a new life, one that wasn't agonizingly painful.

One that didn't have Thorn in it.

Chapter Thirty-five

Thorn kept poking at his feelings for India, the way one might poke a sore tooth. This raw possessiveness wasn't something he ever thought to experience. Planned to experience.

He drove straight back from Piggleston, consumed the entire way by relief, and arrived at Starberry Court just before the noon hour. He needed answers.

"Where is my father?" he asked, cutting Fleming off before his butler could utter a word.

"His Grace is in the library. But, sir—"

"Not now, Fleming." Thorn found the duke alone, sitting before a chessboard, no doubt studying some arcane stratagem. Villiers looked up as Thorn entered. Damn it, he looked completely unrepentant. In fact, he looked amused.

"What in the hell was that about?" Thorn said, keeping his voice controlled. There was no point in howling at the Duke of Villiers, as he knew from childhood experience.

"You knew damn well that I didn't care for Laetitia Rainsford. You sent me on a wild-goose chase."

"You didn't enjoy your trip to Piggleston?"

Thorn had learned—if not inherited—his deadly glare from Villiers; after a moment, the corners of the duke's mouth curled up and he said, "As your father, I thought you could use a lesson in that most perplexing of emotions: love."

"I already knew that I wanted to marry India before you drove me halfway to the next county," Thorn retorted.

"Did you?"

The words hung in the air. It was true that Thorn had decided to ask for India's hand in marriage. But he hadn't understood just how much he felt for her until the darkest hour of the morning, when he'd realized what life would be like without her at his side.

It wasn't a question of bedding her. She was his true north, his other half.

"You are my son," the duke continued, his eyes softening. "I thought there was a good chance you'd inherited my idiocy. By the way, she turned down Lord Brody's proposal of marriage last night."

"How do you know that?" Thorn felt that muscle jumping in his jaw again.

"I kept him company while he drowned himself in a bottle of Cognac," the duke said. "I don't expect he'll be down until well into the afternoon."

"That doesn't mean she'll turn to me. Why would she accept my offer?" Thorn said savagely. "I've nothing to offer her that he hasn't, and in truth, a great deal less."

"She loves you," his father said calmly. "Though the emotion won't be enough on its own. Eleanor fell in love with me, but I had made so damn many mistakes by then that she wanted nothing to do with me."

"I'm no duke," Thorn said bleakly.

"It's my distinct impression that you treated her like the bastard you are. Do you remember how I courted your stepmother?"

"You bought her a ring the size of a swallow's egg, you put on a black coat, and you pretended to be your own cousin."

The duke grinned. "I pretended to be a gentleman, which I am not, duke or no. You'll have to do the same."

"I don't have a black coat."

"Pretend to be a gentleman," his father advised. "Tell her that she resembles a rose; make a formal proposal. But first go to Rundell & Bridge to buy a diamond, and tell them I sent you. She has returned to London, so you can (so to speak) kill two birds with one stone."

"I don't know if India is interested in diamonds."

"What gemstone would she prefer?"

Thorn thought of India's mother's jewels, lost in the Thames. "Nothing I could buy for her. More to the point, like Eleanor, she can marry the highest in the land. You *are* the highest, which means your proposal and mine are hardly parallel."

"She just turned down a duke's heir," Villiers observed. His eyes turned fierce and he said, "You *are* the highest in the land, Tobias. You have more brains and balls than any man in the peerage, and that woman knows it."

Thorn smiled faintly. "You forgot to add that I'm your son."

"All of which were inherited from me, naturally," his father said with satisfaction.

Chapter Thirty-six

129 Maddox Street
London residence of Lady Adelaide Swift
and Lady Xenobia India St. Clair

By late afternoon India had her tears more or less under control. She would find a husband who didn't constantly remind her about the "perfect" woman he planned to marry, but made it clear that *she* was that woman.

The only time she'd seen that sort of look in Thorn's eyes was after Vander joined them in the country. Then she caught him watching her with a possessiveness that had thrilled her. But it hadn't really had anything to do with her. It was about his rivalry with Vander.

Before she met Thorn, she had decided to find a man who would permit her to take charge of the household accounts. The idea of Thorn allowing her to run their life was enough to push a hollow laugh from her throat. She needed to marry a reasonable, measured man.

Thorn had identified the perfect trait for his spouse, and he hadn't wavered from his opinion. He had chosen Lala because she was sweet and always would be.

Just because life hadn't made her sweet didn't mean that a man couldn't love her. She would find a man who would love her just as she was. Neither of her most ardent suitors—Fitzroy and Nugent—would suit; they would be horrified if she lost her temper. Perhaps she should travel to the Continent. Weren't Spanish women famous for having fiery tempers?

India was thinking about black-eyed Spanish men when the door opened and the butler ushered Thorn into her drawing room. She jumped to her feet as her heart threw itself into double time.

He bowed. "Good afternoon, Lady Xenobia."

India took one look at his tousled dark hair and bruised eye and—absurdly—longing ignited in her very blood. There was no other man like him, one whose strength and intelligence swirled around him like a cloak, a complement to his bone-deep confidence. Though perhaps a better word was arrogance.

Belying his battered face, he was wearing a coat as extraordinary as any his father had ever donned: he looked ready to dance attendance on a queen.

"What on earth are you doing here, Thorn?" she asked, affecting a casual tone with effort. "Are you . . . did you catch up with Dr. Hatfield?"

"Not in time."

"Ah." It was no wonder he looked tired. He had lost his ideal spouse. "I'm sorry. You'll find someone else," she offered, feeling the words chip away at her heart.

"I already have."

"Oh."

"I came to ask you to marry me, India. To pay me the very great honor of becoming my bride."

India knew why this was happening. The moment Vander had stepped forward and told Lady Rainsford that they were married, she'd seen the look in Thorn's eyes.

Men like Thorn were ferociously competitive. They didn't give up, and failure was just a temporary inconvenience. In fact, it was likely the competition had escalated once Lala had removed herself from the equation by eloping with Dr. Hatfield. It left India as the bone of contention.

"Why is your eye bruised?" she asked sharply, unable to respond to the question she had longed for—not when it was simply offered, like a business proposition to be accepted or rejected.

"Vander," he said, confirming her guess.

Her heart sank. She stood between two snarling wolfhounds. The story never ended very well for the bone.

"You fought over me," she stated.

"That is irrelevant," Thorn said. "You are the epitome of beauty and grace, India. I cannot imagine spending my life with anyone other than you, and I beg for nothing more than the honor of your hand in marriage."

The words rolled out of his mouth with all the passion of a vicar reciting his third service of the day. He was obviously exhausted, his eyes shaded with some emotion that she couldn't interpret. He took a step closer and held out his hand. "This is for you."

A diamond ring lay in his palm, a lavish, costly ring. India looked at it, and back at his face.

He hadn't come to say that he was in love with her, as she had secretly dreamed. He was asking her to marry him because Vander had claimed her, and Lala had got away.

He was here because he wanted to win. She swallowed

hard. Her heart was breaking. Lala was the golden fleece and India was apparently the consolation prize.

It was as if the world was presenting her with everything she wanted . . . in all the wrong ways.

Her throat tightened painfully, but she refused to cry in front of him. She was the daughter of a marquess, even if her papa was the oddest nobleman who'd ever held the title. She was Lady Xenobia St. Clair.

Somehow she found her Lady Xenobia voice, the cool, businesslike voice that expected—and received—complete obedience. "I'm afraid that I must refuse your very moving offer of marriage."

His eyes burned into hers, so intense in their focus that she felt a bit dizzy. "Why? Did I say it incorrectly?"

"Not at all. It was one of the more eloquent I have received."

A movement caught her eyes, and she saw his right fist clench. The skin was broken over his knuckles, presumably from pummeling Vander.

"Yours is not my first marriage proposal, but it is nonetheless appreciated." Her heart wanted to give in and say yes. Who cared why he was proposing? Maybe he would fall in love with her later. . . .

But every ounce of practicality in her screamed *no*. He wouldn't. Men who slept with an available woman didn't later declare their love. If she hadn't succumbed to him like a trollop, she could have pretended to herself that he would love her someday. She could have lied to herself.

Perhaps.

Frustration burned through Thorn as he stood before India. She was so damned beautiful. Even though she looked pale and was far too quiet.

Abruptly, he decided to discard his father's advice. At this point he should kneel and slip the ring on India's finger, but he had the feeling that she'd back away and he'd be left on his knees like a fool.

He dropped the monstrous ring on a table, and hundreds of pounds' worth of diamond clinked against a teacup.

"I want to marry you, India."

Her eyes met his, steady and grave. "Why? Only yesterday you were courting Lala. You threw yourself into a carriage, by all accounts, trying to stop her marriage. Why are you proposing to me?"

Vander's question resounded in his head. *Why would she want to marry you?* India was a jewel of a woman in a jewel-like setting that he presumed she'd designed herself. She was surrounded by exquisite objects, the patina of age and wealth on every wall.

He might have been dressed like a bloody peacock to come to her, but it was all just show, covering up who he really was: more beast than man. They were beauty and the beast, the lady and the bastard. . . . It was stupid. Impossible.

But the warrior in him reared up. She was everything to him. All that he had thought mattered—his factories, Vander, that damned house—none of it mattered compared to her.

"I want you," he stated, the raw note in his voice telling its own truth.

The air burned as India drew it into her lungs. At least Thorn was honest. He desired her. He didn't pretend to love her, or even declare that she was perfect, the way Lala had been. Her reaction must have shown on her face.

"I'm not talking about intimacies," he added. "In other ways."

Fury engulfed her and there was no stopping it, no telling herself to be adult and compose herself the way a lady should. "The *hell* you're not talking about intimacies," she cried. "You bedded me while you courted Lala. Now she's no longer free and, as you say, you *want* me. That's not good enough. I deserve better."

Finally, it was all clear in her head. Painful, but clear. "I earned my own dowry," she told him. "I told you why. Do you remember?"

He didn't say a word, and she just kept going.

"Adelaide wanted me to debut. Some man would undoubtedly have desired me enough to take me without a dowry: after all, he'd get the daughter of a marquess, wouldn't he? Blue blood sells at a high premium. You know that, since you furnished Starberry Court for Lala."

"India—"

She cut him off, feeling her fingernails digging into her palms. "I earned my own dowry so I could buy freedom to choose the man myself rather than taking the first gentleman who held out his hand."

"Take my hand," he said. His face could have been carved from stone. "I don't care whether you have a dowry or not."

"You don't love me," she said flatly. "Even though you're in the throes of this ridiculous competition with Vander, you haven't lied about that. You don't love me and you don't trust me, which is why you believed that I would give away my own child."

She felt as if her heart were breaking even saying the words aloud.

Thorn's brows drew together. "You are not thinking rationally, India. In fact, I think you are blaming me for the sins of your parents."

"This has nothing to do with my parents!" she cried. "Nothing! If you loved me, you would have come to me after Lady Rainsford made all those accusations, and you didn't."

"I was chasing my own carriage, believing you and Vander were eloping in it."

His voice was so scathing that it took a moment to absorb his words—and to understood why he'd set out after the carriage. "It doesn't matter!" she cried wildly. "Don't you see, Thorn? Don't you see that? That's just more competition with Vander. You're offering this big diamond . . . but that's not what I want. I deserve *better*!"

Thorn was listening, groping through the emotion boiling in India's voice, when he heard words he understood all too clearly: "*I deserve better.*"

Vander was right. Hell, *she* was right.

"I was good enough to bed," he snarled, "but not good enough to marry. Do I have you right, Lady Xenobia?"

Her mouth fell open.

"You're right, India. I didn't want to marry someone like you. I wanted a pleasant relationship. I didn't want a woman who argues with me, who makes me so crazed with lust that I tumble her under the noses of the servants. Do you know what I felt when I thought you'd run away with Vander?" He was shouting now. "Do you have any idea how I felt?"

India would never be cowed, no matter how he shouted. She raised her chin defiantly. "I know exactly what you felt: You felt that you were losing to Vander," she retorted. "That's not enough for me."

A great coldness swept down over Thorn. She wanted better: who the hell was he to argue? "The fact is, India, the last thing I need is marriage to a daughter of a marquess who thinks she's above me, who wants *better*." The words came from some dark part of his soul, and they came with the force that only a bastard could give them.

She stared at him, those beautiful eyes wide and strained. Her beauty hurt his gut, and his voice shifted from cold to lethal. "It would be rank stupidity to marry a woman who lied to me, told me she wasn't a virgin, told me she'd give away her own child. You demonstrated precisely how much you respect me. Would you have lied to a gentleman?"

She flinched as if he'd hit her. He felt exhaustion coming over him like a shroud. India was . . . what she was. And he the same. That brief dream he'd had—of loving and marrying a woman like her—would count as the greatest of his life's stupidities. No more.

India seemed frozen, her face white.

"I bid you goodbye, Lady Xenobia," he said, falling back and bowing with a flourish. "I think we have both said more than we would wish to and more than we ought. I was insane to think of marrying a woman of the titled class. I have no intention of considering it ever again, and I imagine our paths will not cross."

Caught in a storm of madness, he couldn't stop himself. He stepped toward her again and cradled her face in his hands. His soul wrenched with the time he'd wasted, the ass he'd been.

He bent, brushed his lips across hers with the respect that a lord would give a lady.

Then he bowed and turned away again without meeting her eyes. There was no point.

Chapter Thirty-seven

Thorn had barely entered his front door before he started to curse himself for being a fool.

Despite everything he'd said, he wanted India more than he wanted his dignity. She wouldn't lie to him again. Though he didn't give a damn if she did—as long as she was in his house and bed, at his side.

Fred was manning the entry. "Good morning, sir!"

Thorn nodded, unable to summon a greeting.

"Miss Rose's carriage arrived an hour or so ago," Fred said cheerfully. "I believe that Clara plans to take her on a visit to Kensington Gardens this afternoon."

"Excellent," Thorn managed, handing over his great-coat.

"A Mr. Marley is waiting to see you, sir, accompanied by a Mr. Farthingale. Shall I send them into the library?"

At first Thorn had no idea who Fred was talking about,

but then he remembered: Marley was the Bow Street Runner he'd hired to investigate the deaths of India's parents. Farthingale was presumably his partner.

It was bitterly ironic that the man had shown up at this particular moment. It hardly mattered now, but Thorn might as well hear what the man had uncovered.

Mr. Marley was an energetic young fellow, positively trembling with suppressed glee. "It's a pleasure to see you again, sir," he said to Thorn, giving him a brisk bow. He gestured to the elderly gentleman at his side, whose spindly legs and long nose gave him a distinct resemblance to a stork. "This is Mr. Farthingale, the proprietor of a jewelry shop in the Blackfriars."

"Good afternoon, gentlemen," Thorn said, bowing. "Won't you both sit down?"

"You engaged me to make inquiries on behalf of Lady Xenobia St. Clair regarding her father's death," Marley burst out.

"I did," Thorn said, ushering Mr. Farthingale to a settee.

"The Marquess of Renwick drove his curricle off the Blackfriars Bridge eleven years ago, in early 1788," Marley said once they were all seated. "That bit of reckless driving resulted in the untimely deaths of himself and the marchioness, though the horse was better able to fight the current, and kept his head above water until two lads on the bank were able to cut the reins."

Thorn remembered the Blackfriars current well; the marquess couldn't have picked a worse bridge to pitch over in all London.

"You asked me to attempt to locate a valuable article of jewelry that the marquess may have had on his person," Marley continued. "The intervening years between the accident and your query made my investigation extremely difficult, but I decided to visit all the jewelry shops in the vicinity of the bridge. Mr. Farthingale's shop is just outside the liberty of Blackfriars."

The elderly jeweler cleared his throat and adjusted his old-fashioned pantaloons. "I'm afraid that my news will not cheer Lady Xenobia," he said apologetically. "The marquess and his wife apparently died within minutes of their visit to my establishment, a fact that virtually guarantees that the jewels are at the bottom of the Thames. I am not a great reader of the papers, and unfortunately I entirely missed the announcement of their death."

Thorn cursed under his breath. "Am I to understand that the marquess had the jewels in his possession when he departed your shop?"

This prompted an avalanche of detail; Mr. Farthingale had the sort of memory that a historian would envy. "His lordship placed the pouch containing the jewels in his coat pocket as he left," he concluded. "I remember thinking that it was cavalier treatment of such valuable pieces."

"What were they, exactly?"

Mr. Farthingale launched into a description of the pieces as if he'd examined them only yesterday, rather than more than a decade earlier. "A diamond demi-parure, consisting of a necklace and earrings set in engraved silver mounts with gold embellishment. The pieces constituted a substantial set, with hundreds of foil back rose-, table-, and Indian face-cut diamonds of various carats, shaped in flower heads and foliate spray motifs. I dated the pieces to the mid-1600s. I was prepared to pay a generous sum for the set."

"So he meant to sell it?"

"As I informed the marquess, I would have been most happy to have it in my possession. But his lordship merely asked for a valuation. He never returned, and I put it completely out of my mind."

After the two men left, Thorn sank back into his chair.

The Duke of Villiers had bought Eleanor a ring. But India could buy her own jewelry. What she needed was the faith that the man she married wouldn't leave her, as she believed her parents had done.

She would never have enough faith in him: he could imagine that she would test him over and over and he would fail every time, because, damn it, he was as blind as the next man.

India was brilliant and subtle. Her brain darted ahead, planning for eventualities only she could see. In that, he was her opposite. He dealt with problems of the moment, and never bothered to look much further.

He wouldn't even know he was failing her. Yet India's conviction that she was unlovable —and that Thorn didn't love her—had far more to do with her parents than with him. Perhaps if he made love to her every—

He stood up again, his mind reeling. He had just told himself that he planned to *make love to India.*

It was common terminology, after all. Though he never thought of sex that way: he used a rougher term for bedding a woman. Or more jovial ones. He shagged, pumped, screwed, jousted.

He never said anything about love, and he never thought it, either.

Until now.

Finally he identified the emotion that gripped him the night he'd thought India was on the point of marrying Vander. It wasn't possession or lust—or at least, it wasn't only those emotions.

It was love. *He loved her.*

And yet India didn't believe he loved her. She never would . . . unless he took action.

He had to find those jewels and bring them to her.

He had to prove not only his own love for her, but her parents' love.

It wasn't easy to gather the remaining lads together. Dusso was now a senior driver with the Royal Mail, and Thorn had to bribe the office handsomely to give their driver a week's leave. He ran down Geordie in the East End, wretchedly thin and evidently without a job. Bink had a family and lived in Kent on a tenant farm, but he didn't seem to be earning much; Thorn promptly offered him one of the farms attached to Starberry Court.

When at last the four of them were together, Thorn explained what he wanted. "A number of years ago, a carriage went off Blackfriars Bridge, and its two passengers drowned. A leather pouch holding jewels went missing. I want to find that pouch. You three are the only ones I would trust. Hell, I think we're probably the only men in London who have a chance of dragging it back up."

"Yer mugging us!" Dusso exclaimed.

"Giving us the piss," Geordie chimed in.

"I assure you that I am not."

"Bloody hell," Dusso said. "Iffen I'd known you was talking about the river, I wouldn't have come. I'd rather be winding that bloody horn on the coach day and night than that."

"One hundred guineas for each of you," Thorn said, "and five hundred for the man who finds the jewels."

"It'd be like finding a pea," Geordie said, slumping in his chair. "I dream about it at night, you know. Swimming down into the black, stinking water and fearing a dead man's claw is going to pull me down."

Bink scowled at him. "It's no wonder you have the collywobbles if you're letting yourself think about it. I'll do it," he said, squaring his shoulders. "I'm not looking forward to it, mind. The wife complains because I work all day in the fields and still I don't want a drop of water near me after. But I'll do it for my girls."

"I can't possibly do it alone," Thorn said. "I need a team, same as we used to do. Two to dive, and one person above to spot, make sure they both come up. One on the shore in case of trouble."

"I'll be on the shore," Dusso said instantly. "Them boats have no concern for who might be bobbing about in the stream."

Thorn shook his head. "Geordie's on shore."

Dusso looked at Geordie's frail body and nodded. "How much are the joowels worth?"

"I have no idea, and it doesn't really matter. I want to give them to the woman I wish to marry. It was her parents who drowned. Their bodies were recovered but the jewels were not."

"Stolen," Dusso said instantly. "Probably the men as fished out the carriage are sleeping on beds of roses right now."

But Marley had bribed his way into the constabulary records.

"I believe not," Thorn said. "The marquess visited a jeweler in the Blackfriars and went off the bridge minutes later. By the time they fished him out, the man was wearing only his breeches. The jewels were almost certainly lost in the river when his coat was dragged from his back."

"Bloody hell, you's talking of marrying the daughter of a bloody marquess?" Dusso squawked.

The three men stared at Thorn, jaws a-cock. They'd gotten used to the fact that Thorn had grown wealthy. They knew his father was a duke, and that he was always good for a sovereign or two. But this was different.

"I *am* marrying her," Thorn said shortly.

"But is she marrying you?" Geordie asked.

Dusso laughed. "Yeah, a lady agreeing to take on a by-blow? Not likely! No dog in a doublet for the likes of a lady!"

"You always was a gundiguts," Bink snapped. "Why shouldn't she marry our lad? He's as good as any other Englishman."

Thorn intervened. "She'll marry me because I love her." He wanted to believe it.

"Well, aren't you the cork-brained gay-lant," Dusso shouted. "He lurves her. Does she have chicken breasts or a bushel bubby? Has she—"

"Don't speak of her in that manner," Thorn growled, bending forward.

Dusso nodded.

"Iffen you find these here jewels, will she take you?" Geordie asked.

Thorn didn't answer. The truth was that he wasn't sure.

"She'll like him better if he's on his knees with a string of joowels in hand," Bink said practically.

Dusso put his elbows on the table. "I'll help you. For old times' sake."

"I want two hundred guineas," Bink stated. "You said it was only if we went in the water. Geordie here gets a hundred as well, even he don't put a pinkie in that river."

"Five hundred for each of you if we find the jewels," Thorn said. "Two hundred each otherwise, and that includes Geordie. There's many a time that the one on shore has saved everyone in the water."

"There ain't no joowels other than a crown as is worth fifteen hundred guineas," Dusso pointed out.

"They're worth it to me," Thorn stated.

"I remember the Blackfriars Bridge," Geordie said. "It's got a nasty fast current around the corner."

"I expect it was that current that ripped off the marquess's clothing," Thorn confirmed.

"We're not going to find it in an hour," Bink said.

"We'll have it out within the week," Thorn stated. "We could find anything in that damned river. We still can."

"Know it like the back of me hand," Dusso bragged. "Reckon we can get it out today."

Bink looked nervous and cracked his knuckles. "I ain't been in the river ever since."

Silence fell over the table.

"I haven't either," Thorn said.

"You?" Dusso looked astounded.

Thorn shrugged. "I didn't plan on ever going back in either."

"You're a swell, ain't that right," Geordie said. "No need to swim."

Now there *was* a reason to swim. An hour later they were down by the water, all but Geordie stripped to their smalls.

Thorn had avoided the river for years, and the smell—the fishy, murky odor of his childhood—came back like a blow.

He'd forgotten the endless detritus of the river: branches, old clothes, dead rats, wine bottles . . . everything in London seemed to float down its largest tributary, swirling through eddies, scraping by rocks, floating alongside boats, dead goats, and mudlarks.

They clustered on the bank hard by the bridge, as close as possible to where the marquess's curricle had gone into the water. Thorn cast a critical eye at his gang. He'd give his right arm to have Will with them; it was as if there was a silent patch of air that should hold Rose's father. Will would have made sure the marquess's jewels came up from the depths. "You sure you want to go in, Bink?"

Bink was thin but sinewy. He set his jaw. "I ain't looking forward to it, but I've got two daughters. I need that money."

"You all remember how the current fetches up against the bank and smashes into a rock," Thorn said, pointing at the curve. "For God's sake, don't put your foot down in the mud, and watch your hands. Keep your gloves on. It'll make it harder to swim, but I want no sliced fingers."

"Got me a nice teacup there once," shouted the irrepressible Dusso.

The sun was shining, but the Thames didn't reflect the sky's blue; it was liquid gray, the color of silt and debris.

"Exactly where'd the currickle go in?" Bink asked.

"See that newer length of brass there?" Thorn said, pointing to a spot along the bridge's parapet.

"If it went in there," Bink said, his eyes darting from bridge to water, "she would have swung about this way, my guess."

"Driver was thrown out when it hit the water," Dusso said. They were all focused now. They were, after all, the survivors of Grindel's cruel games. He used to throw a shoe in and make them learn the currents by fetching it—or there'd be no dinner.

They used to dive precisely into the spot where housemaids dumped the chamber pots and the kitchen staff dumped the scraps: you never knew when a silver spoon would end up in the mix.

"I think the carriage landed here," Thorn said, pointing.

"Wife and he were caught in the current, along with the joowels. If he lost the bag around there, it would have fetched up on the curve," Dusso concluded.

"Into the shit," Thorn began, but they all interrupted and shouted it together. "Into the shit and bring out the bloody pig!" It was Grindel's old call.

"Here's hoping that hairy-arsed prigger is in a hot place," Bink said, crossing himself.

"He was an arse," Dusso shouted, jumping off the bank, white belly flashing in the sun.

A moment later they were all bobbing at the edge. Thorn knew the river, at least this part of it, like the back of his hand. The pouch's weight would have sunk it in the silt, but not too deep, since the current was strong enough to keep the muck fairly shallow.

"It's too dangerous at the bend," he told his men. "I don't want anyone diving where the current cuts around that rock." The water took on a low whistle as it swept around the curve.

"There might be a pileup there," Bink objected. "Will would have been down there first."

That was true: Rose's father had been a daredevil who always wanted to win more than he'd cared to live. "It's not worth your life," Thorn said. "Your daughters need you. Respect the river, Bink."

They'd learned that lesson the hard way. Their master, Grindel, had been evil; the river itself wasn't evil, but it was temperamental. One day it was tranquil and the next it was a demon dragging a man down to the bottom.

Bink grunted.

"Geordie, keep an eye out," Thorn shouted, and Geordie nodded. "I'll go down with Dusso; Bink, you stay above this time around."

Thorn took a deep breath, reckoned the exact spot on the bank he wanted to explore, and dove deep. The water roared past his ears, and the only reason he sensed the approaching bank was that a deeper dark loomed before him. Out of the corner of his eye he could see Bink's legs waving above like pale fish.

He felt along the muddy bank until he felt his lungs bursting, then kicked up and broke the surface. He got his bearings and realized that he hadn't searched the exact area he wanted.

Dusso surfaced just beside him. "I'll be damned if I

know where to go," he said, gasping. "I've put it all out of my mind and I can't seem to get too deep. My belly's in the way."

"Look there," Thorn said, pointing to the spot he'd picked out. "I'm going to swim over there. If you look up, you'll see my legs."

"I'll go down this time," Bink shouted.

Thorn fought his way through the current and caught the overhanging branch of an alder. "Below me," he shouted.

The two men disappeared, and for a moment the sun glinted on the surface of the water as if it were clean and serene.

Bink came back up, shook his head, took a gulp of air, and kicked his way back down again.

The afternoon passed like that. By the time they gave up, they reeked of the Thames, an noisome blend of fish, potatoes, coal smoke, and rain. It clung to their skin and soaked through their clothes and into the seats of Thorn's carriage.

At home, they bathed and dressed, and he introduced the lads to Rose. That evening, and the next, and the next after that passed as they spun tales of Will's bravery.

By the fourth day, they were all tired. They'd gone down scores of times, but the pouch still eluded them. Only inherent stubbornness kept Thorn in the water. Bink and Dusso were diving, Geordie was on the bank, and Thorn was on the surface.

Thorn hung on to the alder branch, watching the water where the men disappeared. Damn it, he was wasting their time and his own. The bag was either at the curve, where it was worth a man's life to fish it out, or it had washed down the river and fetched up at one of a hundred different spots.

He was a fool. Eleven years is an eternity in the life of a river.

He missed India in a piercing way that shook him to the core. When he'd offered her that diamond ring, he had been consumed with desire: he wanted her back. In his bed, in his arms.

But now he felt as if her absence had ripped him open and stabbed him in the heart. He didn't just love her the way a silly poet loved a maiden. He felt a primal, clawing need every time he thought of her.

It was mad. Or he was mad.

Abruptly he realized that Bink hadn't come back up. Dusso was bobbing near the bank. Damn it, his attention had wavered.

He was about to dive when Bink's head broke the water. The man seemed to have lost a stone in the last four days; his cheekbones jutted from his face. He splashed over to the alder and hung on to it, gasping harshly.

Thorn had stayed in fighting shape, but the rest of his gang hadn't. He made up his mind. "That's it!" he shouted. "We're done. No more. We gave it a good shot. We've been up and down the bank."

"No!" Bink shouted back. "I'm not ready to give up. I know where it is." He pointed directly to the turn in the river, the place where the water ran black and furious.

"We're not going there," Thorn said. "Out of the water!"

Dusso started splashing toward the bank, but Bink shook his head. "I need that money!"

"It was two hundred just for going in," Thorn said, treading water. "Come on, mate. Let's get out of here."

"I ain't taken no charity in my life," Bink said, his jaw setting. "And I ain't going to start now. I'm going after that damn bag." And with that he let go of the branch and began plowing through the water toward the bend.

Thorn shouted, knowing Bink wouldn't hear him—or listen, if he did. Dusso howled something from the bank and Thorn started out to swim, planning to drag Bink back to the bank by force if necessary.

But the man had a good start, and even though Thorn slashed through the water as if it were air, Bink had disappeared below the surface by the time Thorn arrived at the river's bend.

He followed the pale flash of legs down through the murk. Bink was no fool: he was using the current to propel himself against the bank, his gloved hands outstretched to bounce off the looming rock, pushing him lower to a pileup of silt that likely included everything from dead rats to broken crockery.

A stream of curses went through Thorn's mind. What in the hell had he been doing, putting his lads at risk? One wrong move and Bink would be swept sideways, straight into the rock that the water was smashing into with a throbbing roar.

With a powerful kick, Thorn reached Bink, grabbed his arm, and hauled him up.

They broke the surface, both gasping. Bink brought his hand up to the air. It was clutching a slimy, moldering leather hat; he shook it and let it fall. "Damn you," he shouted. "The place is ripe. The pouch is there, I tell you!"

"I don't give a damn. If I hadn't grabbed you, you'd have been driven into the rock."

"Well, you did," Bink said defiantly.

"You're bleeding." A thin red rivulet trailed down Bink's cheek.

"A flea bite. I'm going down again. I'm going to get that damn pouch. You'll marry the bloody marquess or his daughter, and I'll earn me reward." And with that, he slipped beneath the water again.

Thorn swore, and dove. Bink was like a fish. With a grim curse, Thorn swam after, eyes straining to see through the murk. The water was full of silt cast up by Bink's first attempt.

This was the Thames at its worst, black as soot, with a current that clutched with a hundred fingers, no matter how agile the swimmer, seeming to purposefully drive him against a shard of rock or a broken bottle, each perilous in its own way.

The heel of Bink's foot flashed ahead like a fish scale. He was precisely where Thorn had decided the bag had likely lodged, if it was there at all: under the shadow of the rock that the current had cut into, leaving the great bulk hanging above them like a black shelf.

With almost no oxygen left in his lungs, Thorn reached Bink, only to see his body jerk in the way of a man who is trying to tug something free. He was making silt explode into the water, clouds of sediment spreading as fast as smoke.

Thorn swam blindly toward the place where he'd seen Bink's heel. His hand closed on a slick leg, and he felt forward. If a man is caught in spirals of fishing line, tugging could tighten it, trapping the swimmer until, panicked, he choked on sludge-laden water.

Bink knew that as well as he did, and yet he still pulled. Thorn joined in, pulling with every bit of remaining strength he had. Bink lurched backward, kicking madly.

His foot caught the edge of Thorn's thigh and flipped him as easily it might a fish. In that instant the current caught Thorn in a rush of bubbles, turned him over, his vision gone, air gone, and slammed him against the rock. Water rushed to fill his mouth, swept into his lungs.

The world was already black, but the rush of bubbles in his ears stopped, and everything went silent and cold.

Chapter Thirty-eight

*I*n years to come, India never forgot the moment when Fred burst through the door of her sitting room, Adelaide's butler at his heels. "He's dying, m'lady," he gasped. "And the little girl wants you."

For a moment, Fred's words just knocked about in her head like the lyrics of a song she heard recited but never sung.

Dying? How on earth could Thorn be dying? But the fear etched on Fred's face told her that he was not exaggerating.

She sprang from her chair and ran to Thorn's carriage without her pelisse, without her reticule, without Adelaide.

Fred leapt on and the carriage rocked around the corner. India sat, her nails biting into her palms. Her mind turned into a snowstorm, so white and violent that no single thought made it through, nothing besides the beating of her heart. Each beat was a prayer, a cry, a plea.

Thorn couldn't die. The world would be nothing without him. She couldn't imagine it: her heart rejected the idea.

The pain was like a drumbeat marking the minutes.

As the carriage rocked to a halt in front of the house, India leapt out and ran up the path and through the door, past the silent butler, up the stairs, straight to Thorn's chamber. A doctor was bending over the bed.

When she saw Thorn, her knees gave way and she barely caught herself on the bedpost. He was naked, covered below his waist by a sheet. His skin had lost all color; he was white, a powder-white that wasn't right. His lashes were black as coal against the pallor of his cheeks.

Even worse, a huge gash stretched across his forehead. She watched the doctor make another neat, precise stitch, working to close the gaping wound. Blood was running down from the man's hands, soaking into the pillows.

"He's not dead," she said, her voice gasping. "What happened?"

"Mrs. Dautry?" the doctor said, not lifting his eyes. "He still lives." He took another stitch, and another.

"Are there other injuries?"

"Not unless you count drowning."

"*What*?"

"He was pulled from the Thames, as I understand it. It's a miracle those men got him breathing again. But he hasn't come out of it. He should have returned to his senses by now. Could be damage to the lungs. Or brain concussion from the blow." More blood oozed over the doctor's hand, and a woman, likely Thorn's housekeeper, moved forward with a wad of damp cloth.

The world snapped back into focus, and India grabbed her wrist. "Is that towel clean?"

"I do the washing on Monday," she answered, her chin wobbling. "It's only been a day or so."

"I will take it, if you please," India said, softening when she saw the housekeeper's red eyes and the tears rolling down her cheeks. "What is your name?"

"Mrs. Stella," she said.

"I'm Lady Xenobia. I'd be grateful if you could bring me a stack of pristine, unused cloths. Put in an order for ice to be delivered every day for the next week. I also want to make up a poultice of eggs, oil of roses, and turpentine."

She took the cloth and wiped the blood from Thorn's face and neck, carefully avoiding the wound itself.

The doctor glanced up. "If he doesn't return to himself, you'll have no need to treat the wound or ward off fever."

"He *will* wake up," India said flatly.

The man grunted, finished the last stitch, and cut off the string with a small knife. "That's all I can do," he said, wiping his hands with the edge of the sheet. "Either he'll wake or he won't."

"There must be some treatment for head wounds of this nature," India said, eyeing the doctor. His waistcoat was splattered with Thorn's blood.

"Not that I know of. You can try to give him some water, but he won't live long if he doesn't open his eyes. That'll be a sovereign, payable immediately," he added briskly.

"Fred, please escort this man to the door. The butler will pay you," India said, giving the doctor a look that had him scuttling out the door and down the stairs.

India sank onto the bed and took Thorn's hand.

His wound was still seeping blood, but she didn't want to touch it until she had a clean cloth. A doctor had once told her he thought that dirty wounds were more likely to become infected. Lord knows, the Thames was dirty.

"Thorn," she whispered. "It's India."

He didn't stir.

"Please come back," she said, leaning over so that her lips

touched his cheek. "I can't lose another person I love to that river, Thorn." Her throat tightened. "Please, please, wake up."

Fred reappeared, looking anxious. "Mr. Dautry's man is wondering if this would be a good time to wash the river water off and change the bedsheets."

India looked up. "I will do that."

The footman looked horrified, but India impatiently waved a hand at him. "I'll need help with the sheets. What's Mr. Dautry's man's name?"

"Mr. Pendle."

"Please ask Pendle to lay out clean sheets and night clothing, as well as warm water. Mrs. Stella is bringing clean cloths. Meanwhile, I'll go to Miss Rose."

"She's in the nursery," Fred said. He hesitated and said, "It was Miss Rose who insisted that we send a carriage for you, my lady. I hope that was the right thing to do. There was such a commotion when he was brought home that she heard it in the nursery. The duke and duchess are at their country house, so I sent a message to you. And, of course, to the duke as well, but his seat is two days away."

"You were absolutely correct to call me," India reassured him. "I've sat in many a sickroom. Will you please send a messenger to Lady Adelaide to inform her of the circumstances? And where are the men who pulled Mr. Dautry from the river?"

"Messrs. Bink, Dusso, and Geordie are bathing and changing their clothes."

India frowned. "Who are these men? Do you mean to say that they are in residence here?"

"They are former mudlarks," Fred said, "and very proud of it too. They're the ones who saved Mr. Dautry. By all accounts, they got him breathing again."

"I will thank them later," India said. At the moment she had to visit Rose.

When she reached the nursery, she found the child listening as her tutor read aloud from a history of ancient Rome. Rose sat on a straight-backed chair, Antigone perched on the rocking cow beside her.

As India entered, Twink's voice broke off. Rose pulled Antigone from the cow and stood, clutching her doll tightly in her arms. The tutor came to his feet and bowed. In the corner, Clara bobbed a curtsy.

"Mr. Dautry is alive," India said quickly. "The doctor just left."

"Has he woken up?" Rose's voice was tight and high.

"Not yet." India went to her and knelt down. "He's going to be well, darling."

"They said that about my father as well," Rose said.

"May I pick you up?" India asked.

Rose nodded. India scooped her into her arms, carried her over to the sofa, and sat down. The little girl remained bolt upright on India's lap.

"I'm very grateful that you sent a carriage for me," India said, stroking her back.

"Lady Adelaide said that you work miracles," Rose reminded her.

This hadn't been what Adelaide was referring to, but India nodded. "If there is a miracle to be had, I shall do it," she said fiercely. "I promise you that. And if that miracle doesn't happen"—India forced the words out because they had to be said; she could not leave the child in the grip of utter terror—"if Thorn is lost to us, Rose, you will come and live with me."

India felt Rose shudder. "I shall probably be sent to America, to my aunt."

"That's not what Thorn would have wanted—*wants*. He wants you to live here in England. And remember? I announced to half the world that you are my daughter." India's arms closed tighter, and she coaxed Rose back against her shoulder. "I can think of no greater privilege than that."

Rose made a little gasping sound, but said nothing. Still, her body relaxed in the circle of India's arms, and her head sank against her shoulder. "He won't die, will he?"

"Not if I can help it."

India put her cheek against Rose's bright hair and rocked her back and forth. "How is Antigone?" she asked.

"She's not feeling very well," Rose whispered. "She feels sick, as if she swallowed river water too."

"You must soothe her." India put the child on her feet and looked into her eyes. "Tell Antigone that she is loved, and that she will be safe and warm. Tell her that Thorn would want her to be hopeful and never give up, because he isn't the sort of man who gives up, is he?"

Rose shook her head. "Never."

"Neither am I," India said. "I will not give up on Thorn, and neither will you. Now I'm going to return to him and put a poultice on his forehead. If you are worried and want to know how he is, just send Clara to me."

"I won't give up either," Rose said stoutly.

India gave her a hug and ran out the door.

Chapter Thirty-nine

By the time India returned to Thorn's bedchamber, she felt calm again. She was at her best in a crisis, when others fell into hysterics. She stopped to introduce herself to Thorn's butler, who was clearly beside himself with worry.

Between the two of them, they made certain that every member of the household had work to do, from Mrs. Stella to the grooms, who could work scrubbing river water from the carriage.

"You'll meet the mudlarks tonight, my lady," the butler said. "They just left for Cheapside to find a patent medicine that Mr. Dusso knows of."

What on earth had Thorn been up to? Could it be an odd reunion, where the four of them plunged back into the river and revisited their childhood? But she had no time to chat; she hurried back to Thorn's bedroom and shooed out his valet, who had changed the sheets but not yet bathed his master.

She talked constantly as she dipped a clean cloth in

warm water and began to wash Thorn. She told him how much she had missed him, and was missing him now. She might have cried a bit, especially when she pulled back the sheet in order to wash his legs and feet. She had never clearly seen all the scars that covered his legs, the pale slashes that cut through a rough covering of hair without disguising the muscle that lay underneath.

His manhood lay against his leg, looking entirely different than it always had been in her presence. Like him, it was suspended in time.

India kept talking as she washed, softly telling Thorn stories of the more extraordinary households she'd seen.

Every so often she would stop and ladle a spoonful of water into his mouth, holding his head up so that some of it ran down his throat.

Just as she drew the sheet back to his waist, there was a tap at the door and Mrs. Stella appeared, followed by a footman with more hot water. She was clearly restored to her efficient self. "I ordered the ingredients you wanted, and I have Rose and Clara supervising as Cook bakes a special cake for the master."

India smiled at her. "What a splendid idea. Thank you, Mrs. Stella."

When the door was shut again, India turned her attention to Thorn's hair. Blood and river water had dried it into a stiff helmet, so she washed it over and over. All the time she kept speaking to him in a low, soothing voice, though she occasionally stopped and begged him to wake up.

By the time she was satisfied that he was clean, the bed was completely soaked. She pulled the bell and supervised as footmen moved him into the connecting bedchamber, the one meant for the lady of the house. The irony of that did not escape her.

The evening wore on; the butler appeared and asked if

she would like to join Messrs. Dusso, Bink, and Geordie for the meal. She declined, but stepped from the room to greet the gentlemen.

Mr. Bink pressed a brown bottle into her hands. "It's Edison's Magno-Electric Vitalizer," he told her earnestly. "The best stuff in London. It'll jolt him right awake. And if that doesn't work, I'll find some of them tablets they make for rousing one's manhood. That'll do it!"

India thanked him and hurried back to Thorn's bedside. Something deep inside her believed that by talking she was mooring him to Earth, and that if she gave up and left him to silence, he might just drift away.

Late that night, exhausted, she began to slur her words and finally broke into tears.

She *hated* to cry. She had learned as a child that crying did nothing. You could cry for hours, but the house would still be dark and echoing when you stopped. Crying didn't make you warmer, or less hungry.

But now the emotion welled up in her throat and she couldn't stop. When she got enough control to speak again, the words that came were no longer soft and soothing.

"Why—*why* did you go into the river?" she demanded, her voice cracking. "You should never have risked your life when your father and Eleanor love you, when Rose loves you . . . when *I* love you!"

She choked again, appalled to find that she was almost shouting at him, when she should be coaxing him back to consciousness with loving kindness. But she'd used up all of the tender words she had.

"I love you," she said again, her voice breaking on a sob, "but I hate you too, because this is the first time I told you so, and you aren't even listening. I hate you for making me fall in love with you. I hate you for wanting to marry someone sweet and fluffy as a duckling instead of me."

The worst of it was her own role in the drama: she had thrown away the only beautiful thing in her life. Even if Thorn wasn't dying, he was finished with her. And he did deserve better than she.

She had lied to him in their most intimate moments. She had never truly trusted him with her most valuable truths: not with the fact she had never been with a man, nor with the fact that she, of all people, would never desert a child.

Loving him was an anguish that she felt in her entire body, as if two of her bones were grating against each other.

"You broke my heart," she cried. "You broke—you *broke my heart*!"

To her utter horror, she realized that she was emphasizing her points by pounding on his chest. Not hard enough to hurt, but still, it was a sign of what an awful person she was.

"I know I'm not sw-sweet," she cried, tears splashing on the sheet. "I suppose I lost all my sweetness when I was a child. But that doesn't mean that love doesn't hurt just as much. It doesn't mean that I don't need taking care of, as Lala does. Just because I am able to take care of myself doesn't mean that I *want* to!" And with that, she sank down, her face on his chest, her body shaking with sobs.

She was weeping so hard that she scarcely heard a voice whisper, "India."

But she did hear it.

She reared up, saw Thorn's eyes were open, and screamed. "I love you," she cried, her voice rough with tears. "Oh Thorn, I've been so frightened. But you came back!"

"I could hear you yelling, and after a while it seemed easier to open my eyes." His voice was hoarse, but the corners of his lips curled up.

"I'm sorry," she said. "I didn't mean to lose my temper."

"That's you," he said, his fingers curling around hers, eyes drifting shut again. "Love you." His eyelashes lay on his cheeks again, but this time she knew he had been caught by sleep, and not something darker and nearer to death.

Chapter Forty

The next day India left Thorn's side only to bathe and dress, and to see Rose just long enough to reassure her that her guardian was on the mend. Adelaide brought over clothing and wisely said nothing about the fact that even if Lady Rainsford kept her mouth shut about what happened at Starberry, India had now indisputably ruined her reputation, at least among the members of Thorn's household.

After tea, Adelaide poked her head in the door and announced that she was taking Rose on a trip to Hyde Park, and that Thorn's former mudlarks were a good group of men. Apparently they had saved his life by pounding on his chest until he threw up all the water he'd swallowed.

India scarcely listened. She was worried. Thorn hadn't woken again. She could rouse him enough to drink water, but he seemed dazed and said nothing.

By now she had given up all pretense that she wasn't acting precisely as a wife would. She spent the day hanging over Thorn's bed, talking to him, coaxing him, haranguing him, bathing him.

As evening fell, she stripped to her chemise, lay down beside him, and put her head on his shoulder. Fear that he would never truly come back to life was growing in her heart.

She lay beside him for hours, fear steeling her limbs as if a stranger had taken over her body. Finally she fell asleep with her arm tight around his middle, as if she could hold him to this earth by touch alone.

When a warm mouth brushed hers, sliding off to caress her cheek, she just curled up, thinking she was dreaming.

But sometime later her eyes popped open and she found Thorn beside her, propped on his side. He had lost weight, which had only chiseled the dangerous male beauty that moved her as had no other man's. There was nothing dangerous about the look in his eyes.

"I love you," he said, the simple words dropping in the silence. "God in heaven, India. You saved my life."

"Your mudlarks did that," she said, her eyes filling. After a lifetime of suppressing tears, she had turned into a watering can. "Thorn," she whispered, unable to say anything else.

He rolled partly on top of her. "India," he whispered back.

She brought a hand up to touch his face. "Your hair is damp!"

"I know you tried to wake me by yelling," he told her, eyes laughing. "But in the end, very unromantically, I woke because I needed a chamber pot. You were fast asleep, so I went through to my own bedchamber, where my man was rather shocked to see me walk through the door. I just had a quick bath."

"You must eat!" she said, wiggling to get free of his weight.

But he pushed forward one of his legs, trapping her more firmly beneath him. "Fred will bring breakfast any minute."

"You must be starving," India said, her breath catching at his expression. "You must regain your strength."

"Peace, my little whirlwind," he said, lowering his head enough to brush her lips with his again. "There's something I want far more than an egg."

She stilled, her heart melting.

Their kiss made up for days of fear. It was a heart-piercing kiss that seared promises into the bone.

"You are mine," Thorn said fiercely, raising his head.

Another kiss, but India pulled back when it turned slow and erotic. "You must eat," she repeated.

He pushed her hair back from her forehead. "Have I told you how much I love you?"

Her lips trembled. "What if you only love me because I rushed to your side, like the mother you never knew? Or because Vander claimed to marry me?"

Thorn's hand cupped her cheek. "Oh ye of little faith," he said, giving her lips a tiny bite. "I loved you before Vander arrived at the house; I simply didn't realize it. I think I probably fell in love with you the moment you told me I had a shortfall." His eyes gleamed with amusement.

India did not laugh. "But you want to marry a woman like Lala. I can understand. I truly can. I know I'm not sweet."

Thorn's hands gripped her shoulders. "Don't ever say that again, India. You *are* sweet—but you're much more. You're the other half of my heart, and there's nothing docile and childlike inside me. It's not what I want in my wife, my partner."

India managed a wobbly smile.

"I almost came back within five minutes of leaving you,

but I wanted to bring you a gift when I next returned," Thorn said. "It was idiotic, and you can tell me that every day of my life. I had talked myself into believing that I could not come to you again without this." He reached over and took a purple velvet pouch from the bedside table that hadn't been there when India had lain down to sleep beside him the night before.

Velvet pouches rarely, if ever, contained anything other than jewelry, but like the diamond ring, she didn't care. She wanted more than gems. She wanted *him,* his heart . . . his promise. She didn't take her eyes from his. "Are you saying that you—you planned to come back to me, even after . . . even after I told you that I deserved better?"

"Always," he said, his voice deep and true.

"You," she said, her voice cracking, "*you* deserve better than me, Thorn."

"There is no one better than you. You were made for me," he said. The pouch fell to the side as he drew India into his arms, devouring her, convincing her without words that he had no interest in another woman.

Minutes—or hours—later India heard a noise in the corridor and flew off the bed, pulling on her wrapper to welcome Fred, who was carrying a laden tray. Then she climbed back on the bed and sank back in front of Thorn, uncovering the dishes.

"Start with this," she said, holding out a piece of fruit. "You must start slowly. You had no nourishment for two whole days." Thorn ate it, mock-nipping at her fingers. But she ignored him until he had put away two eggs and three toast fingers dripping with butter, and drunk a nourishing cup of broth.

Only when she was satisfied that he had eaten enough for the moment did she send the plates away and curl up beside him again.

"What shall we do now?" Thorn asked. Contrary to every expectation, he looked bright-eyed and energetic.

"You are not leaving this bed," she said severely. "You must *rest*."

"I will stay in bed if you stay with me," he said, giving her a devilish grin.

"None of that! Your body has endured a terrible shock."

His smile deepened and he picked up her hand, placing it below his waist. "Does it seem to you that my body is tired?"

Her fingers curled instinctively around that vital, male part of him. "You *should* be tired," she told him.

"I've been sleeping for two days. There are things I need more than sleep."

India felt color rising in her cheeks. "This is—we shouldn't." She pulled her hand away, rather reluctantly.

"Whether we should or shouldn't is irrelevant," Thorn stated. "You are mine, India, and you are going to be my wife, just as soon as I can get another special license."

Joy filled her heart, but she laughed. "Is this your third proposal?"

"I suppose I should be on my knees," Thorn said, his fingers weaving through her hair. "But that would mean I'd have to move. And I don't want to leave this bed."

She looped her arms around his neck. "I'll pretend you're on your knees."

"In that case, Lady Xenobia India St. Clair, may I have the honor of your hand in marriage?"

Tears fell down her cheeks. Xenobia India St. Clair was rarely speechless, but emotion caught her throat and she couldn't answer.

"You needn't answer, because you've already said yes," he said, his lips brushing hers tenderly.

"When?"

"Every time you smiled at me, it was a *yes*. And when you arrived here determined to save my life, that was another *yes*. And when you shouted at me, and forced me to wake up, that was a third *yes*."

The love deep in his eyes threatened to overwhelm her, and their lips met in a kiss that was irrational in its passion, sinful in its sensuality, raw in its pleasure.

Sometime later, India's robe fell off the bed to the floor and her chemise tore down the middle, the remnants tossed aside. When Thorn's scarred body met hers, she felt as if her heart danced in her rib cage, pounding to a tempo that only the two of them knew.

No one would have believed that mere hours before, Thorn had lain caught in dreamless sleep. He was all tongue and bites and strokes of his hand that drove India from pleasure to pleasure until they were both shuddering, and broken pleas tumbled from her lips. His touch made her head fall back and her mind whirl into a shameless, sensual storm of feeling.

Finally, finally, Thorn poised himself above her. "I think I would like you to say *yes* just one more time," he whispered, lips just above hers. "Will you be mine, India? Will you keep me, in sickness and in health, forsaking all others, as long as we both shall live?"

One tear ran down India's cheek from the pure beauty of it. "In sickness and in health," she repeated, her voice husky, "forsaking all others, as long as we both shall live."

Then he claimed her with a single thrust.

Chapter Forty-one

Quite some time later, Thorn returned the velvet bag to India's lap, insisting that she humor him and open it.

Her mother's necklace and earrings fell into her lap. The settings were tarnished, but there was a flash of diamond, the gleam of old gold. . . .

India's hands flew to her mouth, and a little scream broke from her lips.

"Where did you—" She turned to him, horrified. "You risked your life to salvage my mother's jewels for me?"

He nodded.

"But you hate the river, Thorn. And look what happened: it nearly killed you." Her hand brushed back his hair, caressing the wound that would remain on his brow, a permanent gift of the river. "No jewelry is worth your life!"

"Your parents loved you, just as I love you," Thorn told her. "They weren't leaving you, just as I will never leave you. I shall prove it to you this very afternoon."

India was completely confused. "How could you possibly prove that?"

"You believe yourself to be unlovable," Thorn said, ignoring her question, "but I was in love with you after five minutes in your company, and Vander was only ten minutes behind me. All those men who asked to marry you—the ones you say wanted to marry you for your title—they were in love with you too. Not to mention the stonemasons, and painters, and the rest of the men whose hearts you stripped bare."

"Oh," she whispered.

"I did the same thing as you," he continued.

"What do you mean?"

"I tried to keep you in your place, even to drive you away, because I could not believe that you would love a mudlark and a bastard." His voice was raw with emotion.

A hot flush washed over India, a wave of feeling so deep that she could hardly put it in words. "You humble me," she said, stumbling into speech. "You make me—"

The stones tumbled off the bed. No one noticed.

Later that day, a polite man by the name of Mr. Farthingale appeared in Thorn's library and explained to India and Adelaide that he was a jeweler who had met, years ago, with the Marquess of Renwick.

"Oh," India said, clasping Thorn's hand very tightly.

"I know your shop quite well," Adelaide said brightly. "Just off Blackfriars, isn't it?"

"Yes, it is, my lady," Mr. Farthingale said, inclining his head. Then he gave India a kindly look and said, "Lady Xenobia, I understand that you wish to know more of my encounter with your father."

"Yes, I would," she managed, her heart thumping.

"His lordship was in possession of a diamond demi-parure, which had descended through his wife's family. He asked me to value the pieces, as he was considering sale."

India didn't know what to think, so she nodded.

"The marquess and the marchioness were considering the sale in order to fund their daughter's debut and dowry." Mr. Farthingale paused delicately.

"For me?" India whispered.

"There was a reason your parents didn't immediately sell the jewelry to Mr. Farthingale," Thorn said, smiling at her.

Mr. Farthingale inclined his head, his eyes compassionate. "I believe they would have eventually consigned the pieces to me, but they wished to consult with their daughter, that is, with you, Lady Xenobia, before doing so."

A few minutes later, India rose to say goodbye, feeling lightheaded, as if her head were filled with air. Her parents hadn't been running away from her. They had loved her. They had been thinking of her future.

"Your news was very welcome," she told Mr. Farthingale.

"If you ever wish to sell the pieces . . ." he murmured, bowing.

"Never," Thorn intervened before India could say the same.

The pieces were her only tangible tie to her mother and father, and they represented all that Thorn had given her . . . and that which he had almost lost for her.

After they made love that night, India curled against Thorn's side, staring into the darkness, allowing herself to remember her parents.

Her mother used to throw back her hair and laugh in a deep-throated, joyful way. Her father wasn't much good at being a gentleman, or managing an estate, but she recalled how he'd sat with her for hours, helping her arrange glass tiles in just the right order. He taught her the skills that allowed her to make any room into an enchanting oasis.

She even remembered the way her mother would laugh and say, "I knew you would work it out, poppet," when India went to find them to say that she'd succeeded in locating a chicken for supper, or had made mushroom soup.

Her mother's cheerful confidence had pushed her to learn how to bake bread, how to apply stucco, how to polish silver.

Her parents had been the wind at her back in every house she had reorganized and refurbished, and she had never thanked them, or even realized it.

Thorn had given her parents back to her. They hadn't been conventional, or particularly aristocratic, and certainly not protective. But they had loved her.

The following evening, Messrs. Bink, Dusso, and Geordie had the singular experience of dining at the grand home of a duke and duchess, who were deeply grateful to them for saving the life of their eldest son.

Not only were they seated across from the Duke and Duchess of Villiers, but another future duke, Lord Brody, had also joined the meal. News of Thorn's near demise had spread through London, and Vander had turned up, as he said, "because he knew that Thorn's head was harder than a rock but he wanted to see for himself."

All that nobility at one table meant that Geordie, in particular, had trouble shaping a single word until Villiers's butler took pity on them and brought tankards of ale to the table.

Thorn grinned at his father, who fastidiously declined the ale; his stepmother, who not only accepted it, but was drinking it with every sign of enjoyment; his closest friend, who had accepted defeat with utmost grace; and finally at the woman who would soon be his wife.

Earlier that afternoon the archbishop had reluctantly

given Thorn's solicitor yet another special license—this one not blank but specifying the union of Mr. Tobias Dautry to Lady Xenobia India St. Clair.

They would be married in the morning, the ceremony witnessed by a duke and duchess, and three members of the fraternity of mudlarks. Evander Brody, heir to the Duke of Pindar, would stand as Thorn's best man, even though he was laughingly offering the bride a last chance to become a duchess.

"Never," Thorn growled, pulling his fiancée close in an entirely improper manner and bending his head to drop a kiss on a neck that glittered with diamonds . . . restored through Mr. Farthingale's expert ministrations.

"Those joowels looked like rubbish when Bink fished them up," Dusso told the Duke of Villiers. "I'd never know they was the same, now they're cleaned up."

Dusso grinned, and so did Bink and Geordie. They'd been in the Thames, and it hadn't conquered them.

Thorn felt the same. The river had almost killed him, but it had brought him India, and that was worth everything. If he hadn't been a mudlark, he never would have become the man whom India wanted.

He held her hand tightly under the table.

With a wicked little smile playing around his mouth, the Duke of Villiers began telling India about why he'd sent Thorn off to Piggleston. "I thought that Tobias needed to be made to understand how much he loved you." He raised his heavy-lidded eyes and glanced at his own wife. "He is my son, after all. We're fools when it comes to women."

Eleanor bent near, her hair brushing the duke's magnificently clad shoulder. "My husband was playing Cupid," she said. "He likes to do that."

India laughed, and Thorn thought, once again, that he

could spend his life listening to this woman, this particular woman, laugh.

The night he'd waited in Piggleston, believing India had been on the eve of marrying Vander, had scored him to the heart. But his father wasn't wrong: it had also taught him what he most wanted.

Not just what he wanted, but the only thing that was important in life.

Under the table, he tightened his hand around India's. Then he remembered that he wasn't a gentleman—he was a mudlark, sitting at a table with three other mudlarks.

He caught India's face in both his hands and kissed her. Her arms wound around his neck.

It was scandalous.

Outrageous.

Just right.

Epilogue

May 12, 1807
From Miss Adelaide Dautry at Starberry Court,
to her parents at 40 Hanover Square, London

    Dear Papa,

    I miss you very much. When are you and Mama coming home? Rose has been perfectly horrid to me all day. She says that now she's 14, she shan't play with me any longer. She hurt my feelings, and I did something bad, and now Mr. Twink says I have to write to you and confess. I want to say first that I'm not sorry, because she should have read me a story when I asked, and besides, she doesn't play with Antigone anymore.
    I cut a little bit of Antigone's hair.
    Please come home now. You've been gone for years.

                    Adelaide

From Miss Rose Summers at Starberry Court, to her guardians at 40 Hanover Square, London

Dear India,

I know you left only two days ago, but we've descended to the level of animals here, and civilization is but a dim memory. Remember when we visited Italy, and Papa read aloud The Inferno? That's what Starberry Court is like at the moment. I know you will say that Addie inherited her temper from you, but there is no excuse for this: She cut Antigone's hair short in the front! You know how I feel about Antigone. And now my poor dear has shorn hair and looks like a fever victim.

How can you both spend so much time at Starberry Court? I am positively dying of ennui. I have finished my study of Heraclitus and Xenophanes, but Twink can scarcely have a philosophical conversation when he's busy chasing after Addie. I truly think she should have a governess, as should Peter. For myself, I am counting the days until I can return to school.

Please arrange for the baby to be born tomorrow, as I should like to share a birthday.

Love,
Rose

From Master Peter Dautry at Starberry Court, to his parents at 40 Hanover Square, London

Dear Mama,

Mister Twink says I shud rite but I don't like riting.

Peter

From Mr. Dautry at 40 Hanover Square, London to his butler at Starberry Court

Fred,

Thank you for sending on the children's letters. Please inform our irritating offspring that babies arrive on their own schedule, and their mama and I will return to Starberry Court just as soon as their new sister or brother chooses to make an appearance.

Dautry

Daybreak

"Margot is perfect," India whispered, one finger tracing her newborn daughter's winged eyebrows. "And she's so calm! I suspect she will be a better sleeper than Addie or Peter. Rember how Peter bawled?" The infant had opened her eyes just long enough to reveal that they were gray, like her father's, and had promptly fallen to sleep again.

"I wouldn't count on it." Thorn was measuring one of the baby's tiny feet against his thumb. "I suppose Peter and Addie were once this small, but it doesn't seem possible. Rose is almost at my shoulder, and yet fourteen years ago her feet must have been this size."

"But she was already reading," India reminded Thorn with a choke of laughter. It had become a family joke that Rose claimed to have been reading "ever since I was born."

"Margot, do you already know how to read?" her father asked the baby.

Margot would have said yes (she passionately wanted to be like her oldest sister in everything), but instead she slept on, even when her father pretended to bite her toes, when he put her foot down and kissed her mother, when she was in danger of being smothered as they whispered to each other.

She slept the dreamless sleep of an infant who would never be hungry, who would never scavenge in the Thames, who would grow up in the arms of a family so loving that even after the children had grown and left home, Starberry Court would remain their fulcrum, drawing them back with their spouses, and then their children, and, later still, their grandchildren.

In time, a new wing would be built, at least in part to house the overflow of books (mostly Rose's, though Margot contributed quite a few as well). The kitchen would acquire new iron stoves, the water closets would be replaced by bathrooms with ceramic bathtubs, and the house would be the first in the county to be electrified. Peter's grandson would proudly drive one of the very first automobiles into the courtyard.

No matter the modernizations that Starberry Court underwent, it remained the glowing, comfortable home that India created in 1799: the heart of her family and her descendants, where they learned to laugh, to dance (for the pink ballroom became famous through three counties), to love . . . in short, to *live.*

And even two hundred years later, the chandelier that India had found in Venice on their first trip to Italy still hung in a place of honor in a dining room decorated with swallows.

A Note about Toy Shops, Stethoscopes, and Rubber Balls

I must confess that I toyed—pun intended—with history at several points in this novel. *Three Weeks with Lady X* takes place in 1799, a date predetermined by the fact that Thorn first appears as a mudlark—Juby/Tobias—in two of my earlier novels, *This Duchess of Mine* and *A Duke of Her Own*. I envisioned the boy, once grown, as a man whose years as a mudlark led him to recognize value in materials others had discarded, and at some point I became stubbornly attached to the idea that Thorn and India between them would rescue a failing rubber factory. Rubber's early uses in England included making it into a kind of string, which was then incorporated into fabric, creating a gathered look called "shirring." The problem? The rubber threads melted in the heat, making a shirred bodice a risky proposition.

Unfortunately, the first rubber factory in England wasn't established until 1811, and it wasn't until 1844 that Charles Goodyear patented the vulcanizing process, which stabilized rubber. India's "rubber band" first appeared with that usage in 1849. By 1850, many stores were selling India rubber toys, such as balls (and yes, the various puns on names—India rubber, as well as Rose and Thorn, were deliberate). Obviously, I played fast and loose with the dates of vulcanization in England: in my defense, other methods of curing rubber have been dated to prehistoric times. Indigenous peoples, for example, amazed Columbus's crew with rubber balls.

I also took liberties with Dr. Hatfield's "ear trumpet," which was a simple device at the time, without articulated joints. His trumpet is an early version of the stethoscope, which wouldn't be invented until 1816.

Lest you think that everything in the book was made up by me, the toy shop that supplied Rose with her wonderful doll, Antigone, was indeed called Noah's Ark. It was opened in 1760 by Mr. Hamley in Holborn, London. The bookshop that provided Thorn with fourteen Bibles for Starberry Court's library was the Temple of the Muses bookshop in Finsbury Square. The owner, Mr. James Lackington, specialized in buying entire libraries from grand houses.

Don't miss the next
delicious installment . . .

Pre-order
Four Nights With the Duke
now!

Were you intrigued by
Thorn's father, the arrogant, witty
Duke of Villiers?

Keep reading for a sneak peek at

New York Times bestseller

A Duke of Her Own

Available now in
print and e-book!

London's Roman Baths
Duchess of Beaumont's ball to benefit the Baths
June 14, 1784

"The duke must be here somewhere," said Mrs. Bouchon, née Lady Anne Lindel, tugging her older sister along like a child with a wheeled toy.

"And therefore we have to act like hunting dogs?" Lady Eleanor replied through clenched teeth.

"I'm worried that Villiers will leave before we find him. I can't let you waste another evening chatting with dowagers."

"Lord Killigrew would dislike being identified as a dowager," Eleanor protested. "Slow down, Anne!"

"Killigrew's not eligible either, is he? His daughter is at least your age." Her sister turned a corner and peered at a group of noblemen. "Villiers won't be in that nest of Whigs. He doesn't seem the type." She set off in the opposite direction.

Lord Thrush called after them, but Anne didn't even pause. Eleanor waved helplessly.

"Everyone knows that Villiers came to this benefit specifically to meet you," Anne said. "I heard it from at least three people in the last half hour, so he might have been civil enough to remain in the open where he could be easily found."

"That would deny most of London the pleasure of realizing just how desperate I am to meet him," Eleanor snapped.

"No one will think that, not given what you're wearing," her sister said over her shoulder. "Rest assured: I would be surprised if you attained the label *interested,* let alone *desperate.*"

Eleanor jerked her hand from her sister's. "If you don't like my gown, just say so. There's no need to be so rude."

Anne swung around, hands on her hips. "I consider myself blunt, rather than rude. It would be rude if I pointed out that at first glance any reasonable gentleman would characterize you as a bacon-faced beldam, rather than a marriageable lady."

Eleanor clenched her hands so that she didn't inadvertently engage in violence. "Whereas you," she retorted, "look as close to a courtesan as Mother would allow."

"May I point out that my recent marriage suggests that a more tempting style might be in order? Your sleeves are elbow-length—with *flounces,*" Anne added in disgust. "No one has worn that style for at least four years. Not to mention that togas are *de rigueur,* since your hostess requested the costume."

"I am not wearing a toga because I am not a trained

spaniel," Eleanor said. "And if you think that one-shoulder style is any more flattering to you than my flounces are to me, you are sadly mistaken."

"This isn't about me. It's about *you*. You. You and the question of whether you're going to spend the rest of your life in dowdy clothing simply because you were spurned in love. And if that sentence sounds like a cliché, Eleanor, it's because your life is turning into one."

"My life is a cliché?" Despite herself, Eleanor felt a tightness in the back of her throat that signaled tears. She and Anne had amused themselves for years with blistering fights, but she must be out of practice. Anne had been married for a whole two weeks, after all. With their youngest sister still in the nursery, there was no one to torment her on a daily basis.

Anne's face softened. "Just look at yourself, Eleanor. You're beautiful. Or at least you used to be beautiful, before—"

"Don't," Eleanor interrupted. "Just don't."

"Did you take a good look at your hair this evening?"

Of course she had. True, she had been reading while her maid worked, but she certainly glanced in the mirror before she left her chamber. "Rackfort worked very hard on these curls," Eleanor said, gingerly patting the plump curls suspended before her ears.

"Those curls make your cheeks round, Eleanor. Round, as in fat."

"I'm not fat," Eleanor said, taking a calming breath. "A moment ago you were insisting that I'm out of fashion, but these curls are the very newest mode."

"They might be among the older set," Anne said, poking at them. "But Rackfort's inadequate use of powder makes them anything but. For goodness sake, didn't you notice that she was using light brown curls, even though your hair is chestnut? It's oddly patchy where the powder has worn off. One might even say mangy. No one would think that you are the more beautiful of the two of us. Or that you're more beautiful than Mother ever was, for that matter."

"Not true!"

"True," her sister said indomitably. "I've begun to wonder why our mother, so very proud of her glorious past, allows you to dress like a dowager."

"Is this sourness the effect of marriage?" Eleanor said, staring at her sister. "You wed barely a fortnight ago. If this is the consequence of wedded bliss, I might do best to avoid it."

"Marriage gives me time to think." Anne smirked. "In bed."

"I feel truly sorry for you if your bedtime activities involve consideration of my wardrobe, not to mention Rackfort's lackluster hairdressing," Eleanor said tartly.

Anne broke into laughter. "I just don't understand why you dress like a prissy dowd when underneath you are quite the opposite."

"I am not—" Eleanor flashed, and caught herself. "And I don't understand why you are wasting time fussing over me when you have the very handsome Mr. Jeremy Bouchon claiming your attention."

"In fact, Jeremy and I discussed you. In a slow moment, as it were."

"You didn't!"

"We both agree that men don't look past your dowdy clothing. Jeremy says he never even considered the possibility of courting you. He thought you an eccentric, too pious and haughty even to take notice of him. You, Eleanor! He thought that of *you*. How ridiculous!"

Eleanor managed to bite back her opinion of her brother-in-law. "We're in the middle of a ball," she pointed out. "Wouldn't you be more comfortable sharing Jeremy's charming commentary later, in private?"

"No woman here has eyes like yours, Eleanor," her sister said, ignoring her comment entirely. "That dark blue is most unusual. I wish I had it. And they turn up at the corners. Don't you remember all those absurd poems Gideon wrote comparing your eyes to stormy seas and buttercups?"

"Not buttercups," Eleanor said. "Bluebells, though I don't see how this is relevant."

"Your mouth is just as lovely as it was years ago. Back before the buttercup king himself left for greener pastures."

"I don't like to talk about Gideon."

"I've obeyed you for three, almost four, years, but I'm tired of it," Anne replied, raising her voice again. "I'm a married woman now and you can't tell me what to do. Granted, you fell in love—"

"Please," Eleanor implored. "Keep your voice down, Anne!"

"You fell in love with a man who turned out to be a bad hat," her sister said, albeit a bit more quietly. "But what I don't understand is why Gideon's rejection has resulted in your becoming a squabby old maid. Do you really intend to wither into your grave mourning that man? Will you have no children, no marriage, no household of your own, *nothing*, all because Gideon left you?"

Eleanor felt as if the air actually burned her lungs. "I shall probably—"

"Just when *are* you planning to marry? At age twenty-five, or thirty? Who will marry you when you're that old, Eleanor? You may be beautiful, but if you don't make an effort, no one will notice. In my experience, men are not terribly perceptive." She leaned forward, peering. "You aren't wearing even a touch of face paint, are you?"

"No," Eleanor said. "None." Of course she wanted children. And a husband. It was just that she wanted Gideon's children. She was a *fool*. Seven times a fool. Gideon was not hers, and that meant his children wouldn't be either. How on earth had the years passed so quickly?

"I am not finished," her sister added. "There's not a bit of your bosom to be seen, and your skirts are so long they're practically dragging in the mud. But it's your attitude that really matters. You look like a prude, and you jest and poke at men. They don't like it, Eleanor. They flee in the other direction, and why shouldn't they?"

"No reason." Eleanor resorted to praying that Anne would run out of words, though she saw no sign of it.

"Everyone thinks you're a snob," her sister said flatly. "All of London knows that you swore not to marry anyone below the rank of a duke—and they don't think well of you for it. At least the men don't. In one fell swoop you made almost every eligible man in London think you are a condescending prig."

"I merely intended—"

"But now there's a duke on the market," Anne said, overriding her. "The Duke of Villiers, no less. Rich as Croesus and apparently just as snobbish as you are, since everyone says he's intent on marrying a duke's daughter. That's you, Eleanor. You. I'm married, Elizabeth is still in the nursery, and there isn't another eligible lady of our rank in London."

"I realize that fact."

"You're the one who announced that you'd marry no one below the order of a duke," Anne continued, scarcely pausing for breath. "You said there were no eligible dukes and then one appeared like magic, and everyone says that he's thinking of marrying you—"

"I don't see anything particular to celebrate in that," Eleanor retorted. "Those same people describe Villiers as quite unpleasant."

"You said you'd marry no one but a duke," her sister repeated stubbornly, "and now there's one fallen into your hand like a ripe plum. It wouldn't matter if the duke were as broken down as a cart horse, or so you always said."

Eleanor opened her mouth and then realized with some horror that the Duke of Villiers was standing just behind her sister's shoulder.

"Remember dinner last Twelfth Night? You told Aunt Petunia that you'd marry a man who smelled of urine and dog hair if he had the right title, but no one below a duke."

Eleanor had never met the Duke of Villiers; nay, she had never even seen Villiers, but she had no doubt but that she was facing him now. He was precisely as described, with the kind of jaw and cheekbones that wavered between brutish and beautiful. By all accounts, Villiers never wore a wig, and this man didn't even wear powder. His black hair was shot with two or three brilliant streaks of white and tied back at the neck. It couldn't be anyone else.

Her sister just kept going, with the relentless quality of a bad dream. "You said that you would marry a duke over another man, even if he were as stupid as Oyster and as fat as Mr. Hendicker's sow."

The Duke of Villiers's eyes were a chilly blackish-gray, the color of the evening sky when it threatened snow. He didn't look like a man with a sense of humor.

"Eleanor," Anne said. "Are you listening to me? Aren't you—" She turned. "Oh!"

*T*he Duchess of Beaumont was standing beside Villiers, obviously fighting to suppress her laughter. "Good evening, Lady Eleanor. And Lady Anne, though I really must call you Mrs. Bouchon now, mustn't I? I have been looking everywhere for the two of you. May I present to you His Grace, the Duke of Villiers."

"Your Grace," Eleanor said, sinking into a deep curtsy before the duchess. Anne gave something of a bob, since she was hampered by her toga. "And Your Grace." Eleanor curtsied again, this time before the Duke of Villiers.

Like herself, the duke had eschewed the compulsory toga, presumably with the same insouciance with which he refused to wear a wig. Instead he was wearing a coat of heavy, brandy-colored silk. The cut was simple, but the embroidered vine in coppery silk that danced among his buttons and around the hem turned simplicity to magnificence.

"Lady Eleanor," Villiers said. He looked at her from head to foot, his eyes pausing for a moment on the curls next to her ears. A blaze of humiliation went down her spine, but she raised her chin. If the duke wanted nobility, she had it. Elegance, no. Blood, yes.

When Eleanor had fixed on the idea of insisting that she marry a duke or no one, she wasted no time imagining a potential suitor. She had intended her proclamation to reach the ears of one duke—a *married* duke—so he would realize that even though he had been untrue to her, she would hold true to him. It was a stupid strategy that had hurt no one but herself, obviously.

The Duke of Villiers was altogether a different order of duke from Gideon. She had not known, would never have been able to imagine, such a potent mix of elegance and carelessness. It wasn't the silk embroidery, or the sword stick, or the careless power about him. She hadn't imagined the pure raw masculinity of him: the brooding look in his eyes, the jaded lines around his mouth, the width of his chest.

If Gideon looked like a prince in a fairy tale, Villiers was the tired, cynical villain who would try to usurp the throne.

"I gather that you heard my sister teasing me about my childhood wish to marry a duke," she said. "I do apologize if you felt your consequence reduced by comparison to Mr. Hendicker's sow."

"Oh, Villiers never experiences such awkward emotions, do you?" the Duchess of Beaumont said, laughing.

"I was more intrigued by the idea of being stupider than an oyster," Villiers said. He had a deep voice, the kind that made Eleanor instinctively wary. It wasn't the voice of a man who could be led; he would always lead. "How does one determine the intelligence of such a silent creature?"

"Oyster is Eleanor's puppy," Anne put in.

"In that case, it would depend on Oyster's breed," Villiers said. "Unless you have a pet poodle, I am fairly sure that I exceed expectations on both counts."

RAVISHING ROMANCE FROM
NEW YORK TIMES BESTSELLING AUTHOR
ELOISA JAMES

The Ugly Duchess
978-0-06-202173-1

Theodora Saxby is the last woman anyone expects the gorgeous James Ryburn to marry. But after a romantic proposal, even practical Theo finds herself convinced of her soon-to-be duke's passion . . . until she suspects that James desired not her heart, but her dowry.

As You Wish
978-0-06-227696-4

Includes *With This Kiss* and *Seduced by a Pirate*, two stunningly sensual stories in which gentlemen who rule the waves learn that true danger lies not on the high seas, but in the mistakes that can break a heart . . . and ruin a life forever.

Once Upon a Tower
978-0-06-222387-6

Gowan Stoughton, Duke of Kinross, is utterly bewitched by the emerald-eyed beauty, Lady Edith Gilchrist. But after Gowan's scandalous letter propels them to marriage, Edie realizes her husband needs a lesson and locks herself in a tower. Somehow Gowan must find a way to enter the tower and convince his new bride that she belongs in his arms.

Three Weeks With Lady X
978-0-06-222389-0

To marry a lady, the newly rich Thorn Dautry must acquire a gleaming, civilized façade. Lady Xenobia India vows to make Thorn marriageable in just three weeks. But neither Thorn nor India anticipate the forbidden passion that explodes between them.

EJ4 0414

At Avon Books, we know your passion for romance—once you finish one of our novels, you find yourself wanting more.

May we tempt you with . . .

- **Excerpts** from our upcoming releases.

- Entertaining **extras**, including authors' personal photo albums and book lists.

- Behind-the-scenes **scoop** on your favorite characters and series.

- **Sweepstakes** for the chance to win free books, romantic getaways, and other fun prizes.

- Writing **tips** from our authors and editors.

- **Blog** with our authors and find out why they love to write romance.

- **Exclusive content** that's not contained within the pages of our novels.

Join us at
www.avonbooks.com